Text Classics

JESSICA ANDERSON was born in Gayndah, west of Bundaberg, in 1916, and grew up in Brisbane. She left school at the age of sixteen before briefly studying art at Brisbane Technical College. For most of her life she lived in Sydney.

Anderson wrote stories and adapted novels for radio before she published her first novel, *An Ordinary Lunacy*, in 1963. *The Commandant* (1975) was her third published novel. She liked it the best of her books, she said, 'maybe because I enjoyed writing it the most.'

In 1978 she won the Miles Franklin Literary Award for *Tirra Lirra by the River*, and again in 1980 for *The Impersonators*, which also won the Christina Stead Prize for Fiction. In 1987 her collection *Stories from the Warm Zone and Sydney Stories*, won the *Age* Book of the Year award.

Jessica Anderson died in 2010, aged ninety-three.

CARMEN CALLIL founded Virago Press in 1972 and later became managing director of Chatto & Windus and the Hogarth Press. Since 1995 she has worked as a writer and critic. She is the author of *Bad Faith: A Forgotten History of Family and Fatherland*, and co-author, with Colm Tóibín, of *The Modern Library: The 200 Best Novels in English since 1950*.

ALSO BY JESSICA ANDERSON

An Ordinary Lunacy
The Last Man's Head
The Commandant
The Impersonators
Taking Shelter
Tirra Lirra by the River
One of the Wattle Birds
Stories from the Warm Zone and Sydney Stories

The Commandant
Jessica Anderson

Text Publishing Melbourne Australia

Copyright Agency
Cultural Fund   Proudly supported by Copyright Agency's Cultural Fund.

textclassics.com.au
textpublishing.com.au

The Text Publishing Company
Swann House
22 William Street
Melbourne Victoria 3000
Australia

First published by Macmillan Publishers London 1975
This edition published by The Text Publishing Company 2012

Cover design by WH Chong
Page design by WH Chong & Susan Miller
Typeset by Midland Typesetters

Printed in Australia by Griffin Press, an Accredited ISO AS/NZS 14001:2004
Environmental Management System printer

Primary print ISBN: 9781921922138
Ebook ISBN: 9781921921766
Author: Anderson, Jessica
Title: The commandant / by Jessica Anderson, introduction by Carmen Callil.
Series: Text classics.
Subjects: Women—Australia—Fiction. Australia—History—Fiction.
Other Authors/Contributors: Callil, Carmen.
Dewey Number: A823.3

CONTENTS

The Tales of Strangers
by Carmen Callil

FRANCIS O'Beirne, the young heroine of *The Commandant*, gives a key to the genius of Jessica Anderson: 'I am made up of hundreds of persons, and I never know which will come out.' Open the first page of any of her eight published works of fiction and, each time, she presents you with a different world, all-encompassing, entirely absorbing, real.

Nora Porteous, the narrator of *Tirra Lirra by the River*, Anderson's most popular novel, though not her finest—*The Commandant* is that—adds clarification: 'we were all great story-tellers.' The happiness a consummate novelist bestows upon a reader—the feeling that under no circumstance can you bear not to know what happens next, nor can you bear to come to the end of the tale—this is Jessica Anderson's great narrative gift.

She had many others: a precise command of the ironic and descriptive word, and an observant eye that contemplated human inadequacies in the manner of a knowing yet sympathetic bird. Observing, listening, gave her a formidable grasp of dialogue and the human comedy inherent therein. To all this she added a prose of simplicity and elegance, capable, as it is in *The Commandant*, of great lyrical beauty. For all these reasons Jessica Anderson was a most astute chronicler of the Australia of her time, 1916 to 2010.

She was born Jessica Queale, in a rural Queensland town, but grew up Brisbane. She read omnivorously from the age of three. She was a child with a stammer, but one bursting to tell stories, always writing. Her stamping grounds were the places she knew and loved best: Queensland and Sydney, to which she moved when she was eighteen. In 1916 Australia was a recently federated nation bristling with religious hostilities, exacerbated by the vicious conscription debates of World War I. By 2010 its small cities had exploded into tarmacked metropolises, rattling with computers and other godless inventions. Anderson was an Australian of English and Irish descent, born in a time when travel overseas, often to countries mysteriously called Home, together with some years as an expatriate there, was a part of life for so many. Nora, and Sylvia Foley in *The Impersonators*, are such creatures of exile and return.

Anderson once remarked that, with the exception of Christina Stead, she was almost entirely uninfluenced by other Australian writers, little realising that when she also said, 'I was very much...preoccupied with people who are strangers in their society,' she was following a centuries-old Australian literary tradition, one celebrated in so many bush ballads and stories. The loner, the swagman, the convict, the remittance man, the single women hauled out from the old country to serve the early settlers: all were outsiders, all onlookers. Jessica Anderson found their natural successors, in modern times, in her warring Sydney families, her divorcees, her bohemians, her children.

These are novels of Australia in the twentieth century. To see her dissect the vicious pull of sex and money, read her first novel, *An Ordinary Lunacy*; to see her at play amidst the carnage of sibling rivalry and dysfunctional families, read *The Impersonators*. Her writing is at its most elegiac in *Tirra Lirra by the River,* at its most lucid and wise in her *Stories From the Warm Zone and Sydney Stories*. Social satire is her forte. The harshest of stories shimmer with her sense of humour and her singularly empathetic understanding of character. This kaleidoscope of attributes moves through all her work, but only in *The Commandant* does she combine them all.

First published in 1975, it is one of the very best historical novels we have about colonial Australia in the early nineteenth century. A rarity too because it tells of the penal settlement that became Brisbane, rather than rehearsing again the well-trodden paths of convict Sydney. Moreton Bay penal colony was founded in 1824. Under Captain Patrick Logan, who assumed command in 1826, it was one of the worst, for it took repeat offenders. His brutality was recorded forever in the famous Australian folksong, 'Moreton Bay':

> For three long years I was beastly treated
> And heavy irons on my legs I wore
> My back from flogging was lacerated
> And oft times painted with my crimson gore
> And many a man from downright starvation
> Lies mouldering now underneath the clay
> And Captain Logan he had us mangled
> All at the triangles of Moreton Bay

Anderson does not disguise that she is basing her characters on historical figures and events. Logan, a rigid army man, married Letitia O'Beirne of Sligo, Ireland, the daughter of a fellow officer, a member of that select band of Irishmen, Anderson implies, who sold their patrimony to the devil by fighting for the British. The novel opens at sea, as Letitia's sister Frances ends the long journey to Moreton Bay, where she is presented with 'another kind of country', its convicts 'sub-human, like animals adapted to men's work or goblins from under the hill'. From the deck Frances views the wharf, small houses, chimneys, gardens, barracks: solid British settlement. In the surrounding wilderness, evoked with the lightest of touches, are dark presences watching the construction of frightening objects on precious land.

This was the astonishing epoch when imperial Britain presented the original inhabitants of Australia with two invading species: ragged white men in chains and shackles accompanied by uniformed white men bearing muskets or prayer books. What the Aborigines saw is barely described but throbs through the narrative: something achieved by Conrad in his similar contemplation of Africa, *Heart of Darkness*.

Jessica Anderson has said how much she relished the historical investigation required, and it shows in every meticulously researched episode, in understanding lightly conveyed. Moreton Bay was a penal colony governed by Scots and Irish of the Ascendancy. The convicts they brutalised were mostly Catholic Irish. Here are the origins of the rigid division between Protestant and Catholic which was to continue in Australia until well into the second half of the twentieth century. As deftly achieved is the vivid accuracy of her historical figures. Henry Cowper, alcoholic doctor and wit, and the Jewish convict Lewis Lazarus, a Magwitch-like personage worthy of Dickens, are creations of grand— and on occasion comic—opera. There are many more.

Frances arrives in 1830. It is the early age of science; reform is in the air in England, and in Australia Captain

Logan has become notorious for his unquestioning use of the tortures permitted by law, loathed by all those who watch Gilligan the scourger at work with his lash. A liberal Sydney editor accuses Logan of murder: the matter is to come to trial. Logan is a man of the past, devoted to the 'system of punishment and reform' that he is 'privileged to serve'. Anderson portrays a monstrous product of his age, yet one for whom she evokes some sympathy.

His tragedy is played out within a domestic story which reads like a Jane Austen novel transported to strange lands. Bonnet, shawl, muff and the twitterings of the Logan children are juxtaposed with the genteel social life of the settlement, with its servants, wives and medical officers. Frances is an idealistic seventeen-year-old when she arrives, with an admirer met on the journey out who might offer her everything a young woman should want. There are echoes of the famous opening lines of *Pride and Prejudice* in Letitia's homily to her sister: 'ev'wy woman who wants a husband is in some degree a husband hunter…If she is pwetty, so much the better. If not…' Anderson has transposed her own stammer into a lisp for the delightful Letty, as she gives the red hair to be found in every one of her works to the lieutenant's sardonic wife, Louisa Harbin, adorned with 'a hairpiece like six red dead snails'. Frances, more intelligent, must follow the fate of the convicts, blacks and runaways, and face the sights she is forced to see. Her moral self-education is the dramatic lynchpin of the novel.

The novel closes, as it should, in the Australian bush, and once again, at sea: those two defining elements of our national story. Anderson writes of the natural beauty offered, then and now, to every immigrant Australian, whether convict, commandant, male or female. Lines of inspired description about her native land are threaded through *The Commandant* like an exquisite embroidery, writing rarely to be found in her other work:

> On Henry's right hand a few clumps of tall trees, their rough bark the colour of iron, and their foliage a dun green, stood with the junction of trunk and root shrouded by tall pale grass; and although at his left the river marked out a fissure of brighter greens, none among them were the sappy greens of England and Ireland…It was as if everything here inclined not to the sun's bright spectrum, but to those of the mineral earth and the ghostly daytime moon…

The Commandant was published in England in 1975 when its English publisher put a bodice-ripper jacket on it. Today it can be published in a different way, in a different country, and be seen for the masterpiece it is.

The Commandant

For help in the preparation of this novel, I wish to thank my brother, Alan Queale, who put his library and his detailed knowledge of Australian history at my disposal, and the staffs of the Mitchell Library, Sydney and the Oxley Library, Brisbane. Thanks are also owing to the Literature Board of the Australian Council for the Arts, whose award of a fellowship gave me freedom and encouragement.

J. A.

PART ONE

CHAPTER ONE

'But Dunwich is only a depot. Don't judge us by a depot. Wait, my dear Miss O'Beirne, wait till we get to the settlement. Which with this wind—' Mrs Bulwer drew a hand from her muff and held it into the wind— 'will be some five hours more. It's quite a pretty little place, I assure you. And healthy besides. None of us has gone to our graveyard. Not one. And only one soldier. Quite a contrast with the India stations. At least with Madras. I am sure the rumour that the fifty-seventh is to go to Madras is quite unfounded. Agra. It will be Agra. Agra is delightful. Very little fever at Agra. On the settlement we do have the fever, but not the India sort, not the sort to carry one off. And we have the ophthalmia and the dysentery, though neither is so prevalent with *us*. But of course we have nothing so dreadful as the cholera. The cholera! Do you know how bad it was at home last year? Why, of course you do, you were there.'

Frances said, well, she had been in Ireland.

'Well, Ireland. Ireland is as bad as England for the cholera. Did Letty write you that we have two surgeons on the settlement now? Both young,' she said, on a note of persuasion, and with a sudden bold look at Frances, 'and both such dear clever *good* men.'

Frances sank her chin in her collar and opened her eyes wide. 'Mr Henry Cowper is good?'

'Why, certainly he is.' Mrs Bulwer's note of persuasion deepened into bluster. 'I can't think with whom you associated in Sydney if they told you he is not.'

'But I saw him myself, ma'am, on this very voyage—'

'And so you may have. But you have not yet seen him conducting divine service.'

'*He* conducts—'

'He does. We were sent a chaplain, but he and the commandant— We all have our failings, and our good commandant is sometimes short of temper. Mr James Murray is the other surgeon, the new one. He is single—' she flashed Frances another of her bold looks—'and dines quite often with your sister and the commandant. Oh, you will not be dull, I assure you. And the commandant's cottage is charming. Letty has such taste. Well, I will say no more. You will soon see it all for yourself, and meet your little niece and nephew

4

besides. So come, my dear, let us have a smile. Such a young creature, yet so-o dejected!'

'It's the architecture of my face,' said Frances.

'*Arch*-itecture?'

'Yes. It makes me look dejected when I am only thoughtful.'

'It does not do to be too thoughtful.'

'But—does not do for what?'

'Why, that's a question I hardly know how to answer.' Mrs Bulwer's voice was slower. Without looking away from Frances's face, she withdrew into preoccupation. 'If you're going to ask clever questions, you had better talk to Mrs Harbin.'

'I've hardly seen Mrs Harbin since we left Sydney Heads. She was so sick.'

'We were *all* sick. You don't resemble Letty, do you? Or Cassandra? You are in quite a different style.'

'Letty and Cass take after papa. I resemble mama. Or did, when she was alive.'

Mrs Bulwer responded only with a brief but most reflective murmur. 'H'mmm.' Frances, made uneasy by her continued scrutiny, put a hand to her left cheek, where smallpox had left an area of roughness, and raised herself slightly in her seat to look out over the water. They had disembarked at Dunwich from the *Isabella*, and were now on the deck of the *Regent Bird*, going up Moreton Bay. 'What island is that?' asked Frances.

But Mrs Bulwer didn't even look. 'Green Island. I understand there are two more of you.'

'Yes. It's not very green.'

'Both girls?'

'Yes. Hermione and Lydia.'

'Your poor father,' said Mrs Bulwer, with sudden frank gloom.

'Well, ma'am, he is poor, you see.'

'I meant, of course, unfortunate.'

'I know. But it's being poor that makes him unfortunate.'

'You look much more like Cassandra when you laugh. Oh, we do miss Cassandra. Always so agreeable, so patient and tactful. But never mind, she will be as happy as a bird with her lieutenant, *even* in the Indies. And you will take her place. You will have Letty to help you now. And the commandant.'

Frances murmured an excuse and got up, gathering her shawl tightly around her, and went to the side. Mrs Bulwer's warning voice followed her. 'It does not do to be opinionated.' She pretended not to hear. On the bay were amazing stretches of turquoise and violet, and the sky was empty of everything except a dandelion of sun, mildly blazing, and a meek white crescent of moon. From beneath the frill on the back of her bonnet a strand of dark hair dropped and was caught and extended by the wind. The sun, the boom of sails and the race of water, would have held her there at the side, in a dream or trance, as had happened so often on the voyage out, had not Mrs Bulwer, small and black and compact in her side vision, waited. And with a sense of facing something lately evaded, Frances admitted that also waiting, the more insistent because only inwardly visible, was the commandant. Deliberately, she set herself to visualise him, in five hours or so, descending the river bank to meet the *Regent Bird*.

She saw a tall, straight-backed, cold-faced, gingery man, who walked with a kind of curbed stiffness, and who moved his head restlessly, or as if fretted by his high neck band. And as detail accrued—the scarlet and gold of his uniform, the gloss and weight of the braid—the background her imagination had provided, slope and river and blurred sky, faded away and left him as she had first seen him in reality. Walking like that, he had descended the unkempt incline before her father's house in Sligo, while she, nine years old, had peeped from a window with Bridie and Meg. Later she had met him face to face, but it was only as a dim tallness that she could see him bending from the waist to cate-chise her on her lessons. Her own squirming shyness, and her simultaneous shame of it, had perhaps obliter-ated from those later meetings nearly everything but itself, whereas at the window, safe between the adult softnesses of Bridie and Meg, she had been free simply to gape.

'Here comes Miss Letty's captain.'

'Look at him legging it!'

Bridie and Meg had managed to convey mockery, dislike, and admiration, all at the same time; but in Sydney the Hall girls had said, 'Oh, Logan,' and had refrained from looking at her, or at each other. Another strand of hair fell from her bonnet into the wind. She gathered it all together, wound it on two fingers, and poked it beneath her bonnet as she turned to face Mrs Bulwer.

'How will—they—come up the bay?'

Feeling the occasion to be one for courage, she was sad to be betrayed by her shy voice. And now, forced to persist against Mrs Bulwer's look of cool interrogation, she sounded shyer still.

'I mean—the convicts?'

'Oh, the *pris*-oners? Why, how else but in a boat? And be assured, they will be made as comfortable as is consistent with their condition. As indeed they were on the voyage from Sydney. There is more room between decks on the *Isabella* than one might think. If only she could cross the bar I am sure the journey would be less tedious for everyone. Or if there was a way by land. Of course there *is* a way. The runaways find it. But such a wild rough terrible way it must be, it doesn't bear thinking of. Do sit down, my dear, you will blow away. Did Letty write you about the *Laetitia Bingham*? The commandant had her built on the settlement. I believe there's nothing that man can *not*

8

do, if he puts his mind to it. He named her, of course, after Letty.'

Against such purposeful animation Frances could persist no further, but was left only with the trifling independence of continuing to stand, and of asserting that Letty's second name was Anne, not Bingham. 'So he must have named the boat after their little girl.'

'Indeed? Oh, but I am certain.'

So was Frances certain, but her bonnet now blew off and saved her from insistence. As she twirled on a heel and threw up her hands to catch it, she let go her shawl, which slipped down her back and dropped to the deck. By the time she had retrieved it she saw that Captain Clunie, who had evidently just come up on deck, had picked up her bonnet and was offering it to her with a bow. He was about thirty-five, big and staid, and during a seven-day voyage on which neither had been sick, she had found him almost entirely silent. Frances was seventeen; she was not stupid, but was often absurd. His silences had had the unexpected effect of making her gush. Shamed by this, she had vowed each time never to do it again, yet at each meeting had done it again, and indeed, was doing it now.

'Oh, *thank* you, Captain. You have saved my very life!'

He gave his little blink, his little bow. Mrs Bulwer fluttered up and set herself at Frances's side. Her clothes had so many loose surfaces—shawls, veils, ribbons, capes, fringes—that in the wind she seemed to ripple all over with sharp little black flames. She confronted Captain Clunie with her muff raised vertically on one hand. 'Captain, do tell us your wife is soon to join you on the settlement?'

His wife, he replied, was visiting her parents in Oxfordshire. She would soon sail for the colony, but whether she came to the settlement or not would depend on the length of his stay. He excused himself with another bow, then turned away and set himself to pace the small deck.

Mrs Bulwer set her chin in the end of her muff. 'H'mmm.' But then she saw that Frances, to free both hands for attention to her loose hair, was gripping her bonnet and shawl between her bent knees. She sprang forward. 'Give those *to me*!'

Frances saw in her outraged face the reflection of her own lack of grace and propriety; she unloosed her knees and let her take the bonnet and shawl.

'Now, either go below, or tuck *all* your hair under your bonnet. It is better to look *skinned* than like a *tinker* woman.'

Louisa Harbin, very tall and thin, and clutching about her with long hands a furred and hooded mantle of dark blue, dragged her feet as she crossed the deck to her chair. She had just come up from below. Her big lips were compressed and her deeply lidded eyes all but

10

shut. She sat down in a resigned but gingerly way, shut her eyes completely, and folded her hands in her lap. The fur trim on her mantle, from her habit of clutching it, was worn to the hide on the breast and inside cuffs. Mrs Bulwer clucked with her tongue and hurried over to her.

'Louisa, I am happy to see you so well.'

Louisa opened her eyes. 'I am always a little better, Amelia, in the bay.' Her voice was languid but precise. 'But pray, don't call me well.'

'The great thing is not to give *in* to it. Look, here is Miss O'Beirne.' Mrs Bulwer took Frances by an arm and drew her forward. 'Here is Frances.'

'So it is.' The sick equine face in the dark hood quite pleasantly smiled. 'Frances, do I look well?'

Frances hesitated.

'Thank you, my dear.'

'Well, I did not mean well, Louisa, but well *enough*. You can help us. Did the commandant name the *Laetitia Bingham* after Letty or the little girl?'

'The little girl. He named something else after Letty. I think it was a plain. You are looking at me in great puzzlement, Frances. Why?'

'Your face looks thinner, ma'am.'

'But *not* because she has been sick. She had four teeth drawn in Sydney, and the swelling went down on the voyage.'

'Yes, Frances, I had that lovely fat face when we

11

embarked. I expect you thought me quite bonny. Come and sit here, out of the wind. I am glad to see you brought warm garments. So many don't.'

'Letty told me to,' said Frances, as she sat down.

'The first people,' said Amelia Bulwer, 'brought no warm garments at all. Not for anybody. They say the whole settlement was a-shiver every night from June to September, but the commissariat in Sydney could *not* be persuaded of it. They said it was the tropics, and how could anyone be cold in the tropics.'

In spite of her vivacity, most of Amelia's attention was for Captain Clunie as he passed and repassed. 'But what a difference these days!' she said distractedly. 'Louisa, I have been telling Frances how comfortable we all are now.'

'You've been telling her how good and sweet and amiable we all are. I know you, Amelia. No wonder she looks dejected. You make the place sound insipid.'

'Then see if you can cheer her.'

Amelia fluttered away as she spoke and accosted Captain Clunie. His pause was of the briefest, his bow little more than a headthrust, like the first forward move of a pigeon; but she was not deterred from falling into step at his side, talking and leaning forward to trace the effect of her words in his face.

'How her clothes blow about,' said Louisa. 'Though it suits her. It makes her look less like a porcupine. She is in mourning again. At this rate her Lancelot will soon purchase his captaincy. These journeys are very tiresome. We shall hardly be there before dusk.'

'Mrs Harbin, is it an insipid place?'

'Not exactly. What do you think of our new captain?'

'If I dislike him, it is only because he makes me dislike myself. I seem doomed to act foolishly in his presence. Some people know in advance how they will act, but I don't. I am made up of hundreds of persons, and I never know which one will come out. I am at the mercy of my company. I think I divine what they believe me to be, then can't help acting the part. Which means I respond differently to everybody, and falsely to all but a few. And when I meet one of those few, I am so grateful that I become excited, and talk too much, and put them off. Were you ever like that, Mrs Harbin?'

'Yes,' said Louisa in a startled voice. 'Yours seems an extreme case. But it's true I was slightly like that.'

'I shall change, too. I have determined to change.'

'It would certainly be more comfortable. You must acquire a manner, and refer your intelligence to it, and most of your instincts. That's the way it's done. Of course you must work at it. But you will have Letty to help you now.'

'That's what Mrs Bulwer told me,' said Frances in disappointment.

'Amelia is not always wrong. And I am sure she took the greatest trouble with you. Letty is first in

13

consequence among us, and you share her greater glory besides.'

'Do you mean our cousin Lord Clanricarde? I have never met him.'

'Gracious, don't tell Amelia.'

'But Letty has, two or three times.'

'Better not tell her that, either.'

'I see. Does Letty—'

'Say no more, child. What we were speaking of before is of more interest. At the mercy of your company. It's a striking phrase. How did your company in Sydney affect you?' She turned fully to face Frances, setting back her hood a few inches to disclose a hairpiece of tight titian curls. 'I speak of the Hall girls.'

Frances quickly put a hand to her smallpox scars, then as quickly folded it with the other in her lap. 'I felt myself with them. Never more so with anyone. Except the servants at home, and my two little sisters. And one other, a gentleman. But no,' she said, in her scrupulous way, 'I am apt to deceive myself about gentlemen. I will only say this—that with the Hall girls I felt almost entirely myself.'

'And so you talked too much, and put them off.'

'No. It wasn't like that with them. I think I let them talk too much. We walked all over the Surry Hills, talking and talking.' Frances broke into laughter. 'You should have seen us!'

Her transforming laughter made Louisa look at

14

her with a new kind of attention. 'I did,' she said. 'Not on the Surry Hills, but in George Street. Six Hall girls, of all sizes, and two young men with open collars. The girls were pointed out to me as the daughters of the imprisoned editor. My informant didn't know the young men, or you. But I recognised you when I saw you on the *Isabella*.'

'You can't be a dyed-in-the-wool tory, then. You were so nice to me.'

'Dyed-in-the-wool? I don't think I'm a dyed-in-the-wool anything. From time to time I am reached by these new ideas, but I'm too lazy to disturb myself with them. I confess they could be disturbing. I must tell you this, however—I am not the only one who saw you with the Hall girls.'

'Mrs Darling? When I visited Government House, I fancied she looked at me strangely.'

'I was not thinking of such elevated persons. Amelia Bulwer saw you.'

Amelia, now stationary at the side with Captain Clunie, was still talking. Frances pulled a quick wry childish face. 'Well, I don't care. They may say what they please. Elizabeth and Barbara Hall are heroines, and Mr Edward Smith Hall is a hero.'

'I take it Elizabeth and Barbara are the two eldest, who care for all the others?'

'There are emancipist servants.'

'You don't think it irresponsible of Mr Smith Hall

to get himself jailed, and leave his daughters with former convicts?'

Frances had seen a portrait of the editor. She recalled a thin face, an intense but smiling gaze, a loose cravat. She raised her chin. 'He is in jail in the cause of truth and justice.'

'Gracious, which of your many selves is this?'

Frances was herself conscious of having put it badly, of having been both banal and freakish, the one in the words chosen, the other in the exalted tone. But though tempted by Louisa's invitation to laugh and forget it, she felt obliged to persist.

'I hope it's the best of my selves, ma'am. Mr Smith Hall asks for trial by jury for everyone. He would have no trial by military officers, nor a selected council instead of an elected assembly. And he sets himself against all sentences that exceed the law, and in that respect he spares no one, not Governor Darling himself. You must have heard, ma'am, of Governor Darling's sentence on those two soldiers.'

Louisa had shut her eyes. 'I suppose you are proving your theory,' she murmured. 'After seeing you with those girls I *did* expect you to be like this.'

But still Frances would not stop. 'And you must know that one of them died, and that Mr Smith Hall wrote very strongly about it in the *Monitor*. And that's why the governor hates him, and induces the persons he criticises to bring libel actions. No, not induces. Instructs.'

16

'Do you know which persons are bringing these current libel actions, Frances?'

Frances looked slightly aghast at this sterner tone, but continued with the same childish exaltation as before. 'There are a number. I have heard names. I have forgotten. All I know is that Governor Darling is determined to bring Mr Smith Hall down. And he refuses to be brought down. So he is kept in jail.'

'From where he continues to edit his journal.'

'He is so brave.'

'Any reply I make will sound ridiculous. You have fallen into a nest of radicals.'

'He proclaims himself a liberal tory.'

'What is that? No, pray don't tell me. I expect it is something like a heathen christian. There are plenty of those, though they seldom proclaim themselves.' Louisa was looking at Frances with curiosity and amusement. 'However did you become acquainted with the wretched girls?'

'Through a young gentleman. A passenger with me in the *Hooghly*.'

'One of the young men with open collars?'

'Yes. The dark one. Mr Edmund Joyce.'

'Was he the "one other" you spoke of?'

'He was. He had a letter to Mr Smith Hall.'

'He looked as if he would have a letter to Mr Smith Hall.'

'From Mr Joseph Hume.'

17

'Indeed!' Louisa reflected for a moment. 'Ah, but there will never be a whig government,' she then said with confidence.

'We believe there will be.'

'Very well. But even so, how radical are they?'

'I know nothing of radicals. I speak of reformers. There are reformers among them.'

'Yes, and how they embarrass the rest! And in any case, child, what would be the use? Even if they took the Commons, the Lords would head them off. Here is our bread and gruel.'

But Frances, ignoring the woman who was serving them, said with indignation, 'Is that what you hope for, ma'am?'

'I'm sure I don't care. But facts must be faced.'

'And injustice must rule?'

'You must surely be hungry. Thank you, Madge.'

Frances also murmured her thanks, and looked up into the woman's face. One of the commandant's household servants, sent to serve her on the voyage, she was short and thick, with swarthy skin lined in a random and peculiar manner, and small black eyes that reminded Frances of struggling beetles. Her dress was of coarse grey cotton, but she displayed no number, and round her neck she wore a clean muslin kerchief. Before she bobbed and turned away, Frances detected in her expression something of the tolerance towards herself displayed by Louisa, but while Louisa's was open and ironic, this woman's seemed contemptuous and sly. The gruel was greasy but scented with herbs. Louisa ate and drank with thoughtful slow placidity, but Frances, who felt she had talked herself into a trap she could not define, and who was dismayed because the convict Madge Noakes aroused revulsion in her instead of pity, drank with her head bent and encircled the cup with her hands.

Captain Clunie and Mrs Bulwer were taking their gruel standing at the side.

'Mind,' said Captain Clunie, 'some of Smith Hall's proposals are already in practice at home, but that is not to say they're practicable in a colony partly populated by former convicts.'

'Exactly! It is *not* to say so.'

'Besides, I dislike the ranting of fellows like that.'

'The ranting. Exactly! Here is Madge Noakes to take our cups. Madge, I hope Mr Cowper was able to take some gruel.'

'He could not be woke, ma'am.'

'Is Mr Cowper often in this state?' asked Clunie when the woman had gone. Clunie had not been long in the colony.

'H'mmm. I think I shall only say that in this instance his weakness may be compounded by sea-sickness. Oh—but—such a son for such a father! When I called on the Reverend Cowper in Sydney, I asked when the gospel was to be carried to our poor native blacks. His dear face grew grave. "We don't want a repetition of the Reverend Vincent incident," he said. Not a word of blame for the commandant. He is a saint.'

But at the mention of the commandant Clunie had coolly turned his head. Across the deck, Madge Noakes was taking the cups from Louisa and Frances. 'Why was that girl allowed to roam about like that?' he asked in an offended voice. 'Why wasn't she put with some decent woman?'

'But you were staying with Mrs Pollard,' said Louisa. 'Such a starchy old thing. Yet she let you go about like that. Does she tipple?'

'No!' Frances was forced to laugh at last. 'She was sick. She let me go about with her daughter.'

'Oh. Who had a friend *she* wished to visit. Don't reply. I am not asking you to betray anyone. I find it all very interesting. I am not much in the way of meeting radicals. I expect there is a kind of excitement in the lives of such people. They certainly look excited. All the same, you will change these opinions in two or three weeks.'

'Neither two nor three,' said Frances. 'Never!'

'You contradict yourself.'

'How?'

'You said you were at the mercy of your company.'

20

Frances put a hand to her cheek, frowning and staring ahead of her. Lieutenant Edwards of the fifty-seventh, who had been sent from the settlement to discharge the *Isabella*, had come up on deck and was talking to Captain Clunie, while Amelia Bulwer, with swinging skirts, now paced the deck silently and alone except for her gliding shadow. 'Then I shall have to learn to resist it,' said Frances in an undecided voice.

'Learn to adapt to it. Adapt. These ideas will impede you. But never mind, so quickly picked up, they will be quickly dropped.'

'But were they quickly picked up? I think—they began a long time ago. After mama died, Letty and Cass lived most of the year with our Dublin or Bristol aunts, and papa was—hard to talk to, and Lydia and Hermione were only babies, so I was mostly with the servants, and they were a link with the people about. And there was famine, and in Sligo, some rioting. Which is indeed why Captain Logan was sent there.'

But when she looked to Louisa for a reply, she saw an averted head, deeply hooded again. Rebuffed by what she took for boredom, she got up and went to the side. But almost immediately she ran back. 'Mrs Harbin, we have entered the river.'

The reply seemed to come from cold distances. 'I know. I recognised that clump of pines.'

To Frances's eyes, half-shut against the sun, the thin branches of the pines melted away and left the dark tufts of foliage as if exploding in air. 'They are very curious,' she said timidly.

Louisa's hooded head did not move. 'Quite distinctive.'

'We must be nearly there.'

'Hours yet.'

But Frances, at the side again, saw in the thick brown swirls just below the surface of the water, a first greeting from their destination. Since nobody else seemed in the least excited, she crossed her arms on her breast, over her shawl, and hugged herself. But almost at once, this flush of excitement receded, leaving her face pale and frightened. She stared for a moment at the swirls of mud, then turned and went back slowly to Louisa. Refusing now to be unnerved by that motionless hooded figure, she sat down and spoke softly and earnestly.

'I didn't know it was a penal station.'

Louisa drew back her head. For the first time, she looked angry. 'Impossible!'

'Oh, I *knew*—'

'Certainly you did.'

'I have put it badly.'

'Then put it well.'

'I knew it was a penal station. And I knew it was for those convicted twice, once at home and again in the colony. But I didn't know it was *only* a penal station. I thought of it as a mixture of convict and free.

22

Like Sydney, only smaller. Letty simply didn't think to explain the difference. I didn't know the waters were proscribed for fifty miles around. And the land too. I didn't know that the commandant is coroner and sole magistrate and censor. I didn't dream that every single article that enters is under his scrutiny—all mail, every single thing.'

'And who informed you?'

'Mr Edmund Joyce. We mean to correspond.'

'My dear girl, you are right about the proscription of the land and water, but about the mail, someone has exaggerated. Those are the regulations, certainly, partly because where there are ships there is smuggling. But the commandant will not examine mail sent or received by his own household, or the officers' households either. That's what I dislike about your radicals—their childish suspicions and crude assumptions. It is always the same. Directly one begins to sympathise with them a little, something of this sort occurs, and puts one off. Oh but come now, don't cry because your friends were mistaken.'

Frances wiped her eyes and cheeks. 'I am not. I am crying because I'm afraid.'

'Lord, child! What of?'

'I suppose—of arriving. You don't like it yourself, ma'am, it seems to me.'

'A mood. It comes when we enter the river, and goes as fast as it comes.' Louisa set back her hood. 'See

23

me now, looking forward to my books and my sketching pads, and to tea from a china cup. And as for you, my dear, you are going to your own sister.'

'A stranger. I haven't seen her for eight years. And Captain Logan,' said Frances, passionate through fresh tears, 'is a *perfect* stranger.'

Louisa set a long knobbly hand on one of hers. She said no more, but looked around the great sky as if finding there a confirmation that it was indeed a confounding world into which such young and lonely creatures were venturing every day. And no matter in what bold ignorance they set out, they must observe this detail, and that detail, until it must occur to them, one day, to be frightened. Frances had stopped crying; Louisa patted her hand. Her own two daughters, aged ten and twelve, were with relatives in England. She found it hard to recall their features, a fact she pressed home to her husband by pretending to forget their names. Captain Clunie and Lieutenant Edwards had gone below, and Amelia Bulwer was crossing the deck towards them.

'You have not done much to cheer her,' she remarked. But without a second glance at Frances, she sat on Louisa's other side and spoke close to her ear.

'He has come to relieve Lieutenant Bainbrigge.'

'We all know that.'

'But it is all we know. And what is more curious, it seems to be all he knows. But to send a captain—' she broke off and directed a glance across Louisa at Frances. 'Well, it is of no consequence,' she said lightly.

Frances excused herself and got up and went to the side. 'But to send a captain,' said Amelia, 'to relieve a lieutenant? to become subordinate to another captain? It *is not* natural.'

'You make too much of it.'

'All the same, all the same, I wonder if he has come to take the command.'

'Very likely, if Captain Logan's regiment is for India.'

'If the fifty-seventh is for India, it will not be until next year. This is only August.'

'Or if the commandant is needed in Sydney.'

'To press his libel action? Well, to be sure. But an absence of a few weeks hardly warrants a captain as relief. Indeed, if Captain Clunie is *not* to take the command, it is a perfect riddle.'

'There will be an answer to it in the mailbag, Amelia. Nobody is sent without a covering letter from Mr Macleay.'

Alexander Macleay, colonial secretary in Sydney, was Governor Darling's closest colleague. 'I am sure I hope so,' said Amelia. 'But there has been talk, and one does wonder. Does she, by the by—' she pointed with her muff at Frances's back—'know what the father of her boon companions wrote about her sister's husband?'

'I have not told her.'

'She ought to be told.'

'Leave her to Letty.'

The muff was still pointing at Frances, though Amelia's eyes were watching Louisa's face. 'A delightful young lady. But does she think a little too well of herself?'

'No. Only a little too much. How boring these journeys are. I wish we were there.'

'Dear Victor will be enchanted to see you.'

'I shall be a change from overseers' wives, to be sure.'

Amelia put her muff to her mouth and giggled into it. 'You are bold beyond anything.'

'Glum rather than bold. I shan't be enchanted to see dear Victor.'

'Louisa, at heart he is the best of men. In my Lancelot's opinion he is second to none.'

'I know that, Amelia.'

'Damon and Pythias. How pleasant it is to see them at night, with their pipes. I think, Louisa, the peace of our little community during the next few months will depend on how congenial our good commandant finds our new captain. But I am confident they will get on. Both are Scots, both much of an age, both of a foot regiment . . . Indeed, *I* should not care for the task of establishing seniority. Oh, Louisa, look at that girl. I am not a critical woman, but just look.'

Frances was standing with her elbows on the rail, her chin in her hands, and her bottom stuck out.

'But her ignorance is not her fault,' said Amelia. 'It is the old old sad story, Louisa. Brought up by servants!'

I shall live on that island, said Frances to herself, I shall live there for ever with my beloved husband.

Her continuous search for a sanctuary, which was one aspect of her fear of the gaping world, had been directed by her reading into romantic expression. She had hardly admitted to herself her fear of the world, but that she knew her search to be only a fantasy was apparent in her choice of places, for she never chose any real or practicable place, but was attracted only by glimpses and suggestions and cities in clouds. In this case, the island rising out of the muddy river, though made more pleasant by contrast with flat and undistinguished shores, was only a mound of yellow sand on which grew a small grove of slender trees with thin foliage blowing all one way. In contour as plain as a pebble, it was a token or toy island, and since it was too small and unprovided to live on, it did not combat, by raising questions of ways and means, its ideal occupation by Frances and her husband. Nor did the figure of the husband demand gross definition, but was simply required to exist there, in the featureless blaze of romance. She fell into one of her elated trances. Her

27

eyes, unfocused by staring at the island, could now see only a blurred image of the trees, like tall candles with green flames blown sideways, and presently they too disappeared, and so did the husband, and the dream of retreat itself, leaving her elation in its pure form, a matter of the affinity of her youth with air and water. She reasoned that if she were conscious of being asleep with her eyes open, she could not really be asleep, and yet she did maintain a kind of sleep, holding herself most beautifully at the very margin of the unconscious. And in this state time became so distorted that she could have believed this shortest stage of her journey to be the longest—longer than from Cork to Sydney, longer than from Sydney to Dunwich. But the progress of a new fantasy (that they would sail on like this for ever and ever) was impeded by an anxiety, only faintly jarring at first, but presently formulating itself into two words.

'My hair.'

They would soon arrive. All her hair, as commanded by Amelia, was thrust beneath her bonnet: she must go below and dress it.

'How old are you?' asked Henry Cowper.

'Are you speaking to me?'

'My face is three inches from yours. Who else might I be speaking to?'

Frances repressed nervous giggles. 'I am nearly eighteen.'

'Good Lord. You look as old as your sister.'

'It's my hair.'

'Hair? I don't see any hair.'

'That's what I mean. It was too wobbly underfoot to dress it. I had to poke it all under my bonnet again.'

'Why didn't you get Madge Noakes to help you?'

She was sobered by the memory of Madge Noakes's face gliding into the dark mirror behind her shoulder. 'She offered her help, but I like to do my own hair.'

'Then you ought to get a hairpiece like Mrs Harbin's.' He raised his voice for the benefit of Louisa, who stood nearby with her back turned. 'Mrs Harbin has a hairpiece,' he said, 'like six red dead snails.' Louisa looked at him over her shoulder and pursed her lips thoughtfully. Frances had discarded her shawl, cinched her waist with a wide belt, and was holding a reticule. Lieutenant Edwards sauntered by with his hands at his back, Amelia Bulwer and Captain Clunie stood in tired silence, and Madge Noakes and the Bulwers' servant Maria, holding shawls and cloaks and muffs, talked apart in low voices. There was a slight whistling in the sails, a hurried whispering sound in the wash. Louisa Harbin, still looking over her shoulder at Henry, raised her eyebrows and drawled, 'Lord, Henry, how you smell of rum.'

'I always smell of rum.'

Frances giggled again. Louisa looked at her hands

29

fiddling with the reticule, then stepped back and stood at her side. On the banks of an olive green creek vines like ropes were twisted round gigantic trees with buttressed roots. Frances's eyes searched the dark alleys between the trees, her imagination engaged by their unseen extensions; but she was tired and nervous, and rather cold (for she had discarded her shawl out of vanity), and could not for the moment proceed with fantasy. Then a sudden bend in the river disclosed another kind of country: on one bank pleasant wooded hills, and on the other low fields swarming with men in yellow hoeing between rows of very young wheat. They were so close that Frances could hear the unrhythmic sounds of their shifting irons and the collapsing links of chain. Overseers, carrying heavy sticks, lumbered over the unsettled soil among them, and on the perimeter of the field moved red-coated soldiers, crosses of white webbing stark against their breasts, and bayonets shining and precise against field and sky. All the passengers on the cutter were watching them. Captain Clunie exclaimed at the area under cultivation, and Amelia Bulwer told him in a fast pleased voice of other fields, other crops. In the streets of Sydney Frances had seen iron gangs coming and going from barracks, but she had never before seen so many at once, and nor had she seen them at work. It was their great number, perhaps, or the clumsiness of their fettered movements that made them appear sub-human, like animals adapted to mens'

30

work or goblins from under the hill. She hated herself for her aversion from them, for the recoil of her spirit and the agitation of her heart. She was still standing between Louisa and Henry Cowper. 'Dear God,' she whispered, 'why must they look like that?'

Both turned to look at her. She felt in their attitudes a kind of caution. 'Like what?' asked Henry Cowper.

To spare them, or herself, she temporised. 'They are so—small.'

Henry Cowper shrugged, thrust his hands in his pockets, and with a swing of his shoulders moved away. He stood at a short distance, hands still in pockets, chin sunk in cravat, and his curved legs thrusting his calves against his trousers. Frances wondered how such a weary face could look so childish. 'Mrs Bulwer told me he is good,' she said to Louisa.

'Amelia will never speak ill of anyone, though she sometimes pulls faces.'

'Then he is not good?'

'I am no judge of goodness. I believe he sometimes tries to be.'

The wheatfield was spread across a long point of land. The cutter had passed the head of this point, and had reached the other side, when cries broke out from the field. One man had grasped his hoe near the blade and was bringing it down upon his neighbour's head and shoulders. The attacked man fell, his attacker fell with him, and the rest of the gang drew inwards about them. The soldiers, their feet avoiding the young wheat, began to converge on this congestion of yellow, but before they could arrive it was broken into by two overseers. These, parting the gang, disclosed the two on the ground, one felled, the other propped on an arm like a man at a picnic. The soldiers drew back and watched, while on the cutter, the two convict women, and all the passengers except Frances, were watching in the same manner, impassive yet attentive. But the two overseers bent over the men on the ground and obscured them from view. The rest of the overseers brandished their sticks and shouted something like, 'Hup! Hup!' The prisoners began to work again, and the passengers to turn away.

Henry Cowper came back to Louisa and Frances. 'The fellow picked his time.'

'Do you mean—' began Frances. The shock of the incident had made her voice hoarse; she cleared her throat. 'Do you mean he wanted us to see?'

'No doubt of it.' His voice still held a shade of the sulkiness, or resentment, with which he had met her first emotional response to the prisoners. 'It's a thing they often do,' he said.

The knowledge did not eliminate Frances's pity, but tempered it with an unwelcome reserve. 'It simply shows,' she said, reaching back for that first pity, 'their great desperation.'

'And their great cunning, alas,' said Louisa.

'It is said they kill because they wish to hang,' said Frances.

Henry nodded towards the receding wheatfield. 'There's no evidence that the fellow was killed.'

'No. But I have heard it of others. And read of it, too.'

'In the *Monitor*, no doubt,' said Louisa. 'Miss O'Beirne,' she said to Henry, 'is an admirer of Mr Smith Hall.'

Frances had not imagined he could look shocked. He opened his little blue eyes as wide as possible. 'Oh, I say! I say!'

'Is Mr Smith Hall such a monster?' cried Frances; but Louisa put a hand on her arm and said peremptorily, 'Not so loud!' And Frances, looking about her, caught the cold eyes of Amelia Bulwer, and noted Lieutenant Edwards's blank astonishment and Captain Clunie's quelling little blink. She lowered her voice, but still spoke with passion. 'Mr Smith Hall would not have them worked in chains. And when Mrs Shelley was in Pisa—'

'Mrs Shelley?' echoed Henry with bewilderment.

'The widow of the poet,' interposed Louisa.

'When Mrs Shelley was in Pisa, and saw chained prisoners sweeping the streets, she refused to stay.'

'How did that profit them?' asked Henry.

'Had she money of her own?' enquired Louisa.

'It may have profited them,' said Frances to Henry,

33

'by drawing attention to their condition.' And to Louisa she replied, rather more thoughtfully, 'I don't know about the money.'

Frances herself had eighteen pounds a year, from her mother.

Amelia Bulwer crossed over to them. After glancing unsmilingly from Louisa to Henry, she put both hands on Frances's, over her reticule, and looked her full in the eyes. 'Round the next bend you will see our botanical gardens. And round the one after that—' she brought up her hands and softly clapped them— 'the settlement!'

On the land a loud bell began to ring. Frances, who knew the botanical gardens to be cultivated by prisoners, and was prepared to find them hateful, was surprised by their peacefulness, their boskiness and glow. It was the first stage of dusk, when shadows deepen but the light grows for a while more intense. The banana trees, the citrus and figs, the grapevines and cane, all in separate plantations, covered the whole of the sloping bank. The mustered prisoners, half-hidden by foliage, were visible only as an undulating ridge of yellow, a colour that glowed as innocently, against the violet shadows and vivid greens, as the shaddocks and lemons nearer the shore. The glimpses of red—soldiers' coats—could have been the flowers of Rio, and when she saw, on the crest of the hill, a small octagonal cottage with a pointed roof, she gave a cry of pleasure, and Amelia Bulwer, watching her across the deck, nodded in vindication. The bell had stopped ringing.

Again they were rounding a long point defined by the windings of the river. The gardens lay on its eastern side, and when they left them behind, and came within sight of the western bank, Frances, like Amelia herself, brought up her hands and clapped them. The row of houses set in gardens, the smoking chimneys, the tall flagstaff and spirited fluttering flag, the barge crossing the river, the windmill on the hill, the cluster of people on the wharf, all this seemed to her the essence of home-liness and familiarity. A long line of yellow, flanked by spots of red, was moving in low billows of dust down the hill from the windmill, and more yellow, this time an irregular block, could be seen on the opposite side of the river, which the barge had now almost reached. But did not labourers all over the world walk home at dusk, and wait for ferries on river banks? To fortify Frances's impression that the place was much better than she had lately supposed came memories of Sligo, came her knowledge that free men and women, and their children too, could die of hunger while these men ate. For the man lying in the wheatfield the peasant in the Sligo ditch offered himself as counterpoise.

Now that the cutter was drawing nearer, the figures on the stone wharf, near the neat and solid warehouse, could be defined as a wharfinger and his helpers, two army officers, two women, and two children. One child, a small fair girl, was held in the arms of an old woman in a grey dress and white apron; the other, an auburn-haired boy, stood close by the side of a slender young woman, nuzzling her waist. Frances had no trouble in recognising her sister, for Letty's curls were still cropped close to her head, and she still wore the kind of soft and high-waisted dress that Frances remembered. Quite unexpected, however, was her slender unencumbered figure. Frances turned to Louisa to remark that Letty must have miscarried, but was forestalled by Louisa making the same remark to Henry Cowper.

The two officers, both lieutenants of the seventeenth regiment, were soon identified by Louisa (again in a low remark to Henry) as 'my poor Victor and Amelia's ridiculous Lancelot'. It was nearly dark now. Lights were appearing in the houses, the wharfinger was lighting his lanterns, and the cutter was drawing close to the wharf, when three men came over the crest of the bank: a young soldier, a man in rough clothes holding aloft a torch, and Patrick Logan. Frances had remembered him accurately. With one glance she confirmed his height, his straightness, and the restless carriage of his head, but she now wondered if the curbed fastidious step, which had become in her mind almost his emblem, was not caused by the gradient and roughness of the ground, for it was nearly duplicated by the soldier at his side. For the rest, the torchlight

36

showed him to be heavier, stronger, older, harder. He jumped down to the wharf and walked alone out of the torchlight to stand behind Letty. Frances looked from his face to her sister's, and once again felt the weakening flush of fear. She was too much at the mercy of her company, and was about to discover which of her unpredictable selves would advance to meet these two strangers.

CHAPTER TWO

'Good morning, Louisa.'

'Good morning, Letty.' With one hand on the back of Letty's sofa, Louisa bent for an exchange of kisses. 'I am glad to see you resting.'

'I am ordered to west for an hour each morning and afternoon.'

'Mr Murray's orders are so sensible,' murmured Louisa. Madge Noakes set a chair for her and she sat down.

'Thank you, Madge,' said Letty. 'How did you find Sydney, Louisa?'

'So-so.'

But now that Madge Noakes had shut the door, Letty raised herself on the sofa, and Louisa leaned forward in her chair, and Letty's hair, short, loose, and dark, all but met Louisa's, which even at this early hour was stiff, red, elaborate, and supported by a huge back-comb.

'Louisa, what a welief to have you back.'

'You make it almost a relief to be back.'

'I have had no one to talk to. No one I could *twust*.'

'What about Mr James Murray?'

'Too young. *So* young!'

'Do you really prefer his doctoring to Henry's?'

'Patwick asks me to favour James. He says Henwy is gwoss.'

'Gross indeed! I am often cross with myself for liking him. Was your miscarriage very sudden?'

'Lord, Louisa, it came all in a wush.' Letty leaned back with a sigh. 'I believed my hour had come.' Her sofa was placed to give a view over the garden. She turned her head against its blue silk upholstery to look out of the window, and at once lost interest in everything else. 'I pwayed as hard as I could,' she said absently.

Louisa also looked through the window. Across the wide verandah, through guava trees, could be seen part of the wall, and one window, of the separate building housing the commandant's office. Behind that window Mr Whyte the clerk would be at work. The window of the second room, in which (it was known this morning on the settlement) the commandant was closeted with Captain Clunie, was not visible from the house, but still Letty continued to stare, her pre-occupation and air of anxiety imposing such a waiting hush on the room that Louisa gave a little cough before breaking it.

'I didn't see much of Captain Clunie on the voyage, Letty, but what I saw I liked. I'm sure Captain Logan finds him congenial.'

Letty turned as if she had been waiting for it. 'Louisa, we don't know.'

'We? Does that mean that Captain Logan himself—'

'Has not had time to find out. Exactly! Last night Fwances and I left them with the port, but in five minutes Patwick joined us. Captain Clunie had wetired!'

She spoke in such a tone of doom, and brought down both hands, with such finality, on the rug covering her legs, that Louisa could not help laughing. 'Why should he not retire early? It was a long journey.'

'Ye-es.' Letty gave a sidelong glance through the window. 'Indeed, I told Patwick so.'

'But could not convince him?'

'He has been working so hard.'

'Of course.'

'So many on ev'wy vessel.' With one hand, as thin and delicate as a child's, Letty settled the ribbons at her neck. She wore a merino dressing gown, so new that it must have come on the *Isabella*. 'More than two hundwed last month.'

'I know. Victor says there are more than a thousand now. And the usual shortage of suitable overseers. So of course Captain Logan is overworked, and his mind under stress. He is lucky to have you to soothe his suspicions.'

'You sound as if you are soothing mine.'

'No, my dear Letty. But such feelings do act by contagion. Left to yourself, you would not have been taken aback because Captain Clunie went early to bed.'

'Without explaining his pwesence here? Why a captain should be sent? I believe I should have.'

'But surely the usual letter came with him?'

More doomed than ever was Letty's slow headshake.

'Then depend upon it,' said Louisa, 'it will come by the next ship. In Sydney they say General Darling is indisposed.'

But again Letty shook her head. 'Is Mr Macleay also indisposed?'

'Oh, Letty, Letty! We all know the likeliest explanation.'

'What?'

'Muddle. Gracious heaven, at this place we are familiar enough with *that*.'

Letty's face cleared. She almost smiled. But in the next second her brows contracted again. 'All the same, Louisa, a captain subordinate to a captain? It is not usual.'

But now Louisa refused to do anything but laugh at her. 'You echo Amelia. And that brings me to the purpose of so early a visit. I wanted to get to you before Amelia.'

'Amelia has alweady been.'

'Then that explains it. Gracious, she must have run over in her nightgown and cap. Did she say anything about Frances?'

'Fwances was pwesent.'

'Oh. Poor Amelia.'

'She did seem distwacted.'

'Where is Frances now?'

'With the childwen. She was eager to make their acquaintance. What have you to tell me about her?'

But even as she spoke, Letty, as if under compulsion, turned again to the window. Louisa said, 'Let us begin with your feelings for her.'

Letty turned with reluctance from the window. 'She is my sister. I am willing to love her, but for the pwesent, I confess I find her wather solemn.'

'It is the architecture of her face, she told Amelia.'

Letty's eyes, round, bright blue, and set in spiky dark lashes, were often described as 'starry', and indeed, amusement almost made them so. She said, '*Arch*-itecture?'

'Yes. One sees what she means. Palladian. Handsome, but rather heavy and official-looking.'

'Tell me what I am.'

42

'Rococo. What could be more charming? I of course am Gothic.'

'I wish I were Gothic. So womantic.'

'Oh, but I am Gothic that has been imperfectly understood. Commissioned by an Eastern potentate, perhaps, who has added some wrong thing, like an onion dome.'

Letty laughed so much that she kicked up both feet under the rug, and Louisa, seeing her in such good humour, smiled and said, 'But Frances's character doesn't accord at all with her face. If one can even define her character. She is less like a building than an unmixed pudding. In Sydney she was rather silly. She formed a friendship with the Hall girls.'

Letty's face could change in less than a second. She now looked quite stupid, as if such news were beyond her comprehension. She said, 'Not the daughters of . . . you can't mean the daughters of . . .'

'Yes I do. Dear Letty, pray compose yourself.' For Letty, in one movement, had flung off the rug and bounded to her feet. Her dressing gown was indeed new. It had not yet lost its folding creases. Louisa, even while begging her to compose herself, recalled a rumour heard in Sydney: the Logans were said to be in debt. 'Letty,' she said, raising her voice because Letty was pacing up and down and gasping, 'it is not as bad as it sounds. I was too sudden. I wanted to forestall Amelia, who will no doubt exaggerate the matter. I have come

43

to intercede for the girl. She is a girl of good quality. I like her.'

But Letty, as if she had not heard a word, continued to pace, 'How could she! That Jacobin—scwibbler—who has accused—my husband—'

Her pacing had taken her near the door. Louisa rose, crossed the room, and took her by the shoulder. She put a finger to her lips and looked towards the door. Letty raised a hand to her mouth and looked in the same direction. Louisa unloosed Letty's shoulder and went again to her chair. Letty followed and flung herself on the sofa. 'All the same, Louisa, murder. That cweature has accused Patwick of murder.'

'Madge Noakes listens at doors. I have seen her.'

'They all do. Madge is the best servant on the settle-ment. Her clear starching alone . . .' Letty abruptly sat up, kicked off one slipper, and drew her foot up to the edge of the sofa. She grasped it in both hands and bent to examine it. 'I am gwowing a corn,' she said, and in the next second put her chin on her knee and burst into tears.

Louisa was reminded of Frances's tears on the *Regent Bird*. She and Letty wept in exactly the same way: sudden, profuse, childish. Though there was English in them somewhere, and they attended the established church, and had little of the brogue, Louisa sometimes found them very Irish. At other times they seemed unanchored, without national or religious

44

affiliations at all, an odd condition that Louisa believed could be explained by the answer to a single question: by what sacrifice of what principle of his, or of his forebears, had their father become Major O'Beirne of the British army? But that was not, of course, a question one could ask. 'I don't believe Frances knows about Mr Smith Hall's accusations,' she said. 'The Hall girls spared her that, and she wasn't in Sydney for long enough to learn it elsewhere. All the same, she suspects. No, I shall put it like this. She refuses to suspect. But she has an uneasiness, the kind of vague uneasiness that is killed by clear explanation. It will vanish the moment the matter is explained to her—by you, dear Letty.'

Letty was dabbing at her eyes. 'I shall explain nothing to Miss Fwances. She may go back to Sydney on the *Isabella* with Lieutenant and Mrs Bainbwigge. The cutter sails this afternoon. I shall inform her this minute.'

'And what shall she do in Sydney?'

'Assassinate poor Gen'wal Darling. Become a governess.'

'Assigned, if in that order, to the imps of heaven or the heavenly cherubim. And why should either of them have the advantage of her cleverness, when your Robert needs it?'

Letty laughed, but said, 'No, Louisa, I am angwy. Why can't she be more like Cassandwa? Why did Cass have to go to the Indies?'

'You are less understanding even than Amelia.'

'How so?'

'Amelia saw excuses. The girl has been brought up by servants.'

Letty looked amazed. 'Louisa, that is *twue*.'

'And one must also ask who she came out with. Consider that long voyage, all those long conversations. The fellow passengers of a young person are of such importance.'

'Do you know who she came out with?'

'There was a young man. A Mr Edmund Joyce.'

'And he was a Jacobin?'

'Letty, we are very much behind the times out here, so much indeed that it is impossible to assess how much. I don't think they are called Jacobins any more. However, I know what you mean. I suppose he was, or is. In any case, he wears an open collar.'

'Indeed?'

'I saw him on the street. He looks a gentleman in spite of the collar. He and Frances mean to correspond.'

'In-*deed*!'

'But of course, these days, that doesn't mean they have reached an understanding.'

'I know that *vewy* well. I am not *so* much behind the times. But all the same . . .'

Letty's voice trailed away. She gave a little shrug, and fell into a pensive silence. Louisa could hear the fire crackling in the grate, and from other rooms the sound of children's voices, women talking, a clink of china, while from a distance came a ringing and clanging that never failed to remind her of the smithy in her native Essex village. 'He is vewy likely a lawyer,' said Letty suddenly.

'I can't think what gives you that idea.'

'They are so often Jacobins. But it is well known that young men forget these gweat weforming ideas when they take a wife. And so will Fwances. Poor Fwances!' said Letty, as if Frances were very sick. 'Do you know if he is a young man of means?'

'I have no idea. Ask Frances.'

'I shouldn't dweam . . . well, if one were tactful.'

'I am sure you will be.'

'I had begun to think of her for James. Doctoring is not smart, but it is wespectable. And his family is taking all that land in the south. But he has no means, and is a Catholic, and if this Mr Joyce is not . . . well, we shall see. Fwances has beautiful eyes, and vewy good arms and shoulders, and her smallpox hardly show at all. Cass, Fwances, and me. That would be three house-holds to weceive the two little girls at home.'

'One to spare,' said Louisa, rising to her feet.

Letty also rose. 'In case one of us should die. Or—' she flung out both hands in a gesture of dispersal.

'Or what?'

'Or anything. Who knows? You are going, Louisa?'

47

'I must, against my inclinations. Amelia and I live too close. It is too embarrassing to have her commiserate with me about Mrs Luddle. How can she fail to know that Victor shares the woman with Lancelot?'

Letty folded her hands and gave a moue of sympathy.

'And that they have her at the same time.'

Letty gave a gasp. 'How can you know that?'

'Victor told me himself. He is a poor simple creature, but a pig for all that. Though perhaps,' she added, 'I now find him rather less simple than before.'

Letty fluttered her hands. 'If I could help . . .'

'You can't.'

'If I told Patwick . . .'

'No, no.'

'He is so *stwict*,' wailed Letty in apology.

'Quite.' Louisa was looking into the mirror above the mantelshelf and touching her hair. 'The storm of indignation would be boring for everybody.'

'And besides, Luddle . . .'

'Is one of his few competent overseers. Exactly. He must stay, and so must his wife. It's of no consequence. Let us not add to Captain Logan's worries. If it weren't Mrs Luddle, it would be another.'

Again Letty gave her helpless flutter. 'Oh, Louisa . . .'

Into the mirror, Louisa faintly mocked her.

48

'Oh, Louisa . . .' She gave her face a last, reserved look, then turned to Letty. 'I shall see Frances in the nursery—'

But now, hearing a man's voice in the garden, they moved of one accord to the window. The commandant and Captain Clunie had emerged from the office and were walking towards the gate. Captain Clunie was speaking, but presently his slow loud voice gave way to the commandant's, which was so soft as to be hardly audible to the women. He laughed when he had finished, throwing back his head. Louisa always thought it wonderful how his face, so cold and stoical in repose, could be recast by laughter into this mask of a satyr. It was goatish rather than equine, the Roman satyr rather than the Greek, and like everything else about him, Louisa disliked it.

Both men fell silent before they reached the path beyond the verandah. Hands clasped behind and heads slightly bent, they walked by at a relaxed and companionable pace. The path took them on a winding ascent to the road. At the gate Private Collison stood to attention, and was put at ease. The commandant's house was the last on the road along the river bank. With their backs to the window and the attentive women, the two men stood facing the main settlement, while the commandant, with one stiffened hand, described a slow arc in the air, as if outlining the curve of Windmill Hill. He held it for a few moments at the foot of the hill, then moved it up and down in a chopping movement, talking all the time into Clunie's face, while Clunie nodded and nodded.

Letty was watching as if afraid to breathe, while beside her, Louisa made a sour mouth. The dissatisfactions of her marriage made her slightly resemble those women who disparage the marriages of their friends, continually asking what so-and-so can see in such-and-such a man; but she was saved from the excesses of the type both by her ironic self-awareness, and by an appreciation (also owed partly to the dissatisfactions of her marriage) of the attractions of men. She could usually divine what any woman could see in her particular man: she could now surmount her own distaste and see that Patrick Logan, even when standing still, gave an effect of movement only momentarily checked, of so much energy compressed that he made Captain Clunie beside him look heavy and staid and plumb-weighted.

The two men and Collison moved off towards the settlement. Louisa sighed, and said, 'Well,' and turned rather angrily from the window. 'Well!' said Letty also, in a tone of glad relief. She put her fingertips together and smiled at Louisa. She was pretty at all times, but the infusion of love into her face could make her beautiful. Louisa sighed again. 'Well, we may hope he has taken one of his likings. Continue your rest, Letty. I shall see Frances in the nursery on my way out.'

*

50

Outside the french doors of the nursery, Robert Logan, aged six, was leaning against a verandah post watching two of the gardeners at work. Inside, Frances sat in a child-sized chair across the table from her niece Laetitia, called Lucy to distinguish her from her mother. When Frances turned her head she could just see, above the intervening foliage, the heads of Captain Clunie, Patrick Logan, and the young soldier who had come to the wharf last night. In the commandant's head was the talking mouth, Captain Clunie's head kept nodding, and the soldier's flat and regular profile was unmoving. Frances sat bolt upright, a toy teacup of water in one hand and a saucer in the other. Now the commandant's hand was chopping up and down, and disappearing at every downstroke into the foliage. 'Will you take something, ma'am?' she heard Lucy ask.

She turned to meet an upraised enquiring gaze. Lucy, four years old, was quite comfortable at the little table, but Frances had to sit away from it, lest she tip it up with her knees. 'A little cold meat, if you please,' she replied.

'You must call me ma'am.' Lucy handed her aunt an empty plate. 'This is real meat, not kangaroo meat.'

'It is delicious, ma'am,' said Frances. She peeped from the corner of an eye through the french doors, but the three heads had gone.

'You're not eating your meat,' said Lucy.

Frances made vigorous chewing movements,

and Lucy, watching her closely, did the same. On the verandah Robert called, 'What are you doing, Martin?'

Martin's reply could not be heard.

'No, you're not, Martin.'

Martin must have said he was.

'No, you're not pulling weeds, Martin. Because why? Because you couldn't.'

Martin may have asked why he couldn't.

'Because you couldn't pull a greasy stick from a dog's arse, that's why, Martin.'

Frances rose and went through the french doors. She had already seen the gardeners on her way to and from the privy that morning, and she guessed that Martin was the dark young man, hardly more than a boy, who had stopped his work to watch her from beneath the brim of his cloth hat. She could see him again now, but was careful not to look full at him. All the same, as she took Robert by a shoulder and turned him towards the room, she caught a glimpse of his face twisted into a leer. It seemed directed at her, seemed to announce a victory over her. 'You are hurting me,' said Robert, and indeed, she was gripping his shoulder with angry force.

Lucy was still at the table. With her head on one side, she offered Robert an empty plate. 'A little cold meat?'

'No. It has ants on it.'

'Oh, no,' said Lucy with a threatening simper.

'It has. I hate ants. They taste hot. And anyway, it's only pretence meat.'

Lucy could not say pretence. 'It is not. Is it, Aunt Fanny? What he said?'

'Certainly not,' said Frances. 'Look, I am eating it.' And she sat down and chewed unhappily.

Robert knocked the plate out of his sister's hand. 'It's rotten meat. It's got maggots in it.'

Lucy flung herself on the floor, screaming. Robert crushed the plate underfoot. 'I'm killing the maggots,' he shouted.

Frances knelt by Lucy and raised her, still scream-ing, into an upright position in her arms. Robert ran and put his arms as far as they would reach round them both. 'Don't cry, Lucy,' he said. 'They would have crawled up Lucy's arm,' he said to Frances. 'That's why I did it.'

Lucy stopped screaming and hit him, in a feeble and rather experimental manner, in the face. He laughed, and so did Lucy. 'Aunt Fanny,' said Lucy then, 'make him take some cold meat.'

'Oh, very well,' said Robert, 'I'll take a bit of your old meat.'

The two children went and sat at the little table. Both were pale and beautiful.

'Aunt Fanny,' said Lucy, 'you come too.'

'There are only two chairs.'

'You can sit on the floor.'

Frances was about to sit on the floor when the door was opened by Louisa Harbin. By Frances's rush of relief at the sight of her, by her seeming so familiar, like a relation or an old friend, Frances was able to gauge for the first time the full extent of her own feeling of estrangement in her sister's household. She got to her feet and crossed the room quickly. 'I hope you are well this morning, ma'am.'

'Quite well. I have been with Letty and am on my way home.' Louisa was looking at the two children, who were laughing and rapidly picking all kinds of food from here and there on the table. 'What hair they both have,' she said. 'They could light dark places.'

'I wish I could put my mind to them. I'm so unsettled.'

'That's very natural. I enquired about the man in the wheatfield. A man named Fagan. He wasn't much injured. He is in the hospital.'

'And his attacker?'

'I expect he will be punished. You didn't think to enquire yourself?'

'I thought of it,' said Frances in a low voice.

'I wondered about you last night. Which of your selves came out?'

Frances laughed, but desperately flung out a hand. 'The very worst.'

'The radical?'

'No, no.' Frances covered her face with both hands, then took them away and said, 'The coward.'

'Gracious, child, we all have one of those.'

'Not as absurd as mine.'

'Well,' said Louisa, 'you can't be afraid of Letty.'

Frances considered for a moment. 'I don't think so.'

'Of the commandant?'

'Yes!' Frances beat her fists together. 'It's as if I were nine years old again.'

'Familiarity is the cure.'

'Undoubtedly,' said Frances bleakly.

'Letty will join you soon. Then you will feel better.'

'I think I shall feel worse, because she will think me more stupid than ever. I feel quite wildly unsettled. What is wrong with me? My room is very pretty. She had gone to such trouble. How can anything so pretty be so forbidding? I feel it almost impertinent of me to lie upon the bed. Yet I have been in lodgings, and in ships. But then, they don't pretend to be one's home, do they? Mrs Harbin, if I feel like this, arriving in my sister's house, what must servant girls feel in their first place?'

'I can answer only for myself. I felt exposed and mortified, a horrible hybrid thing.'

Frances simply stared. 'I was a governess,' explained Louisa.

'But a governess is hardly—'

'Frances, never let anyone persuade you of that. Unless you are marvellously lucky, the mistress will consider you one. And the band of servants will not presume to befriend you. Governessing made marriage look very attractive, and with all my present knowledge, Frances, it would make it so again.'

'Mar-tin!' called Robert from the verandah.

'They are not allowed to talk to the gardeners,' warned Louisa.

Frances called Robert as she went to the french doors, and he came back to the room at once, without remark. As she was shutting the doors, the young gardener, who was working nearby with an older man, raised his face to her. In his rough grey clothes he looked ugly and crumpled and stunted, and the face he raised was as unattractive as his clothes. But there was no mistaking the fear in his eyes, and the plea that surely sought mercy for his former spontaneous jeer. The older man went on working without faltering, but with a set and stony look on his face, as if to make clear his dissociation from the boy. Frances recognised him as the man who had carried the torch to the wharf the night before. He was taller than most, bandy and wiry, with a big hooked nose and a prim mouth. Like the overseers in the wheatfield, he wore grey slops and a straw hat.

Frances shut the doors. The children had resumed

their game. 'I wish Letty had warned me,' she said to Louisa.

'Letty is forgetful at present. The children are not allowed to speak to the men, nor are the men allowed to speak to the children. The commandant,' said Louisa, 'would be quite beside himself.'

'Would he have the men punished?'

'I expect so. All the prisoners assigned to the households are of the first class. At the very least they would lose their pay and privileges, so leniency is not a kindness. The children pick up words so fast. You have a young man here who used to help with the bullocks, and the bullock drivers do use the most curious language to urge their beasts on. Some of the officers find it vastly amusing, but not Captain Logan, I assure you. You consider that so amazing?'

Frances's amazement was not for Patrick Logan's prudery, but for the disclosure that there were working bullocks on the settlement. She did not correct Louisa's impression because she was reluctant to reveal her Sydney friends in another mistake. But when Louisa had gone, and she was picking up the plate Robert had broken, she set herself to recall the words of Edmund Joyce.

'You will find when you get there, my dear girl, that there is not a working beast on the place. The prisoners are the working beasts. The regulations are quite clear. Working cattle are not to be employed in labour that can be done by men. And what labour can not be done by men,' he asked bitterly, 'if there are enough of them, and their lives are held so cheap?'

'You are saying, then, that Captain Logan is—'

But he had not let her say what the commandant was. 'Oh, up to a point, he is bound by the regulations.' In speaking of Logan his manner had resembled that of the Hall girls, holding in its evasion a touch of stern pity for her, and an embargo on further questions. It had made her feel both vaguely humiliated and vaguely grateful, but she now asked herself if there had not been something shallow and ostentatious about both his sympathy for her, and his bitterness about the plight of the prisoners.

Lucy had spilled water on her dress, and Robert was complaining of hunger. In reply to Frances's summons on the bell came Elizabeth Robertson. An emancipist, brought by the Logans from Sydney, she was of a type soothingly familiar to Frances: a fat old woman, garrulous and inattentive, with a ruminating mouth and sore feet.

'The pretty plate, it's a shame. Hungry. Well, hungry will have to be fed. The cabbages got that bit of frost on them. And Miss Lucy needs drying off. Frost sweetens them. And put in the pan with that lump of pig fat, and that bit of caraway. Martin come and asked me for caraway. For Gilligan, he says. Get away, says I, Gilligan wants for nothing. His own hut in the garden. All the greens he can eat.'

'Why is he so privileged?' asked Frances.

'Well, miss, he can't live in barracks, for what the men would do to him. Him being scourger too.'

'Gilligan lays it on!' cried Robert. He raised an arm, then brought it down. 'Swoosh!'

'I never give Martin that caraway,' said Elizabeth.

CHAPTER THREE

'Another weak point,' said Patrick Logan.

From a bench he took a circlet of leather, like the top of a boot, and offered it for Clunie's inspection. 'It is necessary,' he said. 'It stops the iron from damaging their legs. And yet, it wears, d'you see? Or can be scraped with a stone, bit by bit, and thinned down. And then they grease their heels, and slip their irons, and run.'

Five musters a day, thought Clunie, and five inspections, and still they run. He did not know whether to be admiring or appalled at such ingenuity and determination. But the commandant had begun to look irritated, and was joggling the circlet as though to hurry him into comment. Although their long discussion in the office had come to a friendly conclusion, it was clear that the commandant continued to be fretted by the ambiguity of Clunie's presence at Moreton Bay. For the most part he was good-humoured and friendly, but now and again his anger flashed. As he proffered the leather circlet he was scowling.

Clunie, himself unable precisely to explain his posting, but not of a nature to be worried by it, took the circlet and turned to the light of the doorway to examine it. They were in the lumber yard. They had inspected the tailors and boot-makers, the tanners, the soap and candle makers, the carpenters and coopers and wheelwrights, and had now entered the foundry and smithy, where nails and bolts and chains were made, where animals were shod and men ironed. Wherever they had gone, the commandant had explained that when he was away at Dunwich, or at the Limestone Station, or the Eagle Farm, Bainbrigge had done this, or Bainbrigge had done that; for having reached their friendly conclusion, no possibility must be mentioned than that Clunie had been sent to take Lieutenant Bainbrigge's place as engineer and second in command. Clunie examined the leather circlet with conciliating care. 'I suppose they will continue to run,' he said, 'as long as you've too few capable overseers.'

'You're right. They're slack. They tire of the details. They're slack.' All irritability gone, he eagerly took the circlet from Clunie's hand. 'See?' He traced with a finger the variation in its thickness. 'They missed that.'

Dismay showed in Clunie's face. 'It's very slight.'

'Enough. Fellow who wore it was out for a week. Came in yesterday with a spear wound in the arm.'

He tossed the circlet on to the bench and led the way further into the smithy. Tall, stiff-backed, his step delicate, his head, restless or watchful, turning this way and that, he impressed Clunie as being rather too much of the commandant. Clunie did not doubt that the manner was natural to him, but considered that for these prisoners and their guards it would have been better modified.

The twenty prisoners who had come in the *Isabella*, and who had been brought up the river that morning in the settlement's second cutter, the *Glory*, were waiting in a row for their irons to be knocked off. Clunie had watched them at exercise on the deck of the *Isabella* and recognised them now by nodding along the line. But Logan was looking them over in the sharp but musing manner of a craftsman inspecting new tools. 'A wretched lot,' he said despondently.

'None was sentenced to be worked in irons?'

'None of these.' A sudden cessation in the hammering and clanging did not make him lower his voice. 'But these three over here—all old hands, quite degraded— I sentenced these to be ironed yesterday.'

All three old hands must have heard this soft laconic statement, but none showed signs of doing so. Two were of the usual deficient height, and one of these was now pointed at by the commandant. 'Bulbridge. You saw him

62

attack another man in the wheatfield.' The third man had a bandaged arm; he was of more than middle height and looked in his thirties. 'And this is the absconder I just spoke of,' said Logan. 'He won't run again.'

Clunie saw that the twenty new arrivals could not take their eyes off Logan, whom they were scrutinizing with a surreptitious greed and terror, but that the attention of the three old hands was fixed on himself. The tallish absconder was standing, waiting for his trousers to be split to accommodate the irons already on his legs, and the two little ones, Bulbridge and the other, sat on the ground, their backs against the wall and their legs extended before them. The commandant, pointing to their ankles, explained that this was a new method, still on trial, to circumvent their trick of making their feet swell before the irons were put on. 'We do them in the coolness of the morning, and sit them down beforehand.'

The two sitting men heard this impassively, but the absconder showed a shade of some expression, not quite irony, not quite a smile, and too exactly controlled to be challengeable. Clunie thought such control remarkable in a man who looked as starved and exhausted as a wandering dog. He was a man with a sunken face, a long turned-up nose with flaring nostrils, and a low seamed forehead between his dirty flaxen hair and his dirty flaxen brows. His eyes, of a light hazel, were bold and quick in spite of being so bloodshot that their

63

restoration was hardly imaginable. Clunie saw humour in the face, and good-humour, but it was a tense face in spite of it, with jumping muscles. In his mixture of comedy and strain, of strength and dilapidation, he reminded Clunie of an ageing fairground tumbler or acrobat. He caught Clunie's eye, and with deliberation twisted his head and one shoulder towards the wall, making visible part of his back. By a forward jerk of his arm he pulled the shirt taut across it; in a second it was covered by stripes of blood. 'Speared, flogged, and ironed,' thought Clunie. He was impressed by the man's spirit. 'He is showing you,' said the commandant with lofty amusement.

He was already turning to go. Clunie walked with him out of the smithy into the yard. 'Who is he?'

'Lazarus One.'

'There are two?'

'There are. Both named Lewis Lazarus.'

'Related?'

'They said not.'

'Curious.'

'Ah, man, everything is curious down there where they spring from. They could have the same mother, and not know it, Lewis perhaps being the lady's favourite name. Or one could have stolen the other's name, not wishing to be sentenced in his own. Why ask? It's not to our purpose. Lazarus Two served his sentence and was shipped back to Sydney. This one will never

64

go back. A lifer. Sentenced at home for robbery. Ticket of leave in Sydney. Robbery again, and sentenced to do the rest of his imperial sentence here. And here the man will die, though he swears he won't.'

'No chance of remission?'

'None in this world. He has run too often. From Port Macquarie and from here. Out for nine months in 'twenty-six. A good bushman. And with the bullocks, the best man on the settlement. You would wonder how he took to the work, a city man like that, born in Hull and taken in London.'

'Are lifers allowed to work with the bullocks?'

'Not according to the regulations, but exceptions are made for skilled men, and skill is judged by me. I could have used that fellow, both here and on my journeys inland. But no, he wanted none of it.'

'What does he want? To be flogged and ironed?'

'Ah, that's irrelevant to the man. He wants to beat the thing, and the thing's the law, and in this place the law is me. He wants to beat me.' Logan's voice was both laconic and morose. 'The devil gets into some of them, and in certain ways they go mad.'

'I am interested in their looks,' said Clunie. 'So many lack stature—'

'The type, the type.'

'—and so many are most vilely wrinkled. Not as you and I might wrinkle, but without logic, if I may put it like that. One seeks a cause.'

But now Logan seemed bored. 'Then seek it with Cowper or Murray. They're our men of science.'

They had reached the big gates of the lumber yard, which at their approach were opened by Private Collison and the sentry. The gates faced the river. Broad and shining, brown and silver, it moved with the strength of deep water on an outgoing tide. It was an exquisite day, cold and sunny, and Clunie could not repress a moment of sickish regret for what lay at their backs. But in this long peace, an officer without a private fortune must reconcile himself to such tasks, and alleviate them by the best means at hand. He said, 'Edwards tells me there's good fowling up the river.'

'There is. Teal, wild duck, swamp pheasant. But go prepared to use your arms. Blacks killed three of a boat's crew up there lately.'

He signalled to Collison and they moved off, the soldier following at a distance that put him out of earshot. 'Will you be using Bainbrigge's servants?' asked Logan.

'If I may.'

Clunie almost smiled at the satisfaction with which the commandant heard that Clunie was willing to be assigned only the number of servants accorded a lieutenant. It was his second marked diplomatic success of the day. The first had been in the office, when he had broken blandly into Logan's maze of angry surmise to say, 'I expect they couldn't think of anything else to do with me. And as for the lack of a letter from Macleay, I'll give you my guess about that. Muddle. Simple muddle.' The word had worked a miracle. Logan had actually laughed. 'My dear fellow, you can't tell us at Moreton Bay anything about muddle. We know it all.'

And now he was saying, 'Good. Very good. Bainbrigge's personal servant is a prisoner. You've no objection to that?'

'None.'

'Very good. We need all the ranks for guard duty. The personal servant I had before Collison was a prisoner. Bishop. A man once of my own regiment. A lifer. Highway robbery. A great strong fellow, oh, he stood out among them like a giant. Scourger, too. Went out with a party of soldiers, and drowned while getting water. Bishop! I've not found another like him, nor ever will.'

The memory of Bishop had quite expunged the commandant's good humour; he sounded morose and bitter. 'And of course, there was great rejoicing, and they said they saw his ghost. They're great ghost seers, you will find. And they tried to claim the credit. Yes, credit is how they saw it, and credit was the word they used. They said he was ambushed and murdered by runaways. I should like to see the two or three runaways that could have held Bishop under water, or the four or five either. It needed two men at the triangles to take his place until one grew practised

67

enough to take the task alone. That's Gilligan. He's my chief gardener too. He's well enough, but there will never be another Bishop.'

'Was it Bishop who is said to have killed the man Swann?'

'*I* am said to have killed the man Swann. Bishop was scourger at that time, but according to the *Monitor*, was only the instrument of my murderous rage.'

'I don't read the *Monitor*.'

'Nor I. It was sent me from Sydney with the suggestion that I prosecute. I didn't need the suggestion. I should have done so in any case. It's a question of my good name. Its precious editor got his information from a former prisoner at this place. Lorry, Lawrie, some such name, I don't even recall the fellow. Smith Hall must be a great fool to put his trust in a convict, former or not. By far the larger part of them are liars and curs, and the man's a fool that thinks otherwise.'

They had turned their backs on the river and were picking their way up the rutted street past the military barracks, a two-storeyed brick building, not yet finished, with corner stones of the local pinkish stone. As they paused to watch the work, Logan whistled softly through his teeth, and after a while gave a nod of satisfaction. Clunie also approved the building, finding it solid and decent and suitable to its purpose. 'It's too bad,' he said, as they walked on, 'that the governor has no power to deal with fellows like Smith Hall.'

'He is stopped by the chief justice. As sure as he devises a method to put the radical editors down, the chief justice rules it repugnant to the laws of England. It's evident he doesn't consider anarchy repugnant to the laws of England. I am sorry for the governor, though to me the Hall matter is of little consequence.'

'It will mean a journey to Sydney.'

'D'you think I object to that?'

'No indeed.' Clunie was startled by the commandant's testy response. 'I meant that you would welcome it.'

'Why should I not? And my wife is delighted.'

But there was still a touch of defiance in his tone. Clunie, who had heard rumours of Logan's debts, wondered now if they were gambling debts to fellow officers in Sydney. It did not take much imagination to see him at the tables, high-strung yet stoney-faced, unable to leave, and nor was it hard to realise how galling such debts would be to his touchy pride. 'The ladies,' he was saying now, 'are always wild to get to Sydney. They miss the pic-nics, and the balls.'

'I hope my wife shall have landed by then, so that she and Mrs Logan may meet.' Clunie spoke with a warmth that was in part an apology for his suspicions. 'And as for Smith Hall, may he be confounded! As will certainly happen. Public opinion has quite turned against him.'

'I know it. His only support is from the eccentric and the low.'

Clunie thought suddenly of Frances O'Beirne. He did not like the girl, having been affronted first by what seemed to him a clumsy flirtatiousness, and then by the crude sincerity of her cry: 'Is Mr Smith Hall such a monster?' But last night at the commandant's table he had detected something else in her, a sort of pitiable heat and confusion. 'Well,' he replied to Logan, 'let us say of the unformed and the undisciplined.'

Logan accepted the amendment with a good-humoured laugh. He was obviously pleased, even excited, by Clunie's expressions of support. 'I wish I could take you out to the Eagle Farm, my dear fellow, but we are damnably short of horses. Two died this year, and for the loss of a third I hold myself responsible. On my expedition in May he broke away from our encampment and was not recovered. So now, except for my grey—and she is my own good beast, I bought her in Sydney—there's only the nag Murray uses. I asked for six. Two were sent, but the voyage was rough and both were injured. I asked again. The result was silence. Oh, you are right when you speak of muddle. The governor is the best of men and the best of soldiers, it's an honour to serve him. But he's as bedevilled by his officials as I am by my overseers. Well, who knows? The next ship may bring horses, and in the meantime you may borrow my mount and ride out with Murray. A thousand acres under cultivation at the Eagle Farm, the whole establishment under Parker, dispensary every day, Murray rides out in the mornings. Oh, sometimes I think I've not done too badly. I'll take you to Spicer now. I've some business with Cowper at the hospital. Spicer's my superintendent of convicts. He'll show you the labour returns, and there are a thousand new regulations. Paperwork is not in my line, I'll leave you to him. But wait, wait, first let me show you something.'

The commandant leading, they veered to the left and crossed obliquely a large paddock. On the other side stood the prisoners' barracks. Clunie supposed this to be their destination, but the commandant halted just inside the gate set in the high surrounding wall.

Here stood a row of slab huts. He set a hand on the nearest. 'A few slab huts,' he said. 'When I came, these were all I had to use. At night I used to hear them trying to get out and run.' He held one foot parallel to the wall, a few inches above the ground. 'Scratching just there, between the slab and the earth, trying to get out and run.'

Clunie nodded, looking only at the commandant's boot. He could not look at his face. The boot seemed poised to stamp on fingers. A fine war, he thought, for a Peninsula veteran.

Logan straightened his figure and folded his arms. 'They questioned my punishments. Too severe. I pointed

71

out that I had no means of solitary confinement. So they let me put the slab on stone foundations.'

He walked past three huts, followed by Clunie, and stopped at the fourth. 'Like this.' He set the tip of a dusty boot on the stone. 'I had this quarried across the river. I found good clay and set up a kiln. I sent men upriver and set up the Limestone Station. Oh, and of course there were letters to write. Letters! But in the end I had my way, I built in brick and stone. These are overseers' huts now.'

He turned and walked into the centre of the large compound, followed again by Clunie, who obediently stopped when he did. Collison had remained at the gate. The commandant, looking up at the barracks, lifted and settled his heels. He did not speak, but Clunie understood him to be saying, in effect, 'And now, look at that!'

The barracks, quite empty at this time of day, seemed spread out for scrutiny and comment. It was by far the biggest building on the settlement, with extreme wings on one storey, and a two-storeyed main block intersected by a central tower of three storeys. On the *Regent Bird* Amelia Bulwer had told Clunie that the two top storeys of the tower were occupied by the chapel, and on the same voyage Henry Cowper had told him that at the ground level of the tower the triangles were set up and the men flogged. Like Louisa Harbin, Clunie had been 'reached by the new ideas', and was aware of what capital, especially journalistic capital, could be made of such a juxtaposition, but his very awareness of this, and his distrust of the kind of person who would make it, helped him to disregard all such influences in judging the building. He saw that it was a stout and well-proportioned building, and in spite of certain crudities of construction he thought it very creditable to Logan—very creditable indeed if one took into account the shortage of skilled labour, the lack of enthusiasm in Sydney, and the smallness (after all) and unimportance of the place itself. It was, in fact, a fine building *for the place*. Clunie, understanding at that moment how life in such an isolated place could warp the judgement and disrupt the sense of proportion, determined on steadiness from the start. He would not overpraise the building. But here was the commandant, with folded arms and teetering heels, his face worshipfully raised, clearly expecting it to be praised according to his own inflated estimate.

'It is of credit to you,' said Clunie, 'in the circumstances.'

Logan's heels settled; his arms tightened across his chest; he turned his head and regarded Clunie along his shoulder, without expression. Then his eyes took on a distant look, and he nodded in gentle, regretful agreement. It gave Clunie the impulse to retreat, to contradict himself in some way or to add some stronger praise; but the commandant might have forgotten him, so completely had he withdrawn his attention.

He had raised his eyes to the windmill. 'The settlement,' Cowper had told Clunie on the *Isabella*, 'is mostly on one point of land. Penis-shaped, we shall say, backed by a high ridge we shall call the Line of Bollocks.' Coarse but accurate, thought Clunie now. The windmill was on that ridge. Logan had spent fifteen minutes that morning explaining to Clunie why the sails had never rotated. The building housed a treadmill.

Logan's silence continued as they returned to the gate, were joined by Collison, and crossed the broad paddock again. Clunie felt it as a silence, not of offence, but of deep thought, and indeed, when the commandant spoke at last, it was in the slow, impersonal tone of self-absorption.

'I think, when you have learned the ways of the place, I shall take a journey inland. My map is not complete.'

'One hears of your explorations in Sydney,' gratefully murmured Clunie.

The commandant looked neither pleased nor displeased, but said in the same abstracted way, 'There's a stream striking out of the river at the foot of the Brisbane Mountain. It runs north-east through the ranges, in my opinion, and reaches the sea. In my opinion it augments itself from the mountains and flows as a fine river to the sea.'

He needs that fine river to the sea, thought Clunie. 'If by being your deputy,' he said, 'I can help in such important work—'

But Logan cut in, alert and wary again. 'After the letter, man. We will wait for Macleay's letter.'

The office of the superintendent of convicts was in a long low building of slab and stone. Clunie was relieved to be delivered to Peter Spicer and left alone with him. While Logan's departing footsteps could still be heard, this plump and jaunty young man was congratulating Clunie on having inherited Bainbrigge's personal servant, a clever fellow who wove his own crab baskets and slung them across the mouths of creeks.

'But not too often in the same place, captain, because the crabs are cunning. Bainbrigge—obliging fellow—always let me have one or two.'

CHAPTER FOUR

'But how did you become learned?' asked Letty.

'I am not learned,' said Frances, laughing.

'Louisa Harbin says you are.'

'She is mistaken, Letty. Mama taught me to read and write, just as she taught you and Cass, and beyond that I know only what I learned from reading her books.'

'Then you can't do awithmetic?'

'Yes. Our Uncle Fitz taught me when he broke his leg at our house, and was bored.'

'Even long division?'

'Yes.'

'Then you are learned.'

Frances laughed again, watching Letty in the mirror. They were in Frances's room. Letty had secured the front of her sister's hair with combs and was now standing behind her chair loosely plaiting the long tresses at the back. Several times it had occurred to Frances to tell Letty that the young gardener had spoken to Robert, but each time she had postponed this duty because she was reluctant to mar the pleasure of the occasion. She knew that the exaggerated respect with which Letty spoke of her learning was in part a humorous pose, but it was exactly the kind of half serious and half mocking game played by herself and her little sisters at home, and it made her feel happier and more at ease than she had believed possible. Laughing, and watching Letty in the mirror, she was waiting for her to laugh in response, but Letty, though smiling with her eyes, pursed her lips solemnly and drew Frances's braided hair into a knot at the back of her head. 'Do you like it like that?'

'It's very nice.'

'Tell me the *twuth*.'

'I don't like it.'

'Neither do I.'

Letty released the hair and it dropped like a shot bird down Frances's back. 'You see?' cried Frances. 'That's all it *wants* to do.'

'It can't be let.'

'I could have a fringe. I could curl it in papers.'

'In this climate the curl would dwop out. And you are too young for a hairpiece like Louisa's.'

'When does it get hot?'

'It will start in five or six weeks.'

'I wish I had curls like yours, and could wear it short.'

Letty sent herself a swift glance of approval in the mirror. 'It is no longer modish . . .' she picked up a strand of Frances's hair and felt the texture . . . 'but Patwick dotes on it.'

Frances hid her eyes by looking down at her lap. The satisfaction in Letty's voice (it had sounded so private) evoked in her this modesty, and with it, a rankling surprise that Patrick Logan could dote on anything. Letty had drawn back a pace and was looking at Frances's hair with her head on one side. 'So I shall keep my short curls,' she said absently, 'until we get back.'

Frances raised her eyes. 'Back where?'

'To where modishness matters. If indeed we ever do.'

'Do you like it here, Letty?'

Letty took the comb and quickly parted Frances's hair with one long stroke from forehead to nape. 'In some ways it has been like an island. We will twy this. Hold that half. No, keep your head *stwaight*.'

She became as brisk and busy as a cook making pastry. Dividing and combing and plaiting, she said, 'Fwances, will you teach Wobert?'

'Indeed I will!' cried Frances in gratitude.

'Are you a good teacher?'

'I don't know. I have only taught Hermione and Lydia, and they are both so clever by nature.'

'I hope they are not too clever.' Letty secured a loose knot at one side of Frances's head. 'Don't look, if you please, until I have done the other half.'

Frowning, she began work on the other half, while Frances obediently watched only her face. The darkness beneath her eyes, purplish near the bridge of her nose, must have been there all the time, though her animation had diverted attention from it. In her pre-occupation two thin lines appeared from her nostrils to the outer corners of her lips. These deepened. A minute passed in silence. 'Are Hermione and Lydia pwetty?' she asked.

'Pretty? They are beautiful.'

'But only childwen still.'

'Yes, but upon my word, they are beautiful. Uncle Fitz thinks so too. He says such girls may rise to great heights in the world, with the right patronage.'

'I hate to think what he means. He is quite diswep-utable. Still, he is worldly, and not a fool. Descwibe their manners.'

'Oh, Letty . . .'

'Then their manners are not . . .?'

'I have done my best.'

'Of course. And they will be as gwateful to you as I am. I am sure there is nothing that can't be mended. Don't cwy, dear Fwances. You are like me, always cwying for nothing.'

But Frances, with a handkerchief pressed to her

eyes, now began to laugh. 'I shan't be able to hear with all this hair over my ears.'

'Never mind. It is charming! There, you may look now.'

Frances regarded herself first with surprise, then with gathering criticism. She raised a hand to her smallpox scars, but Letty took it and drew it away.

'No! About those you must be absolutely *bwazen*. There is nothing else for it. Tell me you like your hair.'

'I don't know.' Frances was turning her head this way and that. The face of the young gardener flashed again in her memory, but again it seemed inopportune to mention him. 'I think,' she said, 'it is too frivolous for my face.'

'Your face will gwow into it. Yes, it will do vewy well.' She lifted and settled Frances's frilled collar. 'Madge Noakes will do your clear starching. She has the twick of making it last in the heat. You must have muslin dwesses. Here it is muslin muslin nearly all the year. Like the seaside at home. You will need at least five more. I had a bolt of white muslin sent from Sydney last month. Are you a good seamstwess?'

'Only a very plain—'

'Well, I am a vewy fine one. And Amelia Bulwer can cut.'

Frances said she would not dream of troubling Mrs Bulwer, but Letty cried earnestly, 'My love, you must twouble her. Or else go dwessed like Mother

Bunch. On eighteen pounds a year you can't get your clothes from Sydney or London.'

'Then I shall have to do as I am. I don't like Mrs Bulwer, and when I don't like a person I hate taking favours from them. It makes my flesh creep.'

'Fwances! That is wicked pwide.'

'I suppose it is pride.'

'You must pway to God to purge it from your heart.'

'Could I not pray directly for five white muslin dresses?'

Letty sank into the winged chair opposite Frances's. '*Fwances*!'

'I am sorry, Letty. I know it is wrong to treat God as a haberdasher.'

'Enough! You are showing a side of yourself I find *most stwange*.'

'It is a new self even to me.' Frances gave herself a glance in the mirror. 'Perhaps it's my hair.'

'It is blasphemy. Patwick would send you back on the next ship.'

'Is Patrick so very—'

'But we shan't mention it to him or to anyone else. You will never do it again. It is fwightfully unlucky to blaspheme.' Letty leaned out of her chair and set a hand on Frances's wrist. 'My love, do let Amelia cut the dwesses. You judge her too soon. How long have you known her?'

'Only—'

'Exactly! She is kindness itself.'

'For convenience's sake, I shall try to think so.'

Letty released her wrist. 'You are vewy sharp, sister.'

'I know,' said Frances unhappily.

'Either too shy, or too sharp. So shy last night you could not find a word to say to Patwick. And yet, today . . .'

Frances put both hands over her eyes. 'I know! I wish I were more like you and Cass. Upon my word I do!'

'Cass was not too pwoud to let Amelia—'

'You are right, it is a kind of pride.'

'Now you are being sensible. We will ask her to cut only *four*. You think I am making a gweat fuss about a little thing. Well, uncover your eyes. I must speak to you on an important matter. I will be quite candid. It is best to be candid about this.'

Frances uncovered her eyes. 'You are going to speak of the company I kept in Sydney.'

'What company?'

'Mrs Bulwer has not told you?'

Letty shook her head. 'If it is something I ought to know, you will tell me yourself, Fwances. No, I was going to speak of husbands.'

'Husbands?'

'Yes. Do you want one?'

82

'I—suppose I do. Yes, I do. But I hardly like to say so, lest I sound like a husband hunter.'

'I said we would be candid. We will be more than candid. We will be bold, and admit that ev'wy woman who wants a husband is in some degwee a husband hunter, though it is a hateful term. Vewy well! What are her weapons? First,' said Letty, holding up a fore-finger, 'her looks. If she is pwetty, so much the better. If not, she may attend her skin and hair with diligence, wub her teeth with salt and chalk, and be fwesh and pleasant in her dwess. Second—' Letty held up another finger '—her manners. It is better to be shy than sharp, but better still to be neither. You must cultivate a weliable manner.'

'That's what Mrs Harbin told me.'

'Louisa is vewy clever.'

'Yes, and so are you, Letty. So I suppose it is true. And I don't know what makes me resist it.'

'Pwide.'

'I suppose that is true, too.'

'To be sure. Now we come to her backgwound.' Letty raised a third finger. 'I am not sure that I ought not to put it first. Because when a man seeks a wife, he first sees the young woman as part of a backgwound. There is a comfortable house, and good food, and pleasant conversation. And always an older woman, a mother or aunt or sister. She is important. By speaking to her more than to the young woman, he may disguise his intentions until they are quite firm, and that gives him a feeling of ease and safety. And as well, she may pwaise the young woman, whereas the young woman may not pwaise herself. And if she twuly loves the young woman, so much the better. She teaches others to love her.'

'And yet,' said Frances, 'you had none of that. Oh, you had it while you and Cass were living with our aunts, but not when you came home on that visit.'

'And met Patwick. No. But there are not many such men. A fine-looking captain may easily find a wife with means, and indeed, having spent his patwimony on his commission, he was looking for exactly that. But once we met, he cared nothing for means or backgwound. He would have had me if I had lived in a twee.'

Frances, lowering her eyes from her sister's face (bemused with memory) considered the commandant in this new aspect, and was forced to grant him the dignity of his love. She raised her eyes. 'Then may not I also meet—'

Letty broke in with surprising sharpness. 'It is foolish to wish for it. Men who make such choices are capable of wecklessness.'

She would not let Frances speak. She raised a hand. Her gravity was a warning. 'I say only that backgwound and guidance are safer.'

'Yes,' said Frances, 'I see that, because whatever I

may crave for myself, I should choose background and guidance for Hermione and Lydia.'

'Fwances, I am glad you say that. So would I choose it for them. I want it for them most earnestly.'

Letty, leaning out of her chair, pleading into Frances's eyes, was earnest indeed. 'In another few years they will need it, and now that both our aunts are dead, who is to give it to them but you and me and Cass? And who knows but that one of us will be dead by then? You know how it is with women—their lives wushing out in their blood. Oh, it can happen so fast, with the world tilting and a shade cweeping over the sun. Oh, let us not speak of it. One can only pway. So you see, when I hear you blaspheme . . .'

'I shan't again,' said Frances in a frightened voice. But Letty had risen, and now walked quickly to the window, and stood with her back turned. As a child Frances had often heard the servants describing fatal childbirth: the screams and beating fists, the live torn bodies, the green bloodless corpses. She now watched her sister with the same expectancy she had once turned on the aghast and whispering servants, as if she awaited from that figure at the window the first notes of Bridie's long wail; but as Letty turned from the window her mouth (though with a wry twist) was smiling, and her hands were extended with a simple expository grace.

'Women,' she said. 'Even supposing they survive,

they are at the mercy of their husbands. I speak of course of those with no means. They may be widowed and left penniless with young childwen. Or a husband may be disgwaced and thought unfit to employ, and then they must all starve, or depend on the kindness of wich welations. Who are not always kindly disposed. Indeed they are not. Oh, but don't speak of it, don't speak of it.' She sat again in the winged chair, arranging her skirt over her thighs. 'It will not happen to you. Let us speak of you. Is there anyone you fancy?'

'I don't know how I can still want to marry, after all you have just said. But there is one young man. His name is Edmund Joyce. But I don't like him quite so much as I pretend. I met him on the voyage out. We were the only young passengers, and he was so pleasant that it began to seem peculiar in me *not* to be a little in love with him. He suggested that we correspond.'

'He ought to first ask Patwick's permission, or mine.'

'Oh Letty, these days—'

'I know. I am not *so* much behind the times. Is he a young man of leisure?'

'He is a lawyer.'

'Ah.'

'That pleases you?'

For Letty's satisfied response had surprised Frances, who had almost said, 'only' a lawyer. However, Letty now modified her satisfaction with a provisional

'Well . . .' and went on to say that though the law was not as smart as the army, it was quite respectable. 'More so, I think, than doctowing. If you and I go to Sydney with Patwick, you may certainly pwesent the young man.'

'*If* you and I go? But if Patrick goes to Sydney, will it not be because the fifty-seventh is under orders for India? So you and I would certainly go.'

'Oh, but even if the wegiment stays in the colony, Patwick must soon go to Sydney. To pwess his charge of libel, you see, against Mr Smith Hall.'

Frances put her left hand to her cheek. 'A charge of libel?'

'Why, yes. It is always a charge of libel with that gentleman, is it not?' Letty reached out and gently lifted Frances's hand away from her cheek. 'Wemember what I told you.'

'In what way did Mr Smith Hall libel Patrick?'

'By accusing him of murder, if you please. Oh yes, I don't wonder you look surpwised,' said Letty, though Frances looked less surprised than stupid. 'He met a convict in Sydney who told him that Patwick had had a man flogged to death. A man named Swann. But that same man Swann died in hospital here, of a disease. And of course there is pwoof of it. Poor Mr Smith Hall. He must have a gweat and noble heart, to be so easily deceived.'

Frances continued to sit like a lump, to frown and

to stare. '*Now*,' said Letty, 'your hair is too fwivolous for your face.'

'But how could Mr Smith Hall have made such a mistake? I think I always knew there was something— something—I couldn't or wouldn't think what. Severity. Yes. But murder? I know he writes about—the power of the commandants at the penal stations. Severity, and sentences exceeding the ones given by the courts. But I thought, I took it for granted, that he wrote mostly about Norfolk Island. Or Van Diemen's Land. Or, if he wrote about this place, I thought it would be something—trivial. But murder. As blunt as that. Was it as blunt as that?'

Letty said yes, it had been quite as blunt as that.

'But how could he make such a mistake? He is a clever man.'

'Is he clever? I am sure he is a good man. I know he is a churchman, and a member of the Benevolent Society. And he is bookish. But to be bookish is not to be clever. You are bookish. Are you clever?'

'No indeed.'

'You will be clever one day. You still lack knowledge of the world.'

A knock at the door sent Letty to open it. 'Yes, Madge,' Frances heard her say, 'you may bring it now. One of the men will help you. And Madge—' Letty's voice took on an edge of annoyance—'secure your kerchief, Madge.'

88

As soon as she came back, Frances said, 'Letty?'

'Yes?'

'Letty, in Sydney I became acquainted with the Hall girls.'

'Indeed? Poor girls. And so many of them.'

'Yes, and all so—so—I was going to say clever, but I suppose I must say bookish. I think you would call them radicals, but I call them reformers. I must tell you I was in sympathy with their ideas.' She broke off to drop into a baffled abstraction, then looked pleadingly at Letty and said, 'And I still am.'

'So am I, I am sure,' murmured Letty.

'And you should also know,' said Frances, 'that Mr Edmund Joyce is a real radical, and proclaims himself as such.'

'Oh,' said Letty, smiling, 'if that is all he does . . .'

'It is not all. At home he wrote about prison reform for one of the radical journals. There was such a great fuss that his father sent him to the colony to stay with an uncle for six months.'

'That sounds as if his father has means. Who is his uncle?'

'A Colonel Anning.'

'Lately of the Buffs! A charming man. And poor Mawy Anning. Their only son—only child indeed—dead of a fever at twenty. How vewy convenient. You will have no need to pwesent Mr Joyce. We are bound to meet him at the Annings'. And Patwick and he will find a subject in common. Pwison weform. Patwick says Newgate is a disgwace. How diff'went the poor things must find it here. No damp stone walls, no bitter cold, no jail fever. Indeed, *we* may be called weformers.'

Frances's eyes, alternately baffled and hopeful, had not left her sister's face. 'But Letty,' she said, 'what of the lash?'

'What of it?'

'Is it not—used too much?'

'Gwacious, when one thinks how it was used in the navy and the army! Why, in the fifty-seventh they were called the Shellbacks. And the Diehards too. And as pwoud of one as of the other.'

'I know.'

'And nor did they always have a medical man pwesent. Here they must be pwonounced fit for the lash. It is a *stwict wule*.'

'I rather think it makes it worse. It adds coldness and deliberation.'

'Oh, Fwances, my love, you are so silly. Would you have them hit in a passion?'

'Yes,' said Frances. Then she said, 'No, of course not.'

'Yea-nay,' scoffed Letty with a smile. 'Pway, what would you have?'

'I don't know.'

'And neither do I, my love. So let us give it up. It is not our concern.'

'But I do know there are persons who say it should not be used at all.'

'Then let those persons come and live in this place,' said Letty with spirit, 'where there are one thousand pwisoners and only one hundwed of us, and let them twy to keep order without the lash. Let them come, I say! On the other hand, if they are twue weformers, who want to help the poor and wetched, I am sure they would find useful work to do here, and would set to and do it, instead of weeping over the pwisoners, and giving them notions above their condition. If they were learned enough, there would be work for them at the school.'

'School?' Frances's astonishment made her sound aggressive. 'A school for convicts?'

'Gwacious, no. For their childwen.'

Frances's astonishment remained. 'There are married convicts here?'

'Certainly. The wives of the first-class convicts are allowed to join their husbands. It is an indulgence for good behaviour, a spur to weform. Your fwiends in Sydney who know so much cannot have known that. In your first letter to Mr Edmund Joyce, pway inform him.'

'Who teaches the children?'

'Amelia does her best.'

'Perhaps I could help.'

'To be sure, if it can be done without offence to

Amelia. Wobert will not occupy much of your time. But you must also have some pleasure. There is the pianoforte, of course. I know you play. I fancy you don't care for cards, but I am sure you dance. Oh, and you must know we are all mad for science on the settlement. You have seen the cases in the hall?'

Frances had indeed seen the row of cedar cases in which, beneath glass, insects were pinned in rows or arranged in a wheel with an especially fine specimen as the hub. At home in Sligo there was a fox's head in the hall, and a fish in a glass case, but she had never liked those, either. 'I may ride, I suppose,' she said.

'Well, we are short of horses . . .'

But now the noise of shuffling and bumping outside made Letty hurry to open the door. 'Be careful, Madge,' she said.

Madge Noakes appeared sideways in the doorway, rocking heavily from foot to foot, her upturned hands supporting one side of a desk. As she turned her back to shuffle into the room, Martin appeared on the far side of the desk. His eyes immediately sought Frances's, but all her attention was fixed on the desk. 'Mama's desk!' she wanted to say, but an instinctive scruple made her suppress any such expression of intimacy and delight in the presence of these two, in whose lives she could imagine neither.

She stood aside to give them room to pass, while Letty, opposite her at a distance of six feet or so, directed the operation. The two prisoners, their backs bowed by the pull of the desk, passed laboriously between them, Madge Noakes brushing so close to Frances that her smell, of sweat and soap and burnt fat, was strong in Frances's nostrils, and the movement of her shoulders, shifting her neckerchief to and fro, disclosed, only inches away, the pale puckered gloss of a horizontal scar.

Martin, passing with his back to Letty, was still trying to engage Frances's eyes. Without looking directly at him, she was aware of his avidity, his determination to make her look; and when she did look, with a slipped glance that seemed, even to her, an accident, she was shocked by his expression of beggarly gratitude. No punishment having come to him, he knew that she had said nothing of the morning's incident, and had assumed that she had refrained for his sake. The heat of his look was telling her so.

Pinned by that look, anger and offendedness seemed her only escape. She would tell Letty the instant he left.

Gingerly, bandying their legs, they set the desk against the wall. It was of mahogany trimmed with brass. A bookcase with glass doors, flanked by pilasters, was set above the pigeon holes, and a pediment with urns on top of all. Memory suddenly brought Frances close to tears. She went forward and ran her fingers across its worn table. Letty came and stood beside her, smiling. Madge Noakes pulled a duster from her pocket and gave the doors a flick. Martin, with a glance at Frances and a swagger of his shoulders, hitched up his trousers.

Letty opened one of the doors of the bookcase. 'Thank you, Madge . . . Martin . . .'

Without the ballast of the desk, Martin's retreating footsteps on the polished boards had a timid straggling sound far more penetrating than Madge Noakes's busy thudding. Frances spoke as soon as she heard the door shut.

'The sight of Martin reminded me. I heard him talking to Robert this morning. Mrs Harbin told me it is forbidden.'

'What did he say?'

'I couldn't hear his words.'

'More to the point, p'waps, what did Wobert say. He picks up their words so fast.'

Frances opened the other door of the bookcase. 'I scarcely remember. I am glad it is still lined with the same green silk. Will he be punished?'

'Alas, beginning to split. See?'

'It hardly shows among the folds. Will he lose his privileges?'

'I expect so.'

'It is not perished at all on this side.'

'Cwying again!'

'Mama's desk!'

94

'If you like, we shall give Martin another chance. Let us say nothing to Patwick. I shall speak to Martin and Wobert myself.'

'Oh, very well. Letty, you ought not to lend it to me. Mama gave it to you.'

'I don't lend it. I give it. Mama didn't know you would be the learned one. She would have wanted you to have it. You must have a place for your books. And you will compose your letters upon it. The cutter takes the mail to the *Isabella* at dawn tomowwow. If you wish, you may sit down now and begin.'

CHAPTER FIVE

The commandant had left Collison at the door of the prisoners' hospital and was walking alone down the corridor. The hospital was seldom busy in winter. As he looked in at the door of each room the eyes of the few men lying on pallets moved towards his own, their faces remaining as impassive as his. In one room, Fagan, the man attacked in the wheatfield, was being attended by a kneeling orderly.

'Knowles, where is Mr Cowper?'

'End room, sir.'

In the end room Henry Cowper was applying liniment to Lazarus's back. 'Don't tell me that,' he was saying. 'Boylan is dead.'

'Ees with the blacks in the bush,' replied the stooping man.

'You lie,' said Cowper. The soldier who had

brought Lazarus, instead of staying at the door, had put himself at the window overlooking the river.

'Sir,' said Lazarus, 'Boylan is in the bush.'

'Then why didn't you stay there, too?'

'Why, happenin' to fall in with the wrong tribe—'

'What, they didn't want you?'

Still stooped, Lazarus pointed to his arm. 'When they done that to me!'

'Sensible savages! Here, I can do no more. Take your shirt.'

'Boylan seized the arm of one, to stop 'im.'

'Boylan's ghost!'

'Sir, Boylan 'isself, I say, though cut and painted like a savage.'

When Logan entered, Lazarus's head was in his shirt, and Cowper was corking his bottle of lotion. When he saw Logan he grinned and slapped the cork home with his open palm. A groan came from Lazarus as the rough shirt settled on his back. His head emerged from the neckband, he saw Logan, and drew himself carefully upright. The guard at the window was standing at rigid attention.

'Why has this man come back to you, Mr Cowper?'

'A fresh outbreak of bleeding, captain.'

'He brought it on himself.' He turned to Lazarus. 'Yesterday you said nothing about meeting an absconder.'

Lazarus, looking fixedly at the wall beside the commandant's head, might have been imitating the soldier. He said nothing.

'Although you were questioned at length.'

Lazarus said nothing.

Logan spoke to the soldier. 'Take him back to his gang.' And to Lazarus he said, 'Tomorrow you go to the treadmill.'

Lazarus and the guard left. 'He shouldn't go to the treadmill yet,' said Cowper.

'Your medical sanction is not needed for the treadmill. Which one was Boylan?'

'Nor is my medical sanction needed for twenty-five lashes or less. Yet now they say twenty-five killed Swann. Don't you remember Boylan? He ran at the end of twenty-eight, from this room, with two hundred of Bishop's stripes on his back. Bishop was drowned three weeks later. Ah, now you remember!' Cowper was peering with curiosity into Logan's face. 'Your memory is very bad, captain.'

'There is usually little enough to distinguish them. Lazarus can't have seen Boylan.'

'As you heard me tell him.'

'Boylan didn't long survive his escape.'

'Well, to be sure, he didn't intend to. Or he wouldn't have run in that state, in that heat.'

'Intentions are irrelevant. The fact is, his body came down the river.'

'Said to be his body.'

'Said to be by you, man.'

'Ah, but was I sober? The thing had been in the river. Did I just give it a name, and go back to my dinner?'

'Whose was it, if not Boylan's?'

'Some are unaccounted for.'

'Dead. Dead, or with the tribes in the north. There's none about here now, and there were none about at that time.'

'One could have been making his way down from the north. It could have been his body.'

'Boylan's. It came down at a logical time after he ran. And you swore to it. Proof enough! I'm not sending men into the bush to take one of their ghosts.'

'Nor would I, captain.'

'And yet,' said the commandant, 'Lazarus is not stupid.'

'Not at all stupid.'

'Perhaps he saw a light-coloured native, with a slight look of Boylan. Boylan? A flat-nosed, heavy-browed Irish?'

'A fair description.'

'Then that is it. Either he is lying to make mischief, or he saw a black resembling Boylan.'

'The commandant has constructed an answer,' said Henry, addressing the ceiling. 'He is wise. He is not of a nature to bear unanswered questions. They are so disorderly. In the same way, he says he has put down buggery among the men, because he cannot endure it, yet knows it impossible to suppress.'

'You are a childish fellow, Cowper.'

'Allowances are usually made. You can't have come about Lazarus and Boylan, because you didn't know about it. What have you come about?'

'The black prisoner. But first, your quarterly declaration. In your absence Whyte told me he has had none from you for a year, in spite of repeated requests.'

'Which particular quarterly—'

'The one declaring you derive no advantage from your situation.'

'That one! Shall I furnish one to cover the four quarters, or four different ones?'

'Ask Whyte. I've no liking myself for all their declaring and counting and listing and classifying. It's like wasps round the ears. But do it! Do it today.'

'I will. What about the black prisoner?'

'Wait. Fagan is still here. Why was he not sent back to work?'

'He wasn't fit.'

'You said he was only bruised.'

'There are degrees of bruising.'

'Because you said it was slight, I let Bulbridge off with a hundred. Fagan goes back to his gang today. Now, the black prisoner. Have his irons been removed?'

'As you instructed.'

'How is he?'

'I'll show you,' said Henry.

He led the way to a small room, unlocked the door, and stood back to let the commandant enter before him. The two pallets on the floor were unoccupied, but an aborigine sat against the wall. Three weeks before, one of a hunting party passing by the settlement, he had been denounced by a prisoner as one of the natives who had speared a boat's crew up the river. Now he sat with forehead resting on drawn-up knees, arms hanging, hands trailing the floor. The flesh of his legs and arms had sunk to the bone, and the grease and beeswax had worn from his hair and left it hanging in limp strands.

One of Henry's hands was in a pocket. With the other he swung his keys a little. 'He will die,' he said.

Hearing his voice, the man raised his head. His cheeks and forehead were symmetrically scarified and the septum of his nose pierced to hold a thin bone. Though he looked directly at the two men his face was that of a man who stares at nothing and whose thoughts have turned so deeply inward that the channels of outer communication have ceased to exist. His head remained upright, as though, having raised it, it was not worth moving it again. The upper part of his chest, revealed by this movement, was as elaborately scarified as his face. Staring at him, the commandant spoke in a hushed yet argumentative voice. 'But he is not old.'

'Murray says he looked young when he was brought in.'

'And he is eating,' stated Logan.

'A little.'

'Enough to keep him alive?'

'Enough to keep another man alive. He is dying.'

Logan scowled with some kind of frustration. '*Why* is he dying?'

'I think, because he wants to.'

The commandant continued to stare with bewilderment and indignation at the man, whose eyes were like holes full of dark shining fluid, telling him nothing. 'A man cannot die,' argued the commandant, 'only because he wants to.'

'They say these can—offensive as that must be, captain, to an officer of the Diehards.'

'Who says they can?'

'Persons who have seen it. I have never seen it before. I am much impressed with the delicacy of the operation. Consider our crude European ways. We must cut or smash ourselves, or immerse ourselves, or blow part of our bodies away—or at the very least, put ourselves in a position where it is likely to be done for us. But these have only to sit, it seems, and summon death, and death obliges. Note the smell, captain. You have smelled death before. Murray doesn't know whether to be disgusted or fascinated, to write a paper for the Royal Society or to stop his nose.'

'Will he recover if he is set free?'

'Reverse that stink? I don't know. If they can work one miracle, perhaps they can work another.'

'I doubt if the evidence against him is strong enough to hold him.'

'It has held him until now.'

'A prisoner's word.'

'You took him captive on that word.'

'I hoped to get support for it. I haven't got it.'

'It is true,' mused Henry, as if to himself, 'that the authorities in Sydney have become marvellously touchy about dead blacks.'

'I can't hold him without that support.'

'Being prodded by London, you know, where they say, in effect, that we must dispossess the natives with kindness. Yes, in London the word is kindness, kindness, all the way. You see, I bring you the gossip. And there is more.'

Logan dropped pale eyelids against this offensiveness. 'We will have to let the man go.'

'You will let him go. I will let him go. But will he go?'

Logan went to the door and opened it to its fullest extent. He went back to the man on the floor. He stretched an arm, the forefinger pointing into the doorway.

'Go!'

There was certainly a flicker in the man's eyes. Perhaps he looked at the door. But he did not move.

'*Go!*'

When again there was no response, the commandant's face became a blotched red and the flesh beneath his eyes began to bulge. Henry, who had been inclined to titter at the first command, grew solemn-faced and stepped quickly between the two men.

'Sir, perhaps he cannot.'

The commandant's arm dropped. His step backwards could have been an admission, the slight inclination of his head a nod of thanks. He took a few steps about the room, then halted and looked along his shoulder at the man.

'He's from a tribe near the Limestone Station. I'll have him carried over the river. At once. He will be given a sack of food. Meat. Sugar. Bread.'

'And you will leave him there?'

'His weapons may be left with him.'

Henry, standing at the window of his office in the hospital, saw the aborigine, on the opposite side of the river, rise slowly to his feet. At that distance he looked like a toy made of dark twigs. The barge was coming back across the river. Standing at Henry's side, Logan was watching from beneath a hand held across his brows. 'He is up,' he said. Then, in a voice strained with anxiety, 'On his feet, is he?'

'Why, on his feet and moving.'

The man was walking unsteadily, but had found the strength to carry the sack of food in one hand, his spear in the other. The commandant was silent. The office clock ticked on the wall. After the aborigine had taken about ten paces he began to lope.

'Upon my word,' said Henry, 'Murray should be running at his side, taking notes.'

The native was moving now at a steady pace. At first he struck puffs of dust from the ground, for he was travelling on the track of the working parties from the Limestone Station; but presently he moved off the track and entered long pale blowing grass that hid him up to his shins. Dark eucalypts stood in this grass. He passed behind a single tree, then out into the blowing grass again, then behind a small clump. Henry, familiar with that tract of land, knew when he disappeared suddenly that he had dropped down to walk along the bed of a shallow creek.

Henry turned away from the window first. 'Gone,' he said, 'to disperse his death among the eucalypts.'

The commandant also turned from the window. 'He was shamming.'

'Oh!' cried Henry. He burst into laughter. 'What a man you are! There's satisfaction in such consistency!'

'Shamming,' said Logan again. 'Men in health cannot will themselves to die. I was in the retreat from Salamanca. I saw many a man lie down in the mud—'

'I know,' said Henry, 'you told me.'

'—lie down in the mud to die. But they were sick men. Or men whose endurance had failed, and who had to rest even though they died for it. But that man was not sick, and he was well-rested. He was shamming. And later, when I was in France, in—'

'In the occupation. You have told me all this. Suicide had become a fad—'

'A fad. Yes, I would call it that. France being a mortified country. Young men were blowing their heads off or cutting their throats, but I saw none sit down in health and waste away.' The commandant started towards the door. 'The black was shamming.'

'Sir, one minute!'

'I have the returns to certify, and those cursed reports to write.'

'In Sydney I was called to the attorney-general's office.'

Logan paused at the door. 'What of it?'

'I was questioned about Swann.'

'Cowper, what does this matter? What could you add to the affidavit you swore here, before me? Swann died of dysentery. You swore to it, and so did Spicer and so did Parker.'

'And I was questioned about Lieutenant Bell.'

'I expected it. I wrote to Macleay and asked that you be examined on the subject. He must have instructed the attorney-general.'

Henry slapped himself on the forehead. 'Why did you do that?'

'Cowper, just before you left for Sydney you told me that Lieutenant Bell had come to you after Swann died and suggested that you support a charge against me of undue severity. You refused. Very proper. Your only mistake was in keeping it from me. While you were in Sydney I decided that your story ought to be disclosed. And what better chance, with you on the spot? Is that amazing? I have nothing to hide.'

'I wish he would come in and sit down,' said Henry in a tired voice.

Logan glanced at the clock. 'I can't hold the mail beyond dawn tomorrow.' But he returned and sat down, while Henry, with exaggerated weariness and decrepitude, let himself down into the chair at his desk.

On the desk was the beginning of a letter. '*My dear father, I write you immediately on my return to inform you of my safe passage and to assure you . . .*' Henry picked it up and dropped it into a drawer of his desk. 'The attorney-general asked me if I could recall Bell's exact words,' he said. 'I said it was too long ago. It is. But I remember the gist of them well enough. And I tell you, sir, that if I were Smith Hall's lawyer, I should call Bell as a witness for the defence.'

'Let him be called!'

'A man of good repute,' said Cowper in a tone of warning.

'Who was moved by personal animosity.'

'That would be decided by the court. If I were Smith Hall's lawyer, I would call Vincent, too.'

'Vincent!' Logan flung back his head and laughed.

'A clergyman.' Again Henry spoke on a note of warning.

'A weak meddling fool.'

'Stationed here for nine months. Recalled at his own request.'

'And at mine. Most urgently, at mine.'

'That is so. All the same, I would call him. And I would call Assistant Surgeon Lister too.'

Logan leaned forward in his chair, put a fist on the desk. 'Why, man, what evidence adverse to me could Lister give?'

'He came to relieve me last year. He found the duties so distasteful that he asked to be returned to Sydney.'

'He believed he would be treating only officers and their families. When he discovered his mistake he came to me in the proper way—' Logan suddenly broke off, thrust his reddening face across the desk at Henry. 'An honourable man!' He thumped the desk. 'A man of my own regiment!'

'Oh, true,' said Henry, 'he wouldn't wish to give evidence against you. But he would be on oath. And who knows what an honourable man may feel obliged to say on oath?'

'Why, man, exactly what he said to me.'

'Or to me—which was that he couldn't stand the floggings.'

'Well, sir, a good man may have a weak stomach.'

'And that he thought them cruel and barbarous.'

'Cowper, you lie!'

Henry drew down his upper lip, scratched delicately beside one nostril, then beside the other. 'I am glad I am sober,' he said then. 'Had I been drunk I would no doubt have challenged you. Well, we are spared that. I shan't ask you to apologise. I know you are incapable of it. It would be almost more trouble than a duel. Besides, you are sorry. I see very clearly that you are sorry.'

Logan gave a single sound, half laughter, half disgust. 'It is the same with Lister's words as with Bell's. You can't recall them exactly, and have distorted the gist.'

'Very well,' said Henry languidly.

'And it is amusing, d'you know? to hear you speak as if I am to be on trial. I am not. Smith Hall is to be on trial.'

'There is no saying what will come out at a trial for libel. The name of Patrick Grady may come out. Now, captain, don't tell me you don't recall Grady.'

'I recall him. But if we are to mull over every mishap—'

'He calls it a mishap,' said Henry to the ceiling.

109

'—every mishap,' repeated Logan, rising to his feet, 'the cutter will go down to the *Isabella* without my report in her mailbag.'

Henry also rose to his feet. 'Ah well, I expect at the worst you may count on me. Like Parker and Spicer, I have my post and my pay, and no doubt I shall protect them. Yes, if the worst comes, and Grady's case comes to light at the Smith Hall trial, I think you may count on me. True, I am of vile repute, but in defence of my post and my pay I shall draw on my father's credit, and use it for all it is worth. Unless a certain mood comes upon me—and it happens sometimes even when I am sober—a perverse mood, a truth-telling mood. Oh, dear me, captain. Oh, gracious, I hope that doesn't happen. But now I will be serious, sir, if only to remove from your face that look of excessive contempt. In the past, my shocking actions made certain persons wish to displace me. I was spared for my father's sake. I would pass on the favour. I make nothing of Captain Clunie being sent in place of Bainbrigge, because it could mean nothing. But you are aware of danger. I know you well, and you show it. You know there is official criticism of the number of runaways. That's the danger at your back door. Don't let it divert you from the one at the front. Smith Hall's at the front. Don't go to Sydney innocent and unprepared. Ah, but you are not listening.' Henry broke into laughter. 'I see you have a speech ready, and only wait for me to finish.'

'Indeed, Cowper, I have listened. Listened with astonishment. Man, you have a maggot—'

But seeing Cowper raise a hand, he broke off. The footsteps approaching in the corridor, tripping and scuffling and accompanied by chatter and broken cries, suggested a group of big children, but it was four women who appeared across the doorway, a washing gang from the female factory. Craning their necks, looking into the office with expectant gap-toothed grins, they saw Logan, and immediately all were silent and every head was turned front to display a rigid profile. Their male overseer, sufficiently in the rear to be warned by the change in them, shouted at them with terrible anger as he passed, warning them to look very sharp. All the footsteps, even and controlled now, continued down the corridor and died away as entered the various rooms.

Henry Cowper was looking with amusement at the commandant's face. 'Polly and Nell and Mary and Margery,' he said softly.

Logan also spoke softly. 'You were once a good friend to my family, but in my efforts to bring order and decency to this place, I have come to see your laxity as my greatest obstacle.'

'But that is an old charge,' said Henry, still smiling. 'Come to the new one. You were about to say I have a maggot in the brain.'

'I was. And I was also about to say that I have

111

no fear of Smith Hall, and will show none, nor any great preparedness either, but will treat him with the same disdain the governor shows to those who slander him. And for the same reason—that my conscience is as clear as his. And I also say this—I have the greatest admiration for the system of punishment and reform that he and I—and you, sir; I would remind you of that—are privileged to serve. It allows for change if change is earned and deserved, but does not foster weakness and dependence. And I have the greatest admiration for the man who administers that system in this colony. Yes, and loyalty, sir. Loyalty to that man and that system. One may criticise the system in detail—I do!—but to criticise it in toto is to talk like a Yankee traitor. Oh, you may blink your eyes, Cowper, and shake your head, and whisper to yourself, and try to make a joke of what I say. But if that system is undermined and brought down, it will be the end of British power. And that, sir, will be the end in this world of justice itself.'

At intervals Henry had been whispering, 'He means it, you know.' He watched the commandant leave the room, then turned and addressed the clock on the wall.

'He really does mean it, you know.'

He took a bottle of rum from a drawer of his desk, uncorked it, and took a long drink. 'It is like talking to a horse,' he said.

He put the rum back in the drawer. 'Who knows he must reply, so gives a noble neigh.'

Shaking his head and tutting, he opened another drawer and took out the unfinished letter to his father.

'. . . *I write immediately on my return to assure you of my safe passage, and to assure you . . .*'

He picked up his pen, frowned as he dipped it.

'. . . *that the first task of my free time will be to compose that Account of the Spiritual State of the Settlement which you have requested of me. At the earliest opportunity I also mean to send my brother Macquarie the promised case of insects which he has awaited so patiently. Unhappily, free time at present is exactly what I lack. The hospital is full, and only ten minutes ago, three beds were set up in the corridor . . .*'

Henry began to droop as he wrote, all his animation draining away. Presently he threw down the pen, jumped to his feet, rushed at the clock, and stopped the pendulum. Back in his chair, he took the bottle of rum from the first drawer and set it squarely on the desk. He opened the second drawer and drew out a handful of letters at random and spread them over the desk. Most were from his father, but some were from his brothers, sister, and stepmother, and some, like the one still directly in front of him, were begun by himself and abandoned. Gloomily drinking, he picked out those from his father and snatched at a phrase here and there.

'May the Lord be with you and grant you abundant . . .'

'. . . would also welcome an account of your own Spiritual Progress . . .'

'. . . now that the governor's eldest son is saying his lessons with me, pro tempore . . .'

Henry then read snatches of his own.

'. . . would have replied before, but a little rheumatism in the hands . . .'

'. . . for poor Macquarie, but unhappily there is no one here at present who understands the preservation of insects.'

'. . . and after Divine Service last Sunday, one man, of the most abandoned type, feelingly thanked me.'

'Oh,' he cried when he read this last. 'Oh, what a whopper!'

Enlivened, he flung them all back into the drawer. He took a long drink, then set before him a clean sheet of paper. He picked up his pen, dipped it.

'An Account of the Spiritual State of the Settlement for my father, who believes in God but not the Devil.

'Your son believes in God and the Devil.

'Murray believes in God and the Devil. When he has supervised a flogging he comes in and sits with his hands over his eyes and shivers like a little dog.

'The Commandant believes in the Devil and King George the Fourth.

'Lieutenant Edwards believes in God the Superior

114

Officer. 'Mrs Bulwer, whom you have met, believes in God the headmaster and the junior dominie His Son.

'The commandant's wife believes in God the lucky charm, like a hare's foot, which belief puts her with all the rest.

'For all the rest, officers and officials and prisoners and soldiers, all, all, are pagans. They believe in ghosts, or arts, or in the dark sensational spirits of rocks and rivers and trees.

'There may be one secret Christian among them, but I have not found him out.

'I forgot to say that the commandant's sister by marriage believes in a God called Reform.

'The iron gangs enter the chapel first, father, so that the official party shall not be subjected to the indecent clanking of their chains as they mount to the gallery. While they mount, the other prisoners file in below, including some wives and children, who have been mustered in the barracks yard with the rest and inspected for cleanliness. Then come the soldiers, some with wives and children too. I wait, with my head bowed. The official party comes last, bright and solemn and mildly stately. Sometimes I am not waiting, but am tardy, and appear as suddenly as a jack-in-the-box.

'Only once have I performed divine service before an enthusiastic congregation. Bishop the scourger was drowned just before Christmas. On Christmas Day the prisoners sang so loud and fervently that the very *roof sang and shouted. The commandant stood in utter silence, as red and puffed as if he would burst. When the singing reached its loudest and most triumphal he abruptly left the chapel. He could not have them punished. "We thought he would be glad, sir," a prisoner told me later, "to hear us joyful because of the birth of our Lord Jesus. Who is Our Redeemer, Sir."*

Henry was now writing fast and contentedly. He would not send the account, but even the fantasy of doing so was enough to release his energies. Though blunt and open with most people, he almost invariably lied to his father, saying what he believed would please him rather than what was true. He was never critical of his father. In common with most others, he saw him as a saintly man, and thought it a mark of his own unworthiness that he was bored, uneasy, and dishonest when with him, uneasy at the thought of him when away, and that even the sight of his handwriting on a letter could fill him with guilt and dejection.

In infancy Henry had been his mother's angel child, his imperfections not then detracting from his graces, which were the obvious ones of a light frame, golden curls, innocent blue eyes, and a cherub mouth. His mother died on the eve of their embarkation for New South Wales, and it was necessary to postpone the journey until the Reverend Cowper could decently take another wife. Henry was nine when they arrived in Sydney, fourteen when his father apprenticed him

116

to Doctor Redfern. With his master, he worked at the hospital in Macquarie Street, where, behind an eight foot wall, treatment was given to convicts, merchant seamen, and the very poor. Doctor Redfern had an outside practice and a smart gig. Henry lived in his house but spent all his working hours in the hospital. At seventeen he was appointed hospital assistant at twenty-five pounds a year and free rations. He did all the dressings, stood by at operations, and distributed the medicines, sometimes to the wrong patients. He was also delegated to attend floggings at the barracks and jail, the older men having discovered that one raw back is much like another. In Sydney at that time the pride of the punished men was in taking it, as they said, 'like a stone'. Between each whirr and thud of the lash was a pause of officially ordained duration, and after his first revulsion had passed, Henry began to find the regularity of the sound soporific. As men were strapped in succession to the triangles, and the compulsory prison audience shifted and coughed, Henry, in a sunny spot, out of reach of splattering blood and shreds of flesh, was often half asleep on his feet.

At the hospital, duty was alleviated in various ways. Opium was stolen and sold outside, spiritous medicines were drunk, convict nurses engaged in sexual romps, and pranks played with cadavers. Into the hospital as a visitor, with a cane and a cutaway coat, came Nobby Clark, a free rogue. He flicked up the tails of his coat and jumped his rump to the edge of a table. He raised his cane. Henry admired him to the point of besottedness. Nobody had ever called him Buck before. With the tip of his cane he counted the buttons on Henry's waistcoat. The colony was a damned miserable place, he said. He and Henry would go to Batavia. 'The Batavian women, Buck! Obedient but frisky!' And he told Henry how they could get the money.

When scandal about the hospital spread, and it came at last to an enquiry, it was said that Henry was in the hands not only of this Nobby Clark, but of two others equally wicked, a convict nurse and an assistant surgeon. Henry himself made no excuses at all. When he heard people speak of the things he had done, it didn't seem as if they were speaking of him. It was as if two persons had inhabited his body, and the one that had dominated from the ages of fourteen to nineteen had died. At twenty, cleared of blame for his father's sake, he left the colony to attend the Royal College of Surgeons in London. At twenty-five he was appointed to the penal station at Moreton Bay at one hundred and thirty-six pounds a year. At that time the bodily vigour of youth was still defending his mind from self knowledge. He could not have said exactly when that defence had fallen, and indeed only knew it *had* fallen because a time came when he could not get rid of the thought that he could easily have been one of these prisoners. If they deserved their present state, then so did he, and moreover, two persons had never inhabited his body, but only one.

It had never occurred to him to censure his father for giving him to such a business at so early an age. Indeed, when he pondered the matter, he thought the act indicated such trustfulness on his father's part that it proved rather than disproved his saintliness.

He was now thirty, and earned one hundred and eighty-two pounds ten a year. The light figure was distorted by a drunkard's paunch, the cherub's mouth puckered and drooped, and the golden curls reduced to a thin mousy pelt. But after sexual activity with a woman the old gentle innocence would revive in his eyes, and these women, who were usually overseers' wives or convicts, were always nudging him, or hugging him, and telling him that he was really just a little boy. Now, as he sat in his office chair, drinking and writing, he hummed snatches of hymns, and occasionally burst into the words.

'Com-ing unto thee . . .'

'*I remember* (he was writing) *that when I first came to this place, and took the services on Sunday, I was ambitious to reach their hearts. What an impertinence! I now think how right they were to ignore me. Indeed, for them it was the only sensible and decent course. More than anything else, father, I believe this will convey to you my Spiritual Progress, or the regrettable lack of same.*'

He had finished. He put down his pen, singing.

'For thy a-bun-dant peace. Good-day to you, Mar-ger-ee.'

'You know it is not Margery,' says the woman who has come in with a broom.

'It is Pol-lee,' sings Henry.

'You know it is,' she says, with a sidelong glance.

CHAPTER SIX

'And this is our Mr Mu'wy.'

Letty held James Murray's right hand in both of hers, and looked not at Frances, but teasingly into the young man's face. He was twenty-three, tall and powerful, with large dark eyes and thin tender lips set in a half smile.

'His family has taken gweat estates in the south,' said Letty.

'The southern highlands,' amended James Murray, turning to Frances and bowing as well as he could with one hand in Letty's.

'Millions of acres,' said Letty.

'Thousands,' said Murray, smiling at Frances.

'—all stwewn with stwange boulders. And this is my dear sister Fwances.'

'Is it of volcanic origin?' asked Frances in an alert manner.

He replied in the same forced tone. 'We believe it is, Miss O'Beirne.'

'Do sit down, my loves,' murmured Letty, herself sitting again on the blue sofa and picking up her embroidery frame. At the other end of the room Madge Noakes and Elizabeth Robertson were setting up the card tables, for there was to be an informal gathering to welcome Captain Clunie and Frances. Letty held her embroidery aslant to the light of the window. The candles were not yet lit. There was a pale fire in the grate and across the wide verandah the green blaze of the evening garden.

'Is there good pasturing in such stony country?' enquired Frances.

'Unless the season is dry, Miss O'Beirne, the country is good for cattle as well as sheep.'

'But not for women,' said Letty. 'The poor wives are hundweds of miles apart. They have no society.' She gave Murray a teasing look. 'Who would be bawoness of the boulders?'

'Not I!' said Louisa Harbin, entering and giving her mantle to Madge Noakes. 'We are better off here. At least we converse.' She advanced into the room arranging her long necklaces of Madras silver. Dressed in white, and so tall, her red hair muted by the dusk of the room, she momentarily gave an effect of beauty. Murray sprang to his feet and bowed. 'James,' she said, in smiling maternal acknowledgement. She sat in one of Letty's silk chairs. 'Victor sends his compliments and apologies. He will come shortly with Amelia and Lieutenant Bulwer. You have been talking to Frances, James. Frances is well-informed. I once thought to be well-informed myself, but had to settle at last for a pitiful ignorance.'

'But you are well-informed, Mrs Harbin,' said Frances.

Louisa sent her a glance of annoyance before turning again to James Murray. 'What is this curious story of a black prisoner?'

Bringing himself to the edge of his chair, and losing his shyness in the interest of his story, he told them of the black prisoner who had been thought near death. Elizabeth Robertson, shuffling about the room with a taper, lighting candles, murmured half-audibly as she listened.

'Dear, dear . . .'

'Well I never . . .'

When James Murray finished he turned both hands upward and looked in turn at the three candlelit faces. 'I won't say a miracle. An inexplicable recovery.'

'But he may not have recovered,' said Louisa. 'He may have died on the way home.'

'No. He was seen this evening by men coming in from the Limestone Station. He had met with a hunting party from his own tribe, and himself had caught a lizard.'

'Dear, dear,' murmured the servant. 'Think of that now. They eat them, the heathens.'

'A black Lazarus,' said Louisa. 'Isn't there a white one among the prisoners? And quite as savage?'

'There is,' said James Murray. 'But let us not compare our black with the Lazarus raised from the dead. In his case there was no divine intervention.'

'But if he wasn't raised,' said Frances, 'he must have raised himself. And how is it possible to use the *will* for purposes of dying and recovery?'

'Only by making it the instrument of a higher will.'

'In any case, a useful facility,' remarked Louisa.

'Especially for wecov'wy.'

'Oh, ma'am,' said James Murray, turning to Letty, 'pray let me repeat that at such levels the will belongs to God.'

Suddenly the servant was fully audible. 'Or to their black devils!'

'That will be all, Elizabeth. You may bwing the childwen for a few minutes when the commandant comes in fwom his office. Amelia, my love!' And Letty rose and went forward to greet the three new arrivals: Amelia, Lancelot Bulwer, and Victor Harbin.

At the servant's cry James Murray had murmured an excuse and hurried to the french doors as if some sudden recollection had sent him to overlook the river. Frances glimpsed his moving lips and the quick touch of fingers to forehead and breast, and the sight brought into her own breast such a surge of homesickness that she impulsively rose and went to stand at his side. He gave her a startled flutter of a smile and turned again to the river. Standing beside him, watching the men on the bank hauling up the small boats, she felt the emanation of his shyness, and by its contagion became tongue-tied. Her confused intention had been to speak to him of Sligo, of Bridie and Meg and the two little girls; but the closest she could get to home, after a struggle, was by saying stiffly, 'You—attended Trinity College, I believe, Mr Murray?'

'I did, Miss O'Beirne. And were you at a Dublin academy?'

'I was not. Though Letty and Cassandra were with the Missis Wollstonecraft. You must have fine memories of your college, Mr Murray.'

Whether from an instinct to please him, or to announce indirectly her longing for home, she had said not 'fine' but something like 'foine'. 'Oh, Miss O'Beirne,' he replied, 'it was the life I was meant for. Had I been provided for, I would have stayed a scholar all my days. For a man constituted as I am, it is a calamity not to be provided for.'

She said, startled yet flat, 'You don't care for this place.'

But he recoiled from such directness, explaining with anxious eagerness that nobody could have been kinder to him than the people here, and no government more generous than the one he had the honour to serve. He spoke of his comfortable quarters, his servants, his horse, his fruit and vegetable garden, his ration of good food. And for anyone of an enquiring turn of mind, what could be of more advantage, he asked, than the strange flora and fauna, the curious river and sea creatures and the grotesque or exquisite insects? Especially the last, he said, especially the insects.

The care of her little sisters had fostered the maternal in Frances's nature. She saw that she had frightened him, and to reassure him became as eager in agreement as he in explanation, so that they made together a false accord that came to an end only by her sudden comprehension of what was implied by the work of the men on the river bank. She had watched, but had been too engrossed to interpret, the stripping and securing of the boats, and the locking of the chains. But now the men were carrying away the oars and sails. She put a hand to her left cheek. 'So we are marooned every night!'

'Not marooned.' He laughed. 'Marooned is not the word.'

'It's the word that came to me. Yes, it is wrong, but it feels right.'

He laughed again. 'We would be more truly marooned,' he said, 'if the boats were seized and used for an escape. That—' he nodded towards the river— 'prevents it.'

'It still makes me feel marooned.'

He moved nearer her. His voice was clear and gentle. 'Miss O'Beirne, don't let it.'

The affection she felt for him was as calm as if it were of old standing. Remembering Letty's injunction about her smallpox scars, she lowered her left hand and clasped it in the other. Patrick Logan, with Collison and Gilligan, came into view. They walked rapidly along the river bank, pausing at each boat while Gilligan bent to test the locks. But the dread and doubt they aroused in Frances was soothed by the presence of the young man at her side. So gentle, so sensitive, yet engaged, in a way, in the same business as Gilligan the scourger, he was surely a guarantee against its excesses. Reeds, he was telling her, grew in profusion up the river, and the men went up and gathered them for basket making. The three on the river bank passed out of sight while he spoke. After a glance over his shoulder he turned again to face the room, and she turned with him, guessing that he would think it improper, or even compromising, to stand apart with her for so long. And indeed, he now raised his voice so that anyone might know that they were speaking only of reeds and flowers.

'You arrived too late in winter, Miss O'Beirne, for the full glory of the acacias.'

Presently they were joined by Letty.

'James, if you are to take Mr Cowper's place at the hospital, so that he may be pwesent here for a short

127

time, pway do so in the first part of the evening, when tea will be the only dwink served.'

'I will leave at once.'

'No, no. You must first be pwesented to Captain Clunie.'

Patrick Logan appeared in the doorway. Frances heard Letty's murmur of pleasure and saw with surprise that as she crossed the room to him she reverted to the fast little gliding step that the provincial Missis Wollstonecraft had thought proper. But even more surprising to Frances was their meeting. He threw an arm about her waist like a yokel, and they kissed.

Behind their disengaging figures Captain Clunie and Lieutenant Edwards appeared. Letty, with a smile for young Edwards, took Captain Clunie by the hand and led him towards James Murray, the only person present he had yet to meet. As Murray awaited them, Frances saw him stiffen his shoulders and run his tongue along his upper lip. Moved to tenderness by his timidity, she failed to see in it a threat to the reassurance she had just received from his gentleness.

'Such a proposition would tempt any man,' said Clunie.

'But even free grants must be stocked,' objected James Murray.

'And sheep are expensive beasts,' said Patrick Logan.

'And cattle more so,' added Letty.

'The sale of my father's commission,' said Murray, 'was barely enough for his first flock.'

'Yes, yes,' said Clunie, 'but all the same, it would tempt any man.'

It plainly tempted the three who had heard Murray's story (augmented by yesterday's mail) of his father's land in the south. Clunie, Logan, and Edwards had all become thoughtful. Just as plainly, it did not tempt the two lieutenants, Harbin and Bulwer, nor Peter Spicer and Mr Commissary Hansord. These four, with Amelia and Louisa, were at cards within hearing range, but none had bothered to turn his head.

Frances, determined to please Letty by taking part in the conversation, but intimidated by Logan's presence, rather blurted out her question.

'Does your father live on his grant?'

'Why, no, he rents a farm near Sydney.'

'A gentleman need not live on his grant,' said Lieutenant Edwards, looking in his frank and easy way from face to face, 'he may put in an overseer.'

'My father put in my brother,' said Murray, with some dryness.

'Who now has gweat gwants of his own,' Letty told them all.

'He had not enough capital to trust it to an overseer,' said James.

'What age is your brother, sir?' asked Clunie.

'Terence is nineteen.'

There was an undertone of excitement in the murmur that went round the group. It infected Frances with the wish to say that Mr Smith Hall's son, whom he was forced to leave on his Bathurst property when he went to jail, was only sixteen. But happening to catch Patrick Logan's eyes upon her, she knew she could not say it, however incidental she might manage to make it sound, for he did have a way of looking, a particular cold blueness, that intimidated her even when, as now, she knew that he was hardly seeing her, but was thinking of something else.

He said to the air, 'Of course, it would be vastly different from farming in Scotland.'

'Patwick farmed in B'wickshire,' explained Letty.

'I farmed in Berwickshire,' he said, as if he had not heard her. 'It was after the war. I had long declared I wanted it above all things, and vowed to do it. So had to do it, even after I knew I could not.'

'Patwick does not mean he was not capable,' cried Letty.

'I don't mean I was not capable. But I was plagued with a restlessness, d'you see? that made me want to escape the place. I was like a man bursting to run, who had taken his solemn oath to stay still.'

'Your oath to whom?' asked Clunie.

'Why, only to myself. Never to my father. No, not as an oath. And yet my father's death released me. Well, it took that death. I went back to the army, and was never so grateful to go anywhere. But up there,' he said, looking at James Murray, 'that's new country. It would be different up there.'

'Different indeed, sir. The obstacles are greater.'

'So are the rewards, man.'

'The rewards are sometimes bankruptcy. And supposing they end transportation?'

'They won't,' said Logan.

'Not for a long time,' said Clunie simultaneously.

'No. And you can say what you please,' said Edwards, scanning the group and speaking in his clear affable voice, 'a man's nothing without land.'

'In peace time, that's so,' said Clunie.

'Are you not tempted, Murray?' asked Edwards.

'Once I have accumulated enough capital—' said Murray, but then gave a deprecating laugh and said that all the same, even then, he would not lightly leave his good post here. Enumerating again his comforts and benefits, he lost the interest of his audience, who barely waited until he had finished before drifting away, the men to the card tables and Letty to the kitchen to instruct her servants.

Alone again with Murray, Frances said, 'Your brother is only nineteen. I know of a young man who manages his father's property at Bathurst. Man? He is a boy. Sixteen.'

'Do you mean that editor fellow? His son?'

'I do. Mr Smith Hall.'

'You do right to speak his name so quietly, Miss O'Beirne. But on this settlement you would do better not to speak it at all.'

'Well, his charges against my brother are monstrous, I suppose.'

'He has become a monstrous fellow altogether. I used to be in sympathy with some of his proposals, but that was in his saner days. Whereas now—Oh, such a style of writing! Such low and scurrilous language! It must lose him the sympathy of all persons of moderation, and most certainly all those of good taste.'

'James . . .' said Letty, approaching.

He bowed. 'I am going at once, ma'am. You will have Cowper instead.'

'It is not a good exchange,' said Letty with sympathy. 'Dine on Thursday, dear James, and help me show Fwances the southern constellations.'

'Tea,' said Henry Cowper. 'Only tea. They know how to drive me back to my quarters. I shall allot them—' he drew his watch from his pocket—'twenty minutes of my time. What were we speaking of?'

'The blacks and the runaways,' said Clunie.

'Yes. You ask what governs their fraternisation. Lewis Lazarus told me the blacks sometimes welcome a runaway as the returned spirit of a dead kinsman. Apart from that, I know nothing. They seem to me perfectly unpredictable. They may kill our runaways, or pet and feed them. They may give them up to the military, or carry messages to their mates in the gangs. Not in words. They're great mimics. Prisoners have told me that when they come to the gangs on the outskirts to give them news of a runaway, they copy the bearing of the man so well that it is known at once who is meant. I used to pass such information to the commandant, but stopped because it made for confusion. The prisoners not being above making up such stories, you see, for the simple pleasure of watching the soldiers march off into the bush for nothing. Of course you have heard the story of our prodigious black patient. What is your explanation?'

'I expect he was shamming.'

'The opinion of all of the military. I have been quizzing them. I once heard a man in Sydney say that the trouble with New South Wales was not too many convicts, but too many incompetents of good family, and too much of the military. That man was Smith Hall. You won't take offence if I say that on that point I rather agree with him.'

Clunie was offended. He gave his useful little blink, however, and smiled. 'I hope you don't agree on any others.'

'Well, certainly not that everyone, emancipist or free, should have leave to publicly spout his opinions. If every man is licensed to say what he thinks, what becomes of Henry Cowper's special licence?'

His clown's licence, thought Clunie. Patiently smiling, he glanced over at the card tables; everyone there was engrossed, either in playing or watching. He looked at the blue sofa, where Amelia Bulwer was talking to Frances O'Beirne, and caught a few of her words.

'The youngest is six . . .'

He turned back to Cowper. 'Would you like a pipe?'

Henry drew out his pipe as they went through the french doors to the verandah. Clunie did not smoke. He clasped his hands at his back. 'You told me on the *Isabella* that Captain Logan stands in real danger from Smith Hall.'

'Was I sober?'

'You are sober now.'

'Oh, I see,' said Henry. 'Having just boasted of my special licence I can't deny it so soon. Well, I shan't. I'll speak my mind. I'll answer any question you want to put. Firstly to curry favour with you in case you take the command, and secondly out of sympathy for your delicate position here.'

'It ought not to be delicate,' Clunie said promptly. 'I've been sent to take Bainbrigge's place. That was my only clear instruction. Though it was implied that if the fifty-seventh goes to India the command would be mine.'

'Or if Mr Smith Hall brings convincing witnesses—'

'Now we are back to our conversation on the *Isabella*. Witnesses to what? To murder?'

Henry sent out puffs of smoke for a long time in silence. 'Returns of punishment,' he said at last, 'are sent to Macleay. Macleay may pass them to General Darling, to the attorney general, or to anyone they concern. So how would any commandant feel? He would feel that not to be stopped is to be sanctioned.'

'Quite. And against that sanction, what harm can Smith Hall's witnesses do?'

'Smith Hall is entitled to trial by jury. And times are changing. Public opinion is changing. Punishment accepted as natural a few years ago is called wicked today by a small minority, and harsh by a larger minority. And tomorrow or the next day, the majority will join the chorus. The tide is on the turn, captain, and he—' Henry did not bother to specify whom he meant—'he is caught in the swirl. And the wonderful thing is, he doesn't know it. Oh, he knows there's some turbulence about. He knows that, and worries by fits and starts. But for the most part, he thinks it's elsewhere, and that he's swimming along as usual.'

Clunie turned towards the lighted drawing room, and through the drifting smoke from Henry's pipe, blue in the darkness, regarded the group at the card tables. 'Perhaps he'll swim through the turbulence.'

'Perhaps he will. But not easily. Spicer told me you examined the returns of labour and punishment.'

'Examined? I looked at them, certainly, for what they could teach me of my duties.'

'What did you make of them?'

'I had never seen returns before.'

'You must have made something of them.'

'They do seem to reflect the order and productivity of the place.'

'Oh, order and productivity, yes. Is that all you noticed?'

But Clunie did not regard himself as having a special licence. He had no intention of saying what else he had noticed. Especially to a drinking man, he would not say he had noticed that to be tried was to be convicted, or that lashes were given only in twenty-fives, fifties, one hundreds, and two hundreds. Why, he had asked himself, were there no thirties, forties, sixties? And as for the jump from one to two hundred, it had made him shake his head in disbelief. At the very least, it suggested a recklessness, a wild impatience, but even to himself, Clunie would not admit so soon that it suggested anything more. And to Henry he only said, 'I've been here two days. The commandant has been here more than four years. He may very well have excellent reasons for what he does.'

'Oh, certainly,' said Henry in mild derision.

Elizabeth Robertson had brought the children into the room, and Clunie saw Logan turn sideways in his chair to lift his daughter on to his knee. Robert, standing before the blue sofa, where Frances O'Beirne still sat with Amelia Bulwer, was proffering a sea shell to his aunt, and in the charming gravity of her acceptance, she met with Clunie's approval for the first time. 'A woman like Mrs Logan,' he remarked, 'must be a considerable influence for moderation.'

'Yes. Even on her husband, perhaps, eventually. Did you see the returns for 'twenty-eight?'

'Yes.'

'A bad year. Not one of us survived it unchanged. Drought. The entire crop failed. Everyone on half rations. Trachoma, dysentery, scurvy. And ship after ship bringing more men to feed rather than food for those already here. It's apparent you came across the name of Patrick Grady.'

'I don't know what makes it apparent,' said Clunie, 'but in fact, I did.'

'You could find it in the hospital register as well, disclosing the same thing. Last year Bowman came to inspect us. Bowman's the chief medical officer. All the records were open to him. Why not? The commandant had nothing to hide. His conscience is perfectly clear. Well, I don't know what Bowman did or didn't come across in the records, but I do know this—he went back to Sydney full of praise for the good effects of the commandant's strict discipline. Those were his exact words. Yet here we have Smith Hall saying one of those effects was murder.'

'Of Swann's, not of Grady's.'

'Oh yes, yes, they've got the wrong man.' Henry spoke almost with benevolence. 'Such things happen. Out of general rumour one name emerges, and it's the wrong name. Perhaps Swann died of his twenty-five, perhaps of dysentery. There's a doubt. There's no doubt in Grady's case. And yet in neither case can it rightly be called murder. Or so I tell myself.'

'Smith Hall's language is undoubtedly excessive.'

'I tell myself that, too. And I remind myself that a soldier died under a sentence by the governor. And I ask myself how that gentleman viewed it. A casualty, sir, a simple casualty. And yet, there have been questions asked at home about that simple casualty. In the House of Commons.'

Henry moved to the edge of the verandah to knock out his pipe, while Clunie, looking into the room, saw that Lieutenant Edwards had risen from the card table and was sauntering about bestowing his broad uncritical gaze on persons and objects and views through windows. Henry rose and came to stand beside Clunie. 'You know I gave my medical sanction to Grady's two hundred?'

'If the man was in normal health, you would not have a case for withholding it.'

'Not officially, no. Yet I wish my conscience were clear.'

'I am sorry to hear it is not,' said Clunie with formality.

'I insist it was no murder, yet perhaps could be persuaded that it was.'

'Cowper, here is Edwards.'

'I shan't talk to a military man about men dying because they want to, and in any case that does rather raise the question of why they should want to.'

'Are we never to hear the end of that black?' asked Lieutenant Edwards, stepping through the doors.

Henry lifted his watch from his pocket and carried it to the light from the door. 'Eighteen minutes.'

He went without another word. Edwards burst into laughter. 'Cowper's a real original.'

'Do you like this station?' asked Clunie suddenly.

Oh, yes, it's well enough. The shooting's good, you know. There's no hunting. One can't hunt kangaroo, though Cowper does. Never lend him a horse, sir. He lamed his, and it had to be shot. It gets beastly hot in summer, of course, but not as hot as Madras, or the Indies. Yes, I like it well enough. The commandant's the best of good fellows, and Mrs Logan is always as you see her tonight.'

'Are Lieutenant Bulwer and Lieutenant Harbin cousins?' asked Frances.

'Why, no, but you are not the only one to remark on their likeness. It pleases them so much, I assure you, they are such friends. We were speaking of the samplers. At first there was no cloth to be had, but I was *not* to

139

be thwarted. "The girls *will* learn fine sewing!" That was my vow. How you would have laughed to see me hunting up old petticoats . . .'

Frances stopped listening again. Amelia had welcomed Letty's suggestion that Frances should help her teach the children, and had not left the topic since. Finding that speaking of the children led Amelia, at regular intervals and by oblique means, to her own virtues, Frances had become bored and had contrived a pattern of murmurs, appreciative or acquiescent, which fell roughly in the right places and left most of her attention free, at first for Henry Cowper and Captain Clunie, and then, after they went to the verandah, for the group round the card table.

She could see only Patrick Logan's back, so was not too much disturbed by the childish dread he continued to arouse in her. Mr Spicer and Mr Hansord she dismissed, not out of lack of interest, but out of frustrated curiosity, for by their very blandness and correctness such men always seemed to her positively enigmatic. Lieutenant Edwards, so handsome and pleasant, it was impossible not to like; but in her glances at the other two lieutenants, Bulwer and Harbin, a concentration of interest had soon appeared, and she now noticed with surprise that the likeness she had just commented on to Amelia was fostered rather than real: a matter of hair dressed in exactly the same style, a similar way of narrowing the eyes and letting the mouth hang open, and gestures they seemed slyly to copy from one another like boys playing jokes before their superiors. Once they both leaned over the table at the same time, heads together, to admire a brooch on Letty's dress, and at another time they turned these same over-admiring glances on Louisa's silver necklaces, exclaiming like birds in the same nest, and causing such an affectation of weariness in Louisa that she seemed to find a playing card almost too heavy to lift. When the children were brought in they bent over them in the same way, but the children had carelessly whirled out of their reach, Lucy to go to her father and Robert to present Frances with the shell she still held in her hand.

Suddenly arrested by a remark of Amelia's, Frances turned back to her. 'But I thought the school was only for the prisoners' children.'

'No, my dear. A few are soldiers' children. But you may judge of their quality by the fact that their parents permit them to learn their lessons beside the others. They are all much of a muchness. It takes the *ut*-most determination to draw them towards the light.'

'What light?' asked Frances, before she could stop herself.

'The light of Mrs Bulwer's own opinions,' interposed Henry Cowper. He had just come in from the verandah.

'I hope I am not so proud,' said Amelia, steadily smiling at him. 'I meant the light of Our Lord.'

'You distinguish, madam?' He bowed and continued on his way to the card table. Letty saw him coming and rose to meet him.

'Henwy, you are leaving so soon?'

'Yes. To give you a chance to serve your plaguey weak punch.'

'Oh, *Henwy* . . .'

Though Captain Clunie left soon after the toasts to Miss O'Beirne and himself were drunk, his early departure drew a very different response from the night before. The commandant, instead of the repressed resentment he had shown then, clasped his hand and cheerfully told him to sleep well, and in Laetitia Logan's animated sweetness he could detect no trace of the flat dismay that for all her gallant wiles she had then been unable to hide.

And yet, what in the situation had changed? Though conscious all day of change proceeding, Clunie had been too much at a stretch in receiving information to sense from exactly what quarter it was coming and in what it consisted. But now, as the door shut behind him, clipping off the sound of Mrs Logan's piano and Lieutenant Edwards's song, and he crossed the verandah and descended to the garden, he asked himself again what had caused such a change. He had received his assigned servants on taking occupation of Bainbrigge's cottage that afternoon, but seeing no danger to himself on the short walk to the command-ant's house, he had come unaccompanied.

The moon was in its first quarter and the road outside the garden rather dark. No change, thought Clunie, had taken place in his own explanation of why he had been sent. In Sydney he had decided that soon after Governor Darling had instructed Logan to pros-ecute Smith Hall for libel, rumours of the intentions of the defence witnesses, combined with news from England of questions asked about his own severity, had made him realise that his personal animosity for Smith Hall had trapped him into rashness. He had realised, in fact, that at the trial the cat may jump in unexpected ways, and had therefore resolved to send Clunie to Moreton Bay in case scandal should make it necessary to remove the commandant.

All this Clunie had gathered from gossip or inferred from the very imprecision of his instructions, but much of what he had heard on the voyage, and had seen and heard today, had confirmed him in his opinion. Moreover, the one apparent contradiction had now been resolved.

Clunie's passage down the rough, dark, and unfa-miliar road was so uncertain that he regretted not having brought a servant, after all, to light his way with a torch. The perplexing contradiction had been that since a soldier had died under one of Darling's punishments, it would be dangerous (to Darling

143

himself) to remove Logan because a prisoner had died under one of his. The solution probably hoped for was the posting of the fifty-seventh to India, but if that did not occur in time to save the situation, and revelations at the trial still made Logan's removal expedient, some reason other than harshness must be found. Given the commandant's efficiency in agriculture and building, his enterprise and courage in exploration, and the positive encouragement to strict discipline given him by the governor, Clunie had not been able to imagine what other reason could be devised. It was not until today that he asked himself what better reason they could give—and what reason more acceptable to London—than that Logan's security measures were inefficient, allowing the escape of men who goaded the natives into aggression. By his worried preoccupation with these two matters, the commandant had given Clunie an answer he himself did not know, but had only sensed, so far, like an animal sniffing danger on the wind.

Clunie was passing the cottage Murray shared with Hansord. The darkened window must be Hansord's, whom he had left at the commandant's house, busy at the buffet supper. Against the muslin curtain of the other, candlelight threw the shadow of a man's head inclined to reading or prayer. Murray had been here only a few months. Pious and sensitive, how would he adapt to his tasks? Clunie felt sorry for Murray in his loneliness, for Logan in his teasing intimations of betrayal, and for the prisoners in their debasement. If he could palliate the condition of any of them without putting himself in peril he would do so. Otherwise, like any other sensible man, he would harden his heart. His weatherboard cottage, built in Sydney and shipped in segments to the settlement, had housed the first and second commandants. As Clunie approached he smelled burning fat and guessed that the light from the servants' quarters came from a cruzie lamp. Tired, he had lost sight of the question asked as he stepped down from the commandant's verandah, but now, ascending the two steps to his own small verandah, the answer came to him.

What had changed was simply the commandant himself. At some point in the day, in a sudden and irrational reversal, Logan had decided that his fears of Clunie were unwarranted, that he was the finest of fellows, and that all was well. Clunie had already convicted him of recklessness and impatience, and now he called him confoundedly moody as well. His door was bolted. As he called for admittance and for light, he decided there was a danger to himself in Logan's moodiness. He would be on guard against it. The two windows nearest the door were suffused with golden light, then the bolts were drawn, and the door opened.

*

145

As soon as the door shut behind Hansord and Spicer (always the last to leave) Big Annie went to the inside privy to take the buckets to the cesspool. She was a daily woman from the female factory, but tonight would sleep in the house. Letty was already in the bedroom and had rung for Elizabeth Robertson to bring warm water. The commandant went through the house testing locked doors, and then took his candle to the back door and waited for Annie to reappear. He saw her safely into the house, and was locking and bolting the door, when the sound of footsteps in the garden made him throw it open again. Frances, breathless, was leaping up the steps. 'I thought,' she said, panting, 'I was locked out.'

'Where have you been?'

'Why—to the privy.'

'How dare you, miss! That is for the use of the female servants. You are to use the one inside.'

'The bucket was gone.'

'When that happens, you must wait. Your sister must have told you that.'

'She did. But I don't care, I don't like using it.' She was combating her fear of him with a childish boldness. 'It is like an invalid stool. Such things are used only in sickrooms. It hardly seems clean.'

He had controlled his anger. 'I will decide what is clean and what is not. Goodnight to you.'

'Well,' said Letty when he told her, 'I can't teach her ev'wything in one day.'

146

'True. But pray explain to her that it is indiscreet by day and indecent by night.' He was unhooking the neckband of his jacket. 'I will not have the women of my household,' he said with his chin raised, 'exposed to the eyes of the gardeners in their comings and goings for such purposes.'

'I will tell her, my love.' Letty had finished washing, and now she picked up a towel and moved away from the wash stand to let him take her place. He undressed quickly, dropping his clothes to the floor. She stood by the fire, watching him as she dried herself with the small white towel. 'Captain Clunie is ve'wy amiable, after all.'

'A fine steady fellow. An acquisition to the settlement.'

'If you had heeded me last night—'

'I know. It was the letter. It was because no letter came.'

No worry was audible in her voice. 'It will come by the next vessel.'

'I know. I know that now.'

When he had washed he shook a towel from its folds and walked about the room as he dried himself. Letty, who left the house so seldom, showed no variation, either in face or body, of the creamy colour of her skin except in the three whiter mounds of breasts and belly still distended by her recent pregnancy; but although the skin of his body was paler than hers—

147

being of that white with a tint of blue—and was quite as tender and delicate as hers, his face and upper neck, his hands and wrists, were red and blotched and coarsened. Once, when she had remarked on this variation, telling him that it was like embracing two different men, he had put a hand on a thigh and looked at the contrast with surprise. He showed very little awareness of any aspect of his appearance other than those dictated by his training. She put on her nightgown and as she tied the drawstrings at the neck she watched the tread of his white supple feet on the confines of a Persian rug. When he tossed the towel on to the wash stand she took his night shirt from the chair by the fire and proffered it with the neck held open by her hands. 'I wish I could take some of that land in the south,' he said as he put it on.

'Where would we get the money? You heard what James said. How would we stock the land?'

'Murray's father sold his commission.'

'By the time we could a'wange that, we may be in India.'

'May we? How do I know? Have I heard from my commanding officer? I know nothing. I hear nothing. I am cut off.'

She saw him threatened again by his irritability and gloom. 'If we must be farmers,' she said coaxingly, let us await a weply from the company. Then you could wesign.'

148

'Clunie says the agricultural company has chosen a manager.'

'How does Captain Clunie know?'

'He heard.'

'Oh, the things people hear . . . we will not know until they answer your letter. They must answer soon.'

'Must they indeed? They are under no obligation. It seems nobody is under an obligation but me, who is obliged always to wait. I will tell you—'

'Patwick—'

'I will tell you this. If Macleay's letter does not come by the next ship, I will write to the governor.' But then he said, as if in indignant reply to someone else's suggestion, 'No! I will not. It would betray anxiety. I won't do it!'

Lines of fatigue had appeared on her face. 'Patwick,' she said helplessly. 'My love . . .' She rang the bell for Elizabeth to come and put the room to rights. 'What will happen?' she wanted to ask. But now, standing on the hearth and watching the fire, he suddenly laughed.

'Cowper is the greatest of fools. He said the black man was dying because he wished to. He said he was impressed with the delicacy of the operation. The delicacy! And he named what white men must do if they wish to die. It put me in mind of the army of occupation, of my time in France. Suicide used to be fashionable. Young fellows—'

'I know,' she said, 'you told me.'

149

'I remember how young fellows—'

She threw her arms about him. 'My love, you have told me one hundwed hundwed times. Hush. Here is Elizabeth. Hush.'

PART TWO

CHAPTER SEVEN

'Do you recall our talk on the *Regent Bird*? When I said I was at the mercy of my company? I shan't say it is no longer true—'

'Wait,' said Louisa. 'First let us walk a beetle. I must get those legs.'

Frances took a beetle from the perforated box and set it on the palm of her other hand. 'But I shall say it is less true.'

'I am sure of it. Come, creature, walk.'

'He always tries to fly first.'

The beetle could not fly because James Murray had sealed its wings with a scrap of spider web. Since it was only a common beetle, he would unseal its wings when it had served its purpose and release it into the perils of its own world. When it found it could not fly it began to walk towards Frances's wrist, while Louisa, eyes darting and hands swift, made sketches of it all over her page. From these she would devise the motion for the anoplognathus beetle she was copying for James Murray. The anoplognathus was big and rare and rotund, with dragon shards of green and gold, and golden globular eyes on either side of a wedged head. But it was dead, impaled on a long pin, and its six legs trailed downward like dry litter, so that the walking beetle was needed to provide for it an exemplar of life. The live beetle passed over Frances's wrist and struggled up the inside of her arm. It was small, and of a plain brown, but James Murray said that all beetles of that class walked in the same way. Louisa had replied that she trusted he was right, because they would never make their fortunes out of insects with unscientific walks. It was their intention to send the drawings, with Murray's text, to a London publisher. James Murray was enthusiastic about the project, and for Louisa, from whose nature enthusiasm was absent, it was something to do. When the beetle arrived at the frill falling from Frances's white muslin sleeve it came to a stop. It was the end of September, already warm enough for muslin; Frances had been at Moreton Bay for more than six weeks. For the last three she had been taking drawing lessons from Louisa, but they usually ended, as this one was doing, by her putting aside her own work to help Louisa. She plucked the beetle from her arm and held it between a thumb and forefinger. 'Again?'

'No. I shall try now to fit his legs to my sketch. If I can find it.'

Frances put the beetle back in the box. 'I am still at the mercy of the children at the school.'

'And of one other,' said Louisa, searching in her portfolio of drawings.

'Yes,' said Frances, 'of him.'

'Why?'

'He has only to give me a blue look.'

'Pass his blue looks. Pass them by.'

'I do.'

'I have seen you. You look as if you might burst. Where can that sketch be?'

'You have not seen me lately. I pass them by very meekly now. Because lately, if I irritate him, he extends his displeasure to Letty. And then the strangest thing happens. She becomes thin and blanched looking—yes, all in an hour—and doesn't hear what one says to her. So now I contrive to be perfectly meek.'

'Strive instead for perfect composure. Here he is. Here is greenback.'

'He is beautiful even without legs. He is a scarab.'

Frances, with her chin on her interlaced hands, watched while Louisa lightly pencilled in the legs beneath the painted body. 'Wrong,' she said. She erased them and tried again, and again, while Frances said nothing, but watched with sober respect. The great change in Frances's manner and appearance was not

155

owing only to pressure by three women. Two weeks after her arrival the *Alligator* had brought a letter from Edmund Joyce, which she had opened with the lightest of expectations because she had begun to forget him.

'*My very dear girl, was ever a wretch more cast down than I have been since your departure? Your absence has taught me how I grew to rely, during our long voyage, on your sweet and eager presence at my side. I curse the fate that took you to that place, and yet do not curse it, because it was needed to teach me your importance. Such an insensible fool I was . . .*'

He had first covered the page horizontally and had then written vertically over his own writing, so that it took her about fifteen minutes to read. By that time she knew it was not a joke, or a mistake, and yet was no less astounded than when she had learned from the first three words that she was his very dear girl. Stunned, moving like a sleep walker, she took it to Letty. The *Alligator* had brought neither the letter covering Captain Clunie's appointment nor the awaited advice from Colonel Allen of the regiment's posting, but Letty surmounted her own distress, read Edmund Joyce's letter, smiled and exclaimed over it, and advised her how to answer it. Frances had already written to Edmund Joyce, as well as to Elizabeth and Barbara Hall, telling them of her work with Robert and at the school, correcting their misconceptions of the settlement, and adding that the cause in which they all believed would not be advanced by inaccuracies. But she had not folded or sealed her letters, and she now sat down at her mother's desk and added a postscript to Edmund's, saying, as Letty had suggested, that though no young lady could help but be pleased and flattered by such a letter, she would take it kindly if he wrote no more like it without first asking the permission of her sister. She was amazed and elated to be loved, but a thread of sobriety in her elation reminded her that if he had failed to write she would have relinquished their friendship with regret but without grief. The elation, however, refused to be quenched by the sobriety, and the next morning, while dressing her hair, she suddenly, and with the greatest of ease, devised a style for herself so becoming that Letty, when she saw it, folded her hands and gasped.

'Why did not I think of that?'

'I can't think how I thought of it.'

After that day, drawing the approval of those about her, she fed on it, and gave it back in looks and manners ever more inducive of their approval, seldom reverting to her former gaucherie except with the children at the school, and (although less often now) with her brother-in-law. Into the mild incessant waters shaping a shore, these were the rough stones thrown, the disrupters of expected tides. However, Amelia Bulwer lodged close enough to the school to hear the rumpus with the pupils and to intervene, and as for Patrick Logan, she could at least be grateful for seeing so little of him. Six more men had escaped, among them Bulbridge and Fagan, who had run together as soon as Fagan had gone back from the hospital to his gang. One of the six was found drowned, and three returned, but Bulbridge and Fagan had got clear away. The commandant was increasingly morose; he took his breakfast and left the house early; he went for days at a time to Dunwich or the Limestone Station. Frances longed for him to go on his proposed journey of exploration.

Only the signal from the next ship to arrive, the *Mary Elizabeth*, revived his spirits. In the mailbag were two letters from Edmund Joyce, one for her and one for Letty. There was no reply from the Hall girls, and again, neither of the letters expected by the commandant arrived. Letty, silent and distracted, could scarcely attend to either of Edmund's letters, and Frances, sensitive to her sister's moods (though ignorant of her particular fears for her husband) withdrew to her room to let her recover. Here she read Edmund Joyce's letter again. Although she had corrected his belief that her mail was censored, it was clear that in some matters he was taking no chances. He had heard a rumour, he wrote, that her brother-in-law was soon to be in Sydney, 'on one business or another', and hoped for the great joy of meeting her. And if the captain's business was such as would not be approved by certain of their mutual friends, why, that need not cast its reflection on them. He had not seen those mutual friends lately because he had been staying with his uncle and aunt at their estate in the Hunter Valley. His uncle and aunt, far from being the tory ogres he had imagined, were perfectly delightful. And he went on to describe his uncle's house. 'A stone house with a wide verandah and a pillared portico such as no English gentleman would be ashamed to own.' His uncle's convict servants were 'happier than most of their kind in England and had a hundred times more chance of future prosperity', and although he had not abated one jot of his former opinions, he began to think that reform was better carried out by individual acts of kindness rather than by 'unleashing the refractory passions of the press'.

By this time Letty had rallied. She came in fluttering her letter from Edmund and pronounced it 'vewy pwop'ly put'. She wrote her reply, also very properly put, at their mother's desk, but this time did not advise Frances on hers. The next day brought a warm change, and Frances was able to wear for the first time one of the muslin dresses cut by Amelia and sewn by Letty and herself. Henry Cowper walked round her in circles, staring. 'I met someone like her on the *Regent Bird*,' he told Letty. 'It must have been her mother.' He had come to bandage Robert's hand because James Murray was at the Eagle Farm. Escorted by Madge Noakes, Frances went to the school. It was Amelia's habit to walk up and down in front of her pupils and speak in a ringing unanswerable voice, but Frances, lacking this authority, kept to the old way of collecting them about her chair and dealing with them one by one. She invariably failed to control them, but on this day, sitting and looking into their upturned faces, she mistook her inner excitement, generated by the warm day and by her new expectations, for love of them, and did not see how they could fail to submit to such benign authority. Ten minutes later Amelia Bulwer rushed into the schoolroom with her servant Maria. With threats and bangs they mustered the shouting turbulent children. They seated them in a tight squad and Amelia then marched up and down in front of them and instructed them in a ringing unanswerable voice. When the bell rang for the midday muster, and the yellow lines of prisoners began to converge on the barracks for their hour of dinner and rest, the pupils were dismissed. In her room at home, Frances stood at the window, untying her bonnet strings and looking with the unsensitive eyes of habit at the roads, trodden out by hampered feet, that lay between her window and the botanical gardens on the other side of the point. She could see, set in treetops, the roof of the octagonal cottage (which she now knew as Hobson's Cottage), but trees to the left of her window hid all the main part of the settlement, hid from her view Captain Clunie entering his cottage, and hid the subsiding billows of dust at the gates of the prisoners' barracks. Her room was on the same side of the house as the nursery. Below in the garden Gilligan was sitting on the ground with his knees raised, peaceably smoking his pipe. She no longer saw Martin working in the garden. The day after she had spoken about him to Letty, the boy who helped with the bullocks had been injured. Martin, partly by Letty's contrivance, had been sent to take his place, and Frances now saw him only in the chapel on Sundays. The official party, respectful in silks and braided uniforms, entered the chapel last, watched by the iron gangs and guards in the gallery, and the prisoners and military below, but not by Henry Cowper, whose head was always bowed as if in preliminary prayer. Here and there in the congregation were children's faces, and Frances, looking about for those she taught, would find her gaze catching on a thin dark face, and as her own eyes continued their search she would feel the intensity of a stare that persisted until Henry Cowper raised his head and said with absolutely uninflected solemnity, 'Let us pray.' Bowing her head allowed her to escape those begging, unnerving eyes. She was thankful that he no longer worked in the garden.

Gilligan rose and knocked out his pipe, and Frances, as she turned from the window, heard voices in the nursery. She flung her bonnet on the bed and ran to see who had arrived. James Murray was kneeling to examine Lucy's knee, which the little girl had set up in competition with Robert's cut hand, while Letty

161

stood nearby with Robert leaning against her. Frances, standing in the doorway in her soft white muslin, drew from James Murray such an exclamation of pleasure and amazement that she laughed and said she would presently decide whether to be complimented or offended. Their friendship had quickly been consolidated, but in his case depended upon the presence of others; when Letty left them alone for a minute or two he would become distracted with nervousness and look often and beseechingly at the door.

To indulge Lucy, he bandaged her knee, and they all took tea and cold meat in the nursery, because, Letty said, invalids must be consoled. The warmth had made the children restless; they would not eat, but fidgeted and chanted. Frances, standing at the french doors, could hear above their chanting Letty and James Murray planning an evening of theatricals. She looked over the trodden roads and longed to ride. But no horses had yet arrived, and presently she turned and proposed a walk. Letty, who had not been out of the house since her miscarriage, protested almost in fright, but was persuaded by Robert's eagerness and Murray's earnest advice. A panama hat was fetched for Robert, a bonnet for Lucy, and parasols for Letty and Frances, and with James Murray as escort, they all left the house and took the road along the river bank. While Letty talked of the proposed theatricals, which she said could be in celebration of Frances's eighteenth birthday in October, they sauntered past the cottages, the hospital, the brick kiln, and the graveyard, and presently came to grassy paddocks bounded on one side by the river. The gangs had gone back to work, and they met with nothing but a water cart drawn by four bullocks and accompanied by two men. One of these was Martin.

'Martin!' cried Robert.

'Martin,' quavered Lucy.

But Murray grasped the boy's shoulder when he would have run to the cart, and Letty held Lucy's hand. Frances bent, as if against a wind, and sheltered her head with her parasol, so that beyond recognising that it was Martin, she was not forced to look at his face. The bullocks were pulling well, but as the two groups drew apart he made his whip crack and cried to them with desperate loudness to get on there.

'Gaah-*on*! You there!'

Before Murray and Robert and the children lay a grassy field, fragrant in the warmth, and when Robert plunged into it a multitude of white butterflies rose and fluttered above the pale flowing grass. 'Elodina parthia,' said Murray. 'So they are here in the north as well!' Martin's whip and voice had almost died away. The wings of the butterflies were thin as tissue paper and veined like leaves. Standing in the long grass, Murray put forward for the first time the idea of an illustrated book on the insects of the district. They seized on it with enthusiasm. Theatricals were forgotten. They turned in their tracks and hurried to lay it before Louisa.

Louisa, as she finished painting the legs of the anoplognathus beetle in brownish-black, could not help looking pleased. In the two weeks since James Murray had put forward his plan, she had worked every day, and now had twenty sketches in her portfolio. When she finished the drawing she laid the brush down very delicately, as if it might break.

'I envy you,' said Frances.

'It passes the time.'

'I can do nothing.'

'Oh, surely, something.'

'Nothing coloured. Nothing that shows.'

'Well, I daresay things that show do get one into less trouble than things that don't. Sketching does seem safer than thinking. Do you still expect a reply from the Hall girls?'

Frances shook her head. 'My letter estranged them.'

'Perhaps it is just as well.'

'Yes.' Frances got to her feet. 'Let me clean your things.'

She tied a painting apron over her dress, assembled Louisa's brushes and water and china palettes on a tray and carried them to the scullery. Louisa's cook was plucking a chicken. Frances refused her offer of help and went herself to fetch water from the cask in the kitchen porch.

Each married officer was allowed two outside servants—always convicts of the first class—to grow vegetables and raise chickens and pigs for his household. While Frances was drawing the water she could hear Victor Harbin's two men talking at a short distance from the porch. Of all the members of the officers' households she was the only one who went into places where she was not expected to go. In the matter of the privy she had been obedient until the warm weather had made evident, at certain turnings of a corridor or during certain shifts of a breeze, a faint stench in Letty's pretty house. Then she had taken to using the outside privy when the commandant was out and Letty was resting, and even after becoming used to the stench, the habit of running out of the house remained. If the servants saw her coming and going, they turned their backs, but sometimes, because she went softly so that she should be undetected from the house, so was she undetected by them. She ranged wider. She ran to the stable to see Fatima, and to the yard to watch a litter of pigs. She went to the orchard for a shaddock or lemon, she drew her own water from the casks. And in this way she had seen things she called inexplicable. Gilligan and the groom, lying in a dark corner of the stable, she could have almost believed to be fighting. Big Annie and Madge Noakes, upright and entwined in the scullery, seemed closer to static play. She called such sights inexplicable, yet knowledge was somewhere in her, for they jolted and frightened her. She could not speak of them without disclosing her own disobedience; she thrust them away from her and seemed to have forgotten them. This was the easier to do because such events were rare. More often, she overheard conversations, and these she had no impulse to reject. Many concerned food, some were vulgar chaffing, but a surprising number were similar to that which reached her now. Victor Harbin's men were discussing the social standing of the various officers they had known. She did not pay much attention until they began to speak of the commandant.

'And 'im,' said one. 'What's ee, after all?'

'You're right, cock. What?'

'Nothin' but a marchin' captain in a foot regiment.'

'Nothin' but that.'

'Now if it was the 'Orse Guards. Or another of the bang-up ones . . .'

Frances bore her water into the kitchen. She was the daughter of a major, accustomed from childhood to hearing such distinctions made, but to hear the prisoners making them puzzled and disconcerted her. She had heard enough to know that they made these distinctions among themselves as well as among the military and civilian officers; and that they should care about such details, that they should care whether one was allowed to wear a straw hat and another was not, that one received one and threepence a week and another tenpence, or whether one's master was this or that in the military scale, altered and confused her first conception of them to such a degree that she no longer knew what to make of them at all. In their concern with such petty matters she felt they betrayed the tragedy of their fate. The only ones she still thought of with her former intensity were the truly ungovernable ones: Lazarus, Bulbridge and Fagan, and others of whom she had heard. Bulbridge and Fagan, instead of two little men scrimmaging in a wheatfield, now appeared in her inner vision, with Lazarus and the others (whom she had never seen in life), as dark, wild, crazed, almost wolfish creatures. She would not have walked past them to the privy, or gone among them to pick fruit or to rest her cheek on the neck of a grey mare, but she could not help hoping that they would win the contest into which they had thrown themselves against such odds. The indignation she had shared with Edmund Joyce and the Hall girls was now absorbed in the hope that Lewis Lazarus would get clear away at his next attempt, that Bulbridge and Fagan would never be taken, and that Boylan (whose name she had overheard several times) was not dead, but was indeed with the blacks in the bush. Guilty about the secrecy and fervency of this hope, she told herself for consolation that Lazarus, or

Bulbridge and Fagan, or Boylan, could not be a danger to 'us' (in which category she did include herself) if they were living deep in the bush with the blacks. Standing at the scullery bench and washing Louisa's brushes, she said idly to the cook, 'Do many blacks come about the settlement?'

'A few, miss.'

'I have not seen even one.'

'They come about the outskirts, miss. But not inside. Not now.'

'And on the outskirts, do they speak to the men in the gangs?'

But now the cook spoke with stony reproach. 'I am sure I don't know what they do, miss.'

Louisa's housemaid ran into the kitchen. 'A ship!' she cried. She was sixteen. She twirled about with her arms held horizontally. 'A ship at Dunwich!'

The cook went on plucking the chicken. 'It will bring me nothink, Jenny.'

'Which one is it?' asked Frances.

The girl came to a standstill. 'I don't know, miss. The men just come down from Signals Hill.'

'It will bring you nothink, neither, Jenny,' said the cook.

'It might,' said Jenny, on a rising note.

Frances cleaned the rest of Louisa's painting things and carried the tray back to the sitting room. Amelia Bulwer had just arrived.

'Frances, my love! A ship!'

'The *Phillip*,' said Louisa.

'Then the prisoners will get fresh meat,' said Frances. For weeks the prisoners in the gangs had had no fresh meat, but the *Governor Phillip*, the largest of the ships that served the settlement, was the one on which stock was most likely to be carried. 'And surely there will be horses,' she said.

'And perhaps a home mail at last,' said Amelia. 'To say nothing of the mailbag from Sydney. Louisa, look at Frances. She knows there will be a letter from her beau.'

'I hope there is one from my sisters.' Frances was learning to protect her privacy. She set down the tray and untied her apron. 'I have not had one yet.'

'It takes so long,' said Louisa, 'from over there.'

'And the post is so expensive,' said Amelia. 'It is one of our many, many benefits that ours is carried free.' She rushed at Frances, took the apron from her and folded it. '*Not* that a certain person in *Sydney* counts the cost!'

She was twitching and tweaking at Frances's clothes as if arranging her for a bridal appearance. Frances found it hard to stand patiently under this behaviour: it gave her the old unbearable feeling that she had been trapped into falsely representing herself; it made her wish scrupulously to explain that there were times when all she could remember of Edmund

Joyce was a long pale chin, and that at other times she thought of him as light and affected, though not in the most common way. In fact it brought out in her character an austerity and stiffness that was quite unnoticed by Amelia (now re-tying her sash) but not by Louisa, who was rolling at Frances her pale amused sardonic eyes. Frances recalled her advice—'Strive to be quite composed'—and stood composedly enough until Amelia finished with her clothes and gave her a little push.

'You will want to run home at once. Here is your bonnet. I will lend you my Maria if Louisa can't spare her Mary.'

'Amelia,' said Louisa in her slow voice, 'the *Phillip* must first be discharged. No mail will arrive until tomorrow. I am sure Frances is quite content to wait for Madge.'

Madge Noakes arriving at that moment, however, Frances did put on her bonnet and leave. Not only was she impelled by the excitement generated by the arrival of a ship, but she was drawn home by anxiety for Letty. She knew the mails were of great importance to Letty; she knew that official papers of some sort were awaited, and had felt a sort of offence when Letty had deflected her questions about them. As she left the room with Madge Noakes she heard Amelia say to Louisa, 'Well, with the commandant at the Limestone Station it will fall to Captain Clunie to discharge the *Phillip*.'

And for a moment the answer to those deflected questions curled like a wisp of smoke in her mind, then as quickly as a wisp of smoke disappeared.

The Harbin and Bulwer cottages were set lower in the bank than the others. Instead of taking the winding steps to the road, Frances and the servant scrambled up the rough bank, Madge going in advance and turning now and again to help Frances, who needed one hand to keep her flounced hems clear of the dirt. 'Let us hope the *Phillip* brings beasts,' remarked Frances on one of these occasions.

'Yes, miss, or what a cry will go up.' They were scrambling on again. 'Fresh meat every Sunday they must have now, or they think they is dying.'

'It's little enough,' said Frances.

'More than what we had in the old days.'

Frances had become used to Madge's deep cracked voice, but not to the dragging delivery that made her sound so strangely complacent. She reached the road and turned to pull Frances up the last and steepest part of the bank. The movement dislodged her neckerchief. 'Secure your kerchief, Madge,' Letty was constantly saying. But Madge would not or could not keep her scars quite covered. Frances lowered her eyes as if in concentration on the release of her skirt. Elizabeth Robertson had told her how Madge had come by her scars, but because of the casual disjointedness of the telling—as if only referring to something already well known—or because Frances's understanding had veered away, she was still uncertain whether Madge's crazed disfiguring struggle had been against the wooden collar attached to her on the ship, or the pillory in which they had later sought to subdue her in Sydney Town. What chiefly remained with Frances was that they had done more than subdue her, and this impressed her afresh as she shook out her skirt and heard Madge say, with contempt and yet with pride, 'They would have thought theirselves lucky to get a few ounces of salt beef in the old days. Us who was about in those days know what is what!'

Frances raised her eyes. 'What do you mean by the old days?'

When directly addressed, Madge always shifted those sluggish brown eyes aside. 'I come in seventeen ninety-six.'

'Thirty-four years ago. You must have been only a child.'

Madge's slight smile, like her gaze, seemed directed elsewhere. 'Sixteen, miss. Old enough to know right from wrong. I doesn't complain.'

'It is as well to be content,' said Frances curtly.

'We has made our beds, miss.'

The wrinkles covering her face were like cracks in a glass pane shattered all over by explosion but still hanging in the frame. Frances gave a shrug, and they set off down the road, Madge ostentatiously adjusting her kerchief. 'I knows I ought to put a bit of a pin in it.'

There was cajolery in the cracked voice. Frances set her lips and turned her head away. On the other side of the river she saw Patrick Logan, mounted on Fatima, approaching the landing stage. From the near shore, the barge was already putting into the stream.

'I always loses the pins,' said Madge Noakes.

'I will give you more,' said Frances, watching Fatima come to a halt with a few, prettily curbed steps.

But now Madge Noakes was also looking across the river. 'Back from the Limestone. And he has rode away again, from Collison and the rest.'

The commandant dismounted, leaving clear to view the lovely arch of Fatima's neck. 'There will be horses on the *Phillip*,' said Frances in a sweetened, hollow voice.

'Horses!' repeated Madge with her cracked laugh.

Fatima dropped her head and stood still and wearily, but the commandant fidgeted, taking a few steps to the left and then to the right, and jerking his head as if irked by pain or discomfort at the back of his neck. Frances guessed that Letty would also be watching him, standing at some window or door of the house she so seldom left. Perhaps she would have risen from the blue sofa to watch, for James Murray, puzzled by her slow recovery, insisted that she still rest twice a day. Frances imagined her hand hovering about the ribbons at her collar, saw the worry gathering in her eyes. 'Only muddle, Fwances,' she had said in reply to Frances's questions. 'All our lives are bound by muddle and mails.' She fragmented the worry with her laugh, and waved it away with her hands, but it always seemed to reassemble, out there in the air, and float back to resettle on her. They were near the house now. Frances could hear the children shouting, almost shrieking, with excitement. And then she saw them. They were rolling down the long incline in the field beyond the house, where recent rain had made the grass so soft and green. Elizabeth stood at the bottom of the slope, and nearby, a gardener raised his head from his work to watch them. She saw that it was Martin, and felt a sharp anger, as if he had come back of his own volition, to dog her with his pitiful presence. But conscious of the injustice of this feeling, she controlled it at once. 'Strive for perfect composure.' He would be a test of her composure. She turned to ask Madge Noakes when he had come back to work at the house, and for how long, but Madge was still looking across the river at the commandant, with eyes that looked black and enlarged, and did not hear her question.

It was astonishing to Frances how quickly his mood could change. In the man who strode into the drawing room there was no trace of the restlessness and discomposure he had shown thirty minutes ago while awaiting the barge. Smiling and enlivened, he crossed the drawing room. Letty, watching his face, rose from her seat on the sofa beside Frances, at the same time putting her sewing into Frances's lap. She hurried to meet him. They came together, clasped hands, hardly kissed. 'The *Phillip*,' he said.

She bent backwards so that she could examine his face. 'I know.'

He turned to Frances with a brief bow. 'Miss Reform! She will bring you the radical journals.'

Letty, to insure against possible outbursts on Frances's part, had revealed her sister's sympathies but had exaggerated them to the point of caricature and had omitted mention of the Hall girls. All the same, with a hand on Logan's sleeve, she now gave Frances an anxious look. Frances put Letty's sewing from her lap and picked up her own. 'I should prefer a letter from Ireland,' she said.

'And another from Sydney,' said Letty. For Logan had been much impressed by the attentions paid Frances by Anning's nephew. That, more than anything else, had made him tolerate her. He laughed now, and agreed that Frances would certainly receive one from her beau. 'And for you, my love,' he said to Letty, 'one from Cassandra.'

His ebullience brought an anxious note to Letty's voice. 'The poor old *Phillip*. You make her sound like a tweasure ship. We must wait and see.' She stroked his sleeve. 'You are covered with dust.'

'Yes. Yes. There has been no rain out there. Oh, we saw the black prisoner near the Limestone Station. Fat and well. Yes, I am dusty. I leave at once for Dunwich. Well, not at once, but in thirty minutes. The *Regent Bird* is being made ready. Ring for Elizabeth, my dear.'

'The hot water is alweady on the wash stand.'

As she followed her husband out of the room, Letty sent her sister a smile that was almost timid, as if begging for her understanding, but Frances did not raise her head from her sewing. As soon as they stood in the passage, and he had shut the door behind them, Letty blocked his path and grasped him by both arms. 'Where is Collison?' she whispered fiercely.

'Oh, back there.'

He released himself as he spoke and walked down the passage so fast that she had to trot to keep up with him. In the bedroom she grasped him by the arms again. 'You came in alone. I saw you.'

'I can't go at that snail's pace.'

She followed him across the room. 'Blacks!' she said.

He sat down and took off a shoe. 'They wouldn't dare.'

But she thrust her face at him again. 'Absconders! They would dare if goaded by absconders. You have said so yourself.'

But he only smiled, shaking his head.

'You mean you have not said so?'

'I don't know,' he said, pleasant and indifferent. 'I may have.'

She sat suddenly on the footstool by the bed. 'Oh, why are you either so melancholy that all is black, or in such high sp'wits that all is golden?'

Walking about the room and undressing, he only laughed. She leapt to her feet and extended both hands. 'Now, see? All is golden. A tweasure ship has sailed into our bay. A letter from Mr Macleay is on her, and so is one from Colonel Allen.'

'Don't forget the one from the agricultural company, since you insist it must come.'

'That too. And all will say pwecisely what you want them to.'

'You have forgotten the horses, the beasts, and a keepsake annual for yourself.'

'And you, Patwick, have forgotten the pwisoners. Pway, how many does she bwing?'

'No more than we can accommodate and control.'

'Lord! All is indeed golden!' When she was really angry, she tended to make a pantomime of it, so that she should not appear stark and ugly. 'Oh,' she said, wailing, 'where is the man of sober good sense? This one—' she extended a graceful arm to point at him— 'believes that Captain Clunie's appointment will be explained by the posting of the wegiment, and yet that we shan't be forced to take the childwen to an unhealthy India station, or else part with them to Scotland. He believes that he will be offered a post at two thousand a year—'

'It is you, my love, who believe that the agricultural company—'

'—and that Smith Hall will dwop his charges.'

Stripped to his breeches, he put both hands on his hips. 'What did you say?'

'That Smith Hall—'

'But it is *I* who make the charge. A charge of libel.'

'I spoke,' she said (she was very alert and sober now) 'of the charge he made in the *Monitor*.'

'That was not a legal charge. Any man may write anything. The only legal charge has been made by me. And as to his dropping it, he can't. It is not in his power.'

She said, 'I did not mean dwop—'

'No, you meant withdraw. Well, that is possible. He may withdraw his words, and he may apologise with all his might, but I shan't withdraw my charge.' He dropped his breeches to the floor and kicked them on to the pile of his discarded clothes. 'Ring for Elizabeth, if you please. My jacket must be brushed.' He poured water into the basin. 'Surely you would not wish me to drop that charge?'

'I don't know.'

'You don't know!'

His astonished voice was half choked with the water he was splashing on his face. She rang the bell, then went to a chest and took out his white uniform trousers, which she laid carefully on the bed. She sat on the stool again, and drooped as if all the energy had gone out of her. 'It is all so much of a bother.'

'A bother!' Raising his dripping face from the basin, he spoke with laughing incredulity. 'A bother! My dear girl, my good name is involved. Can I appear to give credence to a vicious lie?'

'Of course,' said Letty, 'it would be much less of a bother simply to dwop the charge. But how can he? It would seem to give cwedence to a lie. Though I don't mean, Fwances, that poor Mr Smith Hall meant to lie. I think what I do mean, my dear, what I am twying to say, is that it will be difficult for you if we accompany Patwick to Sydney.'

The commandant had left an hour ago for Dunwich, and Letty and Frances were again in the drawing room, Frances sewing a pinafore for Lucy, and Letty a jacket for Robert. The french doors stood open to the verandah, as did the double doors to the dining room, where Martin was putting a new sash cord in a window. He was out of earshot, but his presence made the sisters speak in low voices. 'Then it is known when he is to go?' said Frances.

179

'No. He will be called by the court.'

'Is that the paper you await?'

'Oh no, they will send. That much is certain, though nothing else is.'

Frances gave her sister time to continue, but Letty only gave a brief laugh, then a long sigh. 'Why should it be difficult for me?' Frances asked.

'Well, if you mean to visit the Hall girls . . .'

'I don't. They show delicacy in not replying to my letter. I should be an embarrassment to them.'

'They did not find you so before, knowing what they knew.'

'They liked me. And nor would their sense of justice allow them to discriminate against me for something they believed my brother-in-law to have done. But now we are estranged by my letter and by both our circumstances. When I go to Sydney I shall be one of a party. Loyalty to their father will make them see it as the enemy party, and they must discriminate against me as a member of it.'

'Are you—' Letty flicked a glance at her sister from under her black lashes—'against them?'

'Yes. But oh Letty, how hateful such compulsions are. And how unnatural.'

Letty's sympathetic murmur was mechanical. 'It is stwange,' she said, 'to hear you call those girls delicate, and just. And stwanger still that I quite believe you. Less than a year ago, Cass and I sat here and spoke of those girls. And we decided that they must be perfectly low and wicked. How long ago that seems!'

'Everything seems long ago,' said Frances. 'Ireland, even Sydney, seems many years ago. When I came here I believed I had formed opinions that would never change. Now I seem to be without firm opinions at all. What is the use of forming opinions when you know they will change?' She lowered her sewing to her lap and sent wondering glances through the doors to the river, through the window to the garden and the commandant's office, through the double doors to where dark little Martin stood on his ladder. 'And all *this* will seem long ago,' she said, 'if we go to India.'

'Don't speak of it,' said Letty quickly. 'I have made up my mind. The childwen would have to go to Patwick's mother and sisters. You know how I admire them. They are the best of women, but they are never gay. And there are so many of them, and they are all so tall, it is like being at Stonehenge. Well, I am an army wife, and if they must go they must, but pway don't speak of it yet. Let us speak of you instead. You need not go to India.'

'He has not proposed marriage, Letty.'

'Lord, that tone!'

'What tone?'

'So distant!'

'I am sorry.'

'And so stubborn. He would not have sent me such a formal letter unless he wishes—'

'I don't know what he wishes.'

'I do. It is you who is the myst'wy. Tell me what you wish.'

'I don't know. I don't know.'

At the wail in her voice, the badgered note, Letty raised her brows, shrugged, and said no more. Accepting temporary alienation, both worked in silence until the door burst open and Robert ran into the room, followed closely by Lucy, and then by Elizabeth, shuffling and scolding and trying to hurry. The children had been sent for to try on their garments, but because they were seldom allowed in the drawing room except to be presented to visitors, it always seemed to them a great empty place to explore. Lucy ran straight to open the door of a cabinet, and Robert, after a few runs about the room in appreciation of its space, saw Martin, and ran into the dining room crying his name. Martin sent a pleading glance over his shoulder towards Letty and Frances; and Elizabeth, muttering that Master Robert must come along, waddled in after him. Lucy, knowing she would soon be stopped, very quickly took a tea chest from the cabinet and tried to raise the lid, but when she found it locked, and saw that her aunt was approaching, she seized a teacup instead and ran to the window to hold it to the light. Robert, led back to the drawing room by Elizabeth, broke away and ran to

182

unhook the curtain cord and let the curtain drop over the window. Frances hooked it up again, took the cup from Lucy and gave it to Elizabeth, and managed to grasp Robert and Lucy each by a hand. The children suddenly became tractable, and stood obediently, though with wandering eyes, while their garments were fitted on them.

Then: 'Martin!' suddenly cried Robert again.

Martin was coming through the double doors. 'Excuse me, madam.'

'Yes, Martin?'

'Martin!' shouted Robert.

'I done that one, madam. Which are the others?'

'Martin!'

Robert broke away and flung himself at Martin, gripping him about the waist. 'Mar-tin, Mar-tin,' chanted Lucy, trying to follow her brother.

Letty lifted Lucy on to her knee. 'Come here, Wobert,' she called pleasantly, without looking at him.

Grumbling that Master Robert got too excited, Elizabeth went towards them. Martin dissociated himself from Robert's action by standing still, holding his arms stiffly along his sides, and letting himself be rocked by the violence of the child's embrace. But his live dark begging eyes had fixed themselves on Frances's face, and nor could Frances take her gaze from the young man and the child. For she found it a cruel conjunction: the child was so beautiful, tall for his age, his skin so fresh, his red hair so soft and bright, and his strength the easy strength of good health, while the young man was so parched and pinched, his skin already beginning to wrinkle, and his strength a matter of strain and knotted muscle. She found both horror and fascination in the fact that each seemed to distort the scale of the other, so that the child looked too big and lusty for a child, and the young man too small and pinched for a man.

Lucy, as intent on the pair as her aunt, was still struggling to free herself from her mother's grasp. Letty held her tight, played with her hair, and called calmly to Robert to come with Elizabeth. But Robert was resisting Elizabeth's efforts to part him from his wooden staring playmate. 'We will run away,' he cried. 'Quick, Martin! To the bush!'

He jerked at Martin's arm and made for the door. Frances met Letty's eyes and reluctantly got to her feet to help Elizabeth. Martin pulled backwards in an uncertain manner, but when Robert tugged suddenly at his arm, he lurched forward and fell to his knees. Robert, delighted, dropped beside him, pretending he had also fallen, and rolled about the floor laughing.

'Wobert! At once!'

Robert jumped up. Dodging past Elizabeth and Frances, he ran to his mother, vaulted on to the blue sofa by her side, and bent to rest his forehead on Lucy's knee. He yawned. Martin got to his feet. 'Excuse me, madam.' His voice was constricted with rage. 'Which are the other winders?'

'There are quite a number, Martin.' Letty pointed to the window overlooking the garden. 'You may do this one now.'

When Martin went to get the ladder, Letty bent and said in Robert's ear, 'You are a bad, disobedient boy.' She set Lucy on to the floor, rose from the sofa, and took her children each by a hand. 'Stay until I come back, Elizabeth.' She would not punish them before a prisoner. As she led them from the room, Lucy began to cry.

Elizabeth sat in a chair by the door. 'Ah miss, these feet.' Martin came back with the step ladder. 'I dropped down on purpose,' he said to Frances. 'He never pulled me down, miss.'

Frances was sewing again. 'No,' she said.

'I was scared of pulling *him* down.'

Frances, her head bowed low over her sewing, did not reply.

'So I never used all my strength. Of course not!'

Her reply was almost inaudible. 'Of course not.'

'Martin!' called Elizabeth warningly from the door.

He turned aggressively. 'What's up?'

'Get on with it, lad.'

He said disgustedly, 'Arrr—' and mounted the

ladder. A sudden howl from the nursery, followed by Lucy's thin wail, made Elizabeth absently click her tongue against the roof of her mouth. But Frances paid no attention. She was looking only at her sewing, but also in her field of vision were Martin's big boots on the third step of the ladder. They had scuffled and bumped on the floor when he had fallen to his knees, and there he had knelt, in profile to her, perfectly still for three or four seconds, in a silent anger that had attained dignity. Drawing her thread through her white cloth, while his boots obtruded on her consciousness, she tried to think of something to say to him. To say something was a longing, a true compulsion, but it must express only a plain human sympathy, for to express pity would be to condescend. And perhaps even her sympathy would be better expressed obliquely, by tone rather than words. She would start by saying his name. She would say, 'Martin . . .'

'Yes, miss.'

She raised her head. He was standing on the ladder, looking down at her with expectation, in one hand a frayed and dirty sash cord, in the other a knife. She gave a slight bewildered shake of her head. 'You whispered my name,' he said.

They stared at each other in silence until Frances heard Elizabeth rise from her chair. She gave a more positive head-shake, then, and shaped the word 'no' with her lips.

'By Jesus you did. I heard it. No mistake.' There was no begging in his eyes now, only triumph and belligerence. Elizabeth was shuffling across the room.

'Now now now, lad. Now now now.'

Letty came in. 'What is it, Elizabeth?' But the question was mechanical; she seemed preoccupied. She did not wait for a reply, but sat down and picked up her sewing. 'The *Wegent Bird* will be at Dunwich by now. Elizabeth, the childwen are waiting to be washed.' And to Martin she said, as she began to sew again, 'Thank you, Martin, for paying no heed to my disobedient boy.'

'I never speak to them no more, madam. I know my place. I am not one of your mad devils. Of course not! At least,' he added in a heavier tone, 'I know what is thought to be my place, but which perhaps is not.'

And now, while he put the sash cord in the window, he composed aloud a tale of his origins and life. In reality he was one of a family of thieves, whose father and grandmother were also in the colony, and who came to the settlement so young that Logan had separated him as much as possible from the older men and had put him to school with Amelia. He must have known that these facts were known, or at least available, to his audience, yet there he was, telling this tale of his gentle birth and happy sheltered childhood. Amelia's tracts had left their mark. He told of bad companions who had led him into wicked courses, and hinted at rightful parents renounced because he could not bear them to know of his shame. 'Better they think me dead, see?' He spoke in a manner both headlong and vacillating, bursts of words being followed by a pause, or by a long-drawn 'ah' for fresh invention. Letty's occasional murmur could have passed for either sympathy or interest, and once she raised her head and gave Martin an amiable but rather absent glance; but Frances was quite silent, and did not raise her head at all, for if she did, she believed her feelings would flare out of her face: the shame she felt for having whispered his name, the embarrassment for his present performance, the pity for his person, and the resentment that it should be she, and only she, whom he had singled out to catch, impale, and hurt by his misery. And all the time, both sisters sewed steadily, drawing their work nearer to their eyes as the light began to fade, for both knew that however tiresome, or painful, Martin's tale might be, it could last only until the evening bell.

CHAPTER EIGHT

'All is well with Cassandra?'

'She is well, but her Edward has had the fever. And she is twoubled about the slaves being set fwee.'

'It will never happen.'

'She asks what the poor planters would do for workmen.'

'What indeed?'

'Fwances says they could pay their blacks.'

'Your sister's notions!' As dismissive as his words was the commandant's return to his own mail; he broke a seal. 'They would be bankrupt in a month.'

'That is what Cass says.'

He had begun to read again and did not reply. When reading he resisted voices from outside. He had started from Dunwich at first light and on his return to the settlement had come straight to the drawing room, knowing he would find her resting on the blue sofa. Unsorted mail was piled on a table by his side, and the mail he had already disposed of lay on the floor at his feet. The urgent letters he had read last night at Dunwich.

'But so many people nowadays,' said Letty, 'would disagwee with Cass.'

He gave an interrogative murmur but went on reading. She put Cassandra's letter in the drawer of her embroidery table. He came suddenly to life, dropping the letter he had been reading and reaching for another. 'That was from the Agricultural Company,' he said.

'A wefusal?'

'Yes. Clunie was right. The appointment is made.'

'It is of no consequence now.'

'No.'

He was already reading the next letter. He sat in the low chair in a relaxed but imposing posture. One leg was bent, the other fully extended; the back of his left hand rested on a hip and in his right he held the letter, shifting it now and again (Letty observed) to adjust the focus to his impaired eyesight. In Sydney last year he had been fitted with small round spectacles, but after a week had pronounced them useless and refused to wear them. Letty lay back on the sofa and shut her eyes. A breeze off the river entered the open doors, stirring the muslin curtains and carrying into the far distance the slow clanging and ringing from the lumber yard.

'They say the hill station above Madwas is perfectly charming,' she remarked. 'The mansions they have built there! And I shall make the acquaintance of Lady Wumbold.'

'Mrs Harbin, ma'am.'

Letty was immediately awake and upright. Louisa put her bonnet into Madge's hands and advanced. 'So it is Madras?' She did not wait for a reply, but paused in front of the commandant, who had risen, and extended a demanding hand.

He looked through the letters on the table, found two, and gave them to her. She examined them, pulled a face, and put them into her reticule. 'So it is Madras,' she repeated on a more settled note. She exchanged kisses with Letty. 'Lieutenant Edwards told me. You know Lady Rumbold is his third cousin? But you need no recommendation from him. You carry your own. They say the hill station is charming. When do you leave?'

It was Logan who replied. 'In three weeks.'

'What? Not from Sydney?'

'No. From here. The regiment begins to leave Sydney in March next year.' He was gathering the mail as he spoke and putting it back in its bag. 'I had better take these to the office.'

'Does the cutter sail for Dunwich early tomorrow?' asked Louisa.

'At first light.'

'Then our letters must be at the office tonight.'

'As usual, ma'am. Unless you want to run to the quay in the half light.'

Louisa watched him leave the room. 'Those uniforms,' she said. 'As summer draws near I could pity even my Victor.' She glanced at the open door. 'Though last night in the female factory he took it all off.'

Letty also looked at the door. 'They will alweady know that.'

'But not that I know it.'

'Twue.'

'They got in over the wall, I expect.'

'They?'

'Victor and Lancelot and Henry Cowper. Or perhaps through bricks loosened and replaced. That part of the story they left out.'

'*They?*'

'Victor and Lancelot told me. They are both so pink, I told them they must have looked like pigs on their hind legs. I told them they are beginning to look like pigs even with their clothes on.'

'How could they!'

'I asked them the same question, in the same tone. And they asked me to tell them what else they were to do.'

'Louisa, that is a vewy stwange question.'

'Very. I had never considered the matter in that light. Perhaps I am becoming a bit of a pig myself.

I expect Henry looked like a pig, too. But Henry's piggishness is well established, one thinks nothing of it. But you are not resting. Rest!' cried Louisa imperiously. 'Or James Murray will be cross with me.'

Letty lay on the sofa again, and Louisa took the chair vacated by the commandant. 'They would not have dared,' she said, 'if Captain Logan had not been at Dunwich. I should have rather liked them to encounter him on one of his nocturnal sorties with Collison or Gilligan. Or Bishop, before he drowned.'

Tears sprang to Letty's eyes. 'Lord, Louisa, I am glad he will never do that again. I saw him once through the window, with Bishop. There was a huge moon, like the one last night. And I thought—I can speak of it now it is over—I thought they were like two hunting dogs.'

Louisa, of course, knew that Letty did not think her husband entirely noble, but this was the first denial of his nobility she had ever heard her make. From shining knight to hunting dog was a big drop, but in the face of Letty's tears Louisa hid her startlement. 'It is not his fault,' she said, 'if the regulations insist on these surprise visits to the prisoners.' She would have liked to add that the regulations could be taken much too seriously, but Letty was still crying.

'It demeaned him, Louisa.'

'There,' said Louisa, 'don't cry. As you say, it is all over now. You are going, and so is Frances. And so, later, is Lieutenant Edwards, who is so clear and sunny, like that sky out there, only possibly less hot. Yes, Letty, you may laugh at me, but to be truthful, I am distressed. At these outposts it is a great alleviation to have one or two persons of one's own sex to whom one can speak one's mind. I shall be left with only Amelia. Amelia brings out all my malice. It is one thing to be a pig, but I hardly care to be a malicious pig.'

'Mrs Clunie will soon be here.'

'Yes, she sounds a woman of sense. And there are still my beetles and butterflies. Lancelot begs me to discard my hairpiece. What do you say?'

'Lancelot has taste, Louisa. What does Victor say?'

'That Lancelot has taste.'

Letty looked away. 'Yet never exercises it on poor Amelia.'

'He says Amelia is perfect. Absolutely perfect.'

This startled Letty into meeting Louisa's eyes for a few seconds of that excessive solemnity that serves the purpose of laughter. Letty's gaze moved away to the door. 'She will enter in a moment.'

'Of course, to speak of your posting. "Army life!" she will say. "One must not complain." She sometimes shows sense.'

'I shall begin to complain when the childwen go to Scotland. Today I can only feel glad that all our waiting is over.'

'I told you the covering letter would come.'

'Oh, it has not.'

'You said, *all* your waiting.'

'Lord, Louisa, what does that letter matter now?'

'I did not say it mattered at any time.'

'No. I did. Darling Louisa, don't let us weverse our opinions now. Captain Clunie's appointment explains itself, you see, by the fact of the wegiment going to India.'

Louisa got up, went to the mirror, put one hand over her hairpiece, and looked at herself through narrowed eyes. She did not ask if Governor Darling had known for certain, when he sent Captain Clunie, that the regiment was going to India. 'I have worn a hairpiece for five years,' she said. 'You leave here in three weeks, I take it, so that Captain Logan may press his charge against Mr Smith Hall.'

'Yes. He says it will not occupy more than a few days.' She yawned. 'So little sleep last night, Louisa.'

'Your mind was on the mailbag.'

'Yes. Oh, yes!'

'Will Frances go with you to India?'

'That's the gweat question. There has been no time to speak of it since the mail came. She has gone to weply to her letters. One from our little sisters, Louisa, and three from Mr Edmund Joyce.'

'Three!'

'Three.'

Louisa came back to her chair. 'Then Frances is not for India.'

'I don't know. She is evasive about him.'

'So she is with me. I believe she dreads a decision. I hope she is not like that donkey one hears about—who starved because he couldn't choose between straw and turnips.'

'She opened the letter from our sisters first.'

'Oh?' said Louisa, with contralto significance.

'So . . .' said Letty, shrugging.

'Still,' said Louisa, 'it need not signify. She has not heard from them since leaving home, whereas Mr Joyce has been most regular. Let me see, if the regiment doesn't move out until next March, you will have at least five months in Sydney. More than time enough for them to marry.'

'More than time enough for him to change his mind.'

'And for her, and you, to make him change it back again.'

'We are being bwutally fwank today.'

'Well,' said Louisa, 'it is quicker.'

'To be sure, I should pwefer the childwen to be with Fwances and her husband than in Scotland.'

'Oh now,' said Louisa, laughing, 'perhaps we are being too quick.'

'Louisa, I can't take them to Madwas.'

'Not even to the hill station?'

'Oh, Louisa, let us continue to be bwutally fwank. I shan't be at the hill station except in the hottest months. I shall be on the plains with Patwick. We have not enough money to keep two establishments. Don't evade my eyes, Louisa. It is not like you. It is my pwivilege to be fwank, since it is I who am going there, and who do not want my childwen to go there. And they can't go to Cass. Even Madwas is not as unhealthy as the Indies.'

'Mrs Bulwer, ma'am.'

Amelia, who since the warm weather had reduced her mourning to grey muslin, hurried forward with a gentle purring sound instead of her former important susurration. 'So it is Madras! I heard what you said as I came in. And you are right! Madras is *not* as unhealthy as the Indies. And the hill station! Ootacamund. Sir William Rumbold has built a great house there, and his wife is a daughter of Lord Rancliffe's, and is cousin to our own Lieutenant Edwards. And you will be nearer home, and will have the joy besides of knowing yourself in a country where the missions have gained some ground among the blacks. Yes, well, thank you, thank you, I will sit. Well, what news! And Lieutenant Edwards to go, though not yet. And Louisa and I left to console each other. And no horses! Did you know that, Louisa? Letty? *No horses!* Beasts, however. *Some* beasts, though not enough. And you go in three weeks, Letty, so that Captain Logan may appear at the trial of

Mr Smith Hall. Well, to be sure, it will be unpleasant, but he will emerge unscathed, I assure you. Oh, when you look at me with those big eyes, Letty, I realise I make it sound as if it were to be *his* trial, which you know I do *not* mean. Am I interrupting your rest? Pray, do rest. You look as tired today as my poor Lancelot, who can never sleep when there is a full moon. I am one of the lucky ones, I sleep through everything. Is Frances to go with you to India?'

'Why should she not?' asked Letty.

'I thought she may stop in Sydney.'

'Why should she do that, Amelia?' asked Louisa.

Amelia opened her fan. 'Where *is* Frances?'

'Replying to her mail.'

'Oh.' Amelia largely fanned herself. 'I see. She has run to reply at once to his letter. I see. Well, I must go and reply to mine. You have not forgotten my tea tomorrow? I see Louisa has not. And from you, Letty, I shan't accept a refusal. How many times have you left this house these last six months? Once? Twice? It is *not* healthy. Louisa, persuade her.'

'I agree with Amelia, Letty. Such a rare event deserves another. Do come.'

Of the smaller of the two front rooms of his weather-board cottage Clunie had made an office. The window was only a few yards from the road running along the river bank, and on hearing footsteps he raised his

head and saw through the muslin curtain the commandant and Private Collison. When he saw Collison halt,
and the commandant turn towards the open front door
of the cottage, he quickly folded the sheet of paper he
had covered with figures, put it in a pigeon hole, and
rose to open the office door to the commandant. He
had not seen him since his return from discharging the
Governor Phillip, but Lieutenant Edwards, who had
been sent to give him an account of the cargo, had also
told him that the fifty-seventh was under orders for
Madras.

On opening the door he saw Logan standing with
his hand raised to knock; and the two men simultaneously said, 'Well!' in mutual relief from the suspense
they had shared. Logan handed Clunie two letters
and without waiting for an invitation took the second
chair. Clunie glanced at the letters—from his wife and
his brother—and then took his place at the desk again
and turned his chair to the commandant, whom he
observed now to be showing that gratification, almost
a radiance, that marked his good moods.

It was the custom for officers and their families to
collect their mail from Whyte the clerk, but each time a
mail had arrived, Logan had brought Clunie his letters,
and each time had immediately sat down, and each
time but this had been angry and despondent. It had
been Clunie's opinion that the time must come when
the commandant would vent one of his black moods on

the man whom he must surely suspect, at these times, however obscurely, of being his supplanter. He had devised against this occurrence all sorts of guards and wiles, but had needed none of them. Towards himself the commandant had been steadfastly fair and trusting ever since he had taken the decision, on that first day, to like him. Clunie had at first found this restraint remarkable in such a man, towards such a provocation as himself, but later he came to understand that Logan's friendship and loyalty, once given, however arbitrarily, were practically unshakeable. Clunie could not decide whether this was owing to some sacred and mythic view of friendship and loyalty, or to the commandant's desperate need for both, but whatever the reason, he felt it to be excessive and slightly comical. He also felt it an embarrassment, for he could not return without reserve even the friendship, let alone the queer unreasonable antiquated loyalty. All he could offer were amiability and a willingness to oblige, and to his surprise, Logan seemed to find these quite enough. It was as if, having taken his decision on their friendship, he had also decided never to doubt the quality of what was returned to him.

'Well, sir,' said Clunie now, 'India. When do you leave?'

'In three weeks. I've no instructions yet about Edwards and the men.'

'You go early because of Smith—'

'Smith Hall, Smith Hall. Yes.'

'No need to ask about that covering letter. Since it's superfluous, for you at least, no doubt it's come.'

'It has not. But don't be disturbed,' said Logan, as Clunie abruptly raised his brows. 'I know it's not superfluous for you. But are you not in a position, now, to write and ask for full instructions?'

'I am,' said Clunie, 'and I shall. The lack of the letter is no more curious, after all, than the lack of horses.'

It was an argument he had often used to soothe the commandant during the last six weeks, and with so little success that he was privately amused to see it so readily accepted now. 'The governor is ill-served by his commissariat,' said Logan. 'I am mainly sorry because it will leave you with only Murray's nag on the settlement.'

'By the time you leave, horses will have come.'

'I meant when I go on my inland journey. For of course I must ride Fatima.'

'Of course. Well, my dear sir, we must manage. When do you start?'

'The day after tomorrow. I take Collison and five good bushmen.'

'Cowper says the best bushman on the settlement is Lewis Lazarus.'

'You're not suggesting I take him. A hatred like his would put my life in jeopardy.'

'Do none of the five you are taking hate you?'

'I neither know nor care. I know only that all come to the end of their sentences in a matter of months, and unless goaded by someone as mad as Lazarus, they will do nothing to risk my giving them an extension.'

'I see that,' said Clunie with reserve.

'You believe Lazarus is wasted in the gangs. So do I. But the fellow has chosen. He wastes himself.'

'Yes.' Clunie picked up a paperweight, turned it in his hand. 'All the same, I am sorry to learn he is in the solitary cell, in irons.'

'How else can I have him punished? The day after his last two hundred he threatened an overseer. I can't have him flogged again,' said Logan in apology, 'so soon. And if he is not ironed he bangs the walls and shouts. Now he only shouts. Upon my word, he is lucky not to be gagged as well.'

The paperweight was of polished pink stone. Watching it turn, Clunie said nothing. Logan leaned forward in his chair and spoke softly. 'My dear Clunie, in three days Lazarus will be taken from his cell and put in one of the outlying gangs, still in irons. And while I am inland, and you are my deputy, I must ask that you leave him in irons. Do as you please when I leave the place, but while I am still effectively in the command—as I shall be accounted on an absence so short—my punishments must be maintained in their full severity. Not only because I believe in the efficacy

202

of severity, but because to abate them now would seem that I am trying to pander to my enemies.'

Clunie raised his eyebrows at the paperweight. 'Are you speaking of the Smith Hall matter?'

'They will be attentive to it. I am not afraid of the outcome, and don't wish it to appear that I am.'

'Edwards tells me Bulbridge and Fagan were taken at Port Macquarie.'

'They were. They broke into a house there. Stole food and clothing. The *Phillip* put into the Port on her way here and brought me the news. The *Isabella* was at the Port on her homeward journey. She takes Bulbridge and Fagan to Sydney for trial.'

'Their trial is likely to coincide with Smith Hall's.'

'What of it?'

'Are they liars?'

'They are all liars. And the persons who give them credit are fools. An honest man cannot consider the slander of liars and the judgement of fools.'

'Many honest men do.'

'Then they cease to be honest men.'

'Perhaps they learn to temper their honesty with discretion.'

'And thus risk losing it.'

Clunie, with a sigh, put down the paperweight and leaned back in his chair. 'When do you relinquish the command?'

'I am requesting that I keep it until I leave Sydney

for India. I hope I may regard my stay in Sydney as leave, and draw a commandant's pay till the end.'

'That's perfectly fair and just.'

'Then what is troubling you, man?'

Clunie was on the verge of warning him that a man remaining in official command remains in danger of being removed from that command, and that if Logan wanted to make sure of putting himself out of reach of his enemies, he would do better to relinquish the command on leaving the settlement. But by giving such a warning, Clunie would sound over-eager for the commandant's place and pay. It was only a few months ago, in July, that the commandant's salary had been increased from one hundred and eighty pounds a year to three hundred, and backdated only to April instead of to January, as he had requested. If the talk of his debts were true, it would be important to him to continue to draw this increased pay for as long as he could; he would not lightly give it up. And besides, even if Clunie were to risk appearing avaricious, and give the warning, Logan would take no notice. Why should he wish to put himself out of reach of his enemies? He believed he was already out of their reach.

But although Clunie refrained from giving the warning, he allowed its tone to linger in his voice. 'There will be about five months, then, between Smith Hall's trial and your departure?'

'There will. Time to settle my affairs in the colony

thrice over. But don't think you will be required to act for all that time only as my deputy. No. That applies during my journey inland. But the moment I leave for Sydney you become my relief, and will have a free hand.'

'Thank you.'

'And yet, you doubt it? You sound as if you doubt it.'

'No, sir,' said Clunie with resignation. 'You're mistaken. I don't doubt it.'

He went with Logan to the door. The *Regent Bird* had just arrived, and they stood at the edge of the road and watched the prisoners from the *Governor Phillip* disembarking at the stone wharf. 'A fair load,' said Logan. 'Two mechanics—a carpenter and a shingler. The shingler is sentenced to be worked in irons, but we'll knock them off and put him on the roofs. That tall fellow is one of the colonial born whites.' He laughed. 'A beggarly nativity!'

'Who is Boylan?' asked Clunie suddenly.

'A dead man. A runaway. His body came down the river and was lodged by the tide just down there. I know what makes you ask. You have been hearing he is in the bush. So have I. So has Cowper. Lazarus said he saw him last time he was out.'

'My servant says he was seen a week ago.'

'Who told your servant?'

'One of the other prisoners.'

'Who had it from yet another prisoner.'

'No. Who had it from a native black.'

'Who *claims* he had it from a native black. Or perhaps from Boylan's ghost itself. Well, if I meet that ghost in the bush, I'll hobble it with a cobweb and bring it in. But I am likelier to bring in a real animal. The men will search for the horse lost in May.'

'Could he survive so long in the bush?'

'If he has escaped the spears of the blacks. The season has been good. He would not have lasted a week in 'twenty-eight. I go to Cowper now. I am to have a tooth drawn, else it will plague me on my journey.'

But he had hardly joined Collison before he left him again and came back to Clunie. 'I'm damned relieved, you know, to be off and away. Oh, I've been fretting, man. The place is small, small. And I've been in it too long.'

Clunie thought it just as well that someone was happy to go to Madras; he certainly would not have been. 'Madras has many advantages,' he said.

He watched Logan and Collison walk away. There was no doubting the commandant's relief. Even his body was rejoicing, his limbs released from their usual curbed severity. Clunie went back to his office, took the folded paper from its pigeon hole, and opened it out on the desk. It was an estimation of the money he hoped to save while in the command. At three hundred a year, added to his army pay and his wife's small income, he believed he could save a thousand in three years. He had written to his wife suggesting that if he should get the command, they should use the furniture made in the lumber yard and supplied free, rather than transport their own from home and buy more in Sydney. He had added that he certainly did not intend to buy his own horse, but would await a mount supplied by the government.

He folded the paper again and opened his wife's letter. She wrote that by the time he had this she hoped to have sailed from Portsmouth in the *Hooghly*. She mentioned that she had had a visit from his brother Charles, but made no reply to his suggestion about the furniture. As she had neglected to cite the number on his last letter, he could not tell whether her omission about the furniture was deliberate, or whether she had not received his letter in time to comment on it. The shuttling of the mail over such distances, and at such risk, fostered bafflement and exasperation.

As he put down her letter and took up the one from his brother, a loud fast clanging and hammering started up in the lumber yard, sounding as close, through the thin walls, as if the irons of the newly arrived prisoners were being knocked off in the next room. Clunie thanked God that the Logans would be gone by the time his wife arrived, and that she would be accommodated in a good stout house, at a decent distance from the yard.

His brother wrote that he had recently made the acquaintance of a Mr Johnson, or Johnstone, who had been at Sydney, and who informed him that Moreton Bay, or, as he called it, Brisbane Town, was a truly infamous place, with a hill above the river on which a row of gibbets stood black and awful against the sky for all to gaze upon, and on which gibbets they hanged upwards of six wretches a day, every day but Sunday.

Clunie, knowing his brother's inclination to the new ideas, caught the serious criticism underlying the banter. He was so annoyed by such foolish and dangerous exaggeration that he would have liked to reply at once, but the continued noise from the lumber yard bore its message to him; his reply must wait till evening.

But as he pulled down his cuffs and called for his cap, he was composing his reply.

'My dear Charles, my wife writes that you have had the kindness to pay her a visit. I trust you also had the kindness, as well as the sense, not to transmit to her the pleasantries of your new acquaintance. Kindly tell your informant, Mr Johnson, or Johnstone, that there are no gibbets at Moreton Bay, otherwise known as Brisbane Town. No capital offences are tried here, for which I thank God, all such miscreants being sent to Sydney for trial, where they are hanged, if that be the sentence—'

His servant brought him his cap. He put it on and went through the narrow little hall to the front door.

'—*in as seemly a manner as at home. On the hill stands only a windmill, used as a treadmill until a fault in its construction can be put right, and a small signalling station*—'

Taking the few steps to the lumber yard, he looked sideways, longingly, at the river.

'—*while in the bay fish abound, and up the river is the best fowling in the world. Wild duck, widgeons, swamp pheasants, a kind of teal . . .*'

'One for you,' said James Murray, holding his own letters away to one side, as if Henry might snatch them.

Henry squinted at his letter, groaned, and slid it under the reports on his desk. 'From the hound of heaven. I've lost the Fay's forceps. Have you seen the Fay's forceps?'

'No.'

Drawing his four unopened letters close again, Murray looked at them like a child at a sweet he is saving till last. Henry had resumed his search among the paraphernalia on the long trestle table. Piled higgledy-piggledy here were splints and weights and pulleys, instruments in and out of their cases, and boxes of bandages and ligature silks. Searching, Henry gave such a prolonged and anguished groan that Murray was distracted from his letters.

'Cowper, were you drinking last night?'

'Yes. And shall be tonight.'

'Cowper, for your own sake—'

'Murray, take no notice. Playacting helps make it tolerable. A drinking man would understand. Forceps, damn you, where are you?'

'Then you are not as bad as you appear?'

'How do I know how I appear? Have I your eyes? Let me look at your eyes?'

Confronting the tall young man, Henry looked up into his dark lustrous anxious eyes. He exaggeratedly flinched. 'I am worse than I look! Come and help me find the forceps. I am expecting the noble warrior. He wants a tooth pulled.'

Murray rather absently helped Henry to look for the forceps. 'Forceps! Forceps!' cried Henry cajolingly. 'Ah,' he said, 'I knew you were there, forceps.' He held them up. 'Yes,' he said to Murray, 'the Paladin has a dolorus dentus.'

Murray was laughing. 'Now if you mean to mock me again—! I have never said or written "dolorus dentus" in my life.'

'But you might have. You have corrupted my Latin, Murray—'

'I—'

'—which was formerly exact.' He squinted at the forceps. 'Dusty.'

Murray sometimes had a shade of a spinsterish gossipy tone. 'You know they are going to Madras?'

Henry blew dust off the forceps. 'Yes.'

'That place! Yet they seem as gay as birds.'

'If you're bound for Madras, you don't dare to be anything else. You will miss your amorata.'

'Cowper, you go too far!'

'I always go too far,' said Henry with modesty. He drew out his handkerchief and wiped the forceps. 'If the fever or a tiger doesn't take Miss Frances, a wicked India officer will. You had better propose.'

'Cowper, I have had the greatest kindness from all the family—'

'So have I, indeed, even from the Paladin, in his better days.'

'—but I don't distinguish among them. The sincere friendship I feel for Miss O'Beirne—'

'Murray, if you had my dolorus cerebrus—'

'Dolorus cerebrus!' cried Murray on a shout of laughter.

'—you would spare me the speeches. By the look of your boots you have just come in from the Eagle Farm. I hope you have seen to your nag.'

'Of course I—'

'Because no horses came in the *Phillip*. Take care of that nag, Murray. Lose him, and you will ride out to the Eagle Farm on a bullock cart.'

Murray, suddenly serious, clutched his letters to his

211

breast with both hands. 'I should be forced to refuse,' he said quietly.

'Ha!' exclaimed Henry, with deep enjoyment.

'I should certainly refuse, or be the laughing stock of the place.'

'Ho-ho! Oh, Murray, don't make me laugh. Oh, how it hurts!'

'But the horse happens to be quite strong,' said Murray with a touch of peevishness. 'And there will be another ship shortly. More horses must come.'

'Well, they will come one day,' said Henry in kinder tones. 'Do you know that Bulbridge and Fagan are taken?'

'No. Poor wretches.'

'You may well say so. They broke into a house at Port Macquarie. They go to Sydney for trial.'

Murray reflected for a moment. 'Smith Hall's trial is likely to take place about the same time.'

'Yes. And will no doubt gain added attention. Of a particular kind.'

Almost soundlessly, but with distinct lip movements, Murray asked, 'Could I be called? Is that possible?'

'Possible? My dear fellow, I should think it certain.'

'Cowper, I am deadly serious.'

'No, Murray, no. You won't be called. You haven't been here long enough. If anyone is called, it will be

Henry Cowper, privileged—' Henry bowed, reeled, and clutched the table for support—'in that as in all else.'

'What will you do if you are called?' asked Murray in the same almost soundless way.

'Do?' cried Henry, throwing his arms wide. 'Do?' Both heard the footsteps in the corridor. Henry turned to the door, arms spread, forceps clasped in one hand. 'How do you do, captain?'

'Murray,' said Logan, acknowledging Murray with the word and a nod. To Henry he said, 'You have been drinking, Cowper?'

'No, captain, upon my word. It is Murray's breath you smell. Look into those dissipated eyes! And he is not only a drunkard, sir, but a dangerous amorist as well. Last night he scaled the wall of the female factory.'

Murray was bowing. 'Yes, Murray,' said the commandant. 'You may go. I see you have your mail. Go along, man, and read it.' As soon as Murray went he turned to Cowper. 'Well, you are Clunie's problem now. Your clock has stopped.'

'The ticking was terrible.'

Logan opened the glass door of the clock and tapped the pendulum. 'I go inland the day after tomorrow. Are you fit to pull the tooth?'

'Of course I am fit. Perhaps Clunie will ask for my removal. Well, good, I will go to Batavia at last.'

The commandant set the clock at half past eleven,

waited for it to strike, then set it at twenty to twelve and shut the door. 'I can't answer for Clunie,' he said, 'but it may have come to that if I had stayed.'

'I have never been to Batavia,' said Henry, 'though in my seventeenth year I planned to go there with a scoundrel named Nobby Clark. We intended both to set up as surgeons and exchange our services for diamonds and gold plate.' He rang the bell for the attendant. 'Shall I tell you how we proposed to finance the venture? No. You would order me a retrospective two hundred.'

The commandant was removing his jacket. 'You have been here longer than any of us. I haven't forgotten your help to me when I arrived. I hope you are as helpful to Clunie while he is finding his feet.'

'If I am on mine. Knowles,' said Henry, to the attendant who came to the door, 'bring a ewer of water, a basin, a cup, and three towels.'

The man went. Henry waved a hand at the office chair. 'Well, commandant!'

Logan sat down. 'Clunie is pretty well disposed towards you. It is your lack of—'

'Head back, commandant! Mouth open! Now, which tooth?'

Logan indicated an upper molar. Henry inserted a tobacco stained finger into his mouth, tested the tooth for looseness, and felt the gums about its roots. 'Ah. Very good. We'll soon have her out.'

Logan wiped his mouth. 'Clunie is worried lest he does not have a free hand while I am in Sydney. Because, mind you, I will hold the command until I leave for India. It is a matter of form only, his hand will be free, but he points out to me, in a signifying way, that there will be a biggish space between Smith Hall's trial and my departure, and by that I infer that he is worried.'

'Thank you, Knowles,' said Henry. 'I shan't need you. You may go. What *I* infer by that,' he said, as he tied a towel round Logan's neck, 'is that he's worried for you. He thinks there will be revelations at the trial that will put you in danger of disgrace and removal. Retain the command, and you retain that danger. Relinquish it, and you are in danger only of military disgrace. Come now, head back! Mouth open!'

But Logan sat amazedly scowling. '*Military* disgrace!'

'How like you to fear the lesser danger. The command tries to shelter its officers.'

'Has Clunie said all this?'

'No. Nor needs to. He is a man of sense, and so am I, whatever you may think. And by our similarity I divine his opinion in the matter. And indeed your own blunders and quarrels may be accounted for by the same principle. Nobody thinks as you do any more. Or hardly anybody. Come, mouth open! Head back!'

Slowly the commandant opened his mouth, and

slowly let his head fall back, while his eyes and scowling brows retained their look of shocked and furious reflection. Henry inserted his forceps and tugged at the tooth, and the commandant helped him by setting his feet firmer on the floor, gripping hard on the arms of the chair, and tightening the muscles of his neck to make his head as stable as possible; but his eyes, though they rolled now in his head, never once altered their shocked expression. Henry panted and swore, and muttered that this was harder than he had supposed, but at last, with a relieved breath, he tugged the tooth slightly loose of its socket, and then jogged it, and twisted it, and at last pulled it free.

The commandant's mouth filled with blood. He clapped the towel to his face and leapt to his feet to stand over the basin and spit. Henry turned the forceps and examined the tooth held in its two halves. 'There's a piece of the root still in your gum. You'll find yourself spitting it out. It may be today. It may be in a week.' Aware that the commandant was lifting his head from the basin, he raised his eyes to meet those shocked and furious eyes above the bloody towel Logan held again to his mouth. 'My dear sir,' he said gently, 'you have realised at last that I have tried to tell you the truth. It's my own fault that you've realised it only now. I've always presented it in a bantering way. But would you even have stopped to listen otherwise? Well, in any case, here I am, in all seriousness, telling it at last. I wish you would realise that as well. I've told you it's part of your danger. Now, I will suggest this—go to Captain Clunie and ask him his true opinion of the risk you run at the Smith Hall trial. I think he will give it if asked direct. And I think he will say that Smith Hall's trial could turn out to be tantamount to an enquiry into your administration. And now, pray,' said Henry on a sharper note, watching the blood suffusing the towel and creeping over the fingers that held it, 'pray, spit out that blood and rinse your mouth. You will bloody your jacket.'

It seemed to Henry that the commandant bent over the basin again almost absent-mindedly, standing with his weight on one foot and a hand spread flat on the table beside the basin. The forceps in Henry's hand still held the broken tooth. He turned them again, and again looked at the tooth as he spoke.

'You will have an opportunity in Sydney to demonstrate the clemency of your command. Bulbridge and Fagan are bound to come to trial while you are there. Arrange to be called as a witness. Intercede for them. Confound your critics. Prove yourself capable of mercy.'

When, after a full minute, the commandant had neither turned his head nor replied, Henry put down the forceps and sat with his elbows on the desk and his chin in his hands. The commandant was still bent over the basin, but now stood with his feet exactly together, rinsing and spitting in a rhythm that alone indicated to Henry his restored composure. Indeed, as Henry watched, his chin sinking heavier on his hands and his eyes turning in their sockets with tiredness, those neat, quiet gestures of the commandant seemed to gather to themselves an inviolate complacency. It was no surprise at all when Logan rose at last to his height, put on his jacket, pulled down the waist in front, and declared that in no circumstance would he compromise himself by interceding for two iniquitous rogues who had been granted numerous chances of reform but had proved incorrigible. 'Let the court decide that they hang, or be sent to Norfolk Island.'

Only Henry's lips moved. 'There have been runaways enough in the dock in Sydney who have shouted aloud that they are glad to hang, or to go to Norfolk either, rather than be returned here.'

'Let them shout what they please.'

Henry had sunk so far over the desk that he appeared hunched. 'Do you want the tooth?'

Logan gave his brief laugh. 'No.'

'You're bleeding again. Take another towel.'

Henry's eyes filmed over like a lizard's. He shut them for a moment, and opened them again to see the commandant going towards the door, the second towel, already bloody, clamped by one hand to his mouth. 'Rinse it with salt water,' he called weakly after him. He shut his eyes again. 'Aqua saline,' he whispered to himself.

After several minutes he opened his eyes. 'I thought he had realised it at last,' he remarked, in the same weak voice in which he had just spoken to Logan.

Minutes passed; the big clock ticked; a frown gathered between Henry's brows. In his seventeenth year, to finance the journey to Batavia, he had stolen the hospital medicines and given them to Nobby to sell outside. 'It grows, Buck. The pile grows,' Nobby would whisper. But when the enquiry started, he came to Henry aghast, the rich voice hoarse. The pile had been stolen. Every penny. Every last brass razoo. He wept. 'Nobby is a broken man.' It was his habit to speak of himself in the third person. 'Nobby will drown himself.'

Henry said the money didn't matter, and begged Nobby not to drown himself. Nobby did not drown himself. Dr Redfern and Henry's father then called Henry into conclave in the most serious room in the Cowper house, his father's study. In this brown and shadowed room, this shiningly clean and stuffy room, they sat and waited for him. He did not look at their faces as they spoke, but at Dr Redfern's trousers, his father's gaiters, and at the neat and narrow shoes of both men. Nobby Clark, they were telling him, had spent the money long ago. There was proof in plenty, but to prosecute him would be to implicate Henry.

'I don't believe it!'

Henry can still hear the heroic fury of his own voice. 'I don't believe it!'

219

He did not listen to their proof, or thought he did not. He stood before them, proud and restive, with his head turned aside. And yet, when he ran to Nobby, he found he remembered it accurately enough.

'Ah, bucko, Nobby has enemies.' Nobby's eyes were wet. He shook his head. 'Harry, buck, Nobby has enemies.'

'You will confound them yet, Nobby.'

'That I will, bucko, in spite of their lies. Only—' Nobby held up a warning hand—'your father does not lie. No, Nobby does not say that. No, nor let any man say it. Not even his own son.'

'Then—'

'Buck—'

Henry remembers his face. Red, twisted slightly on the neck, the eyes bulging with sincerity, it advances towards his own across the inn table. 'Buck, that sainted man has been misled. He believes their lies about Nobby.'

'Well, Nobby, *I* don't!'

Knowles came in. 'Clear away, sir?'

'Yes, Knowles.'

Henry watched him clearing away. 'And yet,' he said aloud, 'the hammer had hit head on. The nail had gone home.'

'What's that, sir?'

'The armour once pierced, Knowles, is never whole again.'

'That's so, sir,' said Knowles lightly.

Henry let his forearms down on the desk, sank his head on them, and gave a groan so loud it startled Knowles; it was more like a roar.

'Get you something, sir?'

'No, Knowles. Nothing.'

The clock whirred in its preliminary to striking, and at the same time, the midday bell began to ring.

CHAPTER NINE

Between ships, Frances wrote serial letters, so that when a ship arrived, they needed only postscripts of direct reply, which could easily be written in time for the return mail. She had added the postscript on her letter to Ireland, but on her reply to the last of Edmund Joyce's three letters she had floundered. She was no longer the very dear girl of his first letter, or the dearest girl of his later ones; she was his beloved now, and his own beloved. The progression frightened her. And moreover, the text of his third letter made her serial letter obsolete.

'You write with naturalness on all matters but the feelings I have expressed for you. I trust it is modesty, but fear it is more. I took my good aunt into my confidence and she advises me to ask you direct if you find my ardency unwelcome. I grow daily in the estimation

of my aunt and uncle, who now speak of my taking the place of the son they lost. I do not deserve their regard, and perhaps do not deserve yours, but cannot think you less generous than they. My uncle tells me your brother's regiment is now certainly posted to India. Momentous move! You cannot fail to comment on it in your reply to this. Do you want to go to Madras? Whether or no, you must first come to Sydney. And you must know, my dearest one, that where it takes you after that is for you to decide. Only say in reply that you are glad we are to see each other so soon, and if you can manage no more, in your modesty or horrible propriety, I will make do with that for encouragement.'

She knew it was the chance towards which Letty had been shepherding her, and knew too that she might never get such a chance again. The blundering wonder and disbelief with which she had read his first letter had given way to the realisation that on that long voyage, she had somehow made herself indispensable to him, and that since then, she had been approved by his aunt and uncle. She was young, healthy, literate, of the established religion, much too poor to be forever journeying 'home', and, if more were needed, her cousin Clanricarde would tip the scales. She thought of the good stone house in the Hunter Valley, and of the stables and fine horses described in Edmund's second letter. She thought of Robert and Lucy with the severe Scottish aunts. And she read again the letter from Hermione and Lydia.

223

She could not define exactly why it disturbed her. One day she would understand that such exuberant intelligences, when lonely and undisciplined, are in danger of growing fantastic and rank. Now she could only say that Lydia and Hermione were becoming pert, and needed guidance. She had only to add a postscript to her letter to Edmund. *'My dear Edmund, of course I do not find your ardency unwelcome, and of course I am glad we are to see each other so soon.'* She did write it, then tore it off the end of the page, then tore up the letter as well.

She rose from her mother's desk and wandered in perplexity about the room. She stared at her face in the mirror, yet hardly saw it. She went to the window and saw Martin working in the garden below. Although she had made no noise, he immediately began to turn, and she quickly drew back, shamed not only by having whispered his name, but by a lingering trace of her mood—or hallucination—of the night just past.

She returned to her desk and began another letter to Edmund, but after a line or two lapsed into sketching her left hand. She put down her pen. All she wanted to do was to lay her head on her arms and sleep. She rose again and walked about the room, beating her hands softly together, almost breaking into a wail. When she paused at the window, Martin, as if she threw a long shadow, began to turn with a speed and readiness that hardly gave her time to draw back. It suggested a watchfulness for her, a deep consciousness of her, that not only angered and embarrassed her, but added to her present perplexity a vague guilt.

She had already wasted two sheets of paper. She took out her letter book. If she drafted the letter in pencil, erasures and alterations could be made. After searching for a few minutes for a beginning, she turned aside and looked through the window. From her seated position she could see treetops, and among them, hardly intruding on the sky, the octagonal roof of Hobson's cottage. Drifting, vague, she fell into one of her old fantasies. She would live there for ever with James Murray. With no fleshly feelings, they would live in childish isolation, learning from old books, growing fruit and flowers, taking green shaded walks, and never, never going beyond their garden. But she was no longer capable of losing herself in fantasy. Self-mockery invaded it almost as soon as it began. Wanting to laugh and to cry, she did finally laugh, and turned again to her letter book.

For twenty minutes she wrote, striving for natural-ness, often erasing a word to insert another less formal, and fighting all the time against an urgent languor of the mind, until, having covered a page, she paused to read it over. Whether it was 'natural' or not she could not tell; she saw only that it was false, false, and that the mental languor so hard to overcome was in reality a deep reluctance caused by self-disgust.

She seized her india rubber and erased it all, and when she slammed shut her book and got to her feet, her suppressed wail broke from her at last, soft and entirely bewildered. Distracted, quite forgetful of Martin, she went to the window and found herself looking straight into his uplifted face. He had been waiting for her.

Shock held her there, staring, so that he had time to grin, and to swagger with his shoulders while hitching up his trousers, a cockerel gesture repulsive to her by reason of its very pathos. She withdrew to one side of the window, buried her face in the curtains, and gave a nervous but angry laugh. She gathered the curtains in her hands and pressed them close to her face, as if she would stifle herself. James Murray had told her that on the way to and from the Eagle Farm he sometimes passed prisoners who would surreptitiously grin and salute him, or bow low to him, or otherwise mock his importance as he rode red-faced by. 'But do you not report them?' Frances had asked, herself inclined to smile. 'I can't be the cause of their punishment,' he had replied, and had added with bitterness, 'How well they know their mark!'

Standing with the curtains pressed to her face, she admitted that Martin could be forgiven for thinking her his mark if she went so often to the window, and to prevent herself from absently doing so again, she pulled the bedsteps across the floor, and, crouching so that she should not be seen, set them as an impediment beneath the window. Retreating in the same crouched position, she began to laugh again, but again her laughter was angry, for comical though she knew her crouching shuffle to be, she resented his forcing her to it, and asked herself by what fatality she had drawn upon herself his grotesque and dogged attentions, and why, when her sister, who couldn't pronounce her r's and had the face of a fairy, could command instant obedience and respect, her own larger handsomeness and regular utterance should lack all such authority. And with her sudden conviction that it would always be so, and that some flaw in her character condemned her to a life of powerlessness and mockery and usage by hateful or pitiful persons, her laugh became a cry, and she sank in a heap on the floor, in tears; but on realising that she must even cry quietly, in case he should hear her in the garden, her tears quickly changed to plain anger. If he had been in the room she felt she could have attacked him, but now she could only pound with her fists on the floor and whisper in vehement wonder:

'But I am a prisoner!'

She had been awake for much of the night. Prevented at first from sleeping by the knowledge that she must have whispered Martin's name aloud in the drawing room (for he could not have read her thoughts), she had got out of bed to write in the back of her diary, among axioms and other self advice,

'When in company, I must never never *let my thoughts drift.'* She had gone back to bed then, but the warmth was stifling, and in sudden impatience she had leapt from the bed to thrust aside the curtains and open the window as far as it would go.

The shadow of the flagstaff had dropped out of the moonlit night and laid a broken band across her breast and upper arms. Over in the botanical gardens two segments of the octagonal roof were a flat and brilliant silver, and the brightness of the moon on the intervening land seemed to draw it nearer her window, deepening the ruts in the road and silvering the ridges. She raised her eyes to the sky. A few weeks ago she had said to Louisa, 'I have never seen such a moon in my life before.' And the tone of Louisa's reply, so desirous, so dismissive, had lingered in her mind.

'Oh, the moon, the moon.'

Last night it had travelled in a turquoise aureole so wide and bright that no stars could shine in its proximity, though elsewhere they crowded in crazy multitudes. And in that aureole the moon itself seemed slightly crazy, seemed to roll too fast, to tip unsteadily. And yet, for all its turmoil and speed, the total effect was one of ineffable peace. It fascinated Frances deeply, all but hypnotised her. Deeply breathing, she drew in the smell of a white waxy flower, and of the turned earth and the outside privies, but when, in a spontaneous experiment in total acceptance, she raised both arms and breathed deeper still, the predominant smell was yet another, the warm heavy smell of river mud at low tide.

It could only have been an hallucination that that smell of mud, as if personified, had reached out to her body, extended by her raised arms, and stroked her. The servants at home had warned her to crush her carnal longings, which, they said, would lead her to hellfire, or to bearing a bastard, or both, and from the pulpit she had been given much the same advice. So when, at idle moments, she had been visited by mild voluptuousness, and had combated it with physical busyness, she had believed herself to be obeying these edicts. But in fact she had not known until last night what carnal longings were, nor had taken into account until then the possibility of their gratification outside marriage. Neither knowledge nor feeling had been fostered in her; she had lived among people who shunned erotic display, and what intimations might have reached her from books had been occluded by the web of romance. She had often read of longings for a lover, but 'longing' had been only a word until then, when, with her arms still raised above her head and her body extended, amazed, confused words formed in her mind.

'Why—why—anyone would do.'

These words, formed within sight of the trodden roads and the commandant's garden, chilled her into sobriety, for 'anyone' must include not only the commandant, whose image flashed first into her mind, but Gilligan, Martin, even the poor creatures in the iron gangs. And this image of the convicts, crowding into her mind, discredited the whole emotional mood, making it squalid and fearful.

Ashen mosquitoes had drifted in through the open window. She slapped the stings on her bare arms. She already felt that mood to have been bizarre—so uncharacteristic of her that she was quite sure that nothing of the kind would ever happen again. By the time she went back to bed, hallucination seemed its only explanation. The mosquitoes had kept her awake with their buzzing and stinging, and the moonlight on the white sheets becoming unbearable at last, she had risen, drawn the curtains close again, and then, though hot, restless, and half-dreaming, had slept until early morning.

Now she heard the midday bell, and a panic started in her mind for the letter not yet written, the decision not yet ratified. She raised herself to a kneeling position on the floor and dabbed at her eyes with her frilled sleeve. She knelt there as if in a trance, looking with half-shut eyes at the bed-steps beneath the window (but seeing in her mind's eye Martin standing below as if affixed there for ever) until suddenly, in three seconds, her determination became firm, and the right reply composed itself in her head. She jumped to her feet and went—strode, indeed, with her old graceless stride—back to her desk. She put the letter book aside and took a clean sheet of paper.

'My dearest friend . . .'

The words warmed her, as if they were true, and added to her determination. He belonged to a former and distant part of her life. She could neither see his face nor hear his voice. She was turning him to her own purposes, but for that, and for the bold deceit of the words she was writing, she would make amends by being the best of wives. If she could not love him, she would cherish and obey him. And as his wife, she would never again be anybody's victim. Authority would be hers at last, as it was Letty's (she now perceived) partly, at least, because her husband, even in his absence, left it wrapped about her like an invisible cloak.

'. . . and so, my dear one, rather than offend you again with my sad stiffness, I tore it into tiny pieces, and now have time only to write that your ardency could never, never be unwelcome to me, and as to our early meeting, I look forward to it with all my heart. Pray have the kindness to convey my respects to your uncle and aunt.

Signing herself *'your own Frances'*, she was suddenly overcome by a hard triumphant excited greed for the material things she had never permitted herself to covet, but which now lay in her expectations. She suppressed it out of shame as well as duty, but it left her feeling self-possessed and adult, as if in some way it were needed to sanction her decision. She turned the page to the blank side, wrote Edmund's name and

231

address in graceful copperplate in the centre (did he display her letters to the Annings?), then folded it inwards so that the four corners met and concealed the text. When Madge Noakes presently came in, her arms full of mosquito netting, she was looking for the little brass lamp she used to melt her sealing wax.

'Where is my wax lamp, Madge?'

'Took to be trimmed and cleaned, miss.'

'Pray fetch it.'

She already spoke, she fancied, with the voice of government: calm, benign, unflawed by the personal. But when Madge had been gone for a minute or so, and Martin came through the door, carrying a ladder, and his eyes springing, as always, so eagerly to hers, she did falter, hitched for a moment on that snag of pity and shame. But almost at once, she was able to marshall her new forces.

'What do you want, Martin?'

His look of startlement at her coolness confirmed her need of it. 'Putting in a new sash cord, miss.'

'Is it not your dinner hour?'

'Madam said—' he stopped and scowled, trying to assess the change in her.

'What did madam say, Martin?'

'She said, madam did—' he was slow, surly—'she said, do this now. Have dinner later. Miss,' he added.

Frances glanced at the pile of mosquito netting Madge Noakes had left on the bed. Letty, of course, had ordered the two jobs done simultaneously so that her sister should not be left alone with a male prisoner. 'Very well, Martin,' she said, pondering that while she was still with Letty, she must take care to acquire as much as possible of her unobtrusive ways of management. Edmund and she would have many assigned servants. She would certainly suggest that he pay them as free labourers, but if that were really as impracticable as people said, if it would really lead to bankruptcy, they would still treat them as well as possible: they would forbid the lash, tend them in illness and old age, and she would teach their children with her own.

But Martin had not begun to work. He was standing by his stepladder, and was staring at her. She picked up the letter from Ireland and began to read it again, but saw, at the edge of her vision, that he had put one hand on a hip. She felt his gaze on her neck and began to wish for Madge Noakes to come back.

'I don't eat dinner in barracks,' he said suddenly.

She made one of those murmuring noises, derived from Letty, but did not look up.

'You know I don't. You know I eat it here.'

'Of course, Martin,' she said with mechanical kindliness, intent on the letter she was not reading.

He dropped suddenly to a level of secrecy. 'You're for us, ain't you?'

It startled her into looking up, with all her former uncertainty, into his face. 'For you?' she weakly cried.

233

'Madge Noakes heard you on the *Regent Bird*. With Mrs Harbin. You was for us then. You said you was. Madge Noakes heard you.'

She looked at him blankly, hardly taking in what he said, but thinking of her lost power, for which she could have wept; while he, with a face twisted in bitterness, said snarlingly, 'Ah, but words is cheap. It takes more than words to be *for* a person, don't it?'

Her power had felt so assured; how could she have known it was so fragile. 'I hope, Martin,' she said hesitantly, 'I hope—'

Madge Noakes came in. Passing between them, her eyes moved in their sluggish way from one to the other.

'The lamp, miss.'

'Thank you, Madge.'

She was restored by the composure of her own voice, and by the woman's presence. 'Well, Martin,' she said, friendly yet remote, 'I hope I am for everyone.'

'Has he spoke out of turn, miss?'

'No, Madge. It was nothing at all.'

She held the sealing wax to the flame. 'Let the ladder stop here,' she heard Madge Noakes say. 'I will use it to set the nets on the posts.'

'Ah, you will! And what will I use for the winders?'

'The bed steps is sittin' there.'

'Not high enough.'

'It ain't them that is not high enough, Martin. It is you. You can stop here yourself, and pass me up the nets.'

Frances, her head tilted, dropped the seal on her letter to Hermione and Lydia. In her side vision she was aware of Madge climbing the ladder, and then of Martin, leaning backwards to toss up the soft white mass of netting. But as soon as Madge busied herself with it, he turned with deliberation and fixed his stare on Frances's profile. She was now heating the wax to seal Edmund's letter, and even when he took a step forward, and brought into her range of vision the detail of his face, his scowling brows and silently twisting mouth, she forced herself to remain immobile but for her hand, which continuously turned the wax in the flame. She guessed that either Madge Noakes's remark about his size, or her own retreat into self-possession, had enraged him, but she told herself that her only care must be that her hand should not tremble, and she was proud when it did not do so. When she dropped the seal on Edmund's letter she was pleased by its exact placing and even contours. Madge Noakes's sudden movement with the nets was a flash of soft white, like a great blurred wing. Frances snuffed the lamp and set down the wax. Smiling, she set a thumb gently on the warm seal.

'A hand here, Martin!' cried Madge in a stifled voice. Frances looked up, somehow avoiding the face that still sought to obtrude on her view, and saw that when Madge had thrown the net it had caught on one of the back bedposts instead of on both, and was trailing from there and had enveloped both Madge and the upper part of the ladder. But already, while still calling for help, she was hauling it up with both hands; and Frances, seeing first her boots appear, then the hem of her skirt, could not help laughing. 'Steady the ladder, Martin,' she said cheerfully. She got to her feet and picked up her two sealed letters. But Martin had not moved, and Madge, half-blinded by the nets, must be in danger, after all, of over-balancing. 'Martin,' said Frances sharply, 'steady that ladder.'

Instead he sprang at her. She had already turned to leave the room, so that it was a collision, breast to breast, his furious mouth jabbering hatred into hers and his thin arms clamping both hers to her sides. In her first shock she thought of the knife he used on the sash cords, and fearing it in her back, sucked inwards a breath of fear, a soft scream; and when, in the next moment, the fury in his face became a sort of blind besottedness, and his imprecations a burble of love, she only screamed louder, for the change was so swift that it outdistanced her understanding, and it still seemed to her that she was screaming in fear of his killing her. But when he let her go, and stood back in pale awe, she dropped her crumpled letters to the floor, and put both hands over her eyes, and continued to scream, and did not know why.

More than a decade later, in the physical happiness of a late but loving marriage, she would understand the kind of hysteria that had impelled her that day, and would begin to forgive herself at last; but at the time, the first emotions that emerged from her mindless screaming were anger, offendedness, and fear. And the fear was no longer of murder, but of that lifetime of feebleness and usage she had envisioned so clearly when, after having set the bed-steps under the window, she had lain weeping on the floor. By that time Letty had come into the room. She was also carrying a letter. Showing no surprise, she went calmly and quickly to Frances's side. 'Be silent,' she whispered.

Frances stopped screaming. She drew in great sobbing breaths and looked about her as if just awakened from sleep. Elizabeth Robertson was in the doorway, and Robert and Lucy, at her skirts, were looking from face to face with open curiosity and secret excitement. Martin was standing two yards away from Frances, his feet exactly together, immobile and agog. Madge Noakes had drawn up all the netting and was holding it back from her forehead. With its white coif around her swarthy fissured face she looked like a disreputable abbess.

'Well . . .' said Letty mildly, looking from Frances to Madge to Martin. 'Gwacious,' she said, seeing the children, 'you two must go.'

Elizabeth shooed them away. 'Back to the nursery!'

237

'*Take* them back, Elizabeth.'

Elizabeth went. 'Now, what is this?' asked Letty.

'He touched me,' gasped Frances.

Letty did not look at her. 'Oh, gwacious . . .' she sounded milder than ever. 'Well, you had better go back to the garden in the meantime, Martin. The nets can wait, Madge.'

'But,' said Frances, 'he put both arms around me. Madge, you saw him.'

Madge did not move. Letty picked up the two crumpled letters from the floor and put them into Frances's hands. 'Be silent,' she said again, curt and very low. She turned to the two servants. 'Pway go along, both of you.'

Martin had turned towards the door, and Madge had dropped the netting on the bed, when Patrick Logan appeared in the doorway, holding a bloody wad of towelling to his mouth.

'What is this?'

The words were indistinct, but they were asked at the same time by his eyes. They looked from one to the other, and rested at last, with hostility, on Frances.

'A gweat wumpus,' said Letty, before Frances could speak. She fanned herself with her letter. 'Go along, Madge. Go on, Martin.'

After a quick glance at her, the commandant stood aside and left the door free for them to pass. While Madge was coming crabwise down the ladder, Martin,

238

his mouth hanging slackly open and his eyes dulled, crossed the room, reached the door, and suddenly, with a cry, fell on one knee before the commandant.

'Sir . . . captain . . . I never . . . oh, sir, don't!'

His chin dropped to his breast and he broke like a child into loud sobs. Logan looked for about ten seconds at his bowed head, then spoke to Madge Noakes.

'Madge, fetch Collison. Stand up, Martin.'

He took the towel from his mouth, looked at the blood, then went quickly to the window and spat into the garden. Martin got slowly to his feet and stood, as stiffly as before, facing the door. Frances looked at the two crumpled letters in her hand, then timidly held them to Letty's view, pointing to the addresses. But Letty would look neither at them nor at her.

'They will have to be written again,' whispered Frances.

Letty turned her head away, but Logan, returning from the window, glanced at the letters.

'Well, I shall at least write Edmund's again.'

Letty disdainfully touched the ribbons at her neck. Collison came in.

'Collison,' said Logan, 'take Martin to the lock-up.'

Martin seemed unable to move. Collison, not much older than he, slender, flat-faced, with narrow grey eyes and a glitter of gold bristles on a tanned skin, touched him on the arm. 'Come along, lad.'

239

Like a voice of fate, it set Martin in motion. Nobody spoke as he left the room. The commandant's mouth was bleeding again. He dabbed it with the towel. 'What did he do?'

'First, let me bwing a clean towel.'

He gave a brief impatient headshake. 'What did he do?'

'Embwaced Fwances.'

'*What!*'

His astonishment, his outrage, forced upon Frances what she had been (though hopelessly) evading—the consequences of the incident for Martin. She was about to plead that she was, after all, unharmed, when she saw that Logan's gaze was moving over her not only with anger, but with a fierce and prudish disgust for her person, her flesh. She shrank before it. 'But *I* could not help it!' she cried.

'It is my opinion that you could, miss.'

'What, help it? How? Why?'

'How? Why?' The flash of disgust had vanished, consumed by his anger. 'By your Yankee talk, for a start. Oh, you are overheard, miss. You are overheard. And by your sickly commiseration, which you see fit to display, and which gives them ideas.'

'Ideas to embrace me? That is unjust. That is unkind.'

Letty stepped forward. 'Patwick, it is unkind.'

'And unjust, Letty. He is unjust.'

240

'Well, Fwances, it is twue that you lack tact. To speak of the incident before them both! And you *would* not be silent. And to appeal to Madge to support your word—that above all. As if your word is not enough. I was as angwy as could be. Though not as angwy as Patwick is now. My love, upon my word, I believe you are about to burst.'

But he might not have heard her. The glare he had fixed on Frances had not abated while she was speaking, and now he simply put Letty aside, with surprising roughness, with a push of one forearm. 'All very well! But where has your sister's precious pity led one of the objects of it?'

Frances put both hands to her cheeks. 'Oh . . . Martin . . .'

It was only a murmur, addressed to herself rather than to him, but he replied with passion, looking over Letty's head into her face. 'Yes! Martin! Who has never been in trouble until this day.'

'What will happen to him?'

'He will come before me in the morning.'

'Fwances, a fair exchange.' Letty crossed the room with her fast gliding step. 'Here is Cass's letter. Give me the one from Hermione and Lydia.'

But as Frances made the exchange she hardly looked away from Logan's face. 'And what will happen to him after that?'

'So you expect me to prejudge him?'

'Why—no—'

'Why—yes. You do. Well, I shan't. And nor does the matter concern you.'

'Sir—'

But he had turned his back. She waited while he went to the window again to spit into the garden. In the strength and disturbance of her feelings she had lost her fear of him, but in this enforced interval she had time to regain it, and when he came back from the window her struggle against it was evident in her strained and timid voice.

'Sir, a moment ago you said it did.'

But he had seen the sash cord; he picked it up. 'Who requisitioned this?'

'Oh, Patwick! Nobody.'

'*Nobody!*'

'There was no need. It was left over from last time.'

'What last time?'

'Sir,' said Frances, in the same strained voice, 'a minute ago you said it did concern me.'

'I don't remember requisitioning any sash cord. What? What? What concerns you?'

'What happens to Martin.'

'Oh, Fwances . . .'

'Ah, yes, miss, the doing of it concerns you. It does, to be sure. But the punishment does not. That is in my unworthy hands.'

'He has brought me to no harm,' said Frances in a low voice.

'What did you say?'

'He has brought me to no harm.'

'And so should not be punished?'

She was silent.

'Come—is that what you mean?'

'I don't suggest he should not be warned.'

'You are mad. You are mad. I am to let the thing pass with a warning?'

'Oh, but let the warning be severe.'

'Severe. I see. Miss Commandant!' He bowed. 'Only let me have your instructions!'

Letty stepped between them, her arms flung wide. 'Stop! Patwick, your blood is making me sick. Did not Henwy tell you to wash out your mouth?'

'He did. I was about to do so when I was diverted by the screams of your sister. Your sister is as idiotic as Cowper. Now *there* is her match! Let her marry Cowper. A precious couple!'

'I think, sir,' said Frances, with sudden composure, 'that I may shortly marry Mr Edmund Joyce.'

He looked her over from head to foot. 'Then I wish him joy of his bargain.'

But Letty put her fingertips together and cocked her head in enquiry. 'Then he has . . .?'

Frances turned on a heel and grasped the last of Edmund's three letters from the desk. But Logan

243

was now leaving the room. 'With you at his side,' he remarked as he went, 'he may say goodbye to all expectations from his uncle.'

Frances was shocked by her surge of hatred for him, and by her impulse to pursue him and thrust the letter beneath his eyes. She stared after him as she gave it instead into her sister's extended hand.

'It could hardly be plainer,' said Letty, when she had read it.

'And here is my reply.'

The seal had been broken during her scuffle with Martin. 'Yes,' murmured Letty. 'Yes, it is well put. It will do.'

'I thought you would be better pleased.'

'I am thinking of what Patwick just said.'

'I will change when I am Mrs Edmund Joyce.'

'Change now, Fwances, or you will never be Mrs Edmund Joyce. Who would take a scweaming mad woman, a woman with a weputation for making scenes? Why did you do it?'

Frances shook her head. 'I don't know.'

'They say the climate . . . but Lord, it is not even summer yet.'

'Letty, how can I make amends?'

'By a wesolve never, never to act in that way again. But in the meantime, my dear, don't let us distwess ourselves too much. Patwick will go on his journey. By the time he comes back his anger will have abated.

244

You will see—all will be forgiven. And soon after that, we will leave this place for ever—'

'But Letty—'

'—and will leave your little scene behind us in the wiver mud.'

'But I meant, how can I make amends to Martin?'

'You can't. It has passed beyond that.'

'What will happen to him?'

'You heard Patwick say it is not your concern. I don't make such matters mine.'

'He has never been in trouble before. I am sure he will be shown mercy.'

'Can you doubt it? Do you think so ill of Patwick?'

'No . . . no . . .'

'On the other hand, can such an attack be passed over?'

'No. But will you speak for him?'

'Speak?'

'Intercede.'

'I have sometimes neglected to weport him for speaking to the childwen. It may have been a mistake.'

'Then *I* will intercede.'

'You will make the matter worse.'

Frances sat in the chair at her desk and covered her cheeks with both hands. 'I know!'

'I will intercede on one condition.'

Frances raised her head. 'Letty, will you? What?'

'That you dwop the subject.'

'Very well. But you will intercede?'

'I have told you.'

'You will beg—'

'I have told you. Oblige me by dwopping the subject.'

'But you will—'

'Fwances, no more! I cannot bear it. These last six months have been hard and anxious—'

'Letty, that sounds unlike you.'

'All the same, I am saying it. Listen. They have been hard and anxious. And if now, so near the end, when there are only a few weeks to go, there should be more twouble, more fusses, I could not bear, it. No, forgive me, Fwances, but I could not. Help me in this. Help me and my family. Pway to God to smooth our way out of this place. And as for this—' she folded the reply to Edmund and gave it back to Frances—'you must do it again, of course, on fwesh paper.'

CHAPTER TEN

Letty could not see the garden from where she sat alone in the dark drawing room, but as the voices passed by the open window she could easily identify them. The first four came together: Louisa and Amelia, Victor and Lancelot. All talked and laughed as they threaded their way down from the road through the commandant's garden, but the men, who had been drinking, were louder and more free than the women. No torchlight flared on the ceiling of the verandah as they passed. The moon gave so much light that Letty had tired of its brightness and had turned her back to the window.

The four were still talking when they reached Whyte's office, but their sudden silence then informed Letty that the clerk (with a look and a jerk of his head?) had warned them that the commandant was working

247

on his reports in the office next door. Into that silence sprang an image of her husband sitting at his desk, his right foot advanced and his left drawn back against a leg of his chair. The scrape of his nib would scarcely be audible, for he found writing a nervous business and refrained from forcibly pressing the paper. The candle at his left hand would reveal his swollen mouth and the frequent twitching of that taut little muscle high in his jaw. He would not look up when he heard the group enter Whyte's office. His pen would continue to move irritably, lightly, across the page, or perhaps, without raising his head, he would stop to stare at the paper, as if its whiteness had suddenly struck him blind. That muscle would twitch, and as he wrote or stared, he would whisper a few of the words, while in the outer office the four would put their mail on the counter and silently depart.

And indeed they were now returning through the garden, talking this time in low voices. Wishing for the distraction and support of Louisa's company, Letty went to the window to call her; but she did not want the company of all four, and hesitated because she could think of no excuse to detach Louisa alone.

Victor was speaking.

'She says it makes her hot, yet won't do away with it.'

'But underneath,' said Louisa, 'my forehead is quite blue.'

'Charming!' This was Lancelot. '*Do* do away with it!'

'Lancelot is right, my dear,' said Amelia. 'The new way would become you. Parted in the middle, and looped—'

'Looped?' echoed Louisa.

'Looped,' said Lancelot.

'Why not looped?' Amelia anxiously cried.

'Well, we shall see,' Letty heard Louisa say. 'Henry Cowper did once tell me it was like six red dead . . .' her voice was distant now . . . 'snails.'

Letty withdrew from the window and sat on the blue sofa. Provisions must be made against loneliness; she would try to conceal her surprise at those Louisa appeared to be making.

Frances came in, carrying a candle about which a few moths hurtled. 'I have been looking for you,' she said.

'Why?'

'Has Collison taken the letters to the office?'

'An hour ago.'

'I thought of something to add to Edmund's.'

In the *déshabillé* of nightclothes and rumpled hair she looked beautiful. Letty said benignly, 'His letter will do vewy well as it is. Go back to bed.'

'Yes,' said Frances vaguely. But she did not go. About the wavering red flame of her candle, at the point where it climbed into darkness, many moths had now collected. Some, little bigger than mosquitoes, instantly perished in its heat; some, larger, lingered, went away, returned, and dropped; but a few, larger, stronger, hardier, came to the light, visibly singed their wings, and then flew vigorously away, whether to die or not, Letty could not tell. 'Edmund's letter was not your purpose in seeking me out,' she said.

'No.'

'You said you would dwop the subject.'

'I thought you might have spoken to him by now.'

'You know he did not come to the house for dinner. I have not seen him since it occurred.'

'Is that why you are waiting here?'

'Yes.'

Frances raised her candle so that it shed a fuller light on Letty's face. Almost offendedly, Letty turned aside. Two voices could be heard approaching in the garden. She recognised Spicer and Hansord, and under pretext of listening to them, continued to avoid Frances's light.

'I would have him find that horse, rather than a river to the sea.'

'That horse? My dear Hansord, I'll wager anything the blacks roasted him long ago.'

'Have you tasted horse?'

'What, you take me for a Frenchman?'

They fell silent before they reached Whyte's office, so no warning from the clerk was needed. Frances had not lowered her light. 'Must you stay up?' she said. 'You look fatigued.'

'On mail nights he sometimes sleeps in his office.'

'And then you will be forced to run over the garden, and accost him there?'

'Pway lower your light.'

'Is he angry with you as well?'

'I have told you—I have not seen him since.'

'He is. I can see it in your looks.'

Again Letty turned away. Spicer and Hansord were returning through the garden without speaking. One of them yawned. Frances spoke with soft amazement.

'Marriage is not what they say it is. Not what you say it is, Letty.'

'Pway, go back to bed.'

'Dear Letty, *you* go to bed. Speak to him in the morning.'

Letty would not reveal that she could no longer speak on such matters in the morning, for lately, if anything displeased him at that hour, he would simply dress in silence and leave the house, staying neither to eat nor drink. 'You asked me to intercede,' she said, 'but now it seems you have changed your mind.'

'No. Oh, no.'

'Then let me do it in my own way. Go back to bed. And pway, Fwances, be careful of the wax candles. None came in the *Phillip*.'

251

After she had gone, Letty lay back on the sofa and fell into one of those dozes that do not exclude noise. Captain Clunie and Lieutenant Edwards had not yet brought their mail, and nor had they sent their servants. Henry Cowper, she supposed, would have written no letters, and James Murray would have so many to write, and at such length, that he would not have finished. Poor Mr Scottowe Parker, alone at the Eagle Farm, would not get his mail until James Murray rode out tomorrow, so that his replies, like those of the prisoners—who would have no leisure to reply until Sunday—and most of the soldiers, must wait to be carried in the next ship.

When she heard approaching the light good-humoured voice of Lieutenant Edwards, she did not open her eyes.

'. . . used to be considered almost a sentence of death.'

What used to be? she wondered. But Captain Clunie was now informing her.

'Yes, but not these days. Quite a good hill station. Ootacamund. I believe you've a cousin there.'

'Lady Rumbold is dead, sir.'

'What? I'm very sorry. When?'

'June, my mother writes.'

'Fever?'

'Childbirth. Plenty of fever, of course, too.'

'At Madras, yes. But not at Ootacamund.'

'Yes, sir, at Ooty as well. Mustn't blink at facts. Though not as much as on the plains.'

They had not told Letty anything she did not already know, except that Lady Rumbold was dead. With her eyes still shut, she said a fearful little prayer for Lady Rumbold's soul.

When the two men reached the office, Whyte gave no warning, for Letty continued to hear the tone, though not the words, of Captain Clunie's voice, and presently she heard the response of another voice, which, though scarcely audible, she knew for her husband's.

Either he had finished his report, and would soon return to the house, or he had abandoned it for a moment to talk to Captain Clunie. She rose and went to the window. Lieutenant Edwards was coming alone from Whyte's office. As he passed, whistling, as light and cheerful as if under orders for London instead of Madras, she drew back into the darkness of the room. When she went again to the window she saw her husband and Clunie emerge from the office together and begin to make their way along the path. Hands clasped at backs and heads bent, they approached in the same absorbed and sauntering manner observed by Louisa and herself from this same window on the morning after Captain Clunie's arrival at the settlement.

Her husband was speaking softly and occasionally sending sharp sidelong glances into Captain Clunie's face, but before they were near enough for his words

253

to become distinct, running footsteps from the other direction made them raise their heads and stop. James Murray, carrying a bundle of letters, came running into view, exuberant yet anxious.

'Too late? Am I?'

Assuring him together that he was not, they parted to let him pass between them. And then, instead of walking on, as Letty expected, they remained in that position, in silence, as if they must wait for him to pass again before resuming so private a conversation.

Clunie was grateful for the respite James Murray's appearance had given him. It was too late at night to be asked for the truth. Logan's question had made him wish to escape with some easy lie. 'My dear sir, Cowper is a drunken fool. How could Smith Hall's trial turn out to be—what did he say?—tantamount to an enquiry into your administration? Absolute nonsense, my dear sir. Goodnight!'

But by the time Murray had run between them, deposited his mail with Whyte, and hurried back, confusedly wishing them goodnight as he passed again between them, Clunie had rejected the injustice of such a lie and had determined to be as honest as diplomacy allowed. When Murray was out of earshot he set his face once more to the path and with a hand at Logan's back ushered him into step at his side, himself recognising as he did so something almost paternal in the gesture, as well as something of pity. He said, 'What you tell me surprises me. Yet Cowper has sense. One wonders if the Smith Hall trial could turn out as he says.'

Logan stopped and faced him. 'Think of what you are saying.'

'I have. I am. I wonder if it could.'

'Tantamount to an enquiry into my administration?' His bewilderment made it clear that he had expected only reassurance. 'But why, man? In God's name, why?'

'Have you looked at the journals from home yet? A whig victory no longer seems out of the question. The duke is losing control. For a long time I've been saying—lightly enough, you've heard me—that times are changing, but never really believing in my heart that they were, or ever would. But while I've been so lightly saying it, it seems they have. It came to me very strongly today, reading the journals, and my post as well. You're wondering what this has to do with you. Only this—that it's possible for a man to be judged by the standards of the present for maintaining—in all sincerity, of course—the standards of the past.'

'My standards are those of the governor. My actions tally with his.'

Clunie thrust his head forward and spoke very softly, 'And don't you think there may be an enquiry into *his* administration?'

'It will never happen.'

'Ah,' said Clunie, with mournful humour, 'but so much that will never happen has happened already.'

'Very well! If it does, I, for one, will stand by him.'

This, said with the kind of trite nobility that was apt to make Henry Cowper break into laughter or groaning, goaded Clunie past the diplomacy he had determined upon. 'But,' he said, 'do you think he would stand by you?'

Logan's slow headshake was not in denial, but in wonder. It made Clunie amend his question. 'Do you think he could afford to?'

Again Logan shook his head. 'It is clear,' he said calmly, 'that you don't know him.'

'True,' admitted Clunie. 'But I know something of men.'

'Not of that man!'

'You have so firm a trust in him?

'I have.'

Clunie drew back a little. Such faith was almost convincing. And Logan, moreover, was looking at him with the same superiority and pity he himself had felt when ushering the commandant on to the path, and which he now recognised as the pity one feels for ignorance or vulnerable innocence.

'One expects nothing of Cowper,' said the commandant sadly.

The slight emphasis on the name brought home to

Clunie how much was still expected of himself. Once again he unwillingly took on the responsibility of the commandant's exaggerated regard. 'Sir,' he said, 'there will be a chance offered you in Sydney of showing up the excesses of your critics. Bulbridge and Fagan must come to trial while you are there. You could speak for them.'

'Does it surprise you that Cowper had the same idea?'

Under his steady, slightly smiling, but pitying regard, Clunie felt himself growing flustered. 'I hope you don't imagine we discussed it.'

'Not for one moment!'

'For of course, I wouldn't.'

'I know it!'

'I take it you don't like the idea?'

The commandant found no need to reply. He set a hand on Clunie's shoulder. 'I've my report to finish. Well, not to finish, but to make ready for the post.' With commiseration, with warm forgiveness, he looked Clunie full in the face, then lightly shook the shoulder beneath his hand.

'Goodnight, my dear fellow.'

The mosquito nets had been lowered to cover their bed and in the light of his single candle he did not notice at first that the form under the bedclothes was too small to be Letty. He had taken off his shoes and stockings before he realised, at a second glance, that Lucy had come into their bed and that Letty was not there. With his feet bare but still in his dusty resplendent uniform he went to the bed and raised the nets. Lucy opened her eyes at once.

'Lucy, where is mama?'

But though she seemed to be looking at him in full calm consciousness she was not really awake at all. She was drawing him into her dream, and when she shut her eyes, he continued in its flow.

'Come, little maiden.'

He gathered her up and rested her on one shoulder, and with his light in the other hand carried her back to the nursery. When he laid her on the bed she threw both arms back on the pillow and turned quivering eyelids to his candlelight. He quickly put down his light and drew the nets over her bed.

At Robert's bed he raised his candle and thrust his face into the mosquito nets so that the close weave of the cotton threads should not obscure his view. Robert had pushed the bedclothes down to his feet, but before his father could raise the netting to cover him, he started up and gave a loud cry.

'Robert, it is papa.'

'Go away. I don't like you.'

'Hush. It is only papa.'

The boy looked at him with dazed eyes. 'Oh. It is papa.'

'Cover yourself. It is cooler tonight.'

'I thought you were Bishop.'

'Bishop is dead. Lie down and cover yourself.'

Robert lay softly down. 'I meant his ghost.'

'There are no ghosts. Has mama been in tonight?'

Robert sat up as suddenly as he had done the first time. 'There are ghosts!'

'Hush. You will wake Lucy. Has mama been in tonight?'

'She told us a story. There are ghosts, papa.'

'Lie down and sleep, Robert.'

'Yes, papa.'

The boy lay down; the commandant turned away.

'Papa?'

'Yes.'

'Is Gilligan better than Bishop?'

'Go to sleep, Robert.'

'Papa?'

'Robert, I am tired. Goodnight, my son.'

'Papa, what will happen to Martin?'

'He will be punished according to the law.'

'And the law is just,' said Robert complacently.

'As I have often told you.'

'The law is not like life,' said the boy, still with loud complacency. 'Life is unjust,' he announced.

'Who has been speaking to you?'

'Nobody. Everybody says life is unjust.'

'It sometimes seems so.'

'Then the law is better than life.'

'Someone has been speaking to you of these things.'

'No, papa. I have been thinking.'

'You are only six.'

'I think when I lie awake. I often lie awake.' He had raised himself on both elbows. 'Why are your feet bare?'

'Lie down and sleep, Robert.'

'I am frightened. Why are they bare? May mama come?'

'No. It is too late. Go to sleep.'

'Then leave the door open.'

But when his father reached the door, he cried, 'No, shut it. Or he will come again.'

The commandant shut the door and went through the dark house to the drawing room. The big high room dispersed his small light and at first he did not see Letty. Lying as she was, on her side, pressed close to the back of the sofa, with her face hidden, she might have been a bundle of soft shawls left lying there. But the bundle stirred, her raised hip heaved. As he came nearer she turned on her back and looked first at his face and then at some point beyond his shoulder, on which, when he halted beside the sofa, she continued reflectively to dwell. He raised the candle again.

'Why are you here in the dark?'

She flung a forearm across her eyes. 'Pway put it out.'

'It is too dark, with all the curtains drawn.'

'Put it out. The moths.'

It was true that the moths, more and more of them, were rushing to his light. He blew out the candle and put it on the small embroidery table, then went to the window and pulled the curtains aside to admit a little moonlight. He sat on the edge of the sofa and put a hand on her thigh. 'What is the matter? What are you doing here in the dark?'

'Waiting for you.'

'Uncover your eyes.'

When she did not do so he took her arm and lifted it from her eyes. She did not resist, but would not look at him. 'You heard me talking to Clunie,' he said.

Still looking everywhere but at him, she nodded.

'Nothing in that conversation need distress you. Clunie would not discuss such matters with Cowper, but he can't help but hear Cowper's opinions. Cowper's the source of that infection, and Cowper's half mad. Why were you waiting in here for me?'

'You did not come to the house for dinner.'

'I was working on my report.'

'I believed you were angwy.'

'With you, my love?'

'With Fwances's sister. I thought you might sleep again in your office.'

He stroked her thigh. 'And could not wait for morning to make up?'

But her cold, troubled, and wandering glance showed no response to his fondness. 'I wished to speak to you besides.'

'What about?'

She pushed his hand gently from her thigh and got to her feet. 'In a hopeless cause. I am going to bed.'

But he caught her by one hand and held her there. 'Why hopeless?'

'I was going to speak for Martin.'

'My dear Letty, there's no need. It's his first offence. He will be punished as lightly as is consistent with discipline. Can I do more?'

'Yes.'

'What?'

'Intercede for Bulbwidge and Fagan.'

The commandant dropped her hand. 'That is more than three weeks hence. We shan't discuss it. We were discussing Martin.'

'It is all part of the same thing. If you can't give mercy, how can you ask it?'

'Why should I ask it for two vicious scoundrels. Say no more on the subject, if you please!'

He turned as he spoke and went to the window, and when she said, in confusion and wonder, 'But I meant that then you can't ask mercy for yourself,' he gave no sign of understanding her. Perhaps in the noise of the wooden rings passing along the rod he really did lose the sense of her words, and it was only to the sound of her voice that he imperiously said, 'No more, if you please!' She did not know, and could not find out. Her habit of subservience to him would not let her launch herself against such a tone, and the exclusion of the moonlight made the room too dark for her to see his face.

It was so dark indeed that as he led the way from the room she put a hand on his back for guidance. It was when they walked off the big Persian rug on to the bare polished boards that she realised for the first time that his feet were bare. His tread, always so light, was made inaudible by hers, and to hear only her own slithering footsteps gave her a sense of eeriness, of amused shock—amused because she knew by touch that he was, after all, solidly and warmly there. Touching him brought too a renewal of her strength, and in spite of all sadness and doubt, a rise in her spirits. He was walking hesitantly, fumbling for the wall. She put her other hand on his back and slipped both up to his shoulders, where they had better purchase.

'Else I should feel I were following nothing,' she whispered in the dark.

CHAPTER ELEVEN

'Has the *Regent Bird* sailed?'

'Hours ago, miss.'

Madge Noakes pulled aside the curtains as she spoke. Strong sunlight entered the room. Frances sat up. 'I have slept very late.'

'Madam said to let you be.'

With one hand Frances raised the mosquito net, making a peaked aperture like the door of a tent. Clear sky filled all the window except for a fringe of foliage at the sill—the treetops in the botanical gardens, massively stirring in a slow wind. 'But by now,' she said, still dull with sleep, 'the *Regent Bird* will be at Dunwich.'

'As good as, miss.'

'Has my sister breakfasted?'

'Has started to, miss.'

'And the commandant?'

'Has gone out hours since. There is water on the washstand.'

'Thank you. I will breakfast in a few minutes.'

But after Madge went, the window continued to hold her dull attention. She would have gone back to sleep had not the wind, with a sudden gust, blown one branch clear of the mass of trees and moved it to and fro in a wild tossing. The movement brought her to full wakefulness, seeming to shift some irksome weight in her body, leaving her liberated and full of excitement. The branch waved its signal and subsided, but her joy remained. She let the net drop and fell back on the bed, first to put her hands behind her head and smile, then to break into laughter, push the bedcovers down with her feet, and kick and roll about exuberantly in the big bed. For the first time it occurred to her that between a man and a woman there could be something of infantile play. Last night, looking at Letty's diminished face, she had divined a black area in marriage, an evil, a sort of sorcery; but today in the sunlight, and in the knowledge that her letter to Edmund was irretrievable, she could only think how sweet it would be to roll about in a warm bed in play, to laugh and tumble and bite. She flung up the net, ducked under it, and stood on the mat in the warm wind.

Only then did she remember Martin. Admitting yesterday's events with reluctance, she went slowly to the window and looked out. Nobody was visible in the garden, neither Gilligan nor any of the other men, but now, through bushes bordering the path that led upwards to the road, she caught a glimpse of blue, then of white, then, through a larger gap, she saw James Murray. In white trousers, and a blue coat with red facings, and carrying two lilies of a lighter and more gorgeous red, he passed out of her sight towards the door of the house.

That he was here at this early hour, instead of at the Eagle Farm, might mean that Henry Cowper had gone instead, as sometimes occurred, in which case James would be chief medical officer, whose sanction and supervision was needed for all today's punishments. Frances ran to the wash-stand. She washed, dressed in yesterday's white muslin, tucked all her hair beneath a morning cap, and made for the dining room with little running steps, tying her wide blue sash on the way.

James Murray and Letty sat facing each other in chairs pushed aside from the dining table. He was holding her wrist and looking earnestly at her protruding tongue. Tiptoeing with respect, Frances served herself at the sideboard and carried her plate to the table.

'Very good,' said James Murray at last. 'I believe you begin to mend. Good morning, Miss O'Beirne.'

Letty turned again to the table. 'Fwances, good morning.'

'Good morning, Letty. Good morning, Mr Murray. What a surprise to find you here at this hour.'

'Mr Cowper has gone to the Eagle Farm in my place. Kindly accept this. Tigridia pavonia. I had the bulbs sent from Sydney.'

'And grew it yourself! It is beautiful. The petals are as thin as flames.'

'We are equally favoured,' said Letty, touching the lily by her plate.

'I have another for Mrs Harbin. She wants it for her sketch book.'

'Poor Mrs Bulwer gets none?' asked Frances.

'I have only three.'

'So you have depwived yourself.'

'They don't last long,' said James Murray, looking wistfully at his two lilies lying on the table, 'out of water.'

Letty rang the bell.

'What time does Mr Cowper return?' asked Frances.

'That depends on how much he finds to say to Scottowe Parker.' Murray rose to his feet. 'You have recalled my duty to me. I must leave you.'

'You have so many patients today?' asked Frances with anxiety.

'There are always enough, Miss O'Beirne.'

Madge came in. 'Madge,' said Letty, 'put these in water.'

'Yes, yes,' said James, relieved and smiling, 'you will find they do better in water.'

'Tender hearted even for flowers,' said Frances with a smile.

After James Murray and Madge had gone, Letty looked sideways at Frances. 'You were vewy animated with James.'

'He is so gentle and kindly. If my heart were not engaged, I might have had romantic notions about him.'

'So your heart is twuly engaged?'

'This morning I feel that it is. Unless it is simple relief at having acted with firmness, and sent my letter. I can't swim, I can't fly, so I can't fetch it back. It's gone. The thing's done. The rest is up to Edmund. I feel as if a burden has been lifted from me.'

Letty was looking at her sister with slow, almost sleepy curiosity. 'To be sure, you look happy.'

'So do you, Letty.'

Letty looked down at her plate. 'Well, as James said, I begin to mend.'

Frances did not reply that the improvement was unnaturally sudden, and that last night she had looked ill. She had observed enough lately to understand that the differences between Letty and her husband had now been resolved. Watching her, Frances thought 'happy' not quite a word to describe her. She seemed deeply contented, yet vague, remote. Perhaps she had adopted that distant air to protect her contentment, to keep it private and safe and out of reach of assailment. But of whose assailment could she be afraid, if not of Frances's? And with some shame Frances confessed that her sister's fear was justified. She would have assailed that contentment if she could, if only because she did not understand it. It was ridiculous; it was in crazy disproportion to its cause. 'Is he water?' she wanted to ask. 'Is he food?' But instead she said in an awkward voice, 'I expect Patrick leaves early tomorrow.'

'Not until nine.'

'How long will he be gone?'

Letty shrugged. 'For as long as it takes him to twace his famous cweek. And while he is gone, you and I must kilt up our skirts, and woll up our sleeves, and make all weady for our departure out of this place—me for Madwas, and you, let us hope, to make your home with your Edmund.'

'And the children?'

'That depends on so much.'

The sisters exchanged a lightning glance of complicity. 'So much,' Letty repeated gently.

'I shall be Mrs Edmund Joyce,' said Frances with sudden amazement.

Letty smiled. 'Always pwovided you make yourself acceptable to his uncle and aunt.'

'Oh, I shall. I mean to.'

'I don't know what his expectations are fwom his own family—'

'And neither do I,' said Frances happily.

'—but if he is so weady to let the Annings take him over, I think most of his expectations must be fwom them.'

'Well, I expect so. But pray, don't worry. All will be well.' Frances jumped from her chair. 'Letty! Imagine! I shall have my own mount. I think I fancy a grey. And I believe,' she said, laughing as if she did not really believe it, 'that I shall have a silk evening gown. Silk!'

Again Letty looked at her with that slow curiosity. 'A gweat change fwom last night.'

It so closely resembled Frances's own reflections on Letty that the girl's face changed to a startled thoughtfulness. 'Oh, but last night I still could have got my letter back. And of course,' she admitted, turning her startled look directly on her sister's face, 'there was Martin. Letty, you did speak to him about Martin?'

'Martin will be punished as lightly as is consistent with discipline. That is all he would pwomise.'

'But you spoke,' said Frances, with rough impatience, 'so all will be well. All must be well.'

'Indeed, my love, it must be. For at this time no more can be done. The thing is like Edmund's letter. It can't be fetched back. It's done. Think of it in the same way.' Letty rose from the table and took one of Frances's hands in both of hers, pressing and stroking

270

it as if to cajole her out of her present sober mood into her former merriment. 'Today you may pwactice at being mistwess of a house. I go to take tea with Amelia. All will be in your charge.'

'I may order the dinner? I may choose the pudding?'

'Of course. But now you must go to the school.'

Frances ran to the bedroom to dress her hair. At her dressing table she began to sing, but after the first few notes her voice faltered and became self-conscious. With her arms raised and her hands busy with her hair, she looked into her reflected eyes and recognised the reason for the restraint she had suddenly felt. 'But,' she argued with herself, 'Martin is not lying in wait. I may sing. I may do as I please.'

She knew then that she owed her morning's mood of freedom and gaiety as much to Martin's removal as to the finality of her letter to Edmund. As soon as she had thrust the last pin in her hair she got up and went to the window. Gilligan was not there. Tying her bonnet as she went, she ran in fear to the drawing room. From the window she saw Gilligan and another man working near the commandant's office. The anxiety left her face. She turned and saw Madge Noakes enter the door with polish and dusters. 'Madge,' she said, standing straight and smiling, 'will you first escort me to the school?'

The woman was looking at her with the same

curiosity accorded to her a while ago by Letty. It left in her mind a little rankling guilt.

From the scullery window she could see Gilligan and two other men in the garden, working peacefully, their hatbrims and trouser legs flapping in the wind. From the schoolroom she had kept a watch on the road, and was sure that Gilligan had not passed by. After coming home she had helped Letty to dress for Amelia's tea and had then received from her the household keys, but, at her own entreaty, no instructions.

She was mistress of the house. She had checked the supplies that arrived from the commissary store, she had doled out the tea and sugar to Madge Noakes, had apportioned the beef and vegetables for that night's dinner, and had ordered the pudding. She had often done these tasks for Letty, but without the consciousness of Letty's presence in the house they bore a different character, more intimidating at first but ultimately more satisfying. Pressing on against the passive sarcasm of Madge Noakes's glances, she made several innovations of her own. Big Annie took her cue from Madge and guffawed. Annie, six foot tall and slightly mad, with a pin head and bullock shoulders, was valued for her strength and tractability. Frances found it easy to ignore her guffaws, and equally easy to pass over Elizabeth Robertson's opposition. Elizabeth chewed her lips and mumbled that they never did it that way.

'Well, do it this way today. Madge, there is scum in the water casks.'

'As in the tank itself, miss.'

'This has not come from the tank. It has had time to settle on the sides. Pray strain the water into fresh casks.'

'Miss, how strain it?'

'Through cheese cloths.'

'Water through cheese cloths?'

'Haw-haw!' roared Annie.

'Why not? Annie may do it, and then she may scrub the casks and wash the cloths.'

She left the scullery at a brisk step, inclined to swing and rattle the household keys.

In the nursery Robert was standing at his desk, still engaged in the task she had set him, while Lucy sat at her small table, scribbling with a pencil in a used letter book.

'No, Robert. Your "cat" is more like "cot". Let me show you.'

Robert moved aside to give her room. 'Aunt Fanny, is Gilligan still in the kitchen garden?'

'Yes, I saw him. Now, see, if you bring the tail—'

'Then Martin cannot yet be flogged.'

'—right down to here, and then give it an upward turn, you have made a correct "a". Who said he was to be flogged?'

'Papa.'

'Your papa told you that? Are you sure?'

'No. I am wrong. Punished. He said punished.'

'Well, that is a different thing entirely, is it not?'

'Yes, it is different. He could be put in the solitary cell, on bread and water.'

'Bread and wat-er,' chanted Lucy from her table.

'Robert, Lucy, it is not our affair. Now remember, Robert, the tail of an "a" must make a hook.'

'A hook,' said Robert vaguely.

'I am writing my name,' shouted Lucy.

'Make a row of a's here, Robert.'

'Aunt Fanny, Aunt Fanny, look what I have done.'

'Very nice, Lucy.'

'You are not looking. You are looking out of the window. Look at it. Look.'

'I am. It is very nice.'

'It is a cart.'

'I thought it was your name.'

'No, a cart.'

When the lesson was over, and she had handed the children into Elizabeth's care, and had given her permission to take them into the garden, she went to her room and began to draft a serial letter to Edmund. James Murray's lily was in a vase on her desk, and during the long dreaming intervals in her writing, she sometimes smiled and touched a petal with her pen, or looked with unfocused eyes into its velvety heart. She knew that she was now employing a great deal of craft and guile in addressing Edmund, but it no longer seemed inconsistent with honesty. She felt the glow her own words created in her as the glow of sincerity. She was manufacturing love. Now and again she went and lay on her bed, with her hands behind her head, staring upwards into the white net and the lace, but presently fresh words would form in her head, and she would leap up and seize her pen again. Once she got to her feet and hurried to the scullery. Neither Madge nor Annie was there, but outside in the garden Gilligan and the two men were at work. She returned through the house, silently mouthing the next words of her letter. But she had hardly begun to write when she heard cries from the garden, a joyful hallooing cry from Robert and Lucy's shriller but no less delighted voice. The children were rolling down the grassy bank. In a few minutes the cries had penetrated and dispersed her concentration. Letty would soon be home, and would find them hot and excited. She jumped from her desk and took her bonnet from its peg near the door.

She went into the garden by the back door, and as she passed the place where Martin had stood looking up at her window, the surge of relief she felt was so strong that it entered her limbs and would have impelled her into joyful movement if she had not been troubled at the same time by guilt. Guilt, she realised, had haunted her all day like the sound of an old wooden rattle outside the door of a music room, not loud enough to stop her from hearing the music, but providing all the same an irksome undertone. But now it was growing in volume, and threatening to fracture the music. She would no longer stand it; she would attack it.

'Well, at any rate, he will work no more in the garden.'

The thought was so waspishly swift, and informed by such defensive spite, that it made her slow her pace, and put a hand to her cheek, and wonder at herself.

'Am I really so—so—'

But before she could formulate the question she heard Robert's glad hallooing give way abruptly to a startled cry, and immediately afterwards Lucy's voice rose to a shriek of terror. The grassy bank was still hidden from her sight by a deep shrubbery. She took the path around it at a run.

Robert was sitting on the ground holding his right leg in both hands and watching with curiosity or horror the blood running from a deep jagged gash across the inner side of his calf. Lucy, no longer shrieking, but sobbing wildly, stood beside him, while Elizabeth, trying to run, was approaching the pair at a jerky waddle.

Frances, on their other side, reached them while the old woman was still yards away. Robert raised a pale but stoically composed face. 'Will I bleed to death?'

'No.' She knelt and looked at the wound. 'I am sure none of the big veins are cut. Lucy, be silent.'

Elizabeth came up, out of breath. 'Oh, oh, however did he do it?'

'That doesn't matter now. Pray send one—'

'On that!' cried Lucy. 'He did it on that.'

But Frances gave the broken ring of rusty iron, an old handcuff or leg iron, hardly a glance. 'Elizabeth, tell Gilligan or one of the others to run for Mr Murray.'

'Then I *am* bleeding to death.'

'Robert, you are not.'

'Oh, miss, miss, Gilligan and the rest have all went five minutes back to the potato field.'

The potato field was the farthest in the commandant's fourteen acres. 'I will send Annie,' said Frances.

'Annie is back at the factory.'

'Then Madge may go.'

As Frances rose to her feet she felt a passing pride in her quick and unflustered management of the situation. It helped to compensate her for yesterday's shameful hysteria, and was the more commendable because the wound alarmed her. It looked deep and dangerous, and her calm voice belied her quickened heartbeats.

'Lie down, Robert. Elizabeth, take his leg on your lap and raise it slightly. It's no great matter, but Mr Murray must look at it. Stay with your brother, Lucy. I shall be back in a minute or two.'

But as soon as the shrubbery hid her from their view she broke into a run, for she carried in her vision the swelling and empurpled edges of the cut, and the blood running out so steadily between. Madge Noakes's room was one of three in a wing at a right angle to the house. Madge was as likely to be in the house, but since the room was nearer, Frances thought it best to look there first. She entered and knocked at the same time.

Madge, naked except for a cap, sat in a wooden tub so small that her buttocks and feet were jammed together on its base and her raised calves and legs pressed against either side of her body like the legs of a frog. Twisting her head and washing with a cloth behind her ears, she regarded Frances without much surprise. Frances saw that the scar completely encircled her neck in front, and from her many previous glimpses of it knew that the jagged circle was completed at the back. She looked at the floor beside the tub and spoke very fast.

'I beg your pardon, but Master Robert has cut his leg. Badly. Perhaps very badly. I came to ask you to fetch Mr Murray, but it can't wait till you dress. I shall run to the road and find someone else to go. Dress at once, take the coldest water you can find to the bank behind the big shrubbery, and lay a cold compress on the wound.'

Madge had risen from the tub as Frances was speaking. 'You is not let go out alone, miss.'

'I must go. Do as I say.'

She left without shutting the door. The winding

ascending paths of the garden were an impediment. She pulled her skirts above her knees and held them bundled in one hand, leaving the other free to lever or steady herself while she scrambled up the bank in the short cut to the road.

No one was in sight on the road, no soldier or overseer she could send. The hospital lay half a mile along the river bank, at the other end of the road. She let her skirts down, then plucked them up on either side to leave her ankles unencumbered. She ran. She would find a messenger at Captain Clunie's cottage, which was at only a furlong's distance; she would rouse one of his servants.

The road, though rough, was straight. The sound of her pounding feet, her swishing, billowing clothes, and her panting breath, all increased her sense of urgency. She saw how the blood streaming down Robert's leg rippled slightly as it passed over minute golden hairs. She saw Letty's face; Letty was leaning out of her chair; her mouth was moving. 'You know how it is with women—their lives wushing out in their blood. Oh, it can happen so fast . . .' But how much faster a child's life would rush out; a child's body held such a small quantity of blood. And had she been right in ordering that the leg be raised? Could the blood perhaps return on itself, and clot inside the vein? The thought made her give a gasp of fear. Urgency passed into panic. She had reached Captain Clunie's cottage, but the delay made possible by servants absent, engaged, or even only slow-witted, now seemed intolerable. She ran on.

The shining blue ribbons of her bonnet strings parted at the bow beneath her chin and streamed behind her on either side. Below them the two blue tails of her sash leapt in and out of billowing muslin. Robert's face, as he lay down, had showed awe at his own condition. Lucy had moved in a frightened way to take his hand, and the blood had already begun to soak into Elizabeth's white apron. She had reached the military barracks. There must be a guard somewhere, for two shinglers were working on the roof. They stopped to watch her. But by now the hospital was as close, perhaps closer, than those guards would be. She was glad she had come herself, glad she had not sent Madge, for Madge moved heavily. In her relief at having arrived she allowed her mind to wander for a moment from her mission and to observe in retrospect that Madge's belly as she rose from the tub was as froglike as her legs, but that her skin from shoulders to knees, though of a repulsive soapy sallowness, was marvellously soft and unwrinkled.

But now the hospital struck her as so unnaturally quiet that in her sudden wild fear that help was not at hand after all, the image of Madge vanished and she saw again Robert's tender skin marred by the crude and bloody gash. She had entered and was on her way down a long corridor.

'Mr Murray.'

But she was so out of breath that what she had intended for a shout emerged only as a few gasped syllables. She passed room after room, all giving on to the corridor. The doors all stood open and men on pallets turned amazed eyes upon her. One abruptly sat up.

'Mr Murray.'

It was no louder than before, but out of the room she was approaching came a man in grey slops, his face as amazed as the others, and made as if to bar her way. But when she ignored him—indeed she hardly comprehended his intention—he stepped back as if afraid of her, and let her pass. In the next room James Murray stood in quarter profile to her on the other side of a table on which lay a small thin body covered in blood from neck to heels. A man in grey was holding the ankles with one hand and sponging blood from the buttocks with the other. On the floor by his side stood a wooden pail. James Murray was intent on pouring something from a bottle into a dish. The attendant in grey bent to dip his cloth in the pail, and the legs, released from his grip, flailed aimlessly, and Martin's voice, deep, parched, and croaking, went out into the room.

'Do this to a man—can they? Of course not!'

James Murray turned with his filled basin and across Martin's body saw Frances. Now that the attendant had washed the blood from the buttocks they rose from the rest of that body, from the stringy blood-stained legs and the raw bloody shredded mess of the back, as round and fresh as the buttocks of a child.

'Of course not!' croaked Martin in anguish. He flailed with his legs and beat with his fists on the table before him, while across his body James Murray stared at Frances, his eyes pleading and tragic in his pale face, and Frances looked back into his eyes, and spoke as if talking in her sleep.

'Robert has cut his leg.'

Murray gave the dish to the attendant. 'Knowles, you know what to do.'

Martin saw or heard none of this. He rolled his head about as if it would never again learn to rest.

'Can they? Of *course not!*'

Murray had reached the door. He took Frances's arm, drew her into the corridor, and shut the door. A little colour had come back into his face.

'Miss O'Beirne, is it bad?'

'I don't know.'

'Much blood?'

'Oh,' she said, swaying, 'yes.'

'You ran here. Can you stand?'

She straightened herself. 'Of course.'

'It may need sutures.'

They returned down the long corridor, Murray hastening ahead but half turning all the time to check

Frances's progress. The office was near the front entrance. By the time Frances reached it, Murray had entered it, collected his bag, and had reached the door again.

'Are you revived, Miss O'Beirne? Can you hurry back?'

'No,' she said.

He stood in confusion, looking anxiously up the road and then back at her.

'Pray go ahead,' she said.

'But there is none but prisoners here. Who will escort you?'

'Nobody. Pray hurry.'

'And you—'

'Will come after. And fetch my sister from Mrs Bulwer's on the way.'

'Yes, I see. And you will not go—'

He glanced uneasily at the door of the hospital; she looked at him with amazement.

'Back there?' she asked.

'Yes,' he said in relief. 'You do not mean to do that, do you?'

'Oh,' she said, her amazement growing almost into laughter. 'Oh, how do you think I would dare?'

'No,' he said, giving a little bow. 'Of course not. Well, I will obey. I will hurry.'

He turned and went off, taking the first few yards at a jog trot but then settling to a fast run, leaping in a practised manner from the points of his toes. He was tall and strong, and as fleet, she supposed, as Mercury. She watched him until he had passed the barracks. The shinglers had left the roof. Lagging, she set off down the road, but soon, thinking of Letty, forced herself to a brisker pace. She reached the path to the Bulwers' house and unsteadily descended, holding her body backwards against the incline. Banana trees grew on either side of the path, and their last emergent growth, big flat leaves of the freshest possible green, met above her head. She felt their cool shade on her hot face, and fancied she could feel, as well as see, their green light. 'Once there was a garden,' she thought, 'and people walked about naked, and their skins were as fresh as new fruit.' James Murray's cheek, in quarter profile to her as he poured lotion into his dish, had been very pale. He had been pale even before he saw her, even greyish, even the colour of Madge Noakes's belly; and yet, there he had stood, in his sky-blue coat, pouring his lotion. Frances walked in among the sappy trunks of the banana trees and leaned over to let out her vomit, a lumpy yellow stream on either side of which hung a shining blue ribbon.

Robert's wound, though not as dangerous as Frances had feared while racing past Captain Clunie's cottage, was large enough to need stitching. When Murray arrived he found the bleeding had almost stopped. He sent Elizabeth to change her bloody garments, sent Lucy away in Madge's charge, and carried Robert into the house and laid him on the scullery table. Letty and Frances arrived at the house with Amelia. Amelia, who had sent one of her servants to fetch the commandant, waited in the drawing room while Letty and Frances, informed by Madge Noakes, hurried to the scullery.

By this time the child's pale silent bravery had given way to a high-strung hilarity, for Murray had given him brandy to make the coming pain endurable. Robert laughed and said in a high voice that he hardly felt the needle; he said it was only like the prick of a thorn; but as he said this he fainted.

'He has,' murmured Murray, engrossed in his work and speaking in snatches, 'lost a great deal—' he thrust the needle into the flesh again—'of blood. Don't look, dear madam.'

Letty had already withdrawn her gaze from the ugly wound. She wiped her son's forehead and looked only at his pallid and heavily sweating face, which she thought strangely reduced in size.

'Where is Fwances?' she asked in a low voice.

Murray seemed too intent on his work to reply.

'She bwought the water,' said Letty, 'and then went away.'

'Eight sutures. This is the last.'

'Dear little son,' whispered Letty to the unconscious but groaning boy, 'this is the last. I think Fwances

285

is still sick,' she said to Murray. 'She a'wived sick at Amelia's.'

'There. That is all.' Murray tied the last suture. 'Miss O'Beirne,' he said, 'ran all the way to the hospital to fetch me.'

'Yes. Poor girl. And back with Amelia and me. In the heat.'

'The bandage, if you please.'

The commandant came in. Hurrying forward with his light step, he put a finger to his lips to forestall their explanations. 'Mrs Bulwer told me,' he whispered.

He and Letty watched James Murray bandage the wound, then all three withdrew and stood at a distance from the table.

'Eight sutures,' Murray told the commandant.

'He will be so pwoud,' said Letty on a laugh that turned to a sob.

The commandant put his arms about her, and she pressed her face into his jacket, and laughed and cried. He spoke to James Murray over her head. 'There is no danger?'

'Let us anticipate none.' Murray looked over his shoulder at the child. His look became a stare. 'He is of strong body.' He spoke with detachment, almost coldly. 'And in splendid health, and can count on the most loving of care.'

Letty raised her head to speak to her husband. 'My love, Fwances was so calm, and showed such good

286

sense, and managed the matter so well. But now she is sick.'

'You will look at her, Murray?'

'Well, sir, perhaps Cowper—'

'No, sir! You, if you please.'

'Sir, I should like Cowper to come in any case, to look at Robert. In wounds and such matters he is more practised than I. I wish with all my heart he had not gone to the Eagle Farm today.'

'We are well satisfied, Murray.'

Murray bowed. 'Then pray show it by following me in this. Let Cowper see Robert and Miss O'Beirne.'

'Well, he may see Robert. And my sister if you still consider it necessary after you have attended her. My dear,' said the commandant to Letty, 'go and tell Frances that Murray will attend her.'

'Mama!'

This sent them all hurrying back to Robert. Murray took him by the shoulders and pressed him gently back on the table. 'You must not sit up, Robert.'

'Mama, my leg hurts.'

'Wobert, my love—' Letty leaned over him and made her face glad—'you have had eight sutures.'

He echoed her gladness. 'Eight sutures! Oh, papa!'

'Yes, my boy. Lie still.'

'Papa, I took it like a pebble.'

Letty laughed. But the commandant frowned at this old convict boast, and Murray set his lips. 'Hush, my son,' said the commandant. 'Murray, have you something to make him sleep?'

'He will sleep in any case. Only get him to bed. Look, he is going back to sleep already.'

'I will make his bed weady. Amelia will help me. And then James and I will go to Fwances.'

After she had left the room the commandant said, 'Is there anything in this matter—' he nodded his head towards the drowsy child—'to make me put off my journey?'

'I think not, sir. But ask Cowper.'

'I will see him when he comes to attend Robert. I leave in the morning and have still a hundred things to do. Will you stay with the boy till his mother returns?'

'Gladly, sir.'

Letty had not expected to find Frances in such a strange state. She had been vomiting again, and when Letty and James Murray entered was lying as if unconscious of the mess on her chin and neck, and on the pillow and counterpane beneath her head. Then came that curious exchange between her and James Murray: no words, but a galvanic intimate anguished stare. It suggested to Letty the complicity of secret physical passion, but had yet another element that shocked Letty even as it eluded her.

She advanced quickly, so disconcerted that she hardly knew what she was saying.

'My love, all is well with Wobert . . .'

But Frances turned her head away and vomited on to the pillow again. It was so incredible that she had not even bothered to procure a basin that Letty almost could have suspected her of acting, or of indulging in some perverse whim. She said uncertainly to James Murray, 'First I shall clean her?'

'No.'

Letty saw the young man take a conscious resolve before he stepped forward and put two fingers on the pulse in Frances's wrist. Frances gave no sign of knowing that he was there. Her vomiting over, she lay unmoving, her face still averted, while Murray, his head turned in the opposite direction, seemed to muse and count and consider. Letty went to the washstand and was relieved to find the ewer full. Amelia had gone home; Robert, watched by Madge Noakes, was asleep; Lucy was in the charge of Elizabeth. The house was very quiet except for knockings and bumpings from the kitchen. Annie, sent for in this emergency, was getting ready to cook the dinner. After all, they would not have the dinner that Frances had been so delighted to order.

Murray released Frances's wrist and gave her upturned hand a professional pat. Without turning her head, she curled her fingers into the palm in a spasmodic crippled gesture. He turned abruptly away, his face showing such misery that Letty thought again of passion, and of the sloughs in that terrain. She wondered if he had come to the house during her absence at Amelia's, and if he and Frances had found themselves engaged in one of those accidental sexual encounters, had been lovers for an hour. But even as she wondered, she guessed that they had not.

Murray took her aside. 'I will send medicine.'

'It is only heat and exertion,' said Letty, searching his face with rather stern eyes, 'is it not?'

'Agitation also.' He spoke haltingly, as if divested for the moment of medical authority. 'Is Mrs Bulwer still in the house?'

'No. Why is Fwances worse now than at first?'

'She still had her mission. Her mission accomplished, she could give way to shock. It is the way with most of us.'

'Shock at Wobert's accident?'

'Why, ma'am, at what else? Shall I send for Mrs Bulwer to return?'

Although Frances's face was still averted, Letty saw that her mouth now hung slightly open. 'No,' she said. 'No.'

'But with two sickbeds—'

'Wobert is only next door. And Madge Noakes is with him.'

'She can not provide the kind of nursing either he or Miss O'Beirne needs. It will all fall to you. Send for Mrs Harbin. Miss O'Beirne is fond of Mrs Harbin.'

'I shall if needs be. But pway, leave me now to manage alone.'

'At least let Cowper see her.'

'James, are you distwessed for her?'

'Not distressed, no. But it would be as well.'

'Then Henwy may come. And in the meantime, Madge Noakes will help me clean her.'

But when Murray left, Letty did not ring the bell. She did not wish any of the servants to see her sister in this state, and nor was she willing to enlist Amelia, or even Louisa. Frances's open eyes were as passive as her open mouth, betraying no pain, no passion, no feeling of any kind. Letty no longer suspected her of acting, and had all but discounted her suspicions of James Murray. She now feared that Frances had been struck mad. And if it got about that she was subject to fits of madness, it would certainly undermine her chances of marriage to a nephew of the Annings.

She brought a basin of water and a cloth to the bedside. Frances was quiet and tractable. She turned her head when Letty told her to, and allowed herself to be made clean. Letty kept up a quiet, calm flow of talk—'And now we must do this. And now let us do that.'—as if talking to a child. Frances rolled over and let the soiled counterpane be pulled from beneath her, but when Letty said, 'And now you must lie still, while I go and fetch fwesh bed clothes,' she raised herself on an elbow and grasped her sister's hand. Letty's ministrations had had an effect; intelligence was breaking into her eyes. She said, 'It was the letter.'

'What letter?'

'Well, you see, it must have happened while I was writing to Edmund.'

'Beginning a new letter to him alweady!' exclaimed Letty with approval.

'Yes. Over there. At my desk. And I came and lay here on the bed. Not for long, but very likely for longer than I thought. I don't remember.'

'Never mind. It doesn't matter.'

'But it does. That's when it must have been done.'

'My love, no one blames you.'

'And I thought I was so vigilant.'

Letty was so relieved that she laughed aloud. Frances was not mad after all. She was suffering from heat, exertion, and pangs of conscience made worse than usual by her earnest nature. Laughing, Letty bent forward to embrace her and to assure her again that Robert's injury was in no way her fault, but at the moment of embrace she was deterred by her sister's scowling brows and resisting shoulders. She straightened herself and spoke with persuasion. 'But my love, who could blame you? Wobert is always hurting himself.'

'Robert!'

The anger and contempt with which Frances spoke her son's name was so unexpected, so unprecedented,

292

that Letty was stunned by it, and went on as if it had not happened.

'And if you must blame yourself, my dear, make amends by getting well quickly. Wobert loves you and will need you.'

But Frances, as she let herself drop back on the bed, loudly laughed.

'Robert needs nobody.'

'Fwances!'

Frances raised her voice. 'Robert needs nobody. For him, we run from all quarters.'

'Mama!'

The cry was lusty, and came from the nursery next door. Frances laughed again, but Letty, as if in perfect proof of her sister's assertion, had already reached the door. But on her way out she hesitated, and turned, and flung out a pleading hand.

'Sister, lie still. Sleep. I will soon be back. James is sending medicine for you.'

Robert had been asleep for an hour. He said he wanted to go to the Jericho, and Letty sent Madge Noakes to fetch him a bottle from the scullery. He was still sweating. Letty washed his face and dried his damp hair with a towel. A good pink colour rose to his cheeks and he cried out cheerfully that he was starving. Letty sat by his bed, and Elizabeth Robertson, smiling and munching and trundling, brought calvesfoot jelly and milk. He said he didn't want that; he wanted a piece of roasted cheese. Lucy ran in, and would have jumped on to her brother's bed had Letty not made a barrier with one arm. Lucy began to cry. She was hungry, she said, and wanted a piece of roasted cheese. Henry Cowper arrived, smelling of mint and rum, and sanctioned a piece of roasted cheese for them both. When he removed the bandage from Robert's leg, and the wound was disclosed, Lucy began to weep fiercely. Robert told her curtly to be quiet, and she ran from the room, followed by Elizabeth. It was growing dark. Henry asked for candles, and when Madge Noakes had brought them, and he was examining the wound by their light, the commandant came in.

He put one hand briefly on his son's head. 'Well, my boy.' And to Henry he said, 'What is your opinion, Cowper?'

'Murray has done well.'

'Mr Cowper, Mr Murray gave me brandy.'

'Did he indeed. Well, tonight you may have port wine.'

'Papa, I am to have port wine.'

'Yes, my son.'

'Where is my Aunt Fanny, mama?'

'In bed, my love.'

'Is it late?'

'Not vewy. She is indisposed.'

'Oh.' The boy's gaze became remote, as if he were

trying to remember something. Henry was swabbing his wound with cold water. Robert watched him for ten seconds or so, then raised his head.

'Papa, what happened to Martin?'

'He was punished, Robert.'

'The water, ma'am,' said Henry Cowper, for Letty had suddenly put the dish on the floor, out of his reach. 'Water, if you please,' he said sharply.

The commandant picked up the dish from the floor and put it into his wife's hands. 'My dear,' he said, 'Mrs Bulwer will be happy to help you, and Mrs Harbin too. I have their assurances on it.'

She did not look at him. 'I need no one.'

'You are tired.'

'For the moment I pwefer to manage.'

But the water in the dish was slopping at the sides. 'I will hold the dish,' said Madge Noakes, 'if the candle will do on the table.'

'Nobody need hold it,' said Henry. 'I have finished with it.'

Letty set the dish on the floor. 'Henwy, did James give you the medicine for Miss O'Beirne?'

'In my bag.' Henry began to put a fresh bandage on Robert's leg. 'In the small blue bottle.'

Letty, in a hurry, rose and shook out her skirts. 'I will take it to her at once. Pway attend her when you have finished here.'

*

The wind blowing down the kitchen chimney had enveloped Annie in smoke as she stood lunging with a poker as if trying to stab the fire to death. Letty found a tray. She set it with a glass, a spoon, the medicine, and a lighted candle, and set out for Frances's room. As she passed the nursery she saw her husband and Henry Cowper, standing one at each side of Robert's bed, while Robert, his eyes passing from one to the other, drank port wine.

Expecting to find the disorder she had left, Letty was surprised to find both Frances and the room clean and neat. The soiled linen had been removed and the bed freshly made and covered with a fresh linen counterpane. The ewer stood in its basin on the wash-stand, and clean folded towels hung on both rails; and although the smell of vomit was still present, the window had been thrown open and a warm breeze was flushing the room.

Letty had spent only about twenty minutes with Robert in the nursery. She knew that Madge and Eliza-beth had been busy for all that time, and Annie, very audibly, had been in the kitchen. So Frances must herself have carried off the dirty linen and gone to the cupboard for fresh, must have emptied and washed the basin and filled the ewer with water drawn from the casks, must have made the bed, washed herself, brushed and tied back her hair, and dressed in clean clothes. But the energy needed to do all this had failed her, Letty guessed, when the light faded. She now sat on the bed steps, her feet drawn up on the bottom rung, an elbow on a knee, and one hand supporting her chin. In the other she loosely held one of her wide blue sashes. It was as if she had been struck into impassivity at the moment of picking it up.

She was very quiet; she gave Letty a smile but did not move. Letty came forward with her tray.

'Henwy bwought you this medicine. He will attend you in a few minutes. All seems well with Wobert.'

Frances smiled again. 'I am glad. I did not mean to laugh at him.'

'I know. Will you take the medicine?'

'It was not at him I was laughing.'

'Will you take the medicine now?'

'Of course.'

Letty carried the tray to Frances's open desk and set it down. Here she found a small exception to the order of the room: two sheets of paper had been torn together from a letter book, and then torn four times across. Letty read phrases.

'. . . *live in peace and fidelity* . . .'

'. . . *abate my former immoderate* . . .'

'. . . *hope your dear aunt and uncle may find me* . . .'

On one of the pieces of paper lay a scrap of red pulp, about the size of a grain of corn. The paper beneath it was stained a weak pink. The stem of the lily still stood in the vase, but supported an empty calyx.

Frances took the medicine at a draft, not seeming to notice its bitterness. She handed the glass back to Letty, spread her sash across both her knees, and looked at it as if considering its weave and colour. Letty, holding the glass, looked down at her sister's glossy brown hair, which was drawn back tight and tied at the nape of her neck with an old narrow brown ribbon. 'When you went to fetch James,' asked Letty, 'where did you find him?'

Frances did not look up. 'At the hospital.'

'In the office?'

Frances shook her head. Letty, feeling her altitude a disadvantage, dropped to one knee. Frances was smoothing the sash upon her lap. Letty put a hand on one of hers.

'I think you saw Martin.'

'Yes, I did.' Frances's voice was uninflected. She took the glass out of Letty's hand, drained it of the remaining drop or two, and handed it back. 'Yes, I did see him,' she said.

'He had been punished?'

'Yes, punished.' She spoke in the same uninflected voice. 'Yes, he had been flogged.'

'But,' said Letty, 'you knew.'

'Yes.'

'Knew it likely today. And have always known that—that thing—happened. We spoke of it the day after you came.'

'Yes.'

'It has never been kept secwet.'

'Yes.'

'I don't take your meaning.' Letty was disturbed as well as puzzled by this inconsequent affirmative. Frances made no reply. Her head was bowed over the sash lying across her knees. The breeze stirring one of its loose ends also stirred her hair and the muslin flounces of her skirt. Letty lowered herself into a sitting position on the floor. She was still holding the empty glass. 'I don't take your meaning,' she said again. She wished she could drop the subject, and persisted against her own exhaustion and hovering dread. 'You say first it is known, was known, and yet you say now it has been kept secwet.'

'We knew it in words, yet kept it secret. The words we used in speaking of it were the words that kept it secret. And then we kept it secret in the way we behaved, in our manners and our dress and our pastimes. I don't exactly see what else we could have done. It is very hard to live in their proximity. And in saying this I don't speak of him. He does not keep it secret.'

Letty, comprehending at once that 'he' was her husband, could not help sounding a note of eager commendation.

'Well, there you are! He never has.'

'Oh, but it doesn't excuse him.' Frances raised her

head and looked straight into Letty's eyes. 'In secrecy,' she said, 'in avoidance, at least there is shame.'

The need to escape Frances's eyes made Letty struggle to her feet with uncharacteristic clumsiness. 'I am sure I don't understand you,' she murmured, looking distractedly about for somewhere to set down the glass. 'I am sure your bluestocking talk is too much for my poor bwain.'

'You know it is not.'

When they heard a knock at the door, Frances took no notice, but Letty, eager for the ease of a third presence, first hurried to open it, then hesitated for fear it should be her husband. But as she hesitated, the door opened a few inches, and she heard Henry Cowper's voice.

'May I come in?'

'Come in, Henwy. Do come in.'

She saw that he looked wearier than usual, though his manner was much the same as always—off-hand, affable, his bow slightly sarcastic—until he turned to Frances. Frances had not moved except to coil inwards, it seemed to Letty, so that she sat more crouched, or hunched, on the small set of steps. Only her gaze moved outward, flaring into Henry's face with the same galvanic intimacy she had shown to James Murray.

Henry, like Murray, returned it in kind, but unlike Murray, who had appeared unable to disengage his eyes, he returned it for only a moment. The moment was long enough for Letty to understand that what her sister shared with these two men was nothing so innocent as sexual passion. Theirs was a complicity of incurable knowledge. She found it no less shocking for having defined it. It was a relief to see Henry master it. He mastered it by laughing, by advancing on Frances and saying in a sing-song voice, 'Come now, Miss O'Beirne, what is all this? What is all this fuss and bother?'

Though partly recovered from a difficult day, Henry was still feeling rather tired and testy. He had drunk too much at the Eagle Farm and had been too much bored by Scottowe Parker's complaints. Parker was lonely; he felt ousted. Murray, he said, was so much occupied on his visits that he had no time for conversation, and when Parker was able to go in to the settlement, which, heaven knew, was seldom enough, everybody was so busy that they had no time for him. His isolation and danger were not appreciated. He was forced to carry a big stick for self-protection. He showed Henry the stick, and although he confessed that he had not yet beaten anyone off with it, he said the time would come. Perhaps, he added with gloomy sagacity, it would come for them all.

On his way home Henry had gone to sleep and fallen off Murray's horse. The horse had walked away and he had had to go after it. But as soon as he drew near it trotted away. It played games with him, teasing him, letting him almost catch it and then moving out of reach and trotting around in circles. He cursed it. 'You horse! Fiend from Tartarus! Mistake of Poseidon!' The appellations were ridiculous for such a nag. He began to laugh, but was still angry. Here he was, Henry Cowper, who had once thought to become the richest surgeon-merchant in Batavia, who had meant to loll in a palace—a pavilion, Nobby Clark said it would be—and be waited upon by twenty frisky but docile young wives, yes, here was that same Henry Cowper, dodging around a clayey little clearing, among stunted twisted bushes of an unknown genus, sweating, sick in his stomach and rotten in his mouth, playing games with a skittish old nag. In repudiation of the image, he had dashed at the horse and vaulted on to his back, taking both the horse and himself by surprise.

For a moment he was Buck Cowper again. It was the most adroit and energetic movement he had made for years. But what was that violent rasp across his chest? What was that gong in his temples? And that airy expansion of his cranium? 'But I am only thirty,' argued Henry with indignation. The horse, the fiend from Tartarus, the mistake of Poseidon, was moving meekly on. But Henry's bridle hand shook, and in the other (set stylishly on a thigh) a nerve came alive and passed up his arm and made his elbow jerk. 'One more caper like that,' said Henry in amazement to himself, 'and I'm a done dog.' Yet he hoped he exaggerated.

Immediately on his arrival at the settlement he had been met by Murray with the story of Robert's injury, and of how Frances O'Beirne had burst in upon him when he was about to treat Martin's back. The latter event had filled Henry with fury. He had been drinking a pannikin of water and had almost dashed it in Murray's face. 'God's teeth! Why didn't you stop her?'

'But she *burst—*'

'Oh, burst, burst, burst. Well, damnation to you, what am I to do?'

'See her. She is in a curious state.'

'So am I. I am in no state to encounter a radical virgin.'

'Could it have driven her out of her wits?'

'It has evidently driven you out of yours. And in revenge you are trying to drive me out of mine.'

But in fact Henry was already feeling better. He gave several of his roaring groans, attracting the attention of the orderlies and the giggles of the cleaning gang. He drank a small glass of rum, washed his face and hands, and went to the commandant's house. Here he was further restored by their need of him, and the need on his own part for professional concentration. He reminded himself that in thirty minutes he would be back in his quarters. He foresaw

303

his hand grasping the neck of the bottle. He would sleep tonight, and live another day. But when Letty put the basin of water on the floor, he spoke sharply. 'The water, if you please.'

The port wine made Robert tipsy instead of drowsy. 'Hush, son,' the commandant kept saying. 'I will stay with him until he sleeps,' he said to Henry. 'Pray attend Miss O'Beirne. Mrs Logan is with her.'

Henry turned down his cuffs. He felt some trepidation, but intended to waste no time. He would be brisk; he would stand for no ridiculous sensibility or nervous nonsense.

But Frances's stare unnerved him. Such a jolt it sent through his chest and his pulses, it was like an echo of his physical shock after his vault to the back of the horse. But its agony was of another kind. It was an old agony; Henry had learned to bear it; he was calloused to it. And there was besides something ludicrous about this big young woman sitting crouched on the little bed steps, with her hair pulled back from a face that looked too old again, as it had done on the *Regent Bird*. And Mrs Logan, who could usually be depended upon to pout and charm, looked hardly less stark than her sister. She stood at a loss, a medicine glass in her hand, silently beseeching him for God knew what. Henry burst into his laugh and went forward.

'Come now, Miss O'Beirne, what is all this? What is all this fuss and bother?'

Mrs Logan relaxed. She went quickly to the desk and set down the medicine glass. Frances did not move. Henry halted before her.

'Has the medicine settled your stomach?'

'Yes.'

'And otherwise?'

'I am well. I wish I were not. I wish to be dead.'

'Well, so you will be, in fifty years or more or less.' Henry avoided heartiness, but spoke with the coarseness so often imputed to him. 'I am sorry you saw a flogged back. But the world sees thousands such every day. The young man will recover.'

'I don't enquire after him. I don't presume to enquire.'

'You are too scrupulous, Miss O'Beirne.'

'To bring him to that, and then to enquire after him. No, it would be to insult him.'

'Yours is a sickly tenderness.'

Frances gave a listless shrug, as if to say, if that were so, she could not help it.

'Sickly and finicky, dwelling on itself rather than its object.'

He spoke at random, with an anger he did not intend. Frances shrugged again, but her sister, giving Henry a grateful yet warning look across Frances's head, advanced on her from behind. She would have taken her by the shoulders, Henry thought, would have bent to her ear and added her voice to Henry's

305

argument, had she not been diverted by the entrance of the commandant.

Frances sprang to her feet in one movement like a rope flicked straight. A strong colour rose to her face. She was immediately blazing, accusatory. Anyone but the commandant would have seen it. But he was in one of his abstracted moods, and slightly irritable also. He spoke above her head to his wife.

'My dear, go to Robert. I make him only more restive. He is asking for you. And I can ill spare the time besides.'

Letty went at once.

'Sir!' said Frances.

Henry wondered if the commandant mistook that quiver of rage for timidity, and if in his glance at her he mistook her stiff accusatory stance for some kind of deference. He bowed pleasantly. 'One moment, sister.' He turned to Henry.

'Cowper, is my son's injury serious enough to warrant the delay of my expedition? Murray thinks not, but refers me to you.'

'Putrefaction is the danger,' said Henry. From the tail of his eye he saw that Frances's colour had not receded and that her breath was fast and shallow. 'If there are signs of putrefaction in the morning I will let you know. There are none now.'

'And the boy is strong,' said the commandant in a ringing and reassured voice. He clicked a finger and thumb together and turned with his peculiar sudden radiance to Frances.

'Sister, I thank you for your promptness and coolness.'

'Sir—'

'You and I have had differences. Let us have no more. Let us rest in the knowledge that in important issues we are not at variance. You have been indisposed. I am happy to see you well again.'

'Sir, when I went to the hospital, I saw Martin.'

'Did you indeed? I would not have had that happen. Such sights are not for women. Poor girl. Now I understand your sickness. I have seen it happen even to men. Even to young soldiers. The hospital of course is out of bounds. But on this occasion your trespass is excusable. I beg your pardon—' he bowed—'commendable. It is commendable. And I know you will not go again. By the by, my dear, I allowed myself to be persuaded— no, not persuaded, but swayed—yes, I allowed myself to be swayed by the intercession of your sister. Martin had only a hundred.'

Henry had seen wind go out of sails before. He had often felt the wind go out of his own, cut off by the commandant's rigidity as effectively as by a towering cliff or by dense dying trees crowding a bank. The commandant may have mistaken the inclination of Frances's head for thanks ('Thank you for giving Martin only a hundred.') but Henry knew it for defeat.

307

How often had he himself made that slow obeisance? It shaded into a bow as she sat down again on the bedsteps. She folded her hands and turned on her brother-in-law a long wondering look. She was accepting defeat with incredulity but without complaint, her will paralysed by the commandant's obliviousness.

It was at this point in his own exchanges with Logan that Henry usually laughed. Frances did not laugh. When at last she withdrew her gaze she sank; she coiled inwards again; Henry could see her incredulity give way to hopelessness.

But he also saw that the commandant was now giving her a sharper attention, and he was suddenly reminded of another occasion when they had stood side by side and confronted a similarly passive presence. He had swung his keys and said, 'He will die.' The black man had been sitting on the floor. Perhaps the black man had also said, in his own way, 'I wish to be dead.' To be sure, the statement would be necessary to the operation, whether made in words or not.

The commandant put a hand on Henry's shoulder and walked him to the window. He bent to his ear. 'She is still indisposed.'

'Oh, she is.'

'It is a plaguey nuisance. Robert is used to her. She is needed to help with him. Cowper, persuade my wife to call upon Mrs Bulwer or Mrs Harbin. They are better than nothing.'

308

'. . . *not* to disturb Mrs Logan,' said Amelia's voice in the corridor.

'Sir,' said Henry, 'you have a genie in your pocket.'

Madge Noakes appeared in the doorway. 'Mrs Bulwer. Mrs Harbin. For Miss Frances.'

'Do we interrupt?' cried Amelia.

'No, my dear ladies,' replied Logan in a delighted voice. 'But I will leave you. I must go to my wife. My wife,' he repeated, bowing sideways as he walked quickly towards the door.

'We would not for the world incommode Letty,' Amelia told him.

'You don't, you don't,' said the commandant, going through the door.

'And how is our brave girl?' asked Amelia.

Frances gave a little headshake. Louisa took off her bonnet with both hands and spoke to Henry.

'Strange, in a place so small, I have not seen you at close quarters for weeks. Why are you sober? Have you lost your watch? I have brought one of the London journals for Frances. Frances, my dear girl, it will do you no good to huddle there. You will be easier in a chair. Or do you feel too weak to stand?'

'No,' said Frances, rising to her feet.

'Then take this chair. Amelia, 'bring up the foot-stool for her feet. Henry, how is Robert?'

'Young and strong and doing well. Where are your six red snails?'

'Gone!' said Louisa in tragic tones.

'For ever?'

'For ever! Frances, in this journal they say your precious whigs may soon form a government.'

'Do they?' asked Frances with indifference.

'Oh, they will write anything,' said Amelia in dismissal. 'Anything!'

'Why should they not form a government, Amelia, if they can form a strong one?'

'Oh, Louisa, Louisa!'

'No, upon my word, the only tolerable government is one so strong that its power is secure. Then its adherents can take their ease, and stop being angry and solemn.'

'They seldom stop being solemn,' said Henry.

'But at least it gives them that option.'

'Does this mean,' asked Henry, 'that if a whig government came to power, you would approve it?'

'With all my heart, if it were strong enough.'

Amelia gave a sigh. 'Louisa is such an original.'

Henry laughed. 'Ladies . . .' he said, bowing. As he crossed to the door he saw Frances sit upright and pass the sash round her waist. She would not die simply by wishing to. She was a European, and if she wished to die would have to employ their crude and violent methods. Otherwise, no matter how genuine her wish, something would cajole her back into life. She would read a poem that matched her sadness, she would catch at an idea, be amused by a joke, respond to the admiration of a man, or even, thought Henry (who did not really care for women under thirty), only be charmed by a dress.

While leaving the room and shutting the door he could hear Mrs Logan speaking in the nursery, and as he approached down the dark corridor her words became audible.

'. . . no longer pwesenting her argument in speeches, but in her bodily state. A gween girl, you say! But are all who expwess their disgust gween girls? I have taken my thoughts in these matters from you. My love, have you misguided me all this while?'

Henry had never heard her so anguished, so recklessly loud. It startled him into looking into the nursery as he passed. But he could not see her. The commandant stood with his back blocking the partly opened doorway, and beyond that dark solid back, rimmed by candlelight, Henry could see only, on the opposite side of the room, the fair, sleeping child.

PART THREE

CHAPTER TWELVE

A fast pace was so unnatural to Captain Clunie that
when forced to hurry he bounced and jerked and
became anxious-eyed. On this Saturday afternoon in
late October, bouncing and jerking and rotating his
elbows too high, he was hurrying along the rutted
road towards his weatherboard cottage. He had
been walking at his own deliberate pace from the
brick kilns when he had seen the boat coming down
the river, with the two men rowing and the sleeping
soldier lying in the bilge. On Thursday the same boat
had brought a letter from Sergeant Baker at the Limestone Station.

The commandant having failed in his purpose,
Baker had written, he had begun to bring the expedition back to the Limestone Station when he decided to
ride away alone to look for the horse lost in May. He

told Collison to go on, and to make camp at a certain spot, and to wait there until he joined them.

'*But when he did not come up to that place,*' concluded Sergeant Baker, '*Collison and the others returned to this station, in the hope that he had come here direct. Not finding him here, Collison and five men went out this day to search. Blacks have been seen in the area.*'

To prevent rumour from unsettling the prisoners, and to prevent it from reaching Mrs Logan (already in distress about her son's poisoned leg), Clunie had had the messengers fed in his presence, and after questioning them had told them to take advantage of the tide and row back to the Limestone Station at once.

But now, here was the boat again. He saw one of the men wake the soldier while the other made the boat fast. The soldier sat up; it was Collison. He stepped on shore, where he shook and straightened himself into some kind of precision; but it was apparent, in the clear light of first dusk, that he was still groggy with fatigue, and Clunie was greatly relieved when he proved sufficiently awake to take the path, not towards the commandant's house, but towards the weather-board cottage. When Clunie saw him knock he reduced his pace, but all the same he was red-faced and out of breath by the time he himself reached the cottage.

Collison was waiting in the office. He had been trying to grind his tiredness away with his fists, for his watering, blinking eyes were surrounded by dusty marks. Where he was not dusty he was muddy; he looked ten years older than his twenty-five years. Clunie sat down. 'Sit down, Collison. What news? Is he found?'

'No, sir. But we came upon his traces. We went thirty miles, more than thirty—'

His voice was light and wandering. 'Stop,' said Clunie. 'Collect yourself. Be clear. Who went thirty miles?'

'Why, sir, the search party.' Collison seemed glad to be pulled up and set right. 'Myself, Private Hardacre, four prisoners. We left the Limestone early Thursday. Light baggage and no bullocks. And went in the direction we last seen him take. As he crossed the ford and rode towards Mount Irwin, that was our last sight of him. It was late when we come upon the traces, at the same place the horse was lost the other time. A clearing about as big as the lumber yard, sir. You could see a circle of cropped grass where the mare had been tethered overnight, and the marks at the creek where he had watered her. And there,' said Collison, pointing to Clunie's desk, 'in a tree stump, was the ashes of a fire. And there—' he pointed to the farthest corner of the room—'was his saddle, on the ground, the stirrup leathers cut and the irons gone. And then you could see his footsteps, sir, with long strides, where he had rushed from the fire and mounted the mare.'

Sergeant Baker's note had prepared Clunie for anything. He spoke briskly. 'Any tracks leading away?'

'Sir, too many to distinguish.'

'You searched the area?'

'It was soon too dark, sir.' Collison glanced at the window. 'It was about this time of day.'

'You camped there?'

'Not *there*, sir, you may be sure. But thereabouts, taking turns to watch.'

'And you searched next day?'

'For an hour, sir.'

Clunie raised his brows.

'It being hard to hold the prisoners to the search,' said Collison in apology.

Clunie was silent.

'It sounds like dead silence out there, sir, till you set yourself to listen. They were afraid.'

'So you searched for an hour and then went back to the Limestone Station?'

'Thinking he might have reached there, sir. Hardacre took another search party out today.'

'Very well, Collison.' Clunie rose to his feet. 'Go to barracks. Eat, get an hour's sleep, then report back here to me. I can't stay to get your full story now. The boatmen will talk, and I am fearful of this news reaching Mrs Logan by any other than myself. But in an hour or so I must have the entire story. We will need it to prime the search party that will go out from here. Unless we hear in the meantime that Hardacre has found him, the party will leave at first light. You will go with them.'

'And would want to, sir. And indeed,' said Collison, with a touch of indignation, 'if they had been real men with me, I would have stayed, and beat every bush. I never complained of him, nor called him hard, except sometimes, when it was up to him to call a halt, and him not needing it, no more do we. But perhaps we don't neither, for we endure it, seeing him do so.'

Collison's voice was flagging again; he seemed to be losing the sense of his own words. 'Well, go along, Collison,' said Clunie in kinder tones, 'go and get that rest.'

As Clunie left the house the evening bell began to toll, filling him again with a sense of urgency. But he forced himself to walk at a normal pace, lest he send alarm before him. As he went he looked sideways, with calculation, across the river to the other bank. The light was no longer good, but he could still see the movement of the pale waving grass, the darkness of the clumps of eucalypts, and the muddy gloss of the cleared space at the landing stage. At about this time on Monday a group working on the boats said they had seen the commandant standing in that space, with the grey mare beside him. He had made a signal, they said, and they had run to board the barge to go over for him. But before they reached the barge, one looked again, and saw he had gone.

Clunie had been too busy to pay much attention to this report. The *Isabella* had arrived, bringing sixty-six beasts. She was not built to carry so many; eighteen were dead on arrival. There were no horses. 'I wish it were truly a mare they saw,' he had remarked to Peter Spicer.

'What was it, d'you suppose?'

'Nothing, nothing.'

Clunie had reached the cottage Murray shared with Hansord. He knocked at the door. It was opened almost at once by Murray himself.

'I saw Collison arrive,' said Murray in a low voice.

'He hasn't been found,' said Clunie. 'I am going to Mrs Logan. You had better come with me.'

Murray fell into step at his side. Edwards and Murray were the only two Clunie had taken into his confidence when Sergeant Baker's note had arrived. Now he said, 'I wish I were confident of having done the right thing. When you told me the boy was worse I thought it better to keep her in ignorance. But these two days I've been of divided mind. Should I warn her? Should I not? Well, now I must. Thank God the boy is better today. The commandant went off alone and slept in the bush with the mare tethered nearby. In the morning he was roasting chestnuts when he was surprised. He escaped on the mare.'

'Surprised? By blacks? By runaways?'

'Collison doesn't know.'

'Baker's note spoke of blacks.'

'It did. And the men who brought it said that stones had been thrown at the party by two hundred blacks. They said the men of the expedition told them so. So you see, it came to me at third hand. And of course I don't believe it. Two hundred blacks indeed! In that case, would he have gone off alone? But no matter, no matter—these contradictions can be reconciled later. The present urgency is to tell Mrs Logan. Every prisoner on the settlement will be talking of it soon.'

'They have been muttering of his death ever since they saw him across the river.'

'Since they fancied they saw him.'

'Could it have been him, after all?'

'No, Murray, it could not.'

'They said the mare was with him. Collison says he escaped on her. Could he have made his way back?'

'No, Murray, he could not. Or why would he run off again?'

'Why,' said Murray hesitantly, 'only in a fit of madness.'

'Murray—'

'He has been under strain,' said the young man quickly, 'and is subject to melancholy.'

'Murray,' said Clunie, 'at present, it is better to suppose nothing. Nothing.'

But Murray persisted. 'Sir, it was on Monday they saw him. Three days before Baker's message reached the settlement. Would they have made it up from the whole cloth? I am convinced they saw something.'

'Very well, Murray. His ghost.'

'Sir, that is exactly what they are saying. They say that Boylan killed him, and his ghost has come back to haunt the settlement.'

Clunie heard again the commandant morosely saying, 'They are great ghost seers, you will find.' He was angry with himself for speaking of a ghost to Murray, and angry with Murray for not taking up the scornful intonation of his remark. 'Did they say the mare was saddled?' he asked.

'They didn't say she was not. So one assumes—'

'Quite. But the saddle lies where he slept. Or did the ghost of the saddle have the kindness to rise and fly to the ghost of the mare?'

But Murray was now looking alarmed. 'Then he leapt on her bare-backed?'

'Yes, Murray, he did.'

'Oh,' said Murray. They had reached the commandant's gate. He paused with a hand on the latch. 'Oh,' he said softly again. 'Poor lady!'

Clunie was about to protest, to say that they must not yet assume Mrs Logan to be pitiable, when he heard someone running up the garden path towards them. In the next second Big Annie appeared, running up the short flight of steps cut into the bank. Her knees paddling into her kilted skirts gave the effect of a vigorous rustic dance, her eyes were shocked and eager, her lips intensely whispering. Clunie, in the mood to expect a messenger of disaster, was amused to see only this poor creature on her way home from her work, rehearsing her thrilling news lest she forget its detail, and running lest someone should tell it in the female factory before her.

'Here is one who knows,' he said quietly to Murray.

She gave a cry when she saw them, and fell back in such a dramatic and despairing manner that Clunie almost laughed aloud. As she jumped to one side and bobbed low, a potato fell from the bundle under her arm and trundled off among the bushes. Clunie heard her scuffling to retrieve it as Murray and he continued on their way. 'I hope they have not told Mrs Logan,' he said.

'Have no thought of it,' said Murray. 'All three have been most tender with her, because of the child.'

Murray was right; it was apparent at once to Clunie that Letty was still in ignorance. They found her in the drawing room, with her sister and both her children. The women sat in chairs, Robert lay on the blue sofa, and Lucy played on the floor beside him. All except the little girl looked tired, pale, and peaceful: Robert was out of danger; the incessant work with the compresses, and the long close vigils, were over at last. 'Wobert,' said Letty softly to her son, 'here are Captain Clunie and Mr Mu'wy, kindly come to enquire after you.'

'Thank you, sirs,' said Robert. 'I am out of danger.'

'Robert is not to die,' said Lucy boastfully.

'I will die one day,' said Robert. He was handling a little Chinese box, sliding its lids, one by one, to reveal its many compartments. 'But not for many years,' he said.

'Not for a hundred years,' said Lucy.

'Oh, before then.' But he looked from Clunie and Murray to his mother, from his mother to his aunt. 'Before then?'

'Who knows?' said his mother with a laugh.

'One is always hearing of old men who claim to be a hundred and six,' said Frances. 'But now I think Mr Murray wants to look at your leg.'

Lucy jumped up. 'I will hold the box.'

'I will hold it myself.'

'Let me!'

'No!'

'You see,' said Letty to Clunie, 'how well he is?' She turned to her son. 'Wobert, let Lucy hold the box.'

Robert thrust the box in silence at his sister, who grasped it eagerly and began at once to open its compartments. 'We are allowed to play with it because

Robert was to die. Or else Mr Cowper was to take off his leg. And we are allowed to play in this room, too, and to eat cucumber.'

Frances had knelt by the sofa and was taking the bandage from Robert's leg, while Murray stood and waited. Clunie bent to Letty's ear. 'A word with you, ma'am.'

As she rose he could see nothing in her eyes but courteous enquiry. He questioned again his wisdom in keeping her ignorant for so long, and to make a bridge for his news he said as they crossed the room, 'What I have to say touches you closely. It concerns Captain Logan.'

She halted abruptly and faced him. She was silent, but her eyes asked the question. 'What is it? What has happened?' And, as if it really had been asked aloud, the four at the blue sofa all raised their heads and looked at Clunie as if also awaiting his answer. Bowing, he put a hand beneath Letty's elbow. He turned her about, and as he guided her towards the french doors he bent to her ear again.

'My dear lady, he is missing.'

She halted again, but then in obedience to the pressure of his hand went forward as if in a dream. They went through the doors and stood on the verandah. She put one hand on the rail and looked across the river as he told her the story. The wind that always blew from the river buffeted her short curls and moved them this way and that, and occasionally she raised a hand as if by touching them she could keep them still. She said nothing until he told her of the saddle on the ground, and the severed stirrup leathers. Then she asked, 'Were they cut clean, sir, or hacked?'

He thought it a strange irrelevant question, but in the next second was startled by its cool relevance. 'I don't know,' he said soberly. 'I will ask Collison.' To break her husband's plight to her gradually, he had left the part about the saddle and stirrup irons until last. 'I have told you all I know. I will speak to Collison and visit you again tomorrow. A search party goes out at daybreak.'

She nodded. 'Sergeant Baker's note mentioned blacks. Did he say how many?'

'No.' He hesitated. 'Why do you ask?'

'Wobert told me he heard the women speaking by his bed. They spoke of hundweds of blacks hurling stones at his father.'

Clunie drew a deep breath. 'Well,' he said with control, 'either the women were passing on some wild rumour, or the child was in fever.'

'In fever. Pwecisely! I discounted it on that score. Another day he saw his Aunt Cassandwa.'

'Well, there you are! And we may discount it on the score of reason besides. If there had been hundreds of hostile blacks about, Captain Logan would not have gone off alone.'

326

There was only the slightest pause, but Clunie had the sense of a hitch, a caught breath. But then: 'Pwecisely!' she said again.

'Hardacre's party may have found him already. Let us proceed one step at a time. A message from the Limestone Station is our present hope.'

'Of course.' But she put both hands to her hair as if suddenly distracted by the wind. 'Oh, sir, let us go in.'

'Robert has broken the box,' shouted Lucy, as soon as they returned to the room.

'I have not,' said Robert. His leg was bandaged again, the Chinese box in his hands. 'I have only taken one of the little lids out. See, mama?'

Letty bent over him. 'Yes, yes, I see.'

He was looking into her face. 'Is my father dead?' he asked quietly.

Murray moved quickly forward, but she checked him by a slight movement of one hand. 'Wobert, why do you ask that?'

Now he looked frightened. 'I should not have asked it.'

'Dear little boy, I am not angwy. Tell me why.'

'I heard the women speaking by my bed. I am sure I did. No, I am not sure. But I thought I heard them say that his ghost stood on the river bank, beside Fatima, and that he signalled for the barge, and then faded away.'

'Papa is dead!' cried Lucy. Her mouth became a

wet red oblong and the big hot tears rolled out of her eyes as they moved in terror from face to face. Frances rose from her chair, but Letty, who was nearer, reached the little girl first. She gathered her into her arms and fell with her into a chair, holding her fast and rocking her, her eyes stern and staring, as if she commiserated in the child's emotion but would not deny it. Clunie, after one helpless moment, mouthed at Murray to stay, then signalled to Frances to follow him out of the room.

In the corridor he said to her, 'Your brother is missing.' He told her the story as he had told it to Letty, but with less sympathy, and indeed in rather an angry tone. The whole settlement had heard about her hysteria. Clunie considered that poor Martin, now in a gang, had been punished for her stupidity as much as for his own, and wondered that she had not had enough womanly sympathy even to enquire after him. The incident had made her fall again to her first low place in his esteem, and although she had redeemed herself partly by her untiring work during Robert's illness, he was still wary of her. She was inconveniently intense and had been brought up badly. 'And above all,' he said crossly in conclusion, 'let us have no encouragement for ghosts. If you have any steadiness, Miss O'Beirne, employ it now.'

She was quick to take the rebuke, and so quick to blush for it that he regretted it. 'I am sorry, Miss O'Beirne. You have shown yourself steady this

328

past week. Continue to do so. Scotch that ghost story if you can. Why is everybody so ready to believe in ghosts? I can't make it out.'

'I am not one who is ready to believe in them,' she said. 'At least don't think that of me. If a man and a horse were really seen standing there, let us not draw the worst conclusion, let us rather draw the best. He was dismounted from Fatima, let us say, and began making his way back to the Limestone Station on foot. He missed his way, and is now lost and wandering. And while he wanders, a runaway finds the mare and brings her in, hoping to gain a remission by his action. But at the last moment he loses confidence, and runs off again.'

He could only stare. 'Why, that's quite possible.'

She lowered her eyes. 'Barely possible. I shall advance it as possible enough to scotch the ghost story, but not as possible enough to raise hopes for his safe return.'

'Well,' he said, 'well, I see I can leave it to you.'

It was not until he had let himself out, and was walking through the garden, that his wariness of her returned.

'Too much imagination,' he grumpily told himself, 'and too much logic besides. They must be at war in her. I don't like that. A woman should be peaceful.'

Frances found herself unable to return at once to the drawing room, unable yet to advance with cheerful and unfaithful words upon her sister rocking the little girl, upon Murray watching them with his woeful eyes, and upon Robert as he quietly and reflectively opened compartment after compartment of the Chinese box. Henry Cowper had been right in believing that she would find a way back into life, but wrong in believing that it would or could be anything so trivial as a dress. Indeed her disgust and self-disgust had been so violent, and her wish to die so strong, that only Robert's danger had drawn her back. Pressed into helping Letty to nurse him, she had consented because to refuse would be to make too much fuss. But soon after she had taken her place by his bed, she had found herself leaning forward to tend him in an attitude she recognised as like her mother's when she herself had lain ill of the smallpox. Again and again this occurred, her recognitions of the moments becoming so swift and overpowering that she would fleetingly believe herself to have become that dead woman. Letty nursed Robert by day and she by night, both relieved when necessary by the servants, and in those long nights the memory of her own illness had returned with magical clarity. Like *this* her mother had held water to her lips, like *this* had bent to the candlelight. She came to believe that her mother had left some residue dormant in her which had now awakened and was directing her. The link consoled and quietened her. Her fondness for Robert turned into love. If he had had some dangerous contagion she would have been as unfaltering in the face of it as her mother had been when facing the smallpox she had caught, and of which she had died. In the strength of Frances's demand that Robert should live at all costs, she found a renewal of her own wish to live. But since his recovery she had found that if her wish to live could revive, so could her self-disgust. Her self-disgust, it seemed, was always able to renew itself at the fount of her own nature. When she had heard Lucy cry that her father was dead, one cool plain word had formed in her mind. 'Good.' And now she leaned her forehead against the wall and whispered, 'Dear God, forgive me and grant me thy grace.'

Since taking to prayer at unofficial moments she had at first been inclined to pray by paraphrasing the words of Bridie and Meg at home when they prayed to their Mary. 'Dear sweet God,' she would say. 'Darling little Jesus.' When these words did not make her prayers work she had reverted to the calmer address of the established church. They did not make her prayers work either, but she continued in them because they were what she had been taught, and because she could think of nothing else to do. They had not yet affected what she now thought of as the evil in her nature. They did not bring her peace. Their only obvious effect was an outward composure; she accepted it with gratitude.

When she entered the drawing room again she found that calmness, or its simulation, had also returned here. Lucy had been given the Chinese box and was sitting on the floor sliding back its lids with absorption and satisfaction. Robert lay with his hands beneath his head and his eyes shut. Letty, by the window, was talking to Murray.

As soon as Frances heard her sister's high firm voice, she knew that she had decided that since the wait for confirmation or denial might be a long one, she must collect her forces, and hold herself in control, and busy herself with her duties.

'James is telling me about the compwesses,' she said to Frances.

'They may not be stopped entirely, Miss O'Beirne, but reduced to four a day.'

'As you say, Mr Murray.'

She did not look at Murray as she spoke. Robert's danger had brought them together in daily speech, but though she contrived to address him in the tones of their former pleasant friendship, she could never look into his face as she did so. She found a sort of comedy in the thought that an onlooker new to the scene may have taken her attitude to him for coyness. 'Oh, to get away from this place!' she cried in her heart.

'It is a gweat thing that he is better,' Letty was saying. For Fwances and I may now start to pack.' She looked about the room and threw up both hands. 'But gwacious! Where to begin!'

*

332

Clunie was so surprised that he took off his spectacles, sat back in his chair, and stared at Collison across the table. 'Are you quite sure of that?'

'Yes, sir.' On the table between them was Clunie's unfinished dinner: a plate of pork chops pushed to one side, a dish of cheese, a bottle of port and a glass. In the centre of the table, between two candles, was one of Logan's maps. Collison put a forefinger on the long wavering line which Logan, while tracing it with his pen, must have seen in his mind's eye as the river itself. Collison's forefinger indicated a sharp bend close to the tiny circle against which Logan had written, 'First Camp'. 'It was here,' said Collison. 'As we came up to the ford, here was this hill. At least two hundred of them. They covered the hill. We had struck camp an hour before. He was in advance, but when they roll the stones down, he falls back and waits for us to come up.'

Clunie spoke half to himself. 'Good God.' Too much was happening at once. He had hardly arrived home from his interview with Mrs Logan before Lieutenant Edwards had come to tell him of a signal received from the *Alligator*. He warned himself against fragmentation of his attention. The *Alligator* must wait. He put on his spectacles and leaned forward.

'Did he fire to disperse them?'

'No, sir. He told me to. They moved off but closed in again as we forded the river. And they cried something to us. It sounded like "commidy water". We took it to mean that they wanted him to go back over the water. He laughed when he heard it.'

'He was in a good humour?'

'You would say it put him in a good humour. He was in a bad humour when we set out.'

'From here?'

'From here, sir, and from the Limestone, and from the camp that day. The more so that day because the bullocks were slow. But when they said that, he laughed, and told me to fire over their heads. Which I did, and they dispersed, and he laughed again.'

'Did you see any white men among them?'

'Not to swear they were white. He asked me that same question. And I said I seen one that was thick in the leg, and another with lighter hair, and yet another whose face was paler. But so I might, I told him, and yet all three have been native blacks.'

'What did he say to that?'

'He says, Well, Collison, he says, all the same, this seems to me to be fermented. Someone has stirred these up.'

'Then he must have believed there were whites among them.'

Collison almost shrugged. 'He always blames the runaways for everything bad the blacks do, sir. I been his servant two years, and would like a penny for every time I hear him say it's the runaways stir them up.'

'Did any of the men see whites among them?'

'They wouldn't say if they did, sir. They would call it peaching on their mates.'

'Which they sometimes do.'

'Ah, but which they can't be depended upon to do.'

It was clear that Collison, now that he had rested, was beginning to enjoy himself. He was the man with the information everybody wanted. When Clunie had arrived home from the commandant's house, he had overheard him talking to the servants. 'Now then,' he was saying with lordly roughness, 'you know better than to ask me questions like that.'

Now he folded his arms and said, 'But in my opinion, sir, the captain was right this time. There were whites among them. Or if not among them, behind them. Or else, why else would they go after him, and only him?'

Clunie thought of the boat's crew, all prisoners, speared up the river. 'It is true,' he said in a provisional tone, 'that their attacks usually seem haphazard.'

'Well, there was nothing haphazard about this, sir. It was only him they rolled the stones down upon, only him they told to go back over the water, and only him they must have tracked and tried to ambush at that clearing. Ah yes, and he knew it. After we ford the river he says to me, Collison, I believe the ones known to be with the tribes in the north have come down. Their tribes have come down for one of their great meetings, and those have come with them. And I say, to warn him, Sir, what about Boylan? And he says, speaking offhand, Oh, Boylan is dead. But then he falls quiet, and after a while he says, Why, Collison, did you see one like Boylan? And I had to say, No, sir, I did not. But everyone says he's come down and has been seen.'

The candles were flickering. Clunie guarded them with both hands. 'Shut the window, if you please.'

While Collison shut the window he looked at the map. The commandant's pen had been light and tentative, and the river finished like a hairline on an expanse of paper turned grey by the shaded light. 'Well,' he said, when the soldier came back, 'you are standing in the river. You have fired and dispersed them. What then?'

'They withdrew, sir, but did not go. They followed all that day. We seen them between the trees or like shadders in the long grass. The bullocks go well, for a change, and we go fourteen miles, and come to where the horse was lost, that broke his tether last time. We make camp, and in the morning he says, Collison, take the men and look for that horse. And he rides off on the mare alone.'

'To explore his new creek?'

'No, sir. That is up *here*. Even on the mare he could scarce get so far and back in one day.'

'Did he mention the blacks?'

'No, sir, but I did. Sir, I says, what of the blacks? And he says, Have you seen any today, Collison? I have to say no, and he rides off. He comes back that night, quiet, but well enough, and next day we go to the junction of the river and his new creek, reaching it at night. And in the morning he rides off to explore the creek, and all that day we others just wait there. We see no blacks, though one man—Partridge, sir, I should not want to go with him again—Partridge thinks every kangaroo or native dog is a black. And it is true we see the smoke from their fires in the sky. It gets dark and he is not back. I am thinking I had better cooey or fire a shot, when in he comes. He sits with his arms about his knees, and stares at the fire, and says nothing. And neither do I, because when he is like that, it is better not to say nothing. In the morning he says, Well, Collison, there is not one creek, but two. And I says, And do you consider they both run to the sea, sir? I consider nothing, he replies. But after a while he says, Into mud or sand, most likely, or lost among stones. I see his mood is heavy. And will you trace them again today? I ask. I have done all I can, he says. There is nothing for it now but to go back.

'So we strike camp and set off. Nothing happens that day. He stays with us and the bullocks, walking the mare or dismounting to rest her. We camp at the second ford, and next day we go on and come again to the first ford, the one where they rolled the stones. And he is ahead, and he stops and is looking at the ground. And when I come up, he says, These are tracks. Well,

337

they might have been. They were very indistinct. What is it tracks of? I ask. A horse or a bullock, he says. I will follow it. Take the men and camp at the bend where we camped in May. Wait there till I come up. So I do, reaching it at four p.m. Soon after four one man thinks he hears a cooey. We answer, and then we think we hear it again, and we answer again, and also I fire a shot, in case he is lost. But in my opinion, sir, it is easy to think you hear a cooey in the bush, when none has been made, and if I was asked to swear there was a cooey, I would have to say, I don't know. At any rate, he doesn't return. The whole night goes by, and at dawn I send two men back to search.

'Sir, those two men come back very soon. They seen the tracks of his horse across a small creek, they tell me, going in the direction of the Limestone. Well, it is like the cooey. I wouldn't swear they seen those tracks, or were just in a hurry to get out of the bush, where they were alone, with no gun to protect them. But they keep saying they did, so I think it better to take it as true, and we set out for the Limestone. At noon we see blacks, fifty or sixty. They follow us in the trees and shout, but I don't fire a shot. They don't sound as angry as before. It is more like they are excited. Also they don't come as close.'

'Then they were the same ones?'

'I thought they were, sir, but can't say why. No, and now you ask me direct, I won't say they were. I don't see them as clear as the first lot. They go off in a couple of hours. We go on, and I tell the men to walk in single file after the bullocks, to leave a track he can follow, for I have in my mind all the while that those two might not have seen his tracks at the creek at all. We come to the Limestone, and find him not there. And the rest I told you, how we went out next day, travelling light, and found his traces.'

'Those stirrup leathers, Collison—could you say what was used to cut them?'

'A stone axe, sir, or something like it.'

'Such as the blacks use?'

'Yes, sir. And such as white men use, who live with the blacks. Not all fashion knives for theirselves, nor find the metal to do so. Stirrup irons, and any other thing they might forge to their use, not falling in their path every day.'

'True. Any sign of his pistol?'

'No, sir. He could be carrying it still. May I know who is to lead the search party, sir?'

Clunie could only reply that he didn't know. He had been pondering the question on his way from the commandant's house, and after dismissing Collison he took it up again. The arrival of the *Alligator* meant that either he or Edwards must go down to Dunwich early tomorrow. Bulwer had taken to bed with his intermittent fever; Harbin was the only officer who might go. But there would be prisoners on the *Alligator* (Clunie expected no horses; she was too small for such cargo), and Harbin could scarcely be spared. Moreover, even if he were, by what means would he go? One of the surgeons must go, for the commandant might be found wounded. But Murray's nag was the only horse on the settlement. Of the officer and the surgeon, who would ride, and who go afoot? Well, must either be mounted? Yes, so that if needs be, a message could be carried at speed. He had almost decided to send Murray, mounted, with Collison and five men, and to dispense with an officer, when his servant came in and announced Henry Cowper.

It was close in the room since Collison had shut the window. Henry, already hot from his walk, loosened his collar and spread his legs as soon as he sat down. He eyed the port with longing, but refused Clunie's invitation to drink.

'There are occasions when I regard it as prescribed stuff. I prescribe myself with enough to keep it at a level just below the Plimsoll line. Then I keep topping it off, as it were, but don't let it get any higher. I've just topped it off, and daren't again, because I come with a story, captain, and have need of my senses. Let us begin with Monday's ghost.'

'Cowper, I have had enough of Monday's ghost.'

'Oh, I don't support belief in that apparition, as I told you on Tuesday. I said then that their certainty made me think they saw something in the half light, but not Captain Logan and the mare. But now I believe myself wrong. I believe now that they saw nothing at all, but heard something.'

'I see,' said Clunie with impatience. 'A small confusion of the senses.'

'Not exactly.'

'Oh, Cowper, come to your story.'

'Allow me a minute of drama—' he looked at the bottle—'as a reward for my restraint. May I take the drumming of your fingers as applause for my prologue? Captain, thank you! And now to my story. The commandant is dead. He was murdered on Sunday. Blacks brought the news to the outlying gangs on Monday morning. It reached the settlement in the evening. It reached the men working on the boats. And as they listened to the words, they supplied the action from their imaginations—as all of us do—and then became excited, and continued with their own wild sequel—as all of us do not do. "The commandant is dead," they were saying. "Ergo, there is his ghost."'

'Who told you he was murdered on Sunday?'

'Lewis Lazarus. It may be untrue.'

'Lazarus was sent straight from the solitary cell to one of the outlying gangs. When did you see him?'

'He was brought in this evening with a wound to be dressed. Most likely self-inflicted, so that he could get to me with the story. The belly is an improbable place to be wounded with a pickaxe. He says he fell.

341

You know he lived for months with the blacks. He was made welcome because one black claimed him as his brother returned from the dead. This afternoon this same black brother passed near his gang. He told him that the commandant was taken by surprise while watching white cockatoos, that he was hunted and killed, and that his body was lying in a certain place. Before Lazarus could ask him anything else, according to him, the guards chased him off. So Lazarus then falls on the pickaxe, bleeds harmlessly but in profusion, yells that he is bleeding to death, and is brought in to have the wound dressed.'

'I am glad,' said Clunie, 'that he came to you with this useful information. Mind, I should have thought it simpler if he had asked to be brought direct to me. But pass that! Pass that! Here is a map. Unless the body lies in this area—' Clunie pointed to the blank part of the paper—'he will save the search party much time by pointing out the spot.'

'Captain,' said Henry, 'I am disappointed in you. If such a man asks to be brought to you, do they obediently bring him? And as to pointing to the spot on a map, maps are lines on paper. What have they to do with such as Lazarus, who carries the terrain in three dimensions in his head?'

Clunie was disconcerted not only by the logic of this, but by his feeling that Cowper's disappointment in him, though expressed with levity, was real. However, his impatience with Cowper's half-tipsy circumlocutions remained, and was audible in his voice.

'So I suppose he offers to lead us to the spot.'

'He does.'

'Which will afford him an excellent opportunity to run.'

'It will.'

'Cowper, tell me plainly, do you believe the man?'

'I do.'

'Mr Cowper, in the manner of your replies, you are indulging your taste for drama again.'

'I am.'

'Then you will excuse me.' Clunie half rose in his chair. 'I have the search party to arrange.'

'That looks a very fine cheese.'

Clunie sat back in his chair. 'Pray help yourself.'

'Yes,' said Henry, as he cut the cheese, 'I indulged my taste for drama at the expense of my common sense. For I admit I don't entirely believe the man. I am as much on my guard as you are against their tricks. His motive is one of two—to run, or to get a remission for finding the body. But if I were in command here, I would put my trust in the latter. I would have his irons knocked off, and let him go with the party.'

Clunie was placated by this sober tone. He cut a slice of cheese and put it all at once into his mouth. Eating it, and wiping his fingers on his napkin, he looked beyond Henry in deep reflection. Then he said, 'The white cockatoos.'

'An irrelevant note,' agreed Henry. 'Not the note of a liar.'

'The story of the ambush tallies with Collison's but for the white cockatoos. Such a detail, if true, could come only from the attackers.'

'And what is its purpose if not true?'

'Collison believes that the blacks were goaded by runaways, perhaps even led by them. He's a sensible and steady fellow, and he puts his argument well. He mentioned Boylan. Did Lazarus's black brother mention Boylan?'

'If he did, be assured it will stay between him and Lazarus. Lazarus and Boylan were mates.'

'He mentioned him once to you.'

'There had been no murder then.'

Clunie pushed back his chair and rose heavily to his feet. Henry was cutting and eating cheese as if he could not stop. Clunie went to the uncurtained window and stood with his hands clasped at his back. For a moment he wondered if the light flickering through the trees came from the landing stage, if a boat had brought a message from the Limestone Station to say that the commandant was found. But the light was higher than the landing stage; it was coming from the commandant's garden, and very soon it drew clear of the foliage and showed itself as a light carried by Murray's servant. The moon was in its last quarter; the man was lighting his master from the commandant's house to the hospital; both were walking fast. As Clunie pulled the curtain across the window, he recalled Murray's quiet words—'Poor lady!'—and his own intended rebuke. He turned back into the room. Henry had stopped eating and was sitting with both hands pressed in satisfaction to his belly. 'We must not allow ourselves to conclude that the commandant is dead,' said Clunie. 'We must continue to hope and believe that he will be brought in.'

But as he spoke, he knew that he did not believe it; and he knew by Henry's formal and acquiescent inclination of his head that he did not believe it either. He returned to his chair. 'I didn't see him on the morning he left. Collison says he was out of humour.'

'I saw him,' said Henry. 'He came to ask me a direct question. Would I really give evidence against him if his administration were put to an enquiry?'

Clunie raised his eyebrows high.

'Yes,' said Henry. 'No preamble. Just that. Abrupt as a shot. I had warned him of the possibility before, but perhaps, even the last time, always with too much levity. But this was very early in the morning, the time of day when I am plain and serious. I said I didn't know. I said perhaps the Bible and the oath would make me tell the whole truth.'

'What did he say to that?'

'Nothing.'

'Surely he disputed that the truth *would* be evidence against him?'

'No. He said nothing. Nothing. He nodded his head. Once.' Henry gave a curt nod that was indeed reminiscent of Logan. 'Then he turned on a heel and went.'

Clunie put his elbows on the table and his jaw on his fists. His frowning gaze took in the candlelit map and the opposite rim of the table, on a level with which Henry's white hands now clasped each other on his belly. The footsteps of James Murray and his servant passed on the road outside. 'I gave Captain Logan a promise,' said Clunie. 'I agreed that while I was his deputy, I would see his punishments maintained in their full severity. His request that I do so was the result of a conversation about Lazarus. It applied especially to him. Yet now I must act on a gamble, and order the fellow's irons to be knocked off, and let him go with the party.' Clunie took his elbows off the table. 'Yes, I will do it.' He knew his resolve to be a ratification of his belief that Logan was dead. 'The commandant,' he said, without looking at Henry, 'will understand.'

Henry gave his formal nod again.

'Lazarus understands that remission can come only from the governor?'

'Yes, but knows that the governor will be guided by your recommendation.'

'I shall give him the recommendation he earns.'

'He can ask no more. Collison goes with the party, of course?'

'Of course. Collison, Murray, Lazarus—'

Clunie's abrupt pause made Henry look at him with amusement. 'You are doubtful about that last conjunction?'

Clunie's eyes moved in slow consideration over Henry. Henry unfolded his hands from his belly and spread them with the palms upward.

'Are you fit for it?' asked Clunie.

'If Murray's nag is. I shall ride, I take it?'

'Oh, yes. Someone must be mounted.'

'And so,' said Henry, 'tomorrow, you will go to the Eagle Farm in the bullock cart.'

'Cowper, such considerations are indecent at a time like this. The woman I have just left is perhaps a widow, the children fatherless.'

'I wish only to warn you, Murray.'

'I know what you wish, Cowper. But you will not see me in that bullock cart.'

'Oh, to be sure, *I* will not see you.'

'One of us must be here. Can the hospital be left untended?'

'Captain Clunie thinks you may do both.'

'Impossible! How?'

'Why, Murray, by putting the bullocks to the gallop. Oh, how you will sway and clutch the sides! Oh, how they will cheer!'

CHAPTER THIRTEEN

Under a hot but not torrid sun, and a crescent moon like milky glass, Henry Cowper, with Collison, Lazarus, and four other prisoners walking abreast in his rear, was riding through the open and slightly undulating country northwest of the Limestone Station. The grey slops of the prisoners, like Murray's dusty bay, might have been chosen to accord with the colours about them, but the red of Henry's jacket facings and Collison's coat, that thick ungrained red of woollen cloth, was as clashing in this landscape as blood in a child's hair. For here there were no such positive colours. On Henry's right hand a few clumps of tall trees, their rough bark the colour of iron, and their foliage a dun green, stood with the junction of trunk and root shrouded by tall pale grass; and although at his left the river marked out a fissure of brighter greens, none among them were the sappy greens of England and Ireland or the dense fleshy greens of the coast. There were no mangroves here, nor any of the dark tufted pines to be seen on the shores of the bay and the lower reaches of the river. On these banks all the tangled shrubby things were touched, however slightly, with bronze or silvery-grey, and their flowers, when they bore any, were so small that they were visible only by their slight effect on the general colour of the bush. Among and behind this scrub stood big trees with foliage in similar colours, and with trunks of grey or silvery-grey, or of mauve shading to grey or rust, or of the beautiful colour of pink clay. It was as if everything here inclined not to the sun's bright spectrum, but to those of the mineral earth and the ghostly daytime moon, excepting only those two moving and invasive particles of red.

The sun beating on Henry's shoulders was tempered by a wandering wind. Now and again, listening to the wind and the regular swish of the men's legs in the long grass, he would momentarily feel that his body had become weightless, and was peacefully floating in a vast bubble of warm air. Collison had told him that it was in similar weather of heat and irregular breezes that Patrick Logan had ridden out of the Limestone Station two weeks ago. Henry, who had gone with Logan on a short expedition in 'twenty-six, knew how responsive he was, or used to be, to moving into such pristine spaces as these. It had not lulled him into peacefulness,

as it did Henry, but had induced in him a taut animation and gaiety resembling the state of a man freshly in
love. Away from the balk and perplexity of governing
men, he had moved with enormous relief into government by nature. Collison agreed with Henry that this
was his usual mood on riding out, but this time, said
Collison, he had been 'low', and 'like a lump'.

Henry had not had time to hear Collison's story
before leaving the settlement, but had done so on the
way to the Limestone Station. 'Do you believe him to
be dead?' he had asked at last.

'First show me his dead body,' Collison had
replied.

At fifty yards distance the river bank rose abruptly
to a sparsely wooded hill, on the farther side of which
the river made a sharp turn, and appeared again diagon-
ally across Henry's way. When he drew close enough to
see its shallows he turned in the saddle.

'Collison!' And, after a pause: 'And you,
Lazarus!'

For Lazarus could not be allowed to walk behind
Collison and Henry, as could the other four, all of
whom were due for early release. Although Clunie had
seemed pleased to see Lazarus changed from the yellow
of the gangs into the grey of the first-class prisoners,
he had told Henry not to let him out of range of his
pistol or Collison's gun. When the two men came up
Henry pointed to the river. He had slowed to a walk

and they fell in by his side. 'Is that the first ford?' he asked Collison.

'Yes, sir.'

'Then that must be the hill.'

'Yes, Mr Cowper. We were at about this spot when he comes riding back. Of course I seen them myself by that time, and am coming on fast.'

'Collison,' said Henry, 'two hundred blacks couldn't conceal themselves on that hill. There is not enough cover.'

'I never said they were hid, Mr Cowper. They stood among the trees, but were not hid.'

'In that case he would have turned back before they rolled the stones. Indeed, as soon as he noticed them.'

'As he did, sir. When they move to roll the stones, that was when he first sees them. If I had been in advance with him, I would have seen them before they moved, my eyes being sharp.'

'And his—' said Henry with sudden uncertainty.

'They serve him well for most things, Mr Cowper, but for small distant things he uses mine.'

Henry had always thought himself observant; he was both amazed and abashed. He had seen Logan shifting papers into comfortable range, but had never considered that his distant vision might also be defective. Yet the evidence had been there: he saw again the raised hand beneath which Logan had watched the

351

black prisoner rising from the grass on the other side of the river, and heard again the anxious voice. 'On his feet, is he?' He wondered what else Collison knew, and was so used to knowing, or so barely conscious of knowing, that he did not think it worth mentioning. He said, 'Is that why he asked if you had seen white men among them?'

'It was, sir. Or else he was comparing what he seen with what I seen, which he also does. I don't call him half blind, nor even a quarter so. It's just the little sharp distant things, like the difference between a black face and a white face rubbed with ashes, like they do.'

Lazarus quickly pressed his fingers to his jaw to crush a fly. In the lee of the hill the wind hardly reached them; Collison and Henry had both begun to wave flies from before their faces, and the horse was regularly swishing his tail. Henry spoke in an idle manner that he hoped would take Collison off guard.

'And did you see such a thing?'

Lazarus turned his head and looked at Collison's profile. Such hard attentiveness, thought Henry, was the closest he dared come to a threat, but Collison, not easily unnerved, ignored the stare, or perhaps (not sensitive either) did not notice it. He replied with his usual dogged common sense.

'Not to swear to, sir. I seen nothing I could swear to.'

Lazarus blew his nose, flicked the stuff into the

grass, and wiped his thumb and forefinger on the seat of his trousers. 'I alwuz knew about ees eyes,' he said quietly.

Collison was inclined to jeer. 'Easy to know once you been told. Sir,' he said to Henry, 'we are coming up to where they rolled the stones.'

As Henry looked up at the hill, he narrowed his eyes in an effort to approximate Logan's faulty vision. Fire must have passed over the hill last summer, for although the foliage of the small sparse upright trees had grown afresh, most of the trunks were still charred. The crowd of blacks standing in the shifting shadows of the leaves must have kept as still as the trunks of the trees. Henry wondered if that immobile massing had been a simple show of strength, their first warning to the commandant to turn back, or if Lazarus had just spoken the truth, and the commandant's enemies had discovered his weakness long ago, and on that day, seeing him ride well in advance, had trusted in it to keep them obscure until they released the stones. Henry thought it likely that Lazarus had told the truth; intense hatred is a wonderful sharpener of the observation. And if Lazarus knew, so did other prisoners, and other runaways: Boylan, if he were really alive and in the bush, would certainly know.

'And sir,' said Collison, 'here are the stones theirselves.'

They lay among others at the foot of the hill, in an apparently natural formation, but Collison leapt

353

forward and distinguished them by pushing them with the flat of his foot and showing them not embedded like the rest. They were big and jagged; Henry would have called them boulders. They could have broken a horse's legs and tumbled the rider.

Their pause had given the other four prisoners time to plod up, passive and tired, taking off their hats and wiping their sleeves across their foreheads. The party had left the settlement at dawn, travelled by water to the Limestone Station, and had set out from there a little after ten. Henry took out his watch. It was two o'clock. He turned the horse and took him to the river at a trot, so that every man should increase his pace before stopping to drink at the ford.

At their approach a flock of white and sulphur cockatoos rose screeching from the bushes on the opposite bank. They rose slowly, in almost perpendicular flight, against the background of tall trees, then disappeared rapidly beyond their tops. Like any sudden flight of birds, they seemed to take the spirit up with them. 'Surprised while watching white cockatoos,' he remembered Lazarus saying. And now Collison was saying that he had never seen so many as on his journey with the commandant.

'Not here, but further up, flock after flock. He would stop and watch.'

And would see them as flowing white clouds streaked with sulphur, thought Henry.

'They is stringy eating, the devils,' remarked Lazarus.

The three men were momentarily united by wry memory; all had eaten them. A low tide exposed at the water's edge a strip of sand as clean and golden as an ocean beach. 'Did you cross from this spot?' asked Henry.

'Yes, sir. We have the bullocks in the stream when the blacks assemble on the other side and wave their weapons and shout. We know already they crossed by the marks in the sand. And then I fire. And this same sand was where he seen the tracks on the way back, of the horse or bullock.'

'Was the sand as firm as today?'

'Yes, sir.'

'Then the tracks would have been distinct.'

'As I told him, sir.'

The four prisoners came up once more. 'I have a wasp in me shirt,' cried one to Collison.

'Wasp in your arsehole!' said Collison in disbelief.

'Let him get it out, whatever it is,' said Henry. 'We must stay while they take off their boots.'

All four tumbled to the bank. Lazarus, his boots tied round his neck, crouched in the shallows and gathered water in his hands, deftly, spilling hardly a drop. Henry, brushing away flies, rode over the sand to let the horse drink. Deft as Lazarus, he took a flask from his pocket and took a swig. Collison came up as he was returning it. He stood near the head of the horse, but faced Lazarus and the men, and watched them casually as he spoke.

'I told him they would be distinct. What is it tracks of? I ask him. He is about where you are, on the mare, and he doesn't answer straight away, because he is searching his teeth with his tongue. Then he puts his finger on the tip of his tongue and takes off a particle of that tooth, the one you drew. I know it was that, because he was bleeding a bit from the mouth earlier, and spitting and saying, There is still a bit there, Collison. He looks at it, and makes a face like when you taste blood in your mouth, or something bad. Then he flicks it off his finger. And I say again, What is it tracks of, sir? A horse or a bullock, he says, I will follow them. And that is the last we see of him.'

Henry remembered the commandant's widely opened mouth. He saw the blood beginning to seep out of the socket as the forceps moved the tooth, and his shocked reflective eyes as Henry spoke of his danger and possible disgrace. It was the day after that roistering night in the female factory, and Henry remembered as well his own debility, his reeling head and the flutter in his belly as he sat at the desk, the forceps still in his hand, and urged the commandant to intercede for Bulbridge and Fagan at their trial in Sydney. He saw the commandant striding straightly out, and heard himself groaning to amuse Knowles, and speaking foolish obscure serious words about nails being driven home, and armour that once pierced could never be made whole again. But by that time his reflections on the commandant's obliviousness had been amplified to include his own former obliviousness to the character of Nobby Clark. The horse had drunk enough; he reined in its head and saw in a troubling flash the hem of Doctor Redfern's trousers, his father's gaiters, and two pairs of neat shining narrow shoes against the dark rug. He turned the horse abruptly, with a sudden splashing of water.

'Let us get on!' he said in a loud voice to Collison. 'Lazarus, how far from here?'

Lazarus was standing in the shallows with his hands on his hips, his eyes half shut, and on his face a look of quiet but intense pleasure. He carried this peaceful look to Henry. 'Sir, about five hours.'

'You no longer sound sure.'

'I know only what I wuz told.'

The other men were all crouched about his feet, drinking from their hands. 'Well, you wouldn't be told in miles or hours, I suppose,' conceded Henry.

Collison interposed. 'Mr Cowper, what he says agrees with the facts. From the Limestone to the clearing where we found the saddle is more than thirty miles. We have covered fifteen, so there is more than fifteen to go. We are none of us on a good mare. We won't cover it before dark.'

'Then I suggest we cover as much as we can, and set out at daybreak on the rest.'

It was not until he rode into the stream that Henry realised the significance of what Collison had just said. It was Collison's first intimation that he did not believe his master to be alive, and indeed did not believe him to have got far from the clearing where he had been surprised. The young soldier was wading at the horse's side, his musket held high. Henry glanced down at his face, spruce and narrow, gilded with bristle. He seemed quite unaware of the disclosure he had made, and again Henry found himself reflecting on what Collison knew, and did not know he knew. To be sure, that had been the case with himself long ago, and lately with the commandant, but in his case as in Logan's, ignorance had been caused by effacement of facts in the service of an ideal, however absurd or mistaken, whereas it seemed to Henry that Collison's ignorance was an unexplored darkness that yielded occasionally to accidental beams of light.

On the opposite bank the men found some of the big seeds they called chestnuts. These lay beside their dried exploded pods, their split tan skins revealing flesh of whitish-green. The men scrambled about and pocketed them to be cooked that night, for they caused stomach pains if eaten raw, but finding bigger ones further on, they threw away the first and took these instead, until Collison abused them for the delay and ordered no more to be picked up. But a little later, coming across two native dogs who had brought down a wallaby, he himself helped to chase the dogs away and ordered the men to carry the beast by turns. They had brought only a little salt beef; fresh meat was worth the delay.

Lazarus now took the lead, walking a few yards ahead of Henry while Collison and the others brought up the rear. Henry had noticed that leg irons affected the gait of men in different ways, according to their physical structure and their former habit of walking. After they were knocked off most continued to shuffle for a long time, but some shuffled with the feet slightly apart, as if chafed on the insides of the thighs. On setting out from the Limestone Station Lazarus had walked with just such a peculiar waddle, but in only an hour it had been defeated by freedom and the long grass, and he now walked straight, swinging his arms, his hands lightly clenched. The back of his shirt was covered with flies, but he had pushed the crown of his hat through a hole cut in a square of cloth, so that the suspended corners blew and bobbed and helped to keep them away from his face. Henry was smoking to repel them, and so was Collison, though it was forbidden. The other four also had cloth suspended from their hats, but though they occasionally swiped or shook the dead wallaby, its wound was black with flies, and its eye sockets crawling.

Once Henry called to Collison, and when he ran up, Henry pointed to Lazarus.

'Is he headed towards the clearing?'

'Oh yes, sir.'

Again Henry glanced down at the young soldier; but Collison was puffing away at his pipe, as oblivious as ever, and indeed with a kind of evening contentment, for it was almost dark, and they must soon make camp.

'We could have used our heads,' said Henry with amusement, 'and done without the rascal.'

'Not if he was told the exact spot, Mr Cowper. It's all rough little hills and creeks and gullies round there. You might beat it for hours and pass him by. And besides,' said Collison, taking his pipe out of his mouth and raising his face to Henry, 'for my part, I am glad he is come if it gets him remitted. There is no good of just flogging and flogging a man. He has shown there isn't.'

It was four years since Henry had slept on a blanket on the ground. On the last occasion he had shared a tent with Patrick Logan, and had chivvied him as he sat by candlelight engrossed in his journals and map. Now there was no tent, no candlelight, no companion awake, and both the ground and his bones had grown harder.

All the others were asleep. It was too dark to see

much more of them than their attitudes. Collison lay on his back, as neat as an effigy, and of the four prisoners, who had no blankets, one lay prone; one, Lazarus, sprawled wide on his back, and three lay curled. Two snored. At ten yards distance the tethered horse could be heard pulling grass with his teeth.

Of the dull little worries floating through Henry's mind, one recurred. Why had he not thought to tell Clunie about the lead coffin at the hospital? In case of death in the administrative families, two coffins—one adult and one child-sized—had been made years ago. They had first been kept in the lumber yard, but were removed to Henry's quarters when it was discovered that prisoners had cut squares out of them to make potato graters. Did Murray know they were there? If so, all would be well. Otherwise, poor Clunie would be running about filching a bit of lead here, and a bit there, flashings and suchlike, and even then would not have enough.

Henry knew that if he took a drink from his flask he would be able to say peaceably, 'Well, I can do nothing about it now. Let it be.' But he had already encroached on tomorrow's quota, and did not dare face tomorrow's deprivation if he drank it now.

He had taken his share of the roasted wallaby, but while eating it had suddenly remembered the coffin in his quarters, and the realisation that the commandant had indeed been provident to have it made of lead had made him remember the state of the wallaby while the men had carried it, and he had sickened, and given the meat to Lazarus, who had eaten it with huge chews, standing with a hand on a hip and looking at the sky as if he had never seen stars before. The memory of this ranging way Lazarus had of looking about him, his head turning stiffly but somehow luxuriously, and the sinews of his neck and chin like an inverted claw, made Henry, lying sleepless in the dark, think piteously, 'I am fat and sick and am going to die.'

But having reached this low pitch, he could only turn back. He laughed at himself, sat up, took the flask from his pocket, and shook it. In his new cheerfulness he thought he may have been mistaken in his estimate of its contents. He shook it twice, listening as carefully as he had ever done to a heartbeat. He had not been mistaken. He took only a sip.

He knelt and spread his blanket on the ground, then lay down on his back, expecting peace. And indeed he was all but asleep when he heard himself whispering, 'Damn you!'

He opened his eyes wide and stared, shocked and solemn, into the dark. A sip of drink was worse than none. On the verge of sleep, an image of neat black shoes had flashed on his eyelids, and off-guard, he had cursed. Curled on his side in his bed in his boyhood room, he had opened his eyes and seen two shining narrow black shoes. One was set on the rug, the other swung comfortably aloft. 'Damn you!' he had whispered at those shoes, and his father had uncrossed his legs and leaned forward.

'What did you say, my son?'

'Nothing,' said Henry hoarsely, beginning to remember the previous night.

'Do you remember last night?'

'No,' said Henry.

'My son, the hold that man Clark has upon you is no natural one.'

Henry sat up in bed. 'It's a lie!'

'My poor boy, if you had heard yourself weeping last night because he has abandoned you!'

'What you say is a lie. We have had women. We took them together. Jemima at the hospital. And others.'

His father, showing no surprise, fell swiftly on to his knees and lifted his hands.

'Save me, O God, for the waters are come into my soul. I sink into deep mire, where there is no standing. I come into deep waters, where the floods overflow me.'

It seemed to Henry—schooled from childhood in the psalms, and familiar with the rest of this one—that his father was praying for himself. He pulled the covers over his head and bawled into the sheet that fell back and half stopped his mouth. For weeks he had been dogging Nobby Clark's footsteps. '*I* don't believe what they say about you, Nobby.' And for a while Nobby had been as grateful, earnest, and tearful, as he had been at first. 'Buck, Nobby won't forget that. Nobby knows his pals.' But then he had changed, had begun to scratch behind an ear and say in a gabble, 'Yes, lad, I know, I know.'

'Nobby, what have I done?'

'Nothing, lad. But I'm leading you into bad ways.'

'Never! Ain't we roistering boys?'

'Yes, but look, better go home, lad. Go on.'

So then there was more dogging and pleading, and soon Nobby, when he saw him coming, took to darting into doorways or down lanes. But Henry was not to be shaken off; he argued that Nobby could not have seen him, and that the darting was for some other purpose. But on the night before he lay bawling into the sheet, and his father knelt by his bed intoning the sixty-ninth psalm, he and Nobby, rounding the same corner, had come face to face.

'Nobby!'

Nobby had turned and run, with Henry after him, calling to him and laughing, for this was surely another of Nobby's jokes. He thought as a counter-joke he would cry, 'Stop, thief!' But it occurred to him in time that this would be excessively indelicate. So he only panted with laughter, and called to Nobby to stop, and was about to catch up with him, and end the game, when Nobby darted into a short lane, saw a cart lumbering across the other end, and stopped, at bay.

He fell quickly into one of his jesting fencing positions, making a sword of his outstretched cane. But Henry stopped dead as soon as he saw his face. He was trying to grin but was defeated by fury. His mouth was a mere contortion about his long decayed teeth, his face was purple and blotched, the whites of his eyes aflame with veins. From under his hat fell one strand of lank black hair. Why had Henry never noticed till then that his hair was dyed? He lunged with his stick at Henry's waistcoat. 'Back!' He lunged again. 'Back! Puppy! Milksop! Gull! Back!' He was no longer pretending that this was a joke. At the end of these invocations he squared his mouth and snarled like a dog. He hated Henry enough to kill him.

Henry turned and walked back through the lane, conscious as he went of Nobby's footsteps racing and clattering in the other direction. 'All they said about him is true,' a quiet voice, his own, was informing him. He walked through the town in a daze. 'I have always known it was true,' said the quiet voice, incredulous yet somehow drugged. 'So why would I not let myself know it in words? Why?'

In one of the streets west of the wharves he knocked at the door of a squat little cottage. All he can remember now of the woman who opened it is her name—Honoria—and her celebrated breasts. He had one out before she could shut the door, and had fastened his lips and teeth to it, and they fell together to the earthen floor of the room, she laughing and gasping, and the other men and women in the room roaring and stamping and crying encouragement. A few hours later someone had dumped him on his father's doorstep, drunk, stinking, his clothes torn, his pockets empty.

'I made sackcloth also my garment, and I became a proverb to them.'

'Baw-baw—' sobbed Henry.

'They that sit in the gates speak against me; and I was the song of the drunkards.'

'Baw-baw—' But it was true. 'And I bet his pa does it just as good,' Honoria had cried to that roomful of people.

'Reproach hath broken my heart, and I am full of heaviness.'

But now, under the covers, there was only a crafty silence. Henry had suddenly decided that the only way to redemption was in death; he would leap from the bed, run to the window, and throw himself out.

The recollection of his great leap from the bed brings Henry to his feet under the stars in the dark bush. Collison wakes.

'What's that?'

'Only me,' said Henry, in a hoarse and humble voice.

'Sir, what are you doing?'

'I must piss.'

As Henry walked away from the group his feet cracked twigs, a sound that carried and multiplied so that he might have been one of a number of men walking, far apart but abreast, across that tract of bush. It was a marvel how his delicate little father had reached the window before him. There he stands, as if for ever, barring the way, his arms outstretched and a steadfast and noble look upon his face.

'Let me be,' shouts Henry. 'I wish to die!'

'You will live,' says his father, as if in judgement.

'I will throw you out first.'

'You will not.'

And of course he is right; Henry cannot touch him with violence; the ancient embargo is too strong. 'You will stay in the world,' announces his father, 'to be saved.'

Henry pulls the flask from his pocket. He puts a hand on a hip as he drinks, and rolls his eyes at the stars.

'Make haste, O God, to deliver me. Make haste to help me, O God.'

His silent intonation of the words are of ironic intention, yet there is a residue of sweetness in them too, a melancholy sweetness, like homesickness, that brings no comfort. The comfort seeping into him comes from the flask, which is now quite empty.

'But,' argues Henry, 'it will be only a day's deprivation. We are bound to find him early in the morning.

Collison and the others will bring him in while I ride ahead. If the nag goes well I will be at the Limestone by dark. All depends on finding him early.'

They did in fact find him very early. When they left the camp, in the grey light before sunrise, Henry expected to be led north-north-west, in which direction Collison said the clearing lay. Lazarus took them almost east, but Collison suggested that the convict was making the first curve of an arc that would bring them out near the clearing and would at the same time avoid an unreliable ford.

By sunrise they were walking again through a blond landscape threaded by the darker clefts of creeks from which the cockatoos again rose screeching. Between creeks the country flattened and opened, and while crossing one of these spaces they saw rising above the bank of the next creek several heads. As they rose a splotched oblong of red appeared among their grey. Lazarus, in the lead, stopped dead, and Henry put the spurs to his horse; but Collison shouted, 'Hardacre!' and Lazarus went on again, his shoulders slumping for a moment in what looked like relief, and Henry reined the horse back to his former pace.

But then it was Collison who halted. 'Mr Cowper!' Henry looked back and saw him pointing to a spot at some distance to Henry's right. Again it was red that drew their attention, but this time a mere speck. Henry put the horse to a canter, and now that Hardacre was near, Collison left the prisoners and ran after.

When Collison arrived at the spot Henry was still mounted, looking impassively down on a torn scrap of red coat, and nearby a piece of waistcoat, rust-coloured and stiff as bark with dried blood. While Collison was picking these up, the breeze fluttered a piece of torn paper above the grass. Collison retrieved it, glanced at it, and as he handed it to Henry he looked into his eyes and nodded. There was no mistaking that impetuous yet tentative handwriting. '*After seven hours trav—*' read Henry.

'And yet there is no good you beating around here,' said Private Hardacre, when they joined him. 'We combed the area yesterday.' But Lazarus insisted to Henry and Collison that it was hereabouts he had been told he lay. 'Then go on,' said Henry. 'Lead! Lead!'

Lazarus made off at a run, heading directly north now, and Henry trotted the horse by his side. Collison fell behind, and all the others, with Hardacre, lagged further behind still. For about two miles Lazarus led them over the rough area Collison had spoken of: a terrain of little creeks, some almost dry, and some, occluded by seeping earth, mere waterholes, but all lying deep in gullies, and the open spaces between them smaller and less frequent than before. They had emerged from one gully, and had begun to cross an open space towards another, when Henry saw that

Lazarus had thrown back his head and was sniffing the air, and in the next moment he was himself assailed by the stench. Henry had led the horse through the last gully, but now he mounted and trotted forward, with Lazarus running by his side.

The pall of flies almost hid the grey mare as she lay in the little water in the bed of the creek, though the mound of her belly, hairless, pink, and shining with slime, showed here and there among them. Lazarus hardly glanced at her. Tense and immobile, he stood looking across the creek. Henry followed his glance, saw nothing unusual, rose in the stirrups to gain the advantage of height, but still saw only the low scrub, of medium density, covering the other side. The men behind them, informed perhaps by Lazarus's stance, had begun to shout and run up.

Lazarus signalled for Henry to follow, then turned and ran for a few minutes alongside the creek until he came to a turn in the bank that obtruded so far into the gully, and so nearly reached the other side, that it all but made a causeway. While Lazarus and Henry were crossing, the others, singly or in twos and threes, reached the dead mare, but none lingered for more than a few seconds before turning and running, forced into single file now, Collison in advance and Hardacre after, alongside the gully towards the causeway.

But they had fallen far behind. They were still running on that side of the gully while Henry, led by

Lazarus, was riding through the low scrub on the other.

They found him lying at a right angle to the line of the creek, about ten yards from where the mare lay. At first Henry saw only a rough hump of sticks, such as might collect against the bulwark of a fallen tree, but then, protruding from one end of this hump, he saw two purplish black objects, and by their compact placing and duality discerned that they were a man's heels. Lazarus went forward, and standing wide of the hump, reached over and took the sticks, one by one, and quickly tossed them to one side.

He had been buried face downward in a shallow grave. The native dogs had dug about his feet, and exposed the heels, and when Lazarus got a green branch, and brushed it to and fro to remove the layer of earth covering the body, they saw that he was naked, and that his flesh had turned the dark colours of decomposition, and that the back of his head had been beaten away by many blows.

They did not notice Collison coming up until they heard his step and his hard breathing. He was carrying a pair of shoes, and when he saw the body he set these down, with abstracted care, near his own feet.

Henry spoke low. 'Where did you find them?'

Without looking away from the body, Collison pointed to the bushes a few yards in his rear. Lazarus spoke as quietly as Henry. 'I wiz wrong. In me mind I seen 'im runnin' barefoot.'

But now Hardacre came crashing along, excited, exploding into their stillness, a broken spear held aloft in one hand.

'Well, there it is!' He threw the spear to the ground. 'Blacks. But led by Boylan or another. They make no burials on their own prompting.'

The eight prisoners, Collison's four and Hardacre's four, were not coming up at a run, but were herded together, dragging their feet and finding much impediment in the small scrub. It seemed that they would have liked to turn back, but were drawn forward by the thread of their own vision, for none could unfix his stare from the long dark dusty shape protruding above the trough in the ground.

Henry and Lazarus and the two soldiers, repelled by the smell released by the removal of the earth, had all stepped back a little, and about a yard outwards from them the eight prisoners now came to an uncertain halt. Several fat flies entered this irregular circle of men and buzzed down on to the body, and Henry gave a garbled shout and motioned Lazarus forward to beat them off with his green branch. Lazarus went forward heavily, setting his face into an expression of indifference. The flies clung, and had to be dislodged almost with blows, and even then did not go far, but flew with an angry buzzing about the circle of men. One, buzzing before the face of a prisoner, caused him to throw up an arm and back away, and the heel of his boot catching in a hollow, he fell backwards and tumbled among his companions.

They laughed as they righted him. They called him a clumsy dog and put him on his feet and slapped his back; and then every man began to slap his neighbour's back and to laugh with such growing relief and excitement that Collison's command to be silent went unheard or unheeded, and at last Henry, with another wild uncompleted shout, had to ride the horse among them and brandish an arm as if to warn them of what they could expect.

They grew silent, but still did not try to hide their smiles except by passing their hands elaborately across their mouths. Hardacre, as if he preferred not to witness these antics, looked lazily at Lazarus, who was still waving the branch to and fro above the body; but Collison had become very red in the face and glittering in the eyes, and as Henry backed the horse away from the silent but grinning group, he suddenly roared in challenge, 'Well—and there are worse men than him!'

The smiles faded and died. None of the prisoners spoke, but measured Collison briefly with their glances before looking away. One took off his hat and gazed into the crown. Some shuffled their feet, one cleared his throat. Then the one who held his hat—his name was Odell—glanced at Collison, and away again, and said almost with kindness, 'In my reckoning, there was a worse one on Norfolk.'

He put on his hat and looked in turn at his companions, but all were stony-faced; none would agree with him. Henry, seeing Collison growing angry again, walked his horse among them and made them press back.

'Come now,' he said pleasantly, 'who has blankets? Take out your blankets. I have brought rope in my pack, and needles and thread. He must be made ready and brought in.'

Sullenly, slowly, Hardacre's four took the blankets from their packs. Hardacre came up. 'Mr Cowper, a word.'

They went aside. 'Mr Cowper, could we bury him here?'

'Hardacre, don't consider it.' Henry was the more definite because he himself had just considered it: only immediate burial would give him a chance to reach the Limestone Station by nightfall. 'It would be indecent,' he said, as much to himself as to Hardacre: 'He must have a Christian burial.'

'Sir, you could say the words over him.'

But this had also occurred to Henry. 'That may satisfy decency, Hardacre, but not official custom. And what of his widow? Poor lady! He must be buried where she wishes. No, there's no help for it—he must be brought in.'

'Very good, Mr Cowper, I will try.'

As Hardacre approached the prisoners, Henry

374

saw that they had dropped their blankets in a pile on the ground and were now standing well away from them, as if to announce like this their withdrawal from the business. Collison, alone and watchful on the other side of the pile of blankets, turned his head as Hardacre reached him, but not his eyes. The two soldiers conferred briefly, then both confronted the eight watching men. Lazarus, his green branch now only mechanically swishing, watched both soldiers and prisoners. He was hardly in earshot, but the great alertness of his eyes suggested to Henry that he was preparing to use them for what his ears might miss.

Collison spoke first. 'Smith. Odell. Packer, Costigan. Two of you are wanted to stitch him into blankets, and two to make a stretcher. Each pair to take the tasks turn about, or if you please, to cast lots.'

Hardacre did not allow the pause in which their silence must make its mark and call for its response. 'And you four,' he said fiercely to his party. 'Carter, Ferris, Snell, Reilly. You will take turns, two by two, at bearing the stretcher to the Limestone. From where it goes by water, Lazarus to row the boat. There—none can say the task is not assigned fair.'

But now there was no evading the silence. Two of the prisoners folded their arms. Henry, seeing Collison grow red-faced and restless footed, took the horse a few paces forward.

'*Get—moving!*' roared Collison.

375

'No. We will not.' The man who spoke was Odell. 'I speak for all of us,' he said. 'None will touch him.'

The other seven assented together. 'Punish one—punish all,' shouted one.

'We will not touch him,' repeated another.

'Why will you not?' asked Henry from Murray's horse.

The youngest, a loosely jointed hobbledehoy, gave a foolish but frightened laugh. 'It would bring a curse.'

'It will bring an extended sentence if you don't,' said Henry.

'The new commandant will not extend sentences,' said Odell.

'But if you do,' continued Henry, as if he had not heard Odell, 'it may mean the remission of the rest of your sentences.'

Lazarus dropped the branch and came forward. He halted beside Collison and put the backs of his fingers low on his hips. 'Remissions, is it?' he said. 'Remissions for these eight will mean less for the one who huz earned ees remission already. I know 'em! They 'ave not mercy enough for two, let alone nine. I will bring 'im in alone. I will do it all. Will stitch 'im up, bear 'im to the Limestone, and row the boat. Ee sez often I will end me days on the settlement, and I sez as often that I won't. And I won't. No, I will make sure of remission by earnin' it over again. I will bring 'im in alone. And if ee thinks to defeat me at this stage by stinkin', why, ee is wrong again.'

Henry looked at Collison. 'Collison?'

'Let him,' said Collison, 'since the rest are only dogs.'

'Lazarus,' said Henry, 'you say you can do it alone, but you will do it quicker if some of these make the stretcher.'

Lazarus considered the eight with a workman's speculative glance. 'If I am to bear 'im alone, it is a pair o' poles I need.'

Ferris, the young hobbledehoy, stepped forward. 'I can make a pair o' poles.'

'Strong and light? Braced at the ends?'

'If you want,' said Ferris.

'Let him try,' said Henry, as Lazarus hesitated. 'And let these others chop down and trim the trees needed. We have little hope of reaching the Limestone Station before dark, but at least we shall make camp as near it as possible.'

He dismounted as he spoke. While he opened his saddle bag to get the needle and the bobbin of thread, Lazarus squatted at the pile of blankets, choosing those he needed for the shroud and tossing another to Ferris. The flies had settled in large numbers on the body, but now that it was to be covered so soon, Henry thought it hardly worthwhile for anyone to take the time to swish them away.

By noon all except Lazarus had passed out of the confused terrain of little creeks and waterholes and had entered again the flat grassy country where they had found Logan's torn clothing and the piece of his journal. Lazarus and his load, a hundred yards in the rear, were still traversing the gullies. Occasionally Hardacre or Collison would ask Henry if he were in sight, and Henry would turn, and rise in the stirrups, and announce that he was still coming on. But apart from this, he was unwatched and unguarded, for after all he had done to secure his remission, none believed that he would elect to become a fugitive again by dropping his burden at this stage and bolting.

Workmanlike and quick, with that expression of set indifference the only sign of his revulsion, he had stitched the body into blankets. Taking over then from Ferris, who had joined the poles at the top, he had set them eighteen inches apart, braced them, and lashed a strip of blanket between them. To this he had lashed the wrapped body and near the heads of the poles had carved grooves to embed the ropes by which he would draw it. Where the poles would meet the ground, on their undersides, he carved them into smooth wedges. Henry, who had gone to the clearing where Logan had been ambushed, saw the finished job on his return, and thought how thoroughly it would have been approved by the man for whose transport it was intended.

To offset the handicap of his load, and to protect the others from the smell, Lazarus had set out in advance, but when the wind had veered in the direction of those following, Collison, on Henry's suggestion, had called to him to halt until they passed him.

Henry had not yet begun to feel the effects of his abstinence from alcohol, but he knew it must strike very soon, and the expectation of it made him tense and dejected. Murray's horse had been spelled enough. Alone, he believed he might manage to reach the Limestone Station that night, after all, but if forced to continue at the common pace, he would have a night's camp before him. He found himself rehearsing a speech.

'Collison, I will go ahead, and carry the news, and have them make the boats ready for the morning.'

But how long would it take to make two rowboats ready? He would deceive no one. Besides, Collison was weeping again, and passing a sleeve across his eyes. With Collison a mourner, and the others so silent, tired, and plodding, it was like a funeral procession; it did not seem decent to leave it.

And now, far behind them, Lazarus began to sing. Because they were walking into the wind, it barely reached them. At this distance it sounded like a chant. Perhaps it was one of those slow shanties, such as every man in the colony had heard on the voyage out. Henry turned in the saddle and saw that Lazarus had emerged from the gullies and had begun to walk in the open country.

The flies were troublesome, and there was no tobacco left. Henry had smoked his last pipeful in the clearing where the commandant had been ambushed. Following Lazarus's directions (and marking his trail lest he be lost) he had found it easily: a large grassy clearing, almost surrounded by eucalypts and chestnuts, and sloping away on one side to a deep cool shaded creek.

The saddle had been taken away to the Limestone Station, and the footsteps made by Logan's rush to the mare had been obliterated by those of the search parties, but the circle of cropped grass, though fresh green grass was pushing into it, was still discernible, and the chestnuts still lay in the blackened tree stump and were scattered about it. Before the stump was a log, on which it seemed likely he had sat while the chestnuts were roasting. Henry sat on it to smoke his pipe.

One had only to stop making one's own noise to realise that the bush, which had seemed so silent, was filled with a multitude of sounds, all so small that if one were the flinching or imaginative sort, it would be easy to hear them as stealthy. Logan had been neither flinching nor imaginative, and yet, as he sat watching the chestnuts roasting, the bush around him must have been full of the stealthy sound of men approaching. He must have heard it. How had he interpreted it? Did he, in a last self-deception, refuse to hear it as anything other than what he was used to? Or did he wait, tense and unblinking, for it to prove itself in a rush of feet? And if the latter, was the waiting a conscious gamble with his life, or only the strategy of a soldier?

The suspense imagined by Henry communicated itself to his body. The sounds in the bush no longer seemed separate, but concerted and threatening. Pride made him sit and finish his pipe, but he puffed rather furiously, and it was with relief that he rose at last to knock it out on the stump.

When he heard the rushing noise he simply fled, and even though in his first steps he heard the shrieking, and saw the great flock of cockatoos rising from the creek, and even though a part of his mind was cool enough to remark that he had never seen so many at once, he continued to run, and was thankful indeed to reach the comparative shelter of the bush.

The fear in his breast and throat was so real that it could only be assuaged by his threshing and crashing through the bush as if really pursued. Something, wild dog or kangaroo or big lizard, must have startled the cockatoos into rising, as something must have startled them into rising on that other morning, causing the commandant to leap to his feet and turn in their direction. As Henry crashed through the bush, his was again the only noise audible, but the rushing of wings, haunting his ears, became the rush of a hundred converging feet, and the shrieking became the yells of pursuers closing on their quarry. By the twigs, still green, littering the ground, and the snapped branches hanging raggedly down, he knew he had happened upon the way the commandant must have taken on the mare. His hat was knocked askew. When he emerged from the bush into a clearer space he set it straight and brushed himself down with shaking distracted hands. A heat at his thigh made him thrust a hand into his breeches pocket and pull out his pipe. He had no recollection of having put it there. He wondered then if Logan's pistol lay somewhere among the trees at his back. If so, let it lie; he would not go back. In the distance he heard Hardacre shouting at the prisoners. Truly, the commandant had not got far. Perhaps on arriving at the spot where Henry now stood, he had found himself already cut off from the causeway, or perhaps he had not even known of it. Had he not been forced to put the mare at her fatal jump, he may have escaped, but the mare once down, and himself scrambling out of the gully and running on alone, they had easily caught him. Henry wondered if, in the last shocked strenuous moments of his life, he had seen a face familiar to him, but too much despised until then to be designated as the face of an enemy. Henry did not doubt that the despised face—Boylan's or another's—had been there. Neither he nor anyone else had bothered to dispute Hardacre's assertion that the blacks did not bury their dead. His only question was whether Logan had seen that face as it bore down, and had recognised it as the clinching argument in a conversion that in this life he would never profit by.

Lazarus, who had stopped singing, or chanting, now broke out afresh. But this time it was louder, and carried a note that made Henry turn in the saddle and look behind him in perplexity. He saw that Lazarus had gained on them, and was pulling easily, with both ropes over one shoulder, instead of one over each as before. And his face was raised to the sky, and he was singing.

Henry felt the onset of a familiar anxiety, and a familiar dispersal of his concentration, both of which would be made worse this time by his knowledge that no appeasement was possible until they reached the Limestone Station in the morning. Mistrusting his own ears as well as his judgement, he turned back and looked for instruction at Collison and the others.

Collison was looking angrily over his shoulder at Lazarus; Hardacre, at his side, was whispering to him; and among the eight prisoners appeared signs of fear and uneasy laughter. Henry now understood that while

Lazarus's song might not be cheerful, it was certainly outrageous. Indeed, he heard it now as exultant. He turned about and rode back towards him.

But perhaps it was not exactly exultant either, unless there was such an emotion as funereal exultance. It was wordless, harsh, and full of hate, and yet was not debased, for while exulting in one man's death, it paid tribute to death, and acknowledged the coming death of the singer. Henry came on, hoping he looked fierce, but wishing to weep, for in a flashing comparison he saw this man's hatred against his own small and secret hatred, and this intemperance against his own, which put his craving so much in the forefront of his mind that no grief could be admitted for a man who had once been his friend. Lazarus saw him, stopped singing, and watched his approach in a calm and considering way.

Henry pulled up and waited for him to advance. Furiously he swished at flies, but Lazarus hardly needed the points of cloth flapping from his hat, for the big grey cocoon, splotched now with dark stains, acted as a decoy.

'You were singing,' announced Henry.

Lazarus nodded. 'She draws good and easy on the flat.'

'Oh,' said Henry. The song was beyond his recall, dispersed into the vast sky. Had it in fact derived only from the wild shouts of the bullock drivers when a rough tract of country is surmounted, and the rest been supplied by his imagination?

'Well,' he said curtly, 'you must stop. It's indecent.'

'Yes, sir,' replied Lazarus, in uncaring assent.

'Remember your remission,' cried Henry, trying to be angry.

'Yes, sir.'

But Lazarus was now rather mocking, for their eyes were holding a different conversation: Lazarus saying, 'Then tell me who else will bring him in?' And Henry shrinking and replying, 'Well, just do as I say, that's all.'

When this silent conversation was over, Lazarus gave a humorous nod, and Henry turned and rode back at a canter to the party. For the first time he had tears in his eyes, prompted, he supposed, either by mortification or by his need for a drink.

CHAPTER FOURTEEN

'He is with God,' said Amelia Bulwer.

'Yes,' said Robert, 'with God.' But he was watching Louisa as he spoke, and now swung on his crutches from Amelia's chair to hers.

'Pray, ma'am, what are you doing?'

'Making a sketch of this room,' replied Louisa.

Lucy had tipped a box of blocks on the floor at James Murray's feet. She was sorting them into sizes and did not appear to be listening.

'This room?' asked Robert in surprise. 'Mama's drawing room?'

'Robert is thinking it is not much like it,' said James Murray.

'Because I called it a sketch,' said Louisa. 'I was wrong, Robert. It is a plan.'

'A plan of the floor, Robert,' said Amelia.

'What the floor would look like,' added Louisa, 'if one were glued to the ceiling and looking down upon it.'

Lucy raised her eyes with wonder to the ceiling.

'Oh, yes,' said Robert, with interest. 'And there are the doors, and that gap is the window.'

'Yes. Five foot wide. One would not think it.'

In her bedroom, Letty shrieked. It sounded sudden, but by this time the three adults in the drawing room knew it to be the culmination of a bout of sobbing so low that it hardly reached them. Louisa and Amelia ignored it; James Murray gave a slight respectful frown; and Lucy, her eyes blank and her mouth open, looked towards the door and absently banged two blocks together. 'But why, ma'am?' cried Robert in a high anxious voice, 'Why are you making this plan?'

The shriek died away. 'I am making it for Mrs Clunie, Robert. It is to go to Sydney, to the wife of Captain Clunie's commanding officer, and when Mrs Clunie arrives at Sydney, she will study it, and will know how many of her pieces of furniture will fit into the room, and where. That is what all those figures are for. They are called measurements.'

'I know, ma'am. Aunt Fanny has taught me to measure.'

'Is Mrs Clunie bringing her furniture from home?' asked James.

'Yes, James.'

'But she fears some of it is too massive,' said Amelia, 'and may buy some smaller pieces in Sydney.'

'She would have lived in this house,' said Robert, looking from face to face, 'even if papa had not been murdered.'

Lucy looked at him with her blank eyes, and silently mouthed the word 'murdered'.

'Of course, my dear,' said Louisa, 'because you would have been in India.'

'Do you mean,' said James to Amelia, 'that she will discard the massive pieces?'

'I am hungry,' said Robert.

'I hardly know, James. Surely not dis*card* them. Lend them or sell them, perhaps. Do you know, Louisa?'

'I am hungry.'

'Well, since Captain Clunie doesn't know himself … yes, Robert, Elizabeth will be here in a moment.'

'I am hungry too,' said Lucy with indifference.

'Captain Clunie had a letter from Mrs Clunie by the *Alligator*,' said Amelia to James. 'The *Hooghly* was delayed. She wrote from lodgings in Portsmouth, expecting to sail any hour.'

'Perhaps by now she will be at Rio,' said James.

'Very likely,' said Amelia.

'We have been to Rio,' said Lucy to James Murray.

'I have,' said Robert. 'You haven't.'

'I have!' said Lucy. 'Mr Murray, I have!'

'I *think*—' said James.

'Mr Murray, she was not even born.'

'Lucy will go there soon,' said Louisa.

'Oh, very soon,' said James with enthusiasm.

'Yes,' said Amelia, 'if Lucy goes to Ireland with her mama, Rio is on her way.'

'Captain Clunie,' said Louisa, speaking quickly to forestall Robert, 'showed me a page of Mrs Clunie's letter. She recounted how while she was waiting in Portsmouth her cousin, who is married to a ship's captain, contrived to get her a short voyage on one of the new steam vessels. She said she found it too reverberative. If one stood at a certain spot on the deck, she said, she was sure one would jump up and down minutely for the length of the voyage.'

'Oh!' said Robert, staring in fascination into Louisa's face.

'I suppose there is no necessity to stand in that particular spot,' murmured Amelia.

'All the same,' said James stoutly, 'it is the vessel of the future.'

Lucy had got to her feet and was jumping up and down.

'No,' said Robert, 'not like that. Not big jumps like that.'

'Yes! Yes!' Lucy's voice almost drowned the renewed shrieking from the bedroom. 'Like this! Like this!'

389

'No!' Robert beat a crutch on the floor in frustration. '*Little* jumps!'

Elizabeth Robertson came in.

'Oh dear, oh dear, oh dear. Now what is this? Stop that jumping, Miss Lucy.'

'I have,' said Lucy.

'She has,' said Robert indignantly at the same time.

'Lucy,' said Amelia, 'don't go back to your blocks. You say you are hungry. Elizabeth will give you something to eat.'

'I don't want anything to eat.'

'It is laid out in the nursery, ma'am.'

'Very good,' said Amelia. 'Send Madge to tell me when they have finished, Elizabeth. I will wash and change them and put them to bed.'

'I am making a house,' said Lucy.

'Come, now, Miss Lucy.'

'I don't want to go out there.'

'Lucy, dear . . .' Amelia rose and took her hand, but Lucy pulled it away, grasped James Murray's leg, and cried piteously that she wanted to stay with him. Robert swung over to Elizabeth's side.

'Look, Lucy, *I* am going with Elizabeth.'

'And so will Lucy,' said James. He picked up the little girl, and held her, sobbing, over his shoulder, patting her back with his free hand.

'There is a good pudding,' said Elizabeth, leading the way from the room.

'Are there currants in it?' enquired Robert.

Lucy stopped sobbing abruptly.

'Black with 'em,' said Elizabeth.

Lucy's resumed sobbing was slightly forced. 'Poor mites,' said Amelia, when they had gone. 'But they are young. Their faith,' she said, sighing as she picked up her sewing, 'has not been endangered and eroded by the disbelievers of this world. Perhaps Frances can convey the plans to Sydney, Louisa. I wonder when they will leave. Let me see—the news will go down on the *Alligator*. You know she has been detained for that purpose. I have not written a *single letter*. Well, she will arrive there in, say, eight days. And a ship to carry them is certain to be dispatched at once. That will be another eight days. Sixteen days, and some to spare for bad weather or delays.'

'Three weeks,' said Louisa.

Amelia nodded. 'To be on the safe side.'

James Murray came back, sighing and shaking his head.

'Poor James,' said Amelia, looking at him over her sewing.

He sighed again, and sat down.

'Well, James,' said Amelia, 'it is an ill wind, but it has blown its modicum of good.'

It was their first opportunity of discussing the event without the presence of the children. James Murray nodded in agreement. 'There will be no libel action.'

'That is not what I meant by good,' said Amelia. 'Mr Smith Hall *ought* to be brought to book.'

'Someone else will do it,' said Louisa.

'But who as fit as our late commandant, Louisa, armed with his perfect probity?'

Murray lowered his eyes. Louisa looked with cocked head at her sketching pad. 'Then what did you mean,' she asked, 'by a modicum of good?'

'Why, that they are not for Madras.'

'True!' cried James with relief.

'Madras is *not* healthy.'

'Where will they go?' asked James.

'To Ireland, I expect,' said Louisa.

'*One* . . . may go only so far as Sydney.' Amelia paused, with needle high and thread taut, and gave Louisa a consulting look. 'I understand that to be a possibility?'

'Do you suggest that Miss O'Beirne—' But James stopped in confusion, made too shy by his own boldness to go on.

'Will marry there?' Amelia did not look at Louisa this time, but continued assiduously to sew. 'There has been talk of it. And in my opinion, and I am sure in Letty's, it would be quite the best thing.'

Letty shrieked again. James Murray pursed his lips, and Louisa went on pencilling her measurements. But Amelia shook her head.

'All the same, it does *not* signify that she is out of her mind.'

'That hardly needs saying,' murmured Louisa.

'Grief is not madness,' agreed James Murray.

'Of course not! But my dear James, to refuse to see *you*!'

'She refuses to see anyone,' said James.

'Except Frances, which is *quite* natural.'

'Frances is allowed in,' said Louisa, 'but I doubt if she is seen. She stands helplessly, poor girl, and watches, and can do nothing.'

'So young! How can she find the right words?'

'What are the right words?'

'Louisa, the words of God.'

James bowed his head. 'She will be ready to receive them soon.'

'Carried by whom?' asked Louisa.

Amelia rested her sewing on her lap. 'I would offer myself as a humble receptacle, but would not do so if dear James were of our faith, or if there were another of our faith more fit than I. Now, how we *do* feel our lack of a chaplain!' She raised her sewing again. 'Henry Cowper would of course do his best, but he is a poor substitute at such a time.'

'Henry does not offer himself as a receptacle,' said Louisa. 'At least, not for that. What a good thing Captain Clunie decided there should be no service today. He would have had to take it himself.'

James Murray drew his watch from his pocket. 'I ought not to be so long absent from the hospital.'

But he spoke without urgency, and did not rise from his chair, for he was infected by the general disorganisation. He had not been forced to travel by bullock cart to the Eagle Farm during the absence of the search party: Clunie had kept him at hand not only to attend Robert, but to make sure that he would be present to attend Letty when the news came. No surgeon had been at the Eagle Farm for more than a week: medicines had been sent out by bullock cart with the rest of the stores, and so far at least, no one had been the worse for it. Yesterday James Murray had murmured to Clunie his first suspicion that under Logan too much had been done by rule instead of by need.

The drawing room was neither as pretty nor as comfortable as before. The blue sofa was still in its usual place, but the armchairs were contained by crates, and more empty crates, ready to receive other pieces, stood about the room. A few chairs, sturdy and rough, had been sent on loan from the lumber yard. Two of the shelves in the glass-fronted cupboard had been cleared of china, and a small crate stood open nearby, for Letty and Frances had been on their knees, packing the china, and Lucy, on top of a big crate, had been exulting over Robert, whose injury had prevented the climb, when Letty, as if informed by instinct, had suddenly risen, and had blundered across the room and through the french doors, and had seen the boat.

'The burial—' said Amelia. She broke off, let drop her sewing, and burst into tears. 'No, to be sure, it is simply too dreadful. Try to keep up one's spirits as one may, it is too dreadful.'

James Murray leaned out of his chair. 'He must not be buried here.'

'No,' said Louisa.

'That is what I was about to say,' said Amelia, sobbing into a handkerchief. 'There are prisoners—monsters—who say that if he is buried here, they will have him up.'

'But supposing she wants him buried here?' asked James.

'We must all dissuade her,' said Louisa. 'You are right, Amelia. It is simply too dreadful.'

'Oh, so I am right, am I?' said Amelia, bridling through her tears, the toppling of one barricade having endangered others. ' "Right for once", I think were the words on your tongue. I don't miss your mockery, Louisa. And there is much else I don't miss, that you think I do.'

'Well, dry your eyes,' said Louisa calmly. 'We must not quarrel, you and I.'

'Certainly not, ladies,' said James, trying to laugh.

'Especially at this dreadful time,' said Louisa.

'Indeed! Indeed!' cried James eagerly.

Amelia put away her handkerchief and picked up her sewing. 'The white perpetrator of his murder,' she said in a voice only slightly tearful, 'or perpetrators, if more than one, must suffer the full penalty of the law. But I have said before, and I say now, and I shall repeat as often as needs be, that even at a time like this, the poor blacks must *not* be blamed. *We* must accept their share of the blame, for our failure to send missions among them. The law of man is but a reflection of the law of God. How may they be punished by a law they don't know?'

Louisa and James assented. 'But of course,' said Louisa, 'neither black nor white will be punished unless they are taken first.'

'Inconceivable that they won't be!' said James.

'Or that they will be,' said Louisa.

'Poor Captain Clunie. One sees his dilemma. He has *not* the men to send, yet must make the attempt. Lancelot,' said Amelia, looking only at her sewing, 'longs to go, though still feverish.'

'And Victor. But it is absurd. How will they know where to look? The murderers may be hundreds of miles to the north or west by now, in country as wild and strange as the poles. And speaking of things wild and strange, James, you have not given me your opinion of my flower sketches.'

'Ma'am, I prefer not to.'

'Flowers should not be made to look like fleshly creatures,' said Amelia in a suddenly trembling voice.

'Yet now I have begun to do them in that way,

I can see them in no other. It is very peculiar. How lucky your insects were finished, James, before this mood took me. When one can talk to Letty again, shall we give them into her charge to deliver in London?'

'Why not into Frances's charge?' enquired Amelia.

'Well—'

'So you do think she will end her journey in Sydney?'

'I believe,' said James, 'that she is quieter.'

They all listened.

'Yes,' said James, nodding, 'I don't hear even the sobbing. She is calmer.' He looked at his watch again. 'I shall wait a few minutes longer.'

Letty was certainly calmer. Still wearing the apron she had put on to pack the china, she lay near the edge of the big bed. Her right hand, which had felt so inanimate in Frances's grasp of attempted consolation, was trailing over the edge, and her face was turned away, instead of rearing up at the chin, as before, to gasp and rake in the air needed for the expression of her sorrow. Her breast heaved in sighs instead of her former shuddering sobs, and except for these sighs, she was silent.

Only her feet were unaltered. In white stockings discoloured at the toes, they stuck straight up from the bed and pointed in different ways, like headstones neglected and askew. Frances found them so much a betrayal of her sister's usual practised grace that it seemed an indelicacy to look at them, and as much as possible, she avoided doing so.

Frances no longer stood in uncertainty by the bed. Reconciled to at least a temporary helplessness, she had drawn a chair to the bedside, and was sitting with her elbows on its arms, and her feet on the first steps of the bedsteps, waiting again.

Before, she had been waiting simply for the first crazed sorrow to pass, as she knew it would do, for she had experienced it in some degree in her own life, and because she came from a country where there was much to mourn, had been able to observe it besides in Bridie and Meg and many others. But now, as Letty's sighs became less frequent, and then died, and the silence took over entirely (yet was an active silence, and not to be imagined as the silence of sleep) Frances came to realise that her sister was deep in thought, was in the act at last of clothing her naked grief. And she realised too that her own present wait was not only for Letty to return to her surroundings (as Bridie and Meg, rising, would feel with their feet for their slippers and raise their hands to their hair), but that she was waiting as well for a sequel to the words Letty had said on seeing the boat. She was expecting, not an explanation of them, which she did not need, but some sequel in action.

While packing the china, Letty had been speaking

gently, insistently, and in a voice too low for the children to hear, on what seemed to have occupied her mind most during the absence of the search party, though Frances now believed that it was only by directing her concentration to this one question—and to the future it might hold for her children—had she been able to alleviate her intense apprehension, to make her hands steady to wrap and pack the Irish china, and her voice to insist, against Frances's equally gentle insistence, 'But my love, you must send another letter by the *Alligator*. The coolness of your last weply was almost a discourtesy.'

'I have not refused to marry him. I said I looked forward to our meeting in Sydney.'

'Where you will impose your impossible conditions.'

'Other persons in the colony have no convict servants.'

'No gweat estate is managed without them.'

'Nor does everyone have a great estate, or is heir to one.'

'Fwances, without his uncle, what is he? A stwuggling lawyer.'

'True. Indeed, it would be little better than governessing. So unless I find I love him, which would make the struggle worth something, I shan't marry him. But it will never come to that, because in a choice between his uncle's estate and me, he will choose the estate.'

'Thus showing his good sense.'

'No doubt.'

'Oh Fwances, silly Fwances, let things be. He will accept his uncle's offer, and you will be his wife, and you will have the gweater chance of convict wefom, because you will be among them.'

'But who will reform their masters?'

'Why, if that is needed, you will also be among them.'

'And their master's masters?'

'Can you aim so high?'

'Not alone. No. And besides,' said Frances, more gentle than ever, 'most of those are not capable of reform. They must be removed from office.'

'What! Oh, gwacious, Louisa says there are no Jacobins now, but there is one left, I swear.'

But she had laughed as she spoke, and Frances had smiled in response, and as if in agreed respite, they had consulted on packing the china.

'Spouts are a pwoblem.'

'Mama,' said Lucy, let me look at the tea pot.'

'No,' said Robert abruptly, 'it is to be packed.'

'We could pack it this way,' said Frances.

But Letty had got to her feet and was blundering towards the door. The children, silenced at once, Lucy on the crate and Robert below, were watching her. Frances put down the tea pot and ran after her.

As soon as she saw the boat, Frances turned back

and shut both the french doors, so that the children, still as immobile as she had left them, could not follow.

The tide being low, the boat was drawn in, not to the stone wharf, to which the body would have had to be raised many feet, but to the narrow timber jetty near the house, which advanced far enough into the stream to allow the body to be lifted with comparative ease on to the waiting stretcher.

This transfer was in progress when Frances reached Letty's side. Knowles and another of the hospital attendants were receiving the body from Lazarus, who stood upright in the rocking boat, while Collison and Henry Cowper, in a second boat with the other prisoners, had come alongside to hold the first steady.

Captain Clunie and James Murray stood together on the wharf, and if proof were needed of the contents of that great stained cocoon, it was given by the swift glance of trepidation Murray suddenly sent over his shoulder towards the house, and which, catching on Letty's face, turned into a stare of dismay. Murray's glance was followed by Clunie. He saw Letty, removed his cap, and bowed his head in solemn confirmation.

Frances put an arm round Letty's shoulders and turned her towards the drawing room. She let herself be turned, making little hobbling movements with her feet. Her eyes were glassy and unfocused, the blood had left her face, and she spoke through whitened lips.

'At least, now it will not all come out.'

'No,' said Frances, fully understanding in that moment what the main burden of her sister's worry had been. But it was doubtful if Letty heard her, and indeed if she was herself conscious of having spoken. As Frances opened the door, she pushed past her, and ran across the room to where Lucy, crouching on top of the crate, and Robert, on his crutches at its base, were waiting. Frances thought she was about to embrace them, but when she had almost reached them she halted, as if in confusion and forgetfulness, and simply stared. By the time any of them spoke, Frances had reached them.

'My father is dead,' whispered Lucy.

Frances supplemented Letty's twisting but silent lips. 'Yes.'

'They have all been saying so,' said Robert with a nod. 'They say Boylan got him.'

Letty whirled about to face her sister. She spoke very fast. 'Let them stay only with you or Elizabeth. Or Amelia or Louisa, if they will.' She grasped Frances's hands in hers and vigorously shook them. 'I will see no one.'

'Not me?' cried Frances, her eyes filling with tears.

'No one! No one!' said Letty with ferocity.

In her rush from the room she was impeded by Madge Noakes and Elizabeth Robertson, who came crowding together into the doorway. Elizabeth's face was crumpled in distress, but Madge's was peaceful, and her dark eyes enlarged and steady. She wore neither cap nor kerchief, and was fastening the buttons of her bodice as she came.

Letty clapped both hands over her face. The women stood aside, and with her face still hidden, Letty ran between them. When she reached the corridor, Frances heard the first shriek. She stood distracted, her will divided between her emotions and her instructions, uncertain whether to follow or to stay, until she saw that Lucy had clambered down from the crate and was crossing the room towards the verandah, and that Robert was following her, swinging fast on his crutches.

She brought them back, gave them into Elizabeth's charge, and warned her that they were to stay in the nursery. 'He is with our Lord in heaven,' Elizabeth told them as she led them from the room.

Henry Cowper arrived soon after. Captain Clunie, he said, would be here presently.

'And has sent me ahead. Am I needed?'

Madge still lingered in the doorway. 'You may go, Madge,' said Frances. When the woman had gone she said to Henry, 'She will see no one. That is her wish. Should we obey?'

'In the meantime, at least.'

He sat down heavily, a hand on each of his spread knees, and looked at the floor between his feet. Amelia

403

and Louisa came, having made their own admittance. Louisa was perturbed, and Amelia aghast, at the shrieks now growing in volume.

'*I will* go in,' said Amelia.

'As long as we can hear her,' said Henry, 'it would be better to do as she says.'

'Oh, but it is too terrible. And we have been told almost nothing, you know. Only that he is dead.'

'Captain Clunie will inform you when he arrives.'

But unless they were to sit in complete silence, it was inevitable that some of the story would come out.

'He may have got away—I believe he would have—but he put the mare at a jump over a gully. It was only twelve foot or so. She could have done that and much more. But bareback, without her accustomed guidance . . . To be sure, he would have shouted his "hup!" and she must have all but got him across. He must have been able to clutch at some growing thing, and scramble out and run. While she, poor creature . . .' concluded Henry, with a tired shrug.

When Captain Clunie arrived, and was engaged at once by Louisa and Amelia, Henry moved unobtrusively to Frances's side. She sat in the most distant corner of the room, her face swollen and tear-blotched. She was relieved that this condition seemed to have been accepted as natural by the others, even by Louisa, and was alarmed when she saw Henry approach, for it confirmed her impression that he had observed her (by an accidental flash, it seemed) at the onset of her tears.

He bent over her chair. 'Her neck,' he said, 'was twisted beneath her body. You know what that means? Broken neck? Over in a second?'

But she knew by the very kindness of his tone, and by the embarrassed deliberation with which he had approached her chair, that this was not so. Out of politeness, and in appreciation of his effort, she nodded her head in acquiescence while at the same time pressing her hands to her mouth to suppress the sobs that continued to rise. For she could see Fatima's forefeet scrabbling at the loose earth of the bank, while her hindlegs dropped back into space, could see the roll of her eye, and hear her high whinny of terror. She was shocked that she could grieve for the mare, and not for the man, and it was this shock, and her self-condemnation, that made her compose herself at last.

Louisa and Amelia had gone separately to Letty's room and had both been dismissed with an upflung hand pushing violently at the air as if against their own bodies. But Captain Clunie did not agree with Henry. 'It would be most imprudent,' he said, 'to leave her alone.' Frances had gone in, and had been allowed to stay. She stood by the bed and picked up Letty's hand, admitting her own fraudulence, but glad of its usefulness, for she knew that the marks of strong sorrow on her face had sponsored her permission to stay.

She had been called to the door once, by Louisa, who whispered that she and Amelia and James Murray were waiting in the drawing room, all of them ready to help in any way, and that the children would stay with them till supper time. She had heard Murray speak to Lucy as he carried her down the corridor, and when she went to the window, and drew aside the curtain, she saw that it was beginning to grow dark.

She returned to the bed, and since her sister was so still and quiet, she ventured to say softly, 'Letty . . .?'

There was no reply, but she now saw that while she had been at the window, Letty had crossed her ankles. Reassured, she sat down again, and although the face Letty presently turned to her was dreadful, so puffed that it looked as if it had been pummelled out of shape, and the eyes that gave it so much of its life were sunken and dull, Frances yet trusted in the decorum of those crossed ankles, the ordered contiguity of the feet.

'It is Sunday,' said Letty.

Her voice was husky, scarcely audible; Frances leaned forward in her chair. 'Yes,' she said.

'I have heard no bells.'

'There have been none.'

'Has there been no service?'

'No.'

'On this, of all occasions . . .'

Frances took her sister's hand. 'It was thought

406

better . . .' The lifelessness of the hand she held unnerved her. 'It was decided . . .'

But Letty had caught the suppressed phrase. 'It was thought better not to let them assemble.'

'Captain Clunie—'

'Lest they waise their voices in joyous celebwation,' said Letty in soft bitterness.

But Frances had never heard of the celebration on the death of Bishop the scourger. 'Oh, no,' she said, 'I have heard no talk of that.'

'None is needed. Not for me. I saw Madge Noakes's face. And her neck. She dared, she dared—' Letty pulled her hand from Frances's grasp and covered her mouth for a moment. Then she said, 'She dared, because it was Boylan.'

'Boylan who—'

'Yes.'

'I heard Robert say so, Letty. Only Robert.'

'He wepeats what they all say. And in any case, Boylan is only a name. Be it Jones or Jackson, it is all the same, as long as it was one of them.'

'But,' said Frances, 'it was the blacks.'

'The blacks?' For the first time, Letty showed in tone and face the quickening of calculation. 'Only the blacks?'

'It is believed that one or more runaways were among them,' said Frances. 'But as to leading them, there is no proof of that.'

'But since you mention it, there is talk of it.'

'I don't know, I don't know. If you were to see Captain Clunie . . .'

But Letty had turned her head on the pillow and was looking up at the lace valance of the bed. 'But it is twue,' she said slowly, 'that talk is not pwoof. There is no pwoof perhaps that any were among the blacks.'

'Letty, I will say no more, lest I mislead you. See Captain Clunie. Or Louisa, who has had the whole story from him. My tears,' said Frances, surmounting a twinge of shame, 'took me away for part of it.'

But it was easier to surmount the shame than the pity that recurred when reminded again of the mare's terror as the weight of her hindquarters pulled her back. Tears flowed into her eyes. She made no sound, but covered her eyes with a forearm.

'You weep for me, Fwances,' she heard Letty say. 'But for him, too, I think, as only a monster would not.'

One day, thought Frances, hiding behind her forearm, perhaps I shall be able to.

'But now,' said Letty, 'we must both consider the childwen.'

Frances knew that Letty would not raise the question of her marriage to Edmund at a time like this, but nor did she imagine that the subject was done with. Under cover of her arm, she reaffirmed her resolution in the matter, and having done so, was able to wipe her

408

eyes with her hand and let it fall with the other into her lap.

'Letty, I beg you,' she said earnestly, 'to see Louisa. She and Mr Murray and Mrs Bulwer wait in the drawing room. All wish only to be of use to you. As I do, darling Letty, as far as I am allowed.'

'Why, *I* will allow you.'

Frances, making thanks for the allowance with a deep nod, hoped her silence did not hint (not yet) at what would limit her use to Letty.

'I will see Louisa. And you, dear Fwances—' Letty reached out and lightly touched Frances's arm—'pway take charge of the childwen. Amelia will offer, but we know Lieutenant Bulwer has his intermittent fever. Amelia is too good, and we must not pwesume on her.' Letty raised herself to a sitting position on the edge of the bed. 'Where are my shoes? And pway, ask Elizabeth to bwing warm water. Madge must not come. On no account, Madge.'

The official mail by the *Alligator* had been taken, as was usual, to the commandant's office in the garden. On the arrival of the boat bearing Logan's body, the duty to open the mail passed to Clunie, but immediately to come and go through the commandant's garden seemed too cruelly to emphasise his death, and for this reason (as well as to keep clear of the female turmoil in the house) he had it brought to his little office in the

409

weatherboard cottage. There was not much; he opened it while waiting for Edwards, whom he had called to confer on whether a party should be sent tomorrow into the bush. He himself thought the project hopeless, but Edwards was the only officer of the fifty-seventh left on the settlement; it was a courtesy to ask for his opinion.

The first seal he broke revealed the confirmation of his own succession, 'after Captain Logan should have left New South Wales', to the post of commandant, at three hundred pounds a year, and with the usual allowances and privileges. He had wanted it, waited for it, yet apprehension settled in him like a stone. The covert jubilation of the prisoners was accompanied by an adulation of himself. 'He's a good 'un,' he could almost hear them saying. 'He'll be different.' He certainly did intend to be different, but was fearful of an approval that rose not from deliberation, but merely rebounded from their loathing of another man. The first test of it, he knew, would be his sentence on the men who had refused to touch Logan's body; they were to come before him in the morning.

But his pay as commandant would start immediately, for Captain Logan had undoubtedly left New South Wales, and his apprehension was soothed by the fact that this unexpected money would help to offset his wife's extravagance in the matter of the furniture.

Now that the confirmation of his appointment had

arrived, the mail must also contain an official letter to Logan with the same message. But all he found was a letter addressed to Logan by name, not, as was usual, to 'The Commandant'. Nor did it bear the official seal. Nevertheless, it was by the hand of one of Macleay's clerks—the same, indeed, who had written the confirmation of his appointment. After a moment's hesitation, Clunie opened it.

Governor Darling had requested him, wrote Macleay, to inform Captain Logan that his illness at the time of Captain Clunie's leaving Sydney had prevented the circumstance being made known to him, as was intended. He now informed Captain Logan that Captain Clunie was sent with advice of ultimately replacing him, as his presence here was likely to be soon required in consequence of the trial of the editor of the *Monitor*, and at any rate, before long, to accompany his regiment to India.

The letter continued with the usual request to give Captain Clunie all possible information and assistance, and concluded by saying that the Governor would have no objection to Captain Logan returning to Sydney for the purpose of making arrangements to leave the colony, but that he had no desire that he should relinquish his present situation one moment sooner than might be necessary to enable him to make such arrangements.

Clunie's first thought was that Logan need not have worried, after all. But, like a man who, as he turns away from a friend, sees on his face an ambiguous smile, and sharply turns back to verify it, Clunie had no sooner put the letter down than he seized it and read it again.

And now he frowned, as the man might do who examines his friend's composed face and asks himself if he has been misled by fancy. The governor's wish that Captain Logan should not relinquish his present situation one moment sooner than might be necessary would hardly need stating if it had not been, at some time, in doubt. Or had the doubt been only Logan's, and this the reply to it? Had Logan sat down, weeks ago, just as a mail was about to leave, and written a private letter, asking for his position, and Clunie's, to be defined? If he had, the fact that he had not mentioned it to Clunie was a guarantee that there would be no draft of it in his letter book. Clunie would never know.

Indeed, the one unambiguous part of the letter was the date: October 4th. Clunie had arrived at Moreton Bay early in August. Governor Darling's explanation of his tardiness was not good enough: other correspondence had taken place during his illness, which, Clunie had learned from the *Sydney Gazette*, had not been serious. Clunie could not reject the suspicion that only now, when the fifty-seventh was under orders for India, and Logan's departure from the colony assured, was it safe for the governor to be friendly.

He wondered what Logan himself would have

made of the letter. Reassurance, he guessed, would have been followed by despondency; and a swift and vivid memory of that despondency made him determine that he, at any rate, was not going to bother his head about it further. The only problem it presented now was whether it was private or semi-official, whether it should be given to Mrs Logan or kept with the office correspondence. He thought the former proper, but if she also found it ambiguous, it would fire her grief afresh. Perhaps it was too early to give it to her. He put it aside and began on the rest of the correspondence.

The servant who came in, and whom he expected to announce Edwards, announced instead Mrs Logan and Mrs Harbin. Clunie got quickly to his feet, a hand still on the back of his chair. The man stood alone in the doorway. 'Where are they?' he asked.

'Sir, the sitting room.'

'Oh. Good fellow. When Lieutenant Edwards comes, ask him to wait in here.'

Clunie entered the sitting room with his head enquiringly cocked, his eyes full of concern. They stood together in the centre of the small flimsy shabby room. Louisa was bare headed but Letty had covered her head with a thin black shawl. It hung about her shoulders and cast dark shadows on her face. He had never seen a woman so changed in the course of a day. After a quick look at Louisa, which she answered simply by directing him with her eyes towards Letty, he turned upon Letty his look of full concern. She extended a hand. He took it as he bowed.

'My dear lady. I would have come to you. You had only to send.'

She bent her head. 'Captain, it is more fit that I come to you.'

Again he looked quickly at Louisa, and again Louisa slid her eyes towards Letty. Letty was holding the edges of the shawl together with a hand beneath her chin; he saw that she was an appellant.

'Well,' he said, looking about the room, 'you will sit down. You will take something?'

But they would neither sit nor take refreshments. 'Sir,' said Letty, 'Mrs Harbin has told me something of how my husband died.'

'As I had it from you,' said Louisa to Clunie.

'Oh,' he said, 'and now you wish to know more. It's very natural. But my very dear madam, don't you think it wiser to wait?'

'I wish to know only one thing at pwesent, Captain Clunie.'

'I am at your service, of course.'

'I wish to know that he was killed by blacks.'

'He was attacked by a large number of men, Mrs Logan.' Puzzlement gave his voice a note of enquiry. 'So most could only have been blacks. What part absconders played we don't know.'

'If indeed they played any part,' said Letty.

414

'What proof is there of it?' demanded Louisa.

He looked from one to the other. Their intentions were obviously known to each other; he wished they were known to him. He said, 'There is the burial, Mrs Harbin?'

'It may have been done by a twibe from the north or west,' said Letty. 'Pway, what do we know of their customs?'

'Because we know of none who bury,' said Louisa, 'must it be assumed that there are none?'

'No,' he said, 'certainly not.'

'Apart from the burial, captain, it seems pure surmise.'

'And gossip,' added Letty.

'My dear ladies, I incline to the same opinion.' But he still looked puzzled. 'I wish you would sit down,' he said.

Neither of them moved. 'Captain,' said Letty in a stronger voice, 'weports of the matter will go to Sydney, to the governor and to Colonel Allen.'

'Of course. Mine to the governor will go by the *Alligator* tomorrow. Edwards will send his later.'

'Vewy well, since there is no pwoof that absconders were concerned, I beg you to say firmly that it was done by native blacks, and to leave out all mention of wunaways. Sir, I beg you. To have been murdered by pwisoners, added to what Smith Hall accuses him of—'

415

She turned her head aside and put a hand over her eyes. Without hesitation, Louisa took over. 'And which can now never legally be refuted.'

'Never!' said Letty. She turned again to Captain Clunie. 'Oh, sir, if you had a son, would you like him to believe that his father was so hated by the men in his charge that they plotted to kill him, and at last succeeded? To be sure, it is no disgwace to be killed by bwutal and depwaved men. But their depwavity becomes less and less understood. I declare, by the time my boy is gwown, they shall be deemed he'woes and martyrs.'

'Oh, hardly, my dear lady. These are wild thoughts. And you do know—you must—that in an official report it is usual to set out all the circumstances.'

'But not all the surmises,' said Louisa.

'No,' he agreed. 'And since it is not surmise that blacks were there, I see no reason why I should not say simply that it was the blacks.'

'Thank you, sir.'

'I am happy to be of service.' He could hear Lieutenant Edwards' voice in the hall. He bowed, and then, since neither woman moved, he said uncertainly, 'Well . . .'

'I should be much obliged,' said Letty, 'if you would also avoid all mention of his wecklessness.'

'Recklessness, Mrs Logan?'

'That he rode away alone,' said Louisa, 'after

416

having been threatened by so many blacks.'

'His enemies may say,' said Letty, 'that such wecklessness amounts to a sort of suicide, and that he wished to avoid appeawing against Mr Smith Hall.'

'Ah, no, madam! These *are* wild thoughts.'

'They are not my thoughts, captain. I guess only what wicked persons may say.'

'No person in authority can avoid calumny entirely, Mrs Logan, do what he will.'

'All the same,' said Louisa, 'if a reason could be stated for his riding away—'

But Letty, as if visibly to cut herself off from this indirect tack, took a step in advance of Louisa.

'I am penniless,' she said curtly.

Clunie could no longer hide his discomfort. It was in his silence, and in his stare. What could be the purpose of such a remark? Did she want him to take up a subscription for her? Impossible that she should ask for that.

'More than that,' she said. 'He died deeply in debt.'

He continued to stare as if to divine her meaning in her cold and passive face. But now he felt Louisa's eyes upon him, and heard her say softly, 'Of course, Mrs Logan will have the military pension.'

Her slight emphasis on the word 'military' made their whole purpose clear at last. 'Oh,' he said. He turned on a heel and took a few steps about the room.

Her military pension would be about fifty pounds a year. If his own wife had two children, he should hate her to be forced to manage on that. 'Oh,' he said again.

Suddenly they were all sitting down. He hardly knew how it had happened, except that they were now in conclave, their three chairs drawn together. Louisa's hands were clasped in her lap. Letty's gauzy shawl had dropped to her shoulders. It occurred to Clunie in passing that she might marry again, but that too, he knew, would be likely to depend on how much money she had. 'Of course,' he said, 'you do know—' he was looking at each of them in turn—'that colonial pensions to widows and families are no longer allowed. It's a great shame, in my opinion. The disallowance is too recent to test whether exceptions would be made. But they ought to be, they ought to be.'

'I should think,' said Louisa, 'that when a man loses his life in exploration of benefit to his country—'

'Yes, yes, so do I. Upon my word I do. And I believe, madam,' he said, turning to Letty, 'that you are not without influence at home?'

Over her distorted face there passed such an expression of bitterness and weariness that Clunie was never to forget it, and was to wonder, in later years, if she had had in that moment a premonition of the long-drawn and humbling intricacies into which her role of appellant would take her: of petitions rejected, indefinitely delayed, or simply lost; of favours granted only to be withdrawn, and of the army agent's tax taken from the pittance granted at last. But at the time he thought only that she was exhausted, both by her grief and her worry, and most of all, perhaps, because her worry would not let her lose herself in grief; and he admired her when she said, straightening her shoulders and settling her gauzy shawl, 'No, I am not without influence. For myself, I would not use it. For my childwen, I shall use it for all it is worth.'

'You are right to do so,' he replied. 'And we must remember that even if a colonial pension is refused, there could be a gratuity, or a royal bounty.'

'There are any number of ways,' said Louisa with firm optimism.

'And I feel sure,' said Clunie, 'that you may count on General Darling's strongest recommendation.'

Now that Patrick Logan is safely dead, he added to himself. He remembered the letter from Macleay, and suddenly realised that to hold it back would be to announce his doubts about it. It must be given to her. He no longer believed that it would make her break down; he saw that she had determined on her stand.

'And for what my recommendation is worth,' he said, 'it goes without saying that you will have that too.'

Unsmilingly, she set him right. 'My husband will have it.'

'Of course. *He* will have it. I shall do everything you

419

have asked. It is Edwards' duty, not mine, to inform his commanding officer, but we all know Edwards. A good fellow. A good young fellow. Pray, don't leave for a moment. There is a letter in my office you must take.'

Edwards was waiting in the office. 'I shan't be more than another three minutes,' Clunie told him. 'Yes, yes, smoke by all means.' He took the letter and went back to the sitting room. Both women were standing again, ready to leave.

'Here is something long awaited,' said Clunie. He had decided on boldness. 'It would have removed from his mind every shred of doubt on the governor's benevolence towards himself. Well, too late! But if you have ever entertained any such doubts, ma'am, here it is, to remove them from yours.'

She opened it and held it slightly to one side so that Louisa could read it over her shoulder. Louisa read quickly. When she raised her eyes, Clunie was careful not to meet the shaft of her questioning glance, directed at him over Letty's bowed head. It seemed as if Letty would never finish reading. She must have read it over and over again, but neither by movement nor sound did she indicate what she was thinking.

Her face, when she raised it, was quite expressionless. She folded the letter, and ran the fold between a thumb and forefinger. She folded it a second time, and perhaps, in the deliberate way she passed it between finger and thumb, and in her avoidance of it by crooking her other three fingers, there was some disdain.

She said quietly, 'I shall tweasure it always.'

Clunie bowed low. 'I take it your escort is waiting?'

'My servant escorted us both,' said Louisa. 'If you could provide—'

Clunie was already at the door. 'Edwards!' he called into the passage.

Lieutenant Edwards was delighted to escort Letty. He bounded into the room, bowed as he apologised for smelling of tobacco, and, as he offered her his arm, managed to combine eagerness, sympathy, and deep respect. Louisa and Clunie watched them pass through the door.

'Does she really put such a value on that letter?' Louisa then asked softly.

'I don't know,' he replied. 'Poor lady!' he added.

'Poor lady, indeed! Well, better not to ask. Better to take her at her word. At first, captain, I thought you would never comprehend.'

'About—?'

'About the pension.'

'I was exceedingly dense.'

'I thought you were going to make her state it crudely, word by word. And she would have, you know. Oh, yes, she would have. You are busy, but I must keep you one minute more. It is my turn to ask a favour.'

Clunie sighed; Louisa smiled. 'Though it can hardly be called a favour. I believe all the kindness is on my part. Mrs Logan has taken a great dislike to Madge Noakes. She can't abide her in the house another day. With your permission, I offered to take her.'

'Oh,' said Clunie, laughing, 'I suppose you did. She is the best servant on the settlement.'

Louisa made a face. 'She has those hideous scars, and won't keep them covered.'

'My wife will induce her to.'

'Letty couldn't, for all her clever ways.'

'Then let them show. I doubt if my wife will be much affronted.'

'Ah. Then I shall have her only till Mrs Clunie arrives, so that her skills may be kept burnished.'

'Have her until the week before, so that Mrs Clunie may arrive at a burnished house.'

'Very well. But you are unkind.'

Clunie laughed again. It was amazing how such a plain woman could be so pleasing. And indeed, he thought, looking at her white forehead between the two wings of smooth red hair, there were times when she appeared almost handsome. It was a pity her clothes were so shabby, but Logan had told him that she had not a penny of her own, and unless Harbin, who was a light feckless fellow, got money from somewhere to purchase his captaincy, he supposed (as he bowed her out) that she would always be poor.

'My dear Edwards,' he said, 'I do agree. It seems positively disrespectful. And yet, what can we do? Send a few men? Where shall we send them? And can we spare them from the settlement? The mood here is curious. The commandant's murder has made them bold. And you may be sure of this, Edwards—the murderers are not sitting in the bush, near where they killed him, waiting to be taken. No, the thing is impracticable, unhappily. If we even had horses! But we have one. One!' repeated Clunie, holding up a forefinger. 'And he, poor beast—have you seen him since he returned?'

'Lord, yes,' said Edwards.

They were in Clunie's office, Clunie in a chair turned sideways from his desk, and Edwards, his forehead sweating and his jacket undone, in the armchair in which Logan used to sit. 'I daresay you're right, sir,' he said.

'Well, I repeat, I see Mrs Logan's request as quite reasonable.'

'It is enough that she makes it.'

'The only certain culprits, after all, are the blacks.'

'Yes. Though I'm bound to say,' said Edwards, 'that I see the hand of a runaway in it somewhere. It's not long since that fellow Lazarus said he saw Boylan out there.'

'I questioned him about it this morning. He says he wanted only to see a party sent out for nothing.'

'Do you believe him?'

'I believe I'll never shake him. If Boylan is really

somewhere inland, and should one day be taken, Lazarus will admit to nothing that may hang him. So it's all very fine seeing the hand of a runaway, Edwards, but precious hard to prove it's anything more than imagination.'

'Imagination? Well, I expect that's an infection I caught from Cowper.'

'Oh, Cowper.'

'Don't think me a bird of that feather, sir. When all's said and done, I'm of your mind. In my report I shall hold to the only thing I know. It was the blacks. And you say I ought also to write—'

'You are to write what you wish, Edwards. This is between you and Colonel Allen.'

'Yes, sir. But you think it better that I give a reason for his riding off alone. So do I. Collison says he rode off on the track of a horse or bullock. Isn't that enough?'

'It may be said that he followed it for an unreasonably long way.'

'Well, he rode towards Mount Irwin. I shall say he meant to bring back some basaltic formations. As he may well have done. He spoke to me of basaltic formations a few days before leaving. He talked a great deal about mountains. It wasn't a matter of fine scenery. In fact, you might say,' said Edwards with a laugh, 'that the stonier and lonelier, the better he liked them.'

'Some men are drawn to lonely places.'

'Sir, *you* don't believe his death was a sort of

suicide?'

'I do not. And neither does Mrs Logan. I beg you, Edwards, be clear on this—what Mrs Logan asks is only a provision against what his enemies, what the radical faction, may say or publish.'

'I think Cowper believes it, sir.'

'Indeed?'

'He says there was a last straw put on Captain Logan's load.'

'Does he say what it was?'

'No.'

'Or what the load was?'

'Oh, Cowper runs on, sir. But I take it that part of the load was his having to appear against Smith Hall. Words in court, Cowper says, are more inflammatory than cold facts set down in records.'

'I will see Cowper. I will suggest that he keeps his wild opinions to himself.'

Edwards puffed on his cigar for a moment, then took it out of his mouth and said, 'All the same, to go off alone like that, knowing there were hundreds of hostile blacks about—it *was* damned reckless.'

'Reckless?' repeated Clunie. He recalled his second night on the settlement, and how he had walked alone down the dark road from Mrs Logan's assembly. Reckless was what he had called Logan then. Reckless, impatient, and confoundedly moody. He had been right in every adjective, and could now have added many

425

more. 'Well,' he said, 'it was certainly imprudent. There is no need for you to write to Colonel Allen tonight, Edwards. Your report may go by the next ship. But mine goes on the *Alligator*.'

Edwards sprang to his feet. 'I'll take my leave, sir.'

'Yes, one must say of him,' continued Clunie, 'that he was neither prudent nor fortunate. Goodnight, Edwards.'

Collison, who is guarding the lead coffin at the hospital, is also giving his opinion of the late commandant. He is speaking to James Murray, who stands with his feet and fingertips together, and frowns at the floor.

'Since I been here, they been coming to me and saying he was this, and he was that, but mostly that he was cruel. But he was never cruel in a hot way. It was more that he thought of them as so many building blocks to be put to his use. Some thought nothing of this in him, but some couldn't bear it. And those that couldn't, they say to theirselves, Well, cock, I will make you hate me. Because you can't hate a building block, can you? To show theirselves as more than building blocks, that made them do the mad things they done. Take Lewis Lazarus, for one . . .'

Henry, in his office, can hear the sound of Collison's voice as he writes to his father. He does not look up.

His rum bottle is on his desk, and his pen speeds unfalteringly across the page. This is one letter he will finish in time to catch the mail, for at last he has a subject he can use in a way that is certain to find favour. 'I had an account direct from my son Henry,' his father will say. 'Indeed, he was one of the search party that found the unfortunate man. A dreadful business. Bridget, bring me that letter from my desk.'

Even as he writes, he finds it incredible that he should continue to seek the approbation of this old and secret enemy of the blood, and even as he wonders at himself, his pen continues to speed across the page.

'And as I rode back, I confess there were tears in my eyes . . .'

He grimaces at this, but still continues. He wonders if there is any limit to his abasement, and rather thinks (as he stops for long enough to take a drink) that there is not.

CHAPTER FIFTEEN

It was often remarked by Amelia during the next three weeks that the packing was a blessing.

'Must she do so much?' asked James Murray.

'My dear Mr Murray, unless you expressly forbid it—'

'I do forbid it. She takes no notice.'

'Then pray let her be. She does less than you might think. We all help her. The packing is a blessing.'

The children at the school were given an indefinite holiday, and Louisa's house was in Madge Noakes's hands. Louisa, Amelia, Letty, and Frances spent all of their mornings and some of their afternoons with aprons over their skirts and their hair in caps. Big Annie came every day, barging about with wild laughter which changed into awed silence whenever she encountered Letty.

The packing was a blessing in more ways than one: Letty constantly spoke in praise of Patrick Logan, and as she spoke threw sharp or begging glances over her audience, and at these times Louisa and Frances were able, while agreeing with their voices, to hide their dissenting eyes by bending to the contents of a drawer or by snatching up their aprons to wipe their sweating faces.

The men, of course—usually Murray and Clunie, on solicitous calls—could always bow.

Only Amelia had no need for subterfuge.

'This is a stone he bwought back from his discov'wy of the gweat downs, those he named after Governor Darling.'

Everybody in the room knew that Mr Allan Cunningham had discovered the downs. Murray bowed. Clunie bowed. Frances looked quickly away from the stone in Letty's hand. 'Lucy, put down that dish. And you, Robert—'

While Louisa rose gratefully from her knees and said that she would take the children to Elizabeth.

But Amelia said, 'That stone? Show me! But *of course*, you mean to keep it?'

'I shall keep it for Wobert.'

'Quite right! It will speak to him of his papa's achievements. Well, well, he is a woeful loss to the colony.'

Clunie bowed. Murray bowed.

Amelia and Letty began to work as a pair, while Louisa and Frances, often with the children under their supervision, spent many mornings in the scullery, washing and packing the dinner services. It was now sultry November weather. Letty agreed that the indoor privy should be shut, and that the women and children should use the privy in the garden. 'It is for only a vewy short time,' she said, 'else I should never permit it.'

All changed their clothes twice a day, keeping Big Annie busy with their laundry. Frances had become thin and darker skinned. 'You had better rest and shelter on the voyage to Sydney,' remarked Louisa, 'or you will make a sallow bride.'

Frances laughed. Louisa's assumption that she was to marry Edmund Joyce, and her denials, had become like a game they played to ease the tedium of their work.

'Sometimes I think you are Letty's emissary,' said Frances.

'What is that?' asked Robert.

He was always asking her questions now, with an anxious note in his voice. 'A kind of messenger,' she said. 'I thought you were over there, Robert, helping Lucy with her letters.'

Lucy caught her name. 'Aunt Fanny,' she called, 'I can make a good "N".'

'She can not,' cried Robert, limping over to prove it.

430

'But if you are Letty's emissary,' continued Frances to Louisa, 'it will do neither her, nor me, nor Edmund, the least bit of good. I have no notion what I intend to do, only what I have determined not to do.'

'Which is never to employ slaves,' said Louisa with a bored intonation.

'And never again to strike at anyone whose hands are bound, and who can't strike back.'

'You already sound like a governess.'

'There are worse things to be.'

'There are better.'

'I shall try those first.'

'A governess! The mortification of it!'

'Yes, and that first day, when one feels so strange, and doesn't know what to do with one's hands. But I daresay I should learn to do something with them. When I have learned so much, I could surely learn that.'

'Well, I abandon your education.' Louisa sat in the servants' rocking chair, put both hands behind her head, and lazily rocked herself. She had little capacity for sustained physical work. 'Whatever course you take,' she said, half-shutting her eyes, 'no doubt in ten years or so you will arrive at the state of most of us—simply of making do with what one has. Surprisingly enough—' she opened surprised eyes—'it is an art in which one may progress. I thought I knew all about making do with what one had, but now I find I can do more with it than I dreamed.'

'Your curious new drawings,' said Frances flatly.

'Those too! You speak of what you have learned, but it is nothing to what you have yet to learn. Nothing!'

Frances, who had knelt to empty the contents of a low shelf, sat back on her heels. 'I think I shall refuse to learn it, have nothing to do with it, if it confuses and overlays what I have come to know.'

'Well, perhaps there are always persons like that,' agreed Louisa, rocking again. 'Yes, I begin to imagine a state in which one may collect and make central one's knowledge, and shelter one's flame, so that it shall burn ever higher and hotter. When one thinks of it, nuns must be like that. And so must bigots, I expect. You will become a sort of secular nun. Let us say nothing about your becoming a bigot.'

'I think about it,' said Frances.

'You are conscious of the danger?'

'How could I not be, having lived in this place?'

'What is a bigot?' asked Robert, limping back. Though he had dispensed with his crutches, and limped only slightly, he tired easily, and every afternoon, when Letty took her rest, he was made to rest on the floor beside her sofa.

Delft was sent to take the place of the packed china, and in place of the twin mahogany dining tables, and the cluster of card tables, stood one huge oblong table with thick square legs. Robert, able to climb now, used

432

it as a stage on which he and Lucy improvised plays about kings and queens, wore table covers as cloaks, and were not reprimanded until the covers were needed to be washed and packed.

Frances went one day to the office in the garden to bring Patrick Logan's personal belongings to the house. There were only three: a dented silver ink pot, a silver pen holder, and a round ebony ruler. Captain Clunie, who had moved into the office by tactful degrees, was working at the desk.

'Captain,' said Frances, 'pray, after we leave, may Martin come back to work in the garden?'

He shook his head, looking into her face with eyes full of meaning and reproach.

She blushed, but made herself speak. 'Sir, why not?'

'He has joined the worst men. He has become incorrigible.'

He wished he could add that he suspected Martin of also becoming what they called a 'leman' or a 'lady'. But to do so would be to outrage her innocence. And yet, as long as any part of such knowledge must be hidden from her, she knew nothing. Her innocence was a danger to herself and to others. She was blushing still more deeply, but spoke in a clear voice.

'I know you blame me, sir, for what happened to him.'

'You must take part of the blame, Miss O'Beirne.'

'I do. I shall. But what of the rest?'

'It is his. I admit it.'

'Then let me take mine, and let him take his. But let King George take his share, too.'

'Miss O'Beirne, on this settlement, I am King George.'

'I know it, sir. So, let you take your share.'

Such insolence could be met only by coldness or amusement. Since she was so soon to leave, he chose amusement. 'All of us here serve King George. Would you have us all take a share?'

'I should, sir. It is the whole of my argument. Except my sister,' she added. 'I don't blame my sister.'

After she had gone, he thought that if she were right (which of course she was not), and they must all take some blame for Martin, she ought to blame her sister as well. He wondered on what grounds she made the exemption. Yet, for her sake, he was pleased she was able to make it. Such an illogicality seemed to put her in less danger of becoming a bluestocking.

When more than two weeks had passed since Clunie's report had gone on the *Alligator*, they began to expect the ship that would bring an answer and inform them of the arrangements made for bringing the family and the coffin to Sydney. The *Regent Bird* and the *Glory* were busy plying between the settlement and Dunwich, on each journey carrying crates to be stored in the depot, where they would await the ship.

'The *Governor Phillip* will be sent for you,' said Amelia, when all four were folding the curtains in the drawing room. 'Anything less would be scarcely decent.'

Lucy, playing on the floor, silently turned her face towards them. Unlike Robert, she seldom asked questions, and all were so busy that they hardly noticed, on the perimeter of their conversations, that pale face, those vague but listening eyes.

Letty had put off packing Patrick Logan's clothes, but now at last she had to begin it. She went to the big bedroom accompanied by Amelia, but placed herself apart by her silence, her downcast eyes and heavy, reflective movements.

Soon, even Amelia's voice became quieter. 'Time will show him to have been a martyr.'

Letty quickly raised her eyes.

'His death, Letty my love, will be the clinching argument in favour of carrying the gospel to the blacks, who, in the words of Our Lord, knew not what they did.'

But Letty had returned to her packing.

One of his uniforms had been dispersed in tatters in the bush. She folded the jacket of the other, and put it last into the small wooden trunk that held his remaining clothes. They were remarkably few. In the afternoon, when Louisa and Amelia had gone home, and Letty was resting, Frances, passing the room, looked in and saw Robert standing before the open trunk. He was wearing the jacket, both hands smoothing the breast of it while across one shoulder he considered an epaulette.

He saw Frances. 'I shall have one like it,' he said.

More and more, he spoke in this questioning tone. It was as if his questions had mounted so high in him that they must permeate every word he said.

She went into the room. 'Why, will you become a soldier?'

Again he questioned her with voice and eyes. 'Mama says I shall join papa's regiment.'

'You ought to be with mama now, resting your leg.'

'She fell asleep. I came away.'

He was of such beauty and quality that Frances was moved to calculate whether the interests of such as Martin were really of much importance if set against those of Robert and his kind. But Martin, and indeed, every prisoner on the settlement, had once been a child, and all, all, must have looked at an elder, if only once, and if only for a moment, with eyes as urgently questioning as these. Regretfully, Frances knelt in front of him, kissed his cheek, and slipped the jacket from his shoulders.

'You know you are not to touch such things without leave. Let us fold it exactly as it was.'

But she was not practised in folding military

436

jackets. When she saw Murray passing the door she called to him.

'Pray, can you fold this jacket?'

He held little repugnance for her now. Even if fresh disaster had not broached it, and time had not begun to fade it, and she had not come to feel that she shared his transgression, she could not have held out against the distress in his dark eyes when he looked at her, or his fluttering beseeching smiles. He put the jacket on the bed, folded it expertly, and carried it on the palms of both hands to the trunk. 'There is always the question,' he said, as he set it down, 'of what to do with them?'

'These go with us.'

'When my mother—departed, my father begged my aunts to take her clothes away.'

'Why?' cried Robert.

Frances laid an arm across Robert's shoulders. 'Were you a child at that time?' she asked Murray.

'I was.'

'So was I.'

'And so was Cowper,' said Murray.

She shrugged. 'It is very common.' Her equanimity made her seem rather hard. She took Robert by the hand. 'Have you come to see my sister, Mr Murray?'

'Yes. Does she know there is a ship?'

'I think not. She is sleeping.'

Robert broke away from Frances's grasp. 'A ship! A ship!'

But he was still unable to run. They caught up with him before he reached the drawing room. Captain Clunie had arrived. In one of the settlement chairs, he faced Letty, who was sitting on the sofa.

'Mama,' cried Robert, 'the ship has come.'

Letty sent a drowsy look over his head at Murray and Frances. 'The *Mary Elizabeth*,' she told them.

'Edwards has gone to Dunwich,' said Clunie. 'We must not be sure that she brings a reply to my report. She could have left Sydney before the *Alligator* arrived. But we may hope, we may hope.'

Robert had left the room as soon as his mother had spoken. Frances, who had caught a glimpse of his face, excused herself and went after him. She found him in the nursery, flung prone on the floor with his face hidden in the crook of an arm. Lucy, who had a heat rash between her shoulder blades, was scratching herself against the door jamb and watching him with open-mouthed interest. Elizabeth Robertson, standing above him, was making mild placatory sounds.

Frances knelt beside him and touched his shoulder. He angrily twitched in rejection of her hand. 'Robert,' she asked, 'why did you run away?'

'The *Mary Elizabeth*!'

'What of it?'

'It ought to be the *Phillip*.'

'What do you mean?'

'She is only little. All of us, our goods, and

papa's coffin. We will be herded in her like beasts or prisoners.'

'Robert, if you had not run off, you would have heard what Captain Clunie said. We are not to go in the *Mary Elizabeth*.'

'We are! I knew we would!'

'Robert, come with me.'

'I won't.'

'I will, Aunt Fanny,' said Lucy.

'No, Lucy. Elizabeth is to bathe your back with calamine. Come along, Robert.'

He allowed himself to be raised by an arm, and went sullenly by her side from the room. In the passage they met Captain Clunie, on his way out of the house.

'Captain, pray tell this boy that the *Mary Elizabeth* has not been sent to take us to Sydney.'

'Does he think—?' he asked with amazement, looking at Frances.

She nodded.

'Why, my boy, of course she has not come for that. Most likely she brings news that your transport will arrive in a few days.'

'Will it be the *Phillip*, sir?'

'Very likely, little man, very likely.'

Murray now came out of the drawing room, and he and Clunie left the house together.

'How is the horse?' asked Clunie.

'Cowper says he will not survive. But he says so only to vex me.'

They were in the garden, and had paused at the junction of their two paths, Murray's to the road, and Clunie's to his office. 'Why should Cowper do that?' asked Clunie.

'Oh . . .' Murray hesitated. 'It is his way. For my part, I think the horse will live. And even if he doesn't, if they send the *Phillip* for the family, there are bound to be fresh horses in her.'

'I believe there will be. I put my request in the strongest and clearest terms. I hope it is the *Phillip*. Indeed, if they are to travel with all their goods, it will need to be. Did you ever see such a pile as lies at Dunwich? The boy thought they were to go on the *Mary Elizabeth*.'

'Impossible, sir!'

'Murray, of course it is.'

'To subject her to so ignominious—'

'Murray, Murray, let us not bother even to speak of it. Governor Darling will pay the greatest respect both to the family and to Captain Logan's remains.'

Must pay the greatest respect, he had almost said. But in spite of his conviction that the governor, by supporting the honour of the late commandant, supported his own, he found himself arguing silently but hotly, during the rest of the day, that *of course* they were not intended to travel in the *Mary Elizabeth*. He went alone that afternoon to inspect the prisoners' barracks. The dormitory was utterly empty (for the men slept on the bare boards), and the floor had just been scrubbed. And yet it stank. If there were such a thing as a clean stench, he thought, this was it. He could have permitted himself to imagine it as the stench of bodies from which some vital spirit, or even perhaps the soul, had gradually been drawn. He could have permitted himself to hate and dread it.

But he would give himself no such licence. And nor would he permit himself to believe that his administration would be attended by the muddle, delay, and calamity that had helped to break Patrick Logan. Recrossing the barracks yard, he remembered how he had stood here with Logan on the day after his arrival, and had seen the dangers of isolation. Heated imagination was one of those dangers, and petty rumour was another. *Of course* they would not be made to travel in the *Mary Elizabeth*. He went to the lumber yard, where the carpenters were making a cedar press for his office. He was pleased that the prisoners, even those in the gangs, no longer looked at him with the inflammable adoration that had followed immediately on Logan's murder. 'Hard but just,' was the message he was now satisfied to read in their eyes. He had been careful to make no drastic reductions in punishments, but when men were brought before him on the complaints of soldiers and overseers, he would listen patiently to each of their stories, and would make sure he was seen to cogitate before passing sentence or pronouncing acquittal. When the men of the search party, those who had refused to touch Logan's body, were brought before him, he had not extended their sentences, but had removed, temporarily, their first-class privileges, explaining to them that they had earned this leniency by their willingness to help in other ways, such as cutting and trimming the trees needed for the pair of poles.

Edwards returned from Dunwich at noon on the following day, coming up the river in the *Glory* with the six convicts brought by the *Mary Elizabeth*. Clunie took the mailbag to his office, emptied it on his desk, and rapidly sorted the official mail from the private. He seized on the large letter addressed in the handwriting of Macleay's chief clerk and opened it first.

It was with the greatest regret, he learned, that the governor had received the melancholy news of Captain Logan's murder by native blacks while on a journey of exploration of great importance to the colony. The *Isabella* and the *Governor Phillip* were to sail from Sydney as soon as they could be made ready, the former to bear the remains of the late commandant, and the latter his unhappy widow, bereaved family, and whatever attendants they might need, and who could be spared from the settlement. Preparations were in course for a funeral appropriate to the honourable character, zeal, and chivalrous spirit of the late commandant.

Clunie found that he was smiling, though he had not (of course) expected much less. He quickly read through the rest of the letter. New brasses for the tread-mill had been made from the patterns sent, and were forwarded herewith; Bulbridge and Fagan had been condemned to death; the request for a boatbuilder made by the late commandant would continue under consideration only if he, Clunie, thought such an appointment necessary. There was nothing about horses.

He put on his cap, left the private mail in Whyte's office, then set out across the garden to carry the news to Mrs Logan. Murray was coming from the door as he arrived.

'Your mail is with Whyte, Murray.' He held up the letter and shook it. 'It is to be the *Phillip and* the *Isabella.*'

'Oh, sir, splendid! And sir, the horses?'

'No mention, but let us wait and see what the *Phillip* brings.'

'Very good, sir.'

Clunie shook the letter again. 'So I hope Mrs Logan is fit to travel?'

'Well, sir . . .'

Clunie's question had been only a pleasantry; the smile left his face. 'What?'

'Sir, if I could have leave to go with her . . .'

'Certainly, if you think it necessary. Indeed, this letter carries that permission.'

443

Clunie went into the house, and Murray ran down the garden path to Whyte's office. He collected three letters for himself and two for Henry Cowper, then ascended the path at the same eager pace, taking the steps three at a time. Today his horse had scarcely got him back from the Eagle Farm; he could not be put to that distance for many more days. Murray skimmed through his letters on his way to the hospital, but even on that brief reading seemed unable to concentrate.

He found Henry in the office, working on the hospital records. Clunie had asked him to draw up a table showing which diseases were the most prevalent among the prisoners, and which the most fatal. He liked such work; he looked as cheerful as Murray. 'Only thirty dead this year so far,' he told Murray, 'against nearly one hundred last year. We improve.'

'There are three cases of fever at the Eagle Farm.'

'And another here. The summer is upon us. What's that? Letters.'

He laughed when he saw the handwriting on his letters. 'I am popular. My stepmama also writes.' He put the letters aside unopened. 'What news of transport for the family?'

'The *Phillip* and the *Isabella*.'

'Honours are coming fast for all. And in two ships there are likely to be horses. I hope so, Murray, for your sake. Above all things, I should hate to see you on that bullock cart.'

'You won't, Cowper.'

'No, my dear fellow. Not if there are fresh horses.'

'Or even if there are not. I go to Sydney in the *Phillip*.'

'You?'

'To attend Mrs Logan. So, Cowper—' Murray let his satisfaction shine forth at last—'it won't be me that goes on that bullock cart.'

Henry stared for a while into the young man's face, then burst into laughter. He threw himself back in his chair, helplessly laughing, slowly slapping his chest with a hand.

Murray looked a little angry. Why had it not occurred to him that Cowper would not care—not one jot!—who saw him on the bullock cart?

CHAPTER SIXTEEN

All the administrative people agreed that the dispatch of the two ships, and the governor's plans for the funeral, augured well for the widow's future. 'She is bound to get a civil pension,' Clunie told Edwards. 'But it's as well to be cautious, and not to tell her so. I don't.'

'Mrs Bulwer does,' said Edwards.

'Mrs Bulwer is a soothsayer. She knows the exact route of the funeral, and the names of all who will attend.'

'And that the archdeacon is to officiate.'

'Well, he will, you know.'

The ships were expected daily. Captain Clunie found himself glancing often at the signalling station on the hill. He believed his wife would have reached Sydney, and that one of the two ships would bring him her first letter written in the colony. On visits to the commandant's house he cast surreptitious but calculating glances about the rooms, wondering where she would put this or that piece of furniture. He had become reconciled to her extravagance both by the discomfort and bleakness of the house, and by the longings that filled him in knowing her so near. She was not yet thirty, and they had been much separated; he hoped that during his term as commandant they would have children at last.

After a wait of only five days the signal from the *Governor Phillip* was received. Clunie had the *Regent Bird* made ready at once, and set out for Dunwich, leaving Edwards to take the news to Mrs Logan. Edwards had finished his report to Colonel Allen only the night before. 'I am not much of a hand at reports,' he told Letty, 'but I pride myself it's pretty clear. I conferred with Collison and that fellow Lazarus, then put it down as I would write a journal.'

'Will Lazarus go back to England?' asked Robert.

'I should *hope* not!' said Edwards, smiling in adult conspiracy at Letty and Frances.

'But he came from there,' said Robert.

'Has he a mama?' asked Lucy.

'Be quiet, Lucy,' said Robert. He turned again to Edwards. 'But he is to be pardoned for bringing in papa's body, so why should he not go back there?'

'Because he has forfeited his right to live there,' said Edwards reasonably.

'He has lost his wight to live in England,' translated Letty, 'because he has been bad.'

'Only good people live in England,' said Lucy with satisfaction.

'If only that were so!' said Edwards, with a droll look at Letty and Frances. Both smiled absently. They were working on a black dress—Letty tucking the bodice, and Frances hemming the seams of the skirt—so that Letty might arrive at Sydney correctly dressed.

Robert turned abruptly away from the conversation and climbed up on a chair. His leg was quite healed. When he jumped with a thud to the floor, Lucy climbed on a second chair and also jumped. When both had jumped several times, Edwards sent them an irritated look, and Letty told them sharply to stop, and that she couldn't hear a word Lieutenant Edwards was saying. Obediently both left their chairs and came to loll about their mother and aunt. Presently there was a break in the conversation. 'Will Lazarus live in Sydney?' asked Robert.

'If he pleases,' replied Edwards.

'His mama is in Sydney,' decided Lucy.

Edwards gave his pleasant easy laugh. 'If he has one, she most likely is. But he's a handy fellow, all the same. He says he will cut cedar in the south, and in a few years will buy a bullock team.'

'So many,' said Letty, with a sigh, 'acquire wiches.'

'Will he come with us in the *Phillip*?' asked Robert.

'No,' said Edwards. 'Captain Clunie has recommended—has written, and asked the governor to remit—to pardon him. But first his case must be considered.'

Frances lowered her sewing to her lap. 'Does that take long?'

'I have heard of it taking a year. You see,' said Edwards, laughing as he rose to his feet, 'it is very often like this business of the horses.'

'It is easy for them to acquire wiches,' said Letty dreamily. 'No duty impedes them. But *he* wejected a pwofitable civil post, in order to stay here as commandant.'

Edwards bowed very low. Frances lifted the black cloth and began to sew again.

The *Isabella* had joined the *Governor Phillip* while Clunie was on his way down the river. He arrived back at the settlement on the following morning. Louisa and Amelia, when they went to the office at noon to collect their mail from Whyte, went on to knock at the door of the inner office, so that they might ask for news of his wife. Liberties were possible with Clunie that would never have been thought of with Logan.

'She is well and cheerful,' said Clunie, looking soberly up from his papers, 'and expects to be here in a fortnight.'

'He does *not* appear well and cheerful,' said Amelia when they were outside in the garden.

'I expect it's because there are no horses.'

They went to the house, where they were to help with the last of the packing, and with finishing the black dress. There was nothing now to hinder the departure. The family, with Elizabeth Robertson and James Murray, were to embark on the *Regent Bird* at first light, but before then, by torchlight, the coffin was to be put aboard the *Glory*.

'Our good captain is in a deep dump,' Amelia told Letty, as she took off her bonnet.

'I observed it. He told me he had a vewy burdensome official mail. Look, here is a letter from Mrs Anning. She sends a most pwessing invitation for us all to stay at their Sydney house. Her nephew will be at the wharf to meet the *Phillip*.'

'What it is to have good friends!' cried Amelia, raising her hands and rolling her eyes.

In the office in the garden, Clunie was reading again the part of Macleay's letter that weighed most upon him. The heaviest awful sentence having been pronounced on Bulbridge and Fagan (wrote Macleay), it had been decided that it should be carried out publicly on the settlement, it being thought very desirable that the other prisoners should be informed of the impracticability of the attempt to escape, by them that had made it. Clunie was therefore requested to have erected . . .

450

In the house, the gardeners pick up the last of the boxes and crates to carry them to the *Regent Bird*. Such weight in the handcart creating too much impetus on the steep garden paths, they hoist them on to their shoulders. Clunie, who has begun his reply to Macleay, hears their heavy, uneven footsteps passing his office as he writes.

'. . . *would suggest that the gallows required should be erected in the yard of the prisoners' barracks, and the prisoners assembled at that place, when the sentence on the two condemned men is carried out.*'

By the time the gardeners return for another load, he has finished that part of his reply. He dips his pen, settles in his chair, and goes on, very deliberately, with the next.

'*I take this opportunity of stating that there is not now a single horse of any description on the settlement, and from the extent of the different establishments, and the distance of some of the grazing grounds . . .*'

The footsteps pass and repass. He decides that he will not even attempt to reply to his wife's letter until the evening. In any reply he might make at present, she is certain to detect the heaviness of his spirits. He knows that his spirits will have risen by this evening, for already he is more resigned to the event. He has asked that a hangman be sent from Sydney, so it may at least be hoped that the matter will not be bungled. Regrettably, men must be hanged somewhere, and since it has

451

fallen to his lot to arrange the business, it is hardly his place to shirk it. The wall around the barracks yard is not high enough to hide the top of the gallows, but the two men need not be left hanging long, nor be seen from the commandant's house. The house, thank God, is at a decent distance. This evening, he will call on Mrs Harbin and ask that she release Madge Noakes. He has noticed that since her departure the dust has collected in corners, and on sills and panes of glass. In the morning, directly the *Regent Bird* has sailed, the cleaning and burnishing would begin.

The gardeners' footsteps no longer pass the office. All that is left in the house of the family's belongings are the garments they are wearing, and the clothes and toilet articles that will be packed into baskets in the morning. When the gardeners have gone, and there is nothing left to do except the hem of the black dress (which Amelia is doing), Letty sits suddenly in one of the big plain cedar chairs.

'Something will happen to pwevent us leaving.'

'It can't!' cries Robert.

'My dear Letty!' says Louisa, with a touch of impatience.

'My love,' asks Amelia, sewing as she speaks, 'what can possibly happen?'

'The two biggest ships in the world,' Lucy reminds her mother.

'Not in the world,' says Robert.

But Letty, as if she has heard nothing of all this, shakes her head. 'At the vewy last minute, something will pwevent us.'

Frances is in her room. 'I think it very unlikely,' she says to the children, who have run to her for information. She is sitting on the edge of the narrow cot provided for this last night, and is pondering the mail brought by the *Governor Phillip*. She holds two letters, one from her sisters, the other from Edmund Joyce. Hermione and Lydia write that their Uncle Fitz brought a friend to the house. He told the girls he brought him expressly to see them. The name of the friend was Becket, but Hermione would address him only as Mr Bucket, and upon leaving the room, they both almost died of laughter. Mr Bucket looked at Hermione as if she were eighteen instead of thirteen, and at Lydia as if she were sixteen instead of twelve. No doubt he also mistook calves for cows, and if he came again, Hermione would ask him if he had ever milked one.

Edmund's letter is simply a brief cry of rejoicing that they are to meet so soon. The children have climbed on to her cot and are bounding about on the mattress. 'You are very unruly,' she tells them. She feels that she has too many conflicting duties, too many options. But since this is so, the sooner she launches herself among them, the better. She is impatient to leave.

'Mama says it will happen at the very last minute,' says Robert.

She folds the letters and puts them in her apron pocket. 'Mama is sad, and when we are sad we have such thoughts. Nothing will happen.'

All went well with their departure. At dawn they left the house and walked to the stone wharf. The *Glory* had already taken on the lead coffin and had put into the stream. Frances, who was in advance of the others, caught a glimpse of her as she rounded the first bend, but she was then distracted by Gilligan throwing the stump of his torch in the water, and when she looked again, the *Glory* was not to be seen.

Farewells had taken place the night before, but Captain Clunie was on the wharf, and so were Louisa and Amelia. There was a fair wind, and the *Regent Bird* got away well. Captain Clunie took off his cap, waved it, and walked briskly away. The bell had begun to toll for the morning muster. Louisa and Amelia turned away without waving, and departed at a stroll. They were to wave from the botanical gardens, and had plenty of time to make their way across the promontory. Their easiest way was through the commandant's garden, and as they passed the house they could hear the knock of brooms and the clanking of buckets. The drawing room window was thrown up as they passed on the path beyond the verandah, and for a moment they saw Madge Noakes's face, flanked by thick brown arms still raised to push up the window;

but either she did not see them, or was too busy to bother.

In the botanical gardens, they stood beneath the fig trees and waved long scarves, while the passengers on the *Regent Bird* waved handkerchiefs, scarves, and hats in response. Amelia and Louisa, experienced in farewells, did not sustain it for too long, but turned away after a few minutes.

From the side of the cutter, Frances watched them as they walked up the hill. The yellow line of prisoners was filing down from the crest, and for a few minutes it looked as if they must meet, but from the long line, group after group broke away and moved into the various plantations, until at last Amelia and Louisa, strolling, trailing their skirts, were alone on the path.

Frances had looked for the *Glory* as they sailed into the gardens reach, but she had disappeared. When the *Regent Bird* rounded the next bend, Frances expected again to see her, but again saw only unoccupied water. Robert was also watching for her. 'Where is the *Glory*?' he asked at last.

'Far off by now,' said Murray.

'No,' said Frances. 'I saw her as we embarked.'

They passed the wheatfield, where the wheat was now so high that the prisoners could be seen only as a yellow ribbon moving behind those thousands of green strokes toppled slightly from the vertical. The wheat muffled, just a little, the sound of their irons and chains.

Letty and Lucy were already feeling queasy, and went below with Elizabeth and Murray to attend them. The *Regent Bird* negotiated the next bend, and there, in the long reach that led with only the gentlest of curves to the bay, Frances and Robert caught their first full sight of the *Glory*.

She was sailing easily and lightly, and on her stern deck stood Collison. Down below she also carried six prisoners, who were to be released in Sydney, but when Frances saw Robert's devout and glowing face, she knew that she would say nothing to him about the prisoners, and indeed, she was glad that the *Glory* was making good speed, and would draw far enough ahead to allow them to be taken off before the *Regent Bird* came up with her at Dunwich.

They kept her in sight during all the long journey to the mouth of the river, not losing her even when she passed behind an island. The island was so small, and the trees upon it so slender, that the trees themselves seemed to pass one by one across her length. They lost her when she made the south-east turn into the bay, but saw her again, travelling at a greater distance than before, just after the *Regent Bird* made the same turn. A cold gusty salt wind was chopping at the surface of the bay. Frances went below, where Murray was now ministering to Elizabeth as well, and fetched two shawls and a basket of food.

Huddled into shawls, they ate cheese, dried figs,

and bread. Murray came up on deck for air, and stayed to talk and share their food. A sailor rushed past, and another sailor came and talked to Robert. But the *Glory* was too distant to show signs of any such activity; and Frances, watching Robert's face, wondered if to him she appeared to be sailing unaided, and to be unoccupied except for the coffin which he knew to be in her, and the soldier whose red coat was distinct even at that distance. She supposed that Robert would never think of his father without the image springing to his mind of a lead coffin, honourably attended, in a small boat struggling through the furrows of a rough sunlit bay. She did not know that for her, too, this image was already beginning to take precedence over the cold-faced soldier descending the rough incline, and over all those others that had interposed between that, the first, and this, the last. Because she was not ignorant of the ballast of men in the *Glory*, it would not obliterate those others, but would succeed, at last, in gaining a little mercy for them.

Text Classics

For reading group notes visit textclassics.com.au